Hello everyone

Merry Christmas! Thank you for spending time with me on this festive trip to Hope Farm. In these strange times, it's nice to know that people are turning to heart-warming and uplifting stories to cheer them up and I hope you'll find that here. There's more from Molly, Lucas and those naughty alpacas.

While my novel is entirely fiction, Hope Farm is based on a very real place called Animal Antiks which, like Hope Farm, helps children and young adults with learning difficulties, mental health issues and autism. They do great work and are very gracious in continuing to help me with my research.

I hope you all have a wonderful Christmas and can spend time with your friends and family.

Carole :) xx

If you want to keep up with what's happening – new books, the occasional Live chat and some fab giveaways – I spend far too much time on social media, especially Facebook and Twitter, so you can always find me there. I have a newsletter which you can sign up to at www.carolematthews.com.
I don't share your information and you can unsubscribe at any time. I'm also on Instagram when I remember.

f www.facebook.com/carolematthewsbooks
🐦 @carolematthews
📷 Matthews.Carole
www.carolematthews.com

Also by Carole Matthews

Carole Matthews

Christmas for Beginners

SPHERE

SPHERE

First published in Great Britain in 2020 by Sphere
This paperback edition published by Sphere in 2021

1 3 5 7 9 10 8 6 4 2

A CIP catalogue record for this book
is available from the British Library.

ISBN 978-0-7515-8014-3

Typeset in Sabon by Palimpsest Book Production Ltd,
Falkirk, Stirlingshire
Printed and bound in Great Britain by Clays Ltd, Elcograf S.p.A.

Papers used by Sphere are from well-managed forests
and other responsible sources.

MIX
Paper from
responsible sources
FSC® C104740

Sphere
An imprint of
Little, Brown Book Group
Carmelite House
50 Victoria Embankment
London EC4Y 0DZ

An Hachette UK Company
www.hachette.co.uk

www.littlebrown.co.uk

Carole Matthews is the *Sunday Times* bestselling author of over thirty novels, including the top ten bestsellers *The Cake Shop in the Garden, A Cottage by the Sea, Paper Hearts and Summer Kisses, The Chocolate Lovers' Christmas, Million Love Songs, Christmas Cakes & Mistletoe Nights, Happiness for Beginners* and *Sunny Days and Sea Breezes*, which won Romantic Comedy Novel of the Year at the 2021 RNA Awards. Carole is also the recipient of the RNA Outstanding Achievement Award. Her novels dazzle and delight readers all over the world and she is published in more than thirty countries.

For all the latest news from Carole, visit www.carolematthews.com and sign up to her newsletter. You can also follow Carole on Twitter (@carolematthews) and Instagram (matthews.carole) or join the thousands of readers who have become Carole's friend on Facebook (carolematthewsbooks).

To have been writing a happy, festive book during lockdown and the strangest of times has been something of a challenge! Thank you to everyone who has helped me through it.

Yvette and Michelle, friends beyond compare – for all that you do and for all that you are.

Sharon and Owen for bonkers laughs, as always.

Our neighbours, Lyn and Martin, for regular takeaway roasty dinners in return for gin.

My dearest Sheila for embracing Zoom and doing yoga classes online – they have been a saviour.

To Jean, Lizzie, Hazel and my Tiara Ladies for welcome and much-needed chit-chats.

To my loyal and lovely readers who cheered me up on social media and joined me for a coffee every morning.

To my mum for coping so well and, at eighty-six, taking all this in her stride.

To Sophie Ellis-Bexter and family for the joyous madness of her weekly Kitchen Discos.

And to Lovely Kev for keeping me sane with our daily long walks, general silliness and for being the best person to be trapped in a house with.

Hopefully, better times are just around the corner.

Chapter One

One of the alpacas has eaten the Baby Jesus. I'm not sure which one. Frankly, they all look the picture of innocence, but I know them better.

'I'm going to be watching your poo very closely over the next few days,' I warn them. The thought troubles our troupe not one jot. Johnny Rotten, Tina Turner and Rod Stewart all stare me down. Rod gives a delicate little burp. Perhaps he was the perpetrator. He looks like the sort who wouldn't think twice about scoffing down the Messiah. I will find out.

But, more pressing, what will I now use for the new-born reputed saviour of mankind, destined to be the centrepiece of my nativity tableau? Stupidly, I paid the vast sum of sixty-five pounds on eBay for a lifelike doll which clearly looked tastier than I could ever have imagined. Now all that's left of him is a few chewed remnants of plastic that provide evidence of his untimely demise.

'Did you see the culprit, Little Dog?' I ask. But my faithful one-eyed terrier mash-up simply bares his teeth in his usual rictus grin and doesn't dish any dirt on the alpacas. He knows, though, and he knows that I know he knows.

1

While I'm still musing on it, Lucas crosses the yard and comes to stand next to me in the barn. He's sixteen now and, though he's not my son, he might as well be, as I harbour all of the same maternal feelings for him.

'You OK?' he asks.

I nod towards our troublesome trio. 'These guys will be the death of me.' They all give us doe eyes and flutter their long lashes, feigning innocence. I snort at them. 'Don't give me that.'

'Butter wouldn't melt in their mouths,' Lucas observes.

But we both know better.

I acquired these guys when their owners moved abroad. They're pack animals and came as a job lot. How could I turn them down? I'd never owned alpacas before. I thought they'd be sweet, fun. I was wrong.

Tina is definitely our diva and rules the boys with a rod of iron. She's chocolate-brown with an impressive pom-pom of hair which she likes to toss about. Rod is white with skinny legs and knobbly knees. He's usually to be found humming and gazing into space and is our most contented alpaca. But that's not saying a lot. Johnny Rotten is definitely channelling the punk rocker he's named after. He has a tan coat with hair like a Mohican in a shade that's almost orange. Despite being pampered like the rest of them, Johnny will bite you as soon as look at you. Actually, I wouldn't mind betting that he's the one who chowed down Jesus. *Hmm*.

Before we go any further, I should also tell you how Lucas came to be under my loving care. Here at Hope Farm, as well as taking in tricky animals, we look after disadvantaged kids too. We're not your usual farm. Far from it. We don't have crops or animals that we (whisper) *eat*. Instead, we offer alternative education for students who can't cope or are currently excluded from mainstream schools. I set this place up as a charity a few years ago now and we take in kids – mostly teenagers – who have behavioural difficulties, mental health issues or are on the autistic spectrum. That's how Lucas arrived here too.

Originally, Lucas was brought to the farm by his father, Shelby Dacre, who was at the end of his tether with his wayward son who had been expelled from his private school for anti-social behaviour. Their relationship had been strained since Shelby had recently lost his wife to cancer. Lucas, understandably, was floundering without his mum and getting any form of communication out of him at all was an uphill struggle. In Lucas's eyes his father hadn't mourned his mother sufficiently. Shelby had dealt with his grief by dating much younger actresses and submerging himself in his work. Lucas, at a terrible time, had been largely left to his own devices and had grown angrier which manifested in challenging behaviour. Instead of pulling together, father and son had grown increasingly apart – to the point where Shelby no longer felt able to deal with his disruptive son. That's where I came in.

When he arrived here, I hadn't expected to bond so easily with Lucas. He's difficult, testing, terse, uncommunicative, moody – all of the usual teenage behaviour – but we connected straightaway. He talked to me when he couldn't speak to anyone else. We have kids with all kinds of problems here, but I could instantly see that beneath the angry façade, there was a lost and lonely boy just wanting to be loved. And love him I do.

Equally surprising is the fact that I love his father too. It's fair to say that love found me later in life. At thirty-several, having lived the life of a loner, this was a new experience for me. The fact that I'm a borderline recluse meant I had no idea who Shelby Dacre was when he first rocked up here. But, yes he's *the* Shelby Dacre, star of *Flinton's Farm* soap opera and national treasure. In my defence, I don't even own a telly, so have never watched a soap opera in my life.

3

Falling in love wasn't easy for me, as we're totally different people. But Shelby is such a confident, outgoing character that he's brought me out of my shell and I think I offer him something more real than the world that he generally inhabits. They say that opposites attract and it's certainly the case in our situation. Our lives couldn't be more different. For Shelby, it's filming, glamorous parties and adoration. For me it's recalcitrant kids, awkward animals and a day that always features manure.

We've only been together for a short while, but he has changed my world in so many ways. The best part is that Lucas has transformed from the sullen, uncommunicative teenager he was. Over the last few months, our bond has grown and we've become ever closer. It would kill him to admit it, but he's blossoming here and I feel that he's teaching me as much as I'm teaching him.

Chapter Two

I should also explain that we're fairly new to these premises – Hope Farm mark two – as we lost the original farm when the dreaded railway line, HS2, was set to come trundling right through our home and school. It was Shelby who came to the rescue and for that I'll be for ever grateful to him. He saved me, my animals and the kids who rely on me. He plays a romantic hero in his soap opera and to me he's one in real life too.

When we moved to the new farm, my old dilapidated caravan didn't survive the journey and collapsed into an uninhabitable heap. Shelby insisted on buying me one with all mod cons. You'd love it. It's very shiny. As it turns out, Lucas loved it too. He'd been living mostly alone in a cottage in the grounds of Shelby's manor house, just a short journey from here. After his day at the farm, he'd linger longer, sometimes staying for supper until Shelby or his driver could collect him. I've never crossed that professional boundary before with any of the kids, but Lucas and I got on so well.

When it was clear that Shelby and I were going to be together, I asked if Lucas could stay over occasionally if he wanted to as I now had the luxury of a spare bedroom. It was a weight off Shelby's mind that his son wasn't going home to an empty house when he was working late or away for a few days at some showbiz event. After one night of staying here, Lucas never went back home. Following some relentless cajoling from me he's now an apprentice here, studying Animal Management, and is acing it with minimal effort. He's proved to be both a natural at it and a huge help to me on the farm. I hope that Lucas may have found his niche. He's a bright boy and the only person who sabotages him is himself.

Lucas, however, still blames everything on Shelby and isn't convinced by his father's altruistic behaviour. At best, they have a tetchy relationship. At worst, they go at it all guns blazing while I play the referee. It's something of a work-in-progress. In all other areas, Lucas is an angel – albeit with slightly wonky wings. He's become a valuable member of the team here and the other kids really look up to him.

Yet, despite the turnaround in his behaviour, Lucas likes to look the rebel and is still firmly attached to his signature Goth clothing. Today he's sporting a Sex Pistols T-shirt, ripped bondage trousers and, the only nod to the farming life, green wellies. Even though he's generally outside in all elements, his face is still as white as the driven snow. His black eyeliner and red lippy only serve to make him look paler. He's carrying a bucket and a spade that's nearly as big as him – though with all the physical work he does here, his skinny, gangly frame has started to fill out a little. He puts down his tools and climbs onto the first rung of the metal gate, the only thing that's keeping our alpaca crew from running amok – something they love to do with every given chance. They all come up to nuzzle his hand in turn.

'What have you been doing now?' he says to them. 'You're making Molly frown and you'll give her wrinkles. *More* wrinkles.'

As if I care. I'm a stranger to anti-ageing creams. In fact my bathroom is shockingly short on the usual unguents. The outdoor life is my beauty regime. I like to think of myself as fresh-faced and natural when I'm more likely wind-blasted and sun-baked. Though I think since this bolshie bunch of alpacas arrived they've been ageing me in dog years.

I fill Lucas in. 'You saw our beautiful Baby Jesus? I only put him down for a minute and one of them had him for breakfast.'

'That was short-lived. Naughty alpacas,' Lucas says with a wag of his finger at them. 'There'll be a special place reserved for you in alpaca hell.'

'I don't think you're taking this seriously,' I admonish. 'The Hope Farm Open Day and Nativity is rushing up towards us at an alarming rate and we are woefully unprepared.'

'It'll be fine,' Lucas says with all the nonchalance of a Gen Z teenager who cares not for traditions. 'You worry too much.'

He's right. And I'm the only one that does worry. Everyone keeps telling me it will be fine, but the thought of an open day with nativity combo is already giving me sleepless nights. I don't know why I let myself be persuaded to do this. I'm too malleable by half. I'm not even a Christmas person. Usually I spend it alone with the animals. I don't possess any decorations. I've never had time for it. Much as I try to ignore it, this year, I fear, will be very different.

The whole open day thing was, of course, the bright idea of my trusty sidekick, Bev Adams. She's what I like to think of as my link between Hope Farm and the outside world. Bev has been here at my side for years. She's like a mum and a sister all rolled into one and, with the exception of Lucas, the closest thing to family that I have. When my guardian, Aunt Hettie, died and left me bereft and adrift, Bev was the one who helped to put me back together again. My dear friend is about fifteen years older than me – in her mid-fifties – but is as fit and as strong as a twenty-year-old. If you'd seen her throw hay bales around or wrangle a stubborn sheep, then you'd know. Bev's an ex body-builder and is still in great shape, although the only exercise she does now is here on the farm.

Even though I'm supposedly banned from taking in more rescue animals, we've recently rehomed two donkeys – also Bev's idea: a mother and daughter called Harriet and Hilda. They are sweetness personified and came from a lady who was too old to look after them any more and wanted a caring home for the pair so they wouldn't be separated. Cue an invitation to enjoy bed and breakfast on a permanent basis at Hope Farm. I'm so glad that we took them in, though. However, on the downside, our delightful donkeys do seem to have provided the inspiration for Bev's desire to throw open our doors to the general public and share our work with them in a festive manner. The thought fills me with terror. I'm not what you might call a people-person – unless they are people with troubles.

But there's no holding it back now – Christmas and our nativity are going to happen whether I like it or not.

Chapter Three

'I should get on,' Lucas says. 'Shit to do involving shit.'

'You're mucking out the barn?'

'Yeah. The joy just keeps on flowing here.' He pushes his long black fringe from his forehead and his dark eyes look across at me. 'There are ten kids here today. I'll take them with me. I'm sure they all need more poo to brighten their lives.'

Lucas gives great sarcasm.

'Thanks. I haven't even had time to look at the register today.' I'm so grateful that Lucas is on top of it. Ten kids is a full house for us and a lot to handle. We need the income, but I like to keep the numbers low so that everyone gets the personal attention they need. We have our regulars and I'd like to say that makes life easier, but you never can tell what the day is going to throw up. If they all decide to kick off at once, then it's mayhem.

We have some students for a few days; a couple are here all week. Some are long-term and have good council funding. Others come and go or are with us just briefly. We try to cater for as many needs as possible with the few people we have. The funding for Lucas's apprenticeship is provided by his dad –

something that irks him. But then a lot of things irk Lucas, especially if his father is involved.

'You're doing a great job.' Whenever I look at Lucas, my heart squeezes. As I've said, he's not my boy, but I could not love him more. 'Can I hug you?'

He sighs. 'Do you have to?'

'I'd like to,' I venture.

'If you must.' With a great show of reluctance, he surrenders to my embrace. Then he lingers a little longer than he needs to, which makes me smile. Sixteen-year-old boys need cuddles as much as anyone, even though they pretend they don't. I hold his skinny, all-angles body tightly.

'Enough,' he says. 'You're breaking my ribs now.' Lucas peels himself away from me and sets off towards the barn with a casual wave. 'Laters.'

'See you at lunch,' I shout as he goes. 'Chickpea curry.'

'Be still my beating heart,' he shouts back.

Watching him walk away, my chest fills with pride. I'm pleased to tell you that Lucas is in a good place. Or as good a place as a slightly surly, overly sensitive, passive-aggressive teenager with authority issues can be.

We've been at our new home – which should rightly be known as Hope Farm Two – since the end of summer. As I said, we were ousted from our previous land due to that terrible thing called 'progress' when our troubled children and misfit animals were kicked out of the way in favour of HS2. Even now I can't bring myself to talk to you about it without muttering darkly and using my worst swear words. The diggers rolled in as we moved out and I haven't been able to go back and look at the scars they will have created on the beautiful landscape. They've destroyed ancient woodland and untrammelled countryside, but commuters will soon be able to get from and on to Birmingham twenty minutes quicker, so that's all right then. That sound is the gnashing of my teeth.

Still, silver linings and all that, this place is amazing. When I feared that, literally, all hope was lost, Shelby stepped in and found us this fantastic replacement. Thanks to him, we have a beautiful slice of Buckinghamshire countryside which we now call home and, dare I say, it's probably better suited for our purposes than our previous home.

We need somewhere tranquil and private, a sanctuary away from the prying eyes and interference of neighbours. Our kids need peace and quiet while they try to overcome their individual challenges. We attempt to cater for all needs and the kids learn through interacting with our animals. Our daily activities teach them teamwork and allow them to flourish at their own pace in a safe environment. Some haven't had the best start in life or have come from chaotic backgrounds. They need stability and a place to grow.

The downside of providing this idyll is that it all costs – handsomely – and we're a teeny-tiny charity always struggling for funds. This new farm was only made possible by our patron and my other half, Shelby Dacre, but we need to raise the money to keep it going.

As I said, at the grand age of thirty-eight I fell in love for the very first time with someone who – given his reputation for dating ludicrously young and beautiful starlets – I'm still aston-ished even looked my way. Some days, I have to pinch myself to check that Shelby's actually here and in my life. Except, at the moment, he isn't. Well, not very much. The soap is filmed every weekday and is, more often than not, starting early and finishing late. Recently there have been a lot of meetings in London, too. Many things, it seems, conspire to keep him away from the farm and, consequently, from me.

Because he's got so much on his plate, I don't want to

always be calling on Shelby for help to keep this place running, so I know that finding extra cash is essential. Bev is our chief fundraiser – as well as everything else she does to help me out. I just wish that she hadn't come up with something so . . . exposing. She's already got us going into care homes with our alpacas and I've barely got used to that. The residents, of course, love to see them. On paper, it's a great idea. But, as you've probably already gathered, those guys love to look for trouble and I don't want to be responsible for having a bunch of traumatised pensioners on my hands.

My default setting is to hide away; I just want to be alone here with the students, my needy animals and my heart-throb boyfriend. Is that too much to ask?

Apparently so.

Chapter Four

'I'll be back to see you later,' I tell the alpacas. 'I won't forget.'

In unison, they hum innocently at me. Not buying it.

It's a bright, sunny day and, even though it's frosty underfoot, it's the kind of day that makes you feel warm in your heart. The kind of day that makes you wonder why everyone can't live on a farm. I take a quick tour of our animals to make sure they're all OK. As dawn is a little later in the winter, we all have a bit of a lie-in and the animal part of the Hope Farm team are just rousing themselves.

All the animals here have been rescued for one reason or another. They've been neglected, sometimes abused, or they've outgrown their welcome or their cuteness. Most have sad stories in their past. But they're here now and are treated with care, kindness and respect. Some might say they're spoiled and pampered. But why not? We all deserve a bit of TLC in life, whether human or animal. The students who come here are taught how to look after the animals and, together, can make the world seem like a better place. Half the kids have never even seen a real hen, let alone cuddled one.

As well as taking on the new donkeys, I've adopted another

dog to add to my growing pack. I know. But what could I do? Betty Bad Dog has been in and out of various rescue homes as she proves to be too much of a handful for one family after another. She's also here as a last resort and, my goodness, is she living up to her name. We've tried to re-christen her as Betty Good Girl in the hope she'd turn over a new leaf, but I'm not sure that she's fully embracing it. She loves to tip over the food bins and tries to lick sheep inappropriately whenever she can. But she's cute with it – which is a good job. Betty's still young – an indeterminate age – and has all the 'exuberance' of youth. She's huge, but that doesn't stop her from trying to sit on anyone and everyone's lap. She's pale like a golden retriever, sturdy like a Rhodesian Ridgeback. She permanently has one ear up and one ear down and looks as mad as cheese. Mischief seems to be the only thing on her mind. Her favourite misdemeanours include drinking unguarded cups of tea, chewing tissues, particularly the used variety, and weeing on everything when she gets over-excited, which is quite often. Still, she gets along very well with Little Dog and three-legged Big Dog, so I'll take that.

Accompanied by my doggie companions, I carry on with my morning round. I've brought some pig nuts for Teacup our giant 'miniature' pig and I lean over the door of his stall to say, 'Morning, big guy. How's it going?'

Teacup heaves his substantial bulk to his feet and I throw him some breakfast and scratch his ears. Our lovely pig came to us when he'd outgrown his owner's pocket-size garden in Hemel Hempstead. He's enormous and built like a tank. Not even one of his trotters would fit in a teacup and I'd like to string up any breeder who sells these monster animals to tiny homes. My advice is never, ever get a pet pig unless you live on a farm.

Teacup's closest companion is our dear little lamb, Fifty, who can often be found sleeping alongside him in his stall. This morning, Fifty is still out for the count, snuggled into the hay, and shows no signs of being ready to face the day. Fifty has the run of the yard. He seems to self-identify as a human or a dog rather than a sheep and we're happy to go along with that. Gender and, apparently, species are more fluid these days. Fifty is a very handsome sheep with a brown face, doe eyes and large, flappy ears – a sheep made by Aardman. We indulge him, not only because he's cute, but he was an orphaned lamb with damaged legs who we thought would never make it. He thrived through sheer will and determination, plus daily massages of lavender oil and being fed only the finest of foods. He still limps a bit, but that doesn't stop him controlling the dogs in the yard – even Betty, to some extent. Occasionally, before I had a soap star sharing my bed, I used to let Fifty sleep with me alongside Big Dog and Little Dog. Now, because Fifty got fed up of being squashed by excess of dogs, he's happier in Teacup's quarters, but I do miss him sometimes.

In the next pen along are the other sheep. I don't even like to count them now as we take on too many waifs and strays. I know it's more than thirty. I hope it's less than forty. Our main guy is Anthony the Anti-Social Sheep who has to have his own specially reinforced pen as he is a grumpy, middle-aged man of a sheep and will head-butt anyone he can of any species – humans are a speciality. Many a time, Anthony's horns have made contact with my rear end, to my detriment. He'll take any chance to catapult man or beast across the farmyard or field. Even when he's outside we have to put him in his own paddock for the safety of all concerned. Anthony has to be handled with iron resolve and kid gloves, but I still love him dearly despite his curmudgeonly tendencies. We took away his 'gentleman's playthings' in an attempt to make him less testy – with only limited success. He is more cross with the world than a pampered sheep needs to be.

The rest of the sheep are, more often than not, named by the students. As well as Midnight, Fluffy and Teddy, we've got most of Little Mix, One Direction and, from our impressionable young girls, members of Korean pop sensation BTS. We've also got a pen full of cuddly bunnies including two Flemish giant rabbits called Ant and Dec who are over a metre long and the size of dogs. Despite their heft, unlike our naughty alpacas, they are no trouble at all. They generally sit there being passive and agreeable in return for lettuce and carrots. The kids, of course, all love them and I have to strictly ration the cuddles otherwise I'd never get anyone to perform any of the other more onerous tasks that need doing as part of their education.

I open the door to the barn and there's a frenzied dash for the door that we call the morning 'rush hour'. The ducks, hens and geese that are kept in there overnight scuttle to freedom as if they've never seen daylight before. Dick the Cock struts out and stretches as if he's only just woken up. He treats me to an ear-splitting crow.

'It's nine o'clock, Dick,' I point out. 'We're all up before you.' So much for him heralding in the dawn. Since we've moved to our new premises, our cockerel does like a lie-in. Though, once he starts to crow, he never stops.

We have two guard geese, Snowy and Blossom, who patrol the farmyard on a daily basis and nip the legs of anyone who disses them. Sometimes they wear jaunty neckerchiefs, courtesy of Bev, when the mood takes them to let her tie them on. If they're not in the mood, you can't get near them.

Our dear hens are a motley crew too: there's Bouncer, the matriarch of the hen house, one-eyed Mrs Magoo, Peg the one-legged hen and Gloria Gaynor who is a champion of surviving fox attacks. They're all ex-battery hens so they are extra spoiled now they're here. We've got a few dozen at the moment and I'm not sure that any one of them has a full complement of legs, eyes or feathers. When they arrive they're in a terrible state – devoid of plumage and hope – and require a lot of nurturing.

Sometimes, if I'm lucky, I catch the occasional glimpse of Phantom – our feral farmyard cat with half a face who lives in the barn. Occasionally, I'll see him skulking along the hedge or sitting in the rafters. I've given up trying to tempt him into contact with cat food as he seems to prefer surviving on the rodents he catches – and I'm glad to have such an energetic mouser as he saves me a fortune in pest control. We didn't adopt Phantom, he chose us to move in with. Neither I nor the vet have managed to get close enough to him to manage a proper examination. He must have had a road traffic accident or something to cause the loss of his face and he walks with a goose step. Occasionally, I'll see him having a fit in the barn, but I daren't approach. He always seems to recover and, despite his issues, he seems in reasonable shape. I just wish he'd let me get closer to him.

As I'm checking our pygmy goats, one of our students comes wandering into the barn. Penny is one of our newer arrivals and has a very difficult home life. She sidles up beside me and stares over the fence at Dumb and Dumber.

'Hey,' I say. 'Thought you were helping Lucas?' Like most of the teenage girls we have here, she likes Lucas – a lot.

'I'm too tired.'

None of them particularly like mucking out and some will do anything to get out of it – which is fine – but I can tell that Penny's not trying to pull the wool over my eyes. There are shadows like bruises under her eyes and her face is paler than normal. She does look exhausted and world-weary.

'Lucas said you were in the barn and to come and find you.'

'What can I help with?'

She shrugs at me.

'Trouble at home?'

'Yeah. Usual.'

Penny's father likes to use her mother as a punchbag and, when it gets too bad, Penny's disruptive at school or, if that doesn't work, she runs away. Who can blame her? Would you want to live like that? Her father is a management consultant and her mother works for a small double-glazing company in the local town who don't seem to mind her frequent absences due to her 'clumsiness'. They live in a nice home with a manicured lawn and dark secrets. Bev goes along to the meetings with social services and tries to explain that it's not Penny who's the root of the problem. We have her for three days a week, so we do our best to pick up the pieces and be kind to her.

Penny looks so lost and lonely that it breaks my heart. I want to scoop up all these waifs and strays and hold them close. Some people just don't deserve the kids that they're blessed with.

'You could do my rounds with me,' I say. 'If you want to.' Little Dog bares his teeth in his mad grin. 'He'd like it.'

Penny bends to fuss his ears and I see a solitary tear fall. 'OK.'

So, I put my arm rounds her insubstantial shoulders and we head off towards the fields.

Chapter Five

Penny and I climb over the stile which is set into a thick hawthorn hedge. The dogs squeeze through a low gap in the hedge and are already running ahead of us, sniffing at the grass, the trees, tails wagging. Occasionally, they come back to herd Penny and me, to make sure that we're following. They must walk twice as far as us.

Away from the shelter of the farm buildings, we're treated to the full extent of the crisp, cold day. There's freezing mist hanging over the ground, but I love a good walk on a fresh and bracing winter's day.

'Warm enough?' I ask Penny.

'Yeah.' But she shivers slightly, so I take off my scarf and she winds it round her neck.

'Better?'

A grateful nod, a ghost of a smile.

This really is an idyllic spot of Buckinghamshire's finest countryside. We have gently rolling hills which take us down to a narrow ribbon of river, fringed with weeping willows, that meanders through the land. There's an ancient wood to the right hand side and, at the far end of our area, we have a large pond surrounded by trees. Bev wants to introduce walks with our animals for people with mental health issues. It's a fantastic idea and this would be the perfect spot. Though I'm not sure that letting some of our badly behaved animals loose on people with troubles would be good for my own mental health.

There's no doubt that the countryside here is soft and soothing – and with the added bonus that there's no threat of a pesky high-speed railway rushing through. If anyone thinks of doing that again here, then the world really has gone mad. We have this land on a ten-year lease courtesy of Shelby and his business partners.

I like this time to myself when I can see how everyone is and I'm not crowded by things that I have to do or say. Until Lucas came into my life, I was always happiest on my own. I was brought up on our original farm by Aunt Hettie and was never one for mixing with humans. I always preferred to be with animals. You know where you are with a pig. Today, though, I'm grateful that Penny has sought me out.

'Things not improving at home?'

Bev says that every time they have a meeting with social services, the father swears it's the last time.

Penny shakes her head. 'Nah.'

'Is your mum OK?'

'They were going at it again last night. She's got a black eye this morning. She put loads of make-up on, but I can still see it. She says it's nothing. They must think I'm deaf too.'

'Social services can help her to leave.'

'They've tried,' Penny says, her voice flat. 'She won't do anything.'

'She's probably frightened to,' I tell her.

'I'd be more frightened to stay,' she counters and then falls quiet.

We walk up the hill to the field where our massive Shire horses are kept. I see that the fence is broken. Again. Another job and more expense. Sadly, fence breakage is a regular occurrence. Our two ex-police Shire horses, Sweeney and Carter, like to lean on the fence. The fence is not so keen – with a couple of thousand pounds of muscle against it, the fence is never going to win.

Someone has put them in with the Shetland ponies, which means that they won't break the fence here as they could just step over it. Sweeney and Carter are huddled together in one corner. Carter suffers from seasonal affective disorder and despises cold weather and grey days. It's a job to try to get him to come out of his stall at all from October to March. Sweeney is as jumpy as they come, having been involved in policing more riots than he should have. The slightest noise makes him bolt across his field. But they are good companions for each other and now that Lucas is here permanently, we take them out together for an exercise ride across the land. Which means I've regained my love of riding and Lucas, who seems to be a natural at everything he turns his hand to, has proved to be a skilled rider.

The miniature Shetland ponies we have are always a big hit with the students. We've got three now. Ringo and Buzz Lightyear have been joined by Beyoncé who, though she's relatively new, keeps both of her boys in check. They, of course, both dote on her and jostle for her attention. She only has to flick her long blonde mane or waggle her comely rump and they come running.

'Have you fed Beyoncé yet?' I ask Penny.

'No.'

I've got a pocket full of carrots for the horses. Pulling them out, I hand half to Penny.

When I shout their names, they amble over to be fed. We

give them all a rub on the snout, especially Ringo who suffers from sweet itch. He's allergic to his own hair and, as there's nothing sweet about it, is always grateful for a good scratch. The itchy little pony now has his own celebrity hairdresser, Christian Lee – a good friend of Shelby's and generous supporter of the farm. Christian lives near here and comes once a month to layer Ringo's fringe into a gorgeous, swishy bob to keep it away from his skin. His mane and tail are styled and kept short too. I'm sure that Beyoncé seems more than a little jealous of his locks.

Occasionally, Christian – who despairs of me – cuts my own unkempt hair into a neat, brown bob and I keep having to check in the mirror that I am really me. When Christian's not looking, more often than not, I take the kitchen scissors to it.

Beyoncé pushes the boys out of the way and hogs the fence, nuzzling Penny's hand.

'She likes you,' I say to Penny and get a nervous smile in return.

Horses and ponies fussed and fed, we head back down to the barn walking at a leisurely pace. I want to give Penny time to talk if she needs to, but she seems happy just to be quiet. Her situation is a difficult one and only her mother can resolve it.

'Shall we go and warm up in the tea room? The others will probably be there now.'

'Yeah.'

Little Dog pumps his stubby little legs and runs ahead of us, stretching out his body. At some point, while I wasn't watching, he rolled in something unspeakable, so his brown and white coat is tipped with caked-on mud. At least, I hope it's mud.

Today, Big Dog has joined us, but more often and probably quite sensibly during the winter he decides to stay at home sleeping next to one of the radiators in my caravan. He's another enormous dog, this time shaggy. Lucas says he's an Alsatian/ Dire Wolf cross. He also tells me that this is a *Game of Thrones* reference but, as I don't have a television, I can neither confirm nor deny this.

What I can tell you is that Big Dog has a number of issues. People in red jumpers can throw him into a frenzy of barking. He only has three legs and it never used to stop him doing anything, but as he's got older he's begun taking his time and is sparing with his choice of activities. And who can blame him? That exemplifies the ethos of this place. Each animal or person goes at the pace they're comfortable. No one is rushed or pushed. Taking things slowly generally brings out the best in everyone, I find. I used to be a teacher in a mainstream school and pretty much hated everything about how the system was set up. With large, unruly classes, constant examinations and a one-size-fits-all approach, it seemed to bring out the worst in everyone – pupils and teachers. And I was no exception. I had to get out before I blew a fuse. So that's how I found myself running a small charity supporting educational needs for the disenfranchised and sidelined. Because I was once someone who needed help, I can see it in others too.

Chapter Six

On our way to the tea room we pass the barn and I can see that mucking-out is in full progress. Wheelbarrows are being loaded with used hay ready to be replaced with a fresh new batch. Lucas is getting stuck in with everyone and there's a cheery atmosphere in the air – never a given. Each day presents us with a different challenge and it's a blessing when all of our students are in a good place and their time here is without major incident. It looks as if we've got Lucas's hardcore fan club in today. He's a big hit with the students here. They see him as anti-authority – which quite often he is – and hang on his every word. Only Lucas can get the other students mucking out without protest.

Penny and I stop to watch as they finish up. Two of our long-term girls are here today – Lottie and Erin – and it's fair to say that they don't like getting their hands dirty. Apparently, as they tell me on a regular basis, glittery manicures and manure are not the best of mixes. However, they also rather like being with Lucas, so they're getting on with it today, glittery nails or not.

They both look like angels, but have mouths born of the

gutter. Both girls have chaotic home lives and as soon as they seem to be settling, their parents seem to do something to send them into a downward spiral again. Here the two teenagers cling together and seem to bring out the best in each other. When they do have a meltdown, they like to do it as a joint affair to really challenge our resources.

Jack's here too – one of my own favourite students. Not that I should have favourites, but he's easy company and if you give him a task he'll see it through with meticulous attention to detail. Jack is on the autistic spectrum and has also been with us for a long time now. He couldn't cope with the bustle of mainstream education, but he's done very well here as he loves the quiet, structured routine of the farm. His favourite job is making tea, which he does with military precision, and I've started to encourage him to help Bev in the kitchen in a more formal way. If I had some extra funding, then I think we could soon give Jack a paid job here and it would be a delight to see him gain some more independence. Perhaps it's something I could talk to Shelby about.

As well as Penny, we have some more relatively new students too and the idea is that, as part of their learning, the kids who have been here longer look after the newer ones. That's how it works in theory. Some fit in straightaway, for some it takes much longer, but one thing I've learned over the years is that you can't force it.

'Good morning,' I say to everyone. 'How's it going?'

Lucas leans on his spade. 'OK. We'll be done soon.'

'Excellent. I'll go and get the tea ready.'

'Cool.'

'After break, Alan might need you to give him a hand with mending Sweeney and Carter's fence. It's been knocked over again.'

'No worries.' Lucas, too, is unusually sunny-natured today.

There must be something behind it but I don't know what. Hopefully I'll find out, but you can never tell with Lucas. Even though I think he trusts me now, he still likes to hold his cards very close to his chest.

Another new thing is that once a week, I have a volunteer coming in to do arts and crafts with the students and she's due in later. I don't know what Anna has planned for them, but at some point we should make Christmas cards and decorations – bunting and stuff, I suppose – to adorn the barn for our open day. Time is of the essence and I guess we need to make a start on it before Christmas has been and gone. There are plenty of holly bushes on the farm if she wants to do something with a natural feel. It's nice that the kids have some indoor activities to occupy them when the weather is bitterly cold and it's not so easy to let them loose on the farm. They also have regular, structured lessons every afternoon – maths, English, history – which they are, to a man, less keen on.

'I'm going to put the kettle on,' I say to Penny. 'Want to come down with me?'

'I'll wait here,' she says and stands a little bit closer to Lucas, who is oblivious to her presence. Poor Penny, I think. I'm not sure her adoration is returned.

'I'll see you later. You know where I am if you want to chat.' Then to Lucas, 'Ten minutes for tea.'

He nods and then turns to finish supervising the kids. It makes me smile to see him organising them so efficiently. They don't play him up like they do the grown-ups. Lucas is seen as very much on their side.

As I leave them to complete their task in the barn and head to the workshop, I dwell further on Christmas. It's rushing up with alacrity and I don't even know what Shelby's plans are for the holidays. We haven't had that discussion yet. I can't see him wanting to spend it in my caravan, as cosy as I find it. He has a beautiful home not far from the farm: Homewood Manor. But it terrifies me. It's like a palace. I've only been there a few times – reluctantly at that – and it's very fancy. The place is filled with expensive furniture, tasteful paintings and things that look as if they might smash easily. I always feel as if I'm making it untidy just by being there. The air inside is still and smells of nothing, so I'm always aware that my natural and unavoidable *eau de farmyard* is somewhat amplified. It's not somewhere I can relax and I know that Shelby finds it difficult to understand my reticence.

He's filming today and they're under great pressure, he tells me. As well as the daily episodes to shoot, there is to be a feature-length special that will air on Christmas Day and the schedule is tight. He finds it difficult to grab a few minutes to call me, but he does so when he can.

Today, I hope it doesn't run too late as he's promised to have supper with Lucas and me. I'm always on tenterhooks as, if he cancels – especially at the last minute – it can send Lucas into a terrible sulk. Unfortunately though, more often than not, Shelby's either too late to eat with us or he doesn't come back to the farm at all, preferring to stay in a hotel near the set where *Flinton's Farm* is filmed.

I only went to the set once – that was more than enough. It's like a proper little village to look at – except there's nothing behind the façade. Lucas would say the same about his dad – that's he's all image with very little sincerity behind the front. I like to think that I've seen a different side of Shelby. Between you and me, I think he's growing tired of the celebrity life. Its shallowness doesn't give him the comfort and support that he needs. He likes to escape the pretence of *Flinton's Farm* and come back to an actual, down-to-earth farm. I think that's why we're together, though I might not be the best judge of this. I'm not like the usual, high-maintenance, starry women he's used to. Far from it. Instead, I hope that I can offer him an alternative type of life. However, while he's terribly supportive of us financially, I have to admit that he doesn't much care for getting his hands dirty. The problem is that he's massively allergic to anything with fur, fluff or feathers. I do think that if the animals didn't make him sneeze and sniffle he'd love to spend longer here and get more involved with the mucky end of it all, but Lucas doesn't believe it for one minute. He thinks that Shelby simply wants to drift about feeling benevolent. Even though he's made great progress since he came to the farm, Lucas's relationship with his father still hangs by a thread. Shelby daren't put a foot wrong. Even the slightest word out of place and Lucas reads far too much into it. But I'm working on them both and, hopefully, one day they'll be fully reconciled. I have my fingers crossed when I say that.

Chapter Seven

I'm pleased to say that I'm not the only one at Hope Farm who has found love. Bev and Alan, who works here too, have recently become an item. They're also an unlikely pairing.

In contrast to Bev, Alan is the strong, silent type. He does all kinds of jobs for me, particularly ones that involve heavy lifting or a hammer. I'd like to say that he's become chattier now that he and Bev are madly in love, but conversation is still a strange bedfellow for him.

I swing into the workshop and he pauses in his sawing when he sees me. 'All right?'

'I'm fine. You?'

Alan nods.

He used to be quite scruffy in an ageing-hippy kind of way. Now love has found him, he has the air of the older Kris Kristofferson with either a flowing, freshly shampooed mane or a neat plait. Today is a neat-plait day. Before they were a couple, the main source of entertainment for Bev and me was to guess which band T-shirt that he'd be wearing each day. Now he and Bev dress in identical outfits from the merch stand, so Lucas and I have taken over the mantle of daily guessing. This isn't so much fun for Lucas as, apart from the Sex Pistols, he's never heard of any bands prior to 2001, which pretty much rules out most of the bands that Alan and Bev know. You'd think that this would increase my chance of winning, but that's yet to materialise. This is mainly due, as I've said, to the fact that I don't have, and never have had, a telly, so I am woefully ill-informed about popular culture in general. Hence the embarrassment when Shelby and I first met as I'd never actually heard of *him*, despite his character, Farmer Gordon Flinton, being a long-standing fixture on our screens.

Alan breaks into my musing to state, 'Horses have done the fence again.'

'Yeah. I've just been up there. Lucas is mucking out the barn, but he can give you a hand with it when he's done.'

The tiniest inclination of the head says that's a good idea.

'What are you making?'

'Manger for Baby Jesus.' Taxed by our exchange, Alan returns to his sawing.

I can't begin to tell Alan what dastardly fate has befallen our poor Jesus. I fear it would tip him over the edge. So, instead, I offer, 'It looks very nice.'

Bev can find the right moment to tell him that we are in need of a replacement.

As I go to leave, my dear friend turns up. 'Hello, my lover.' She twines her arms around Alan and presses her full-chest Whitesnake band logo against his. Neither Lucas nor I were even close to this level of heavy metal, so no band T-shirt winner today.

They snuggle together and make coochy-coo love noises to each other.

'Get a room, you two,' I say. 'That's gross.'

'You're only jealous because your man's not here,' Bev says.

'This is true.' I haven't seen Shelby for days. 'Can I tear you away from each other? You and I need to have a conversation about this looming nativity stuff and Christmas in general.'

'There's nothing to worry about,' Bev assures me. 'I have it all under control.'

For the record, there is no evidence of this.

'Come to the caravan, you can reassure me over a cup of tea.'

'Talk you down off the ledge?'

'Yes, that's the one.'

With a last press of her fulsome bosom against Alan, she says, 'Later, lover!' and peels herself off him. It's a good job that none of the kids are around. They'd be scandalised by such displays of affection in 'old' people.

Bev comes to link her arm through mine and we walk across the yard.

'I have to put the tea on for the kids first,' I tell her.

She checks her watch. 'Is it that time already? Where do the flipping days go?'

Normally, our day starts with greeting our students in the tea room, but I missed out today due to the mysteriously eaten Baby Jesus crisis. Our morning meeting gives us an opportunity to see what mood our kids are in and if they have any problems that we need to work through with them during the day. We also get together again for lunch and a hot meal usually cooked by Bev.

The tea room on our new farm is lovely. It doesn't have a leaky roof and the windows actually keep out draughts. Luxury. When we moved here, I got the students to decorate it with photographs of themselves and their activities. We have a budding photographer here in Tamara, who's thirteen going on thirty-five. Tamara has mental health issues and spends her time on Instagram obsessively following celebrities. I try to give her other subjects to focus on in an attempt to tear her away from taking copious selfies of herself and her friends here. They are typical teenagers in that every moment of their day has to be documented for social media. We try to frame it in a more constructive way and encourage them to provide content for our social media accounts and not just do it mindlessly – see how modern we are? Not me, obviously. But Bev says we need to be 'outward looking' and 'media savvy.' Who am I to argue?

Photography is definitely Tamara's forte and we try to encourage it as a way of development. I'm no expert, but I think she's good. Bev managed to persuade one of the local shops to donate a decent camera to us and we take it in turns walking with Tamara across the farm to help her take some shots. Tamara nearly faints with delight on the rare occasion that Lucas offers to take her. It's another thing that Bev sees as a potential fundraiser. She's convinced that local camera clubs will cough up a few quid to get close to our animals and have access to our land. She might be right. It would be nice if we could get someone who knew about photography to come and mentor Tamara on a regular basis. Another thing to add to our wish list.

Bev and I go into the tea room together and I get the kettles going while she puts out the cups. Minutes later everyone arrives en masse, shouting, laughing and talking over each other, and our moment of peace is turned to bedlam. We dish out tea and biscuits. I'm pleased to note that Lucas is with Penny and he's making her giggle. I like the sound of that.

When they're all happy and we've sorted out any problems and they've devoured all the biscuits and we've organised their next tasks, Bev and I take our leave. Of course, she can't do that without smothering Alan with kisses again.

'I can't get enough of him. That man is grrrrrrrr . . .' She growls at me, yanking at me playfully as we go out of the door.

I'm sure Bev's experiencing a hormone surge. 'I'm assuming that's a good thing.'

'It's a wonderful thing.'

'You can have too much love,' I say.

'You can't,' she replies. 'I've been a desert for many years and Alan is my rain. I'm slaking my thirst.'

'I *think* that's nice,' I say as I ponder the image.

'It's lovely,' she states categorically. 'You should be doing the same.'

'I prefer little sips,' I counter.

Little Dog barks excitedly as he follows Bev and me as we head towards my caravan.

Bev laughs. 'Where is The Great Shelby, by the way?'

'Filming. A Christmas special.'

'Oh, smashing,' Bev says. 'Last Christmas found him in bed with Slack Sally who runs the café.'

'Right.'

'The village pub burned down too.'

'Were the two things connected?'

She tuts at me. 'Don't be silly.'

Bev is a big fan of *Flinton's Farm*, but I confess that I've still never watched Shelby's soap. She does, however, insist on giving me a blow-by-blow account of nearly every episode and I struggle to keep up with the number of women in the fictitious village who he seems to have had affairs with. We did – on my one ill-fated visit – take our alpacas there to have a 'starring' role in the soap, but they behaved appallingly, running amok on the village green, knocking over actors and cameras with gay abandon. They were summarily sacked off the site before getting anywhere near the screen and have never been back since. Their moment of stardom was brief and traumatic for all concerned.

'I can't help but mention that Shelby's hardly here these days.' Bev frowns at me. 'There's nothing wrong?'

'Other than the fact that he's still allergic to all of the

animals?' We both smile at that. It's a constant source of amusement – more than it should be – that someone who has made his living at portraying a farmer sneezes at the sight of a sheep and is, therefore, completely useless with any of the animals. To be able to help for just an hour he has to mainline antihistamine. When he spends any length of time here, his eyes take on a permanent red hue – not ideal for his television work. 'It's difficult for him. He has a lot on. I understand that.'

'There's always something. This or that keeps him in London. It sounds like a lot of excuses to me.'

I have no answer to that. I know it's not ideal, but I don't want to put extra pressure on Shelby. Our relationship is fairly new and, as such, we're still finding our way to blend his life and mine. I'm simply grateful for the time that we have together.

Chapter Eight

We arrive at my caravan. Big Dog is snoozing in a patch of sunshine by the door and wags his tail in greeting, but can't quite summon up the energy to get up and greet us. Bev fusses him before we both step over his bulk and go inside.

Bev shrugs out of her coat. 'I remember the days when you could see your own breath in the old van. It was colder inside than outside. This is the bloody Ritz in comparison.'

I'd always viewed my previous caravan home as shabby-chic, but I have to admit that it was probably more shabby-condemned. Shelby refused to stay in it, mainly due to its lack of amenities and excess of dog hair. The first thing that Shelby did was order me a fancy-dancy mobile home which has all the mod-cons. I have a proper kitchen with a working oven and, miracle of miracles, a shower which produces hot water, lots of it – something I haven't had for a very long time. Strangely, part of me misses the home-rigged, outdoor bucket shower that used to serve as my bathroom. This shower might have hot water, but it doesn't come with a view of the valley beyond or the starry sky above me. Perhaps I am seeing with eyes that are more sentimental than realistic and should remember the freezing mornings when I cursed having to do my ablutions al fresco.

In my des-res van I also have central heating – which I am loathe to use in case it makes me soft, and only put it on to assuage Lucas. I've also got a posh bedroom that's off-limits to anything with fur, which has definitely put out the noses of my dear doggies, but it does mean that Shelby can stay here when he wants to and still be able to breathe. There's also another proper bedroom, which means that Lucas can live with me, and that, beyond any of the other convenient amenities, is the thing I'm most grateful for. Though when I do poke my head round his bedroom door – on the rare occasion I risk doing so – it looks like a glimpse into my old caravan. Lucas favours his floor as a wardrobe, the bed is always crumpled and I have to beg him to change the sheets. What surfaces you can see are scattered with scribblings of his poetry and, though he rarely deigns to perform for me, I do like to hear him read it out. He still won't share his poetry with his father either, which is a great sadness to Shelby. Sometimes, I sneak a peek at the record-ings he puts on YouTube without him knowing. His poems are angry, rapped out with passion and I love them all. We make slow progress and he'll sometimes take a poetry class for the kids – which they love – but it's a talent that he's frustratingly reluctant to share. I'll keep trying though.

I put the kettle on – electric, not half an hour to wait for it to boil – as we're hooked up to mains electric here too. Told you it was fancy.

'I've invited the new mayor to the Christmas open day,' Bev says when she's settled in the window seat with her mug.

'What?' I nearly spit out my own tea. Sliding into the seat opposite, I lean on the table between us.

'He's great, by all accounts. Not that new, I suppose. He's been in office for a bit now. Can't remember when. I haven't met him yet, but I've heard very good things about Matt Eastman.'

'But why have you asked him?'

She shrugs. 'I thought he could shake hands, cut a ribbon, turn on the lights? I don't know. Do the sort of things that mayors do.'

'Won't that be Shelby's job?'

'Well. Ordinarily. But these aren't ordinary times. Golden Boy isn't here all that often, is he? Can we rely on him?'

'I'm sure we can.' I feel myself bristle slightly, which is unfair. Bev, as always, is only saying what she sees. 'I gave him the date for his diary.'

'The other attraction of the mayor is that he has some cash to flash in supporting local charities,' she breezes on. 'I thought he might like to throw some our way. It can't hurt to have him turn up and cut a ribbon. If Shelby is here they can fight it out to the death over the scissors.'

When I break it to Shelby, I'm sure he'll appreciate the benefit of having one of our local dignitaries here, even though it gives me the collywobbles.

Bev draws a notebook from the pocket of her discarded coat and consults it. 'The local branch of the WI have kindly agreed to do mince pies and cakes for us.'

'That's nice.' We're trying to foster relationships with our neighbours and community clubs as some local people view our work with suspicion. They assume the place is full of knife-wielding druggies and, to be fair, we have had our share of those over the years, but it's not our main work. We're more likely to help with mental health and behavioural issues.

'I've organised some flyers to be printed that we can put around the village.'

'How many people do you think will come?'

'No idea, but we could only accommodate a hundred, max.

Parking is the issue. As long as it's not too soggy we can open the field by the road. Alan can supervise that.' She writes it in her pad.

'What are my jobs?'

'I'll leave you in charge of panicking,' she says. 'You do it so well.'

I have to laugh at that. Principally, because she's right. 'I *am* looking forward to it,' I insist.

'You're not. You're dreading it. Already, it's bringing you out in hives and we've got aaaaages to go yet.'

We haven't. Just so you know.

'I need to find another Baby Jesus,' I confess. 'The alpacas have eaten the one I bought off eBay.'

'They are bastard things,' Bev says affectionately. 'We'll have to improvise. Do you think we could get Little Dog to lie still in a manger?'

My canine chum pricks up his ears at the sound of his name. 'No.' He's good, but not that good.

'Plan B then,' Bev says and scribbles furiously again.

'Shall we teach the students a Christmas song?'

'Yeah. They'd like that and it will keep them out of mischief for a few hours.'

'We've got a craft session this afternoon. Card-making.'

'Joy.' Bev can do many things, but arts and crafts are not her idea of fun.

'I thought the kids could make a Christmas card for someone. If they want to.' Unfortunately, not all of our charges are in settled homes with their parents. Some are in foster care or council-run homes.

My friend nods her approval. 'That would be a nice thing.' Bev jots it down and then closes her notebook. 'Better get on. Chickpea curry for lunch and I've got healthy shizzle to chop.'

'Sounds great. I've got Jack pencilled in to help you.'

'He's such a darling,' Bev says. 'One of our success stories.'

'Life would be a lot easier if everyone was like Jack. I'd take a dozen of him every day.'

Bev puts on her coat. 'I still can't get used to seeing you in such civilised surroundings.'

'I know. I have an oven that actually works and everything. I'm very grateful to Shelby.'

'Don't be *too* grateful. He's got pots of cash, he can afford to keep you in a modicum of luxury.'

'I just wish he was here more often to share it with me.'

'Talk to him,' Bev says. When I start to protest, she holds up her hands. 'I'm sure all is absolutely hunky-dory as you say, but he's probably used to being top of the pile, not beneath a couple of mild-mannered donkeys, three badly behaved alpacas, half a dozen horses of assorted variety, forty-odd needy sheep and more bunnies than you can shake a stick at. Not to mention all the hens, ducks, geese and dogs we take care of. Make a fuss of him. Men like that kind of thing.'

'I'm so useless at this romance stuff, Bev.'

'That's because you haven't had enough practice.'

'I haven't had *any* practice!' It's true. Before I met Shelby, there was very little boyfriend action in my life. I've always preferred animals. Sometimes, I wish I were more sophisticated, more worldly wise, but, on a farm, no one cares about that and I've let my social skills slide.

'Have a shower, do your hair, dress nicely,' Bev advises.

'What about the evening feed?'

'I'll do that before I leave,' she says. 'Lucas can help.'

'But—'

Bev cuts me off. 'What I'm saying is make a bit of effort, Mols.' She huffs at me. 'Look like you care.'

'I *do* care.'

'Then make sure Shelby realises that. The man's a star. He's used to people falling at his feet.'

'I've never done that.'

'It wouldn't hurt every now and again, would it?' She kisses my cheek and leaves the caravan.

And I stand there contemplating which out of my two pairs of jeans might be considered in the category of 'dress nicely'.

Chapter Nine

When the day is done, Lucas comes back to the caravan. He's hardly stopped working all day and as he stands in the doorway kicking off his wellies, I see that he looks tired.

'Hey. Busy day?'

'Yeah,' he says. 'I spent most of the afternoon repairing the fences with Alan. I'm knackered. What's for dinner?'

'I'm making some Mexican wraps filled with peppers and onions accompanied by an avocado salsa thing and rice. Sound OK?'

He comes to look over my shoulder at it. 'Cool.'

Lucas has gone vegan, so I'm having to up my cooking game. I'm trying to do the same to show solidarity, but I had no idea how much I'd miss proper cheese. The vegan substitute I've bought tastes like a bar of soap. And, if you ask me, soya milk smells of sick. We're currently trialling oat milk, but it makes tea taste of porridge so I've taken to drinking it black. I hope Shelby doesn't mind the absence of dairy. Perhaps cutting it out might help his allergies.

'Is Dad coming for supper?'

'I hope so. He's in the middle of filming the Christmas special, though, so your guess is as good as mine.'

Lucas rolls his eyes.

'I've cooked plenty just in case. Why don't you have a nice hot shower?'

He kicks his toe against the carpet in his grubby socks. They have a hole in each of the big toes and I've no idea how that boy ruins so many. As I still have a morbid terror of supermarkets, I get Bev to bulk-buy them for me in ASDA. I have come to realise that teenage lads get through an inordinate amount of socks, food and toilet roll.

'Will Dad be here tomorrow?'

'I doubt it.' Two nights on the run is unlikely. 'Why?'

His face is arranged to reflect studied nonchalance. 'Just thought I might invite someone back. Maybe for tea.'

This takes me by surprise. It will be the first time that Lucas has asked to bring anyone here. 'Who?'

'No one.' Instantly defensive.

'OK. Does "no one" have a name?'

'Yes.'

When that name isn't forthcoming, I venture, 'Is "no one" a boy or girl?'

Lucas huffs. 'Don't get on my case.'

'Asking what your friend's name is and whether they're male or female isn't getting on your case, it's being interested in your life.'

'My friend's name is Aurora,' he parrots in a cartoon voice. 'And she identifies as a female.'

'Does that mean she *is* a female?'

'God, you are *so* last century.'

'Quite probably.' I can do nonchalant too. I stir my peppers. For a moment, I hoped it might be Penny and that she and Lucas had formed a friendship. God knows she could do with one. But I've never heard mention of this Aurora before. 'So where did you two meet?'

'At poetry club,' he reluctantly admits.

'Ah.' Of course, it can't really have been anywhere else.

I drive Lucas to a slightly grimy pub in our nearest town, Aylesbury, once a week where poetry club takes place in an upstairs room. I've no idea what goes on as I'm not allowed inside and I have to drop Lucas at the door and pretend that I don't know him. However, it looks as if he hasn't spent *all* his time reading his poetry there.

'What's she like?'

'If you want any more information, you'll have to apply electrodes to my testicles.'

'Lucas.' I give him a look. 'I'm interested.'

'Nosey,' he counters. 'Anyway, I'm not asking *anyone* to come back if *he's* here.'

'I'm sure your dad would be pleased that you'd got a girl-friend.'

'She's not a girlfriend. Aurora's a friend. That's all.' His pale cheeks colour up with two bright pink spots and he says Aurora in a slightly dreamy way. 'And if anyone meets him they go all ga-ga because he's on the telly. Then that's that. It gets in the way.'

'I didn't go ga-ga,' I point out. 'I didn't even know who he was.'

'That's because you're a weirdo,' Lucas says.

I risk giving him a swift kiss on the cheek. 'Takes one to know one.'

Channelling his inner five-year-old, Lucas rubs away my kiss and stomps off to the shower.

I smile to myself. Boy, girl or whatever, Lucas is bringing a friend home and that's a big step. He must be very keen. When we moved here, he had a brief flirtation with a young actress, but that didn't progress much beyond lengthy phone calls and the occasional WhatsApp chat session. It would be nice if he'd found himself a friend. He's a loner, like me, and that's not always all it's cracked up to be.

Chapter Ten

I fluff up my hair, put some mascara on and don a clean jumper and jeans. Even Bev would deem me presentable. However, I'm not sure Shelby will recognise me if he turns up now.

I check on dinner, drain the rice and keep it warm in the oven. The dish of cooked peppers goes in there too. There's still no sign of Lucas – who's yet to reappear from the shower – and there's no word from Shelby either, so I twiddle my thumbs for a few minutes before deciding to quickly nip out to check on the animals. I know that Bev was in charge of the evening feed, but I like to say goodnight to all my boys and girls before bedtime. I realise that I should have thought of this before I changed into my 'good' clothes, but needs must and I'll only be five minutes. I can't get dirty just looking at animals.

I shout out to Lucas, 'Back in five!' and pull on my waxed jacket and my welly boots. The temperature has dropped again and as I step out of the warmth of the caravan, my breath billows out in front of me in blousy white clouds. The inky sky is studded with a mass of stars. Who needs Christmas decorations when you've got this?

I hurry over to the barn. Everyone is already settled for the night. All is calm, all is bright – as they say. There's a lovely fug of animal smells in the air, the odd snuffle and the rustle of the hay as bodies shift and vie for space. This is, of course, when I'm at my happiest.

'Hi, everyone,' I whisper. 'Just came to see if you were all OK.'

The sheep have been brought into the barn as it's cold and they look like fluffy hummocks as they're all squashed together in sleep. Even Anthony is settled – though kept apart from everyone else – and he raises his head in acknowledgement. Then I hear a goat bleat. Our pygmy goats – four of them now – are housed further along the barn in their own escape-proof pen, allegedly. Dumb and Dumber were our original pair and they've been joined by two more rescue goats, Laurel and Hardy. They are talented escape artists, all of them, and I swear that they egg each other on. Another bleat and it definitely sounds a bit off. A goat in distress rather than a cheery one. Damn.

I leave the sheep and hurry along to their pen and, sure enough, Dumb has somehow managed to get himself stuck in the cargo net that forms part of their – rather optimistically named – adventure playground. His front legs are tangled in the net and his frantic wriggling is only making it worse. At this moment, I should stop to think about the situation and the fact that I'm wearing inappropriate clothing for goat-wrangling, but I don't. Instead, I charge straight in, thinking only of getting the distressed goat unravelled.

'Come on, boy,' I say soothingly. 'How the heck have you managed to do this to yourself?'

Dumb kicks against me. The other goats, convinced I'm trying to murder him rather than release him, start to charge and headbutt me in the knees. Laurel is taking particular umbrage at my well-intentioned interference. I could do with Lucas's help, but I don't think he'd hear me even if I shouted and, obviously, I didn't think to bring anything as useful as my phone. Not that I've got enough free arms to use it.

'Stop that,' I say, crossly as I try to hold Laurel at bay with one leg while clinging onto Dumb with both arms and all of my strength. 'I'm trying to help.'

I manage to heave Dumb out of the net despite him struggling and kicking his hooves at the air. For a little goat, he's surprisingly heavy. So I turn him round and put his front legs over my shoulders and hang on to his little goaty bottom. In his excitement at being released, Dumb decides to wee all down my front and distracted by the warmth of his grateful outpouring through my nice, clean clothes, I don't notice that, from the far side of the pen, Laurel has his head down and is taking a run at me.

Before I know what's happening, the horns of a tiny goat have connected with the back of my knees and I crumple to the floor amid the straw and goat droppings. Dumb lands softly but right on top of me, squeezing all the air out of my lungs. Dumber and Hardy, seizing their opportunity, hit me when I'm down and I get a muddy hoof to the face.

'Ouff!' I lie there, breathless in the dirt with a bleating goat on my chest, wondering how much I'll ache tomorrow.

Laurel, his work done in disarming me, starts to eat my hair.

At that moment, there's the honk of a car horn from the gate. This is Shelby. With such perfect timing, it has to be. So, instead of greeting him in my nice clothes with my nice hair, I'm covered in straw, dirt, goat wee and poo.

Bev will be very cross when I tell her.

Chapter Eleven

By the time I've re-asserted my authority over the goats and have sorted them out, Lucas has gone to open the gate and let Shelby in. Already, this isn't going quite as I'd imagined. I don't know much about romance, but I'd thought that, having had an absence of nearly a week, we might rush straight into each other's arms.

Instead, covered in goat and barn detritus, I approach Shelby rather more cautiously as he's climbing out of his shiny red Bentley. From the day he first rocked up in it, that car is something that never ceases to look incongruous in my farmyard. He always looks out of place too with his swept back, dirty-blond hair, movie star looks and immaculate clothes. Shelby is tall and handsome. I think if you saw him in the street, even if you didn't know he was a soap star, you'd think he was someone special. He has that air.

'What the hell . . . ?' Shelby says when he sees the state of me. The look of delight I had hoped for on his face is closer to horror.

'I'm sorry,' I say. 'Very sorry. Animal issues.'

'What else?' He shuts his car door with more of a slam than I think necessary.

Lucas, leaning on the gate, says, 'Jesus, Molly. Even for you . . .'

'I know. I know.' I try brushing myself down, but I'm not sure how much difference it makes. Whatever the opposite is of 'immaculately groomed', I'm it. 'I could have done with an extra pair of hands. Four tiny goats overpowered me.'

In fairness to Shelby, his eyes say that he might like to hug me, but his body is backing away from me.

'I'll take a quick shower,' I promise – fully appreciating how easy it is for me to do that these days. 'Dinner is ready. I won't be five minutes.'

Shelby stifles a sigh. It's obviously not the welcome he'd hoped for either – though it may have been the one he expected. I think Bev's right when she says he likes to have top billing rather than be at the bottom behind alpacas, pigs, sheep, cats, dogs, horses, ducks, goats, hens, etc.

We head to the caravan and I try to keep downwind of him. Goat wee has a fragrance all of its own. When we're inside, I say, 'I'll literally be five minutes. Help yourself to tea, a glass of plonk or whatever. I'll dish up dinner when I'm back.'

I leave Shelby and Lucas looking awkward with each other.

In the bedroom, I strip off and realise that I don't have any clean jeans or shirts. I go through at least one set of clothes a day and my mammoth laundry session was planned for tomorrow. As I jump into the shower, I wonder what I can wear. I can hardly go out there in my pyjamas. I quickly wash myself down, using a ton of minty shower gel to try to minimise the eau de goat wee. I do my hair too just in case Dumb's aim wasn't true. When I'm dry, I fling my wardrobe door open and look despairingly at the contents. The only thing still hanging there is the beautiful charity shop dress that I bought back in the summer for Shelby's posh fundraiser. It's a gorgeous wisp of a dress – black with pastel-coloured roses and with a floaty skirt. I put it on and feel a million dollars, if slightly over-dressed for the occasion of Mexican-style wraps in a caravan. I pull a brush through my wet hair – it will have to air-dry – and venture back out into the living area. Shelby and Lucas are sitting by the window, both of them on their phones. They look up when I enter and both of them seem rather startled.

'Going somewhere nice?' Shelby asks.

'I've run out of clothes,' I admit. 'It was this or nothing.'

His smile and the twinkle in his eyes say that he might have liked it to be nothing but as Lucas is here – even if he is engrossed in social media once again – we check ourselves.

'I could take the three of us out,' Shelby offers. 'You look beautiful. Seems a shame to waste it. We could go to the local pub?'

'No.' Lucas looks up from his phone. 'I can't bear the panto-mime of you turning up in a pub. Everyone stares at us.'

I have to say that Lucas is right. You can't go anywhere with Shelby and him not be recognised. Even if people don't directly approach him, they giggle behind their hands and try to take surreptitious selfies with him in the background. Shelby doesn't seem to mind all that much. I guess he's got used to it, but I find it traumatising and I know that Lucas absolutely hates it too. He's had many years of being overshadowed by his father's fame and, while things are on a reasonably stable footing, I don't want to put their fragile relationship in jeopardy.

'The food's ready,' I say. 'All I have to do is dish up.'

Lucas returns to his phone and I make a placating face at Shelby. 'Do you mind?'

'No,' he says. 'Not at all.' But he does sound a bit grudging. 'It will be nice to have some family time.'

I put the wraps, the rice and the veggies on the table between us. I like it when we eat together. It's a rare occasion and some-times Lucas forgets to be cross and actually talks to his father.

This is one of those times – though they steer clear of Lucas's poetry, which is always a bone of contention.

'How's the coursework going?' Shelby asks as he helps himself to rice.

Lucas shrugs. 'Good.'

'He's doing very well,' I chip in.

Shelby smiles at his son and the pride in his eyes is unmistakable. I only wish that Lucas could recognise it. Shelby might not be the best dad in the world, but he does try and Lucas cuts him no slack. It's a tightrope we all walk.

As I look across at Shelby, I realise that he does need to be loved. Overtly. It must be down to all the adoration he's had over the years. He's shown me some of the letters he gets from his fan club. These ladies are seriously dedicated. They adore him. Some of the things they say to him are . . . er . . . quite *personal*. One of the original attractions of little old me and my basic lifestyle was that he could be real, be himself. There are no trappings of stardom here – far from it. The animals and the kids don't care who Shelby is. And, if I'm honest with you, I don't either. I love him for who he is, not what his job is. But it bothers me that his default setting might be 'adoration'. He says it's not, but how can I know for sure? Do I show him enough how I feel?

We finish dinner and Lucas disappears to his bedroom.

'Alone, at last,' Shelby says in the manner of a Victorian villain.

'I don't like to get smoochy when Lucas is here.'

'You don't like to get smoochy at all,' Shelby points out.

It's true that I'm not a cuddly person, generally. I can do it with friends, but I find it harder when it comes to lurrrrve. Even after all this time with Shelby, I'm awkward with displays of affection, though I understand that in his profession they are much more open and free.

'We could go for a walk,' I suggest.

'It's freezing out there.' Shelby looks less enthralled than I am by the idea.

'We could wrap up warm. There's a full moon. It might be romantic.'

'OK.' He still doesn't look convinced. 'I suppose I'll be all the more grateful for the warmth when we get back.'

'You're staying tonight?'

'I have my supply of antihistamine and an overnight bag in the boot.'

'That's great.'

'Well . . .' he says, hesitantly. 'There's something that we need to talk about.'

'Right.' That doesn't sound good. 'I'll get our coats.'

Instantly, my tribe of dogs appear, having clocked the word 'walk'. With a sigh in his voice, Shelby says, 'Looks like it'll be a romantic walk for five.'

Chapter Twelve

Shelby and I step out into the night and the dogs run ahead of us as we cross the yard and climb over the stile. I've brought a torch, but I don't think we'll need it as the moon is full and bright and our eyes will soon adjust to the darkness.

It's cold and I wish I was wearing my usual jeans and jumper rather than a floaty dress with my wellies. There's a very good reason why I don't usually dress like this. We hold hands as we walk across the field, down to the river, and it's good to feel Shelby's strong fingers curled around mine. The ground is hard with frost beneath our feet. The air is sharp, fresh and freezes your lungs if you breathe too deeply.

Shelby shivers. 'To think we could be in a nice warm pub.'

'This is better for you. Bracing.'

'It's that all right,' he agrees.

'Townie,' I tease.

'Yeah,' he says. 'I need to talk to you about that.'

I wait with bated breath and a thousand things go through my mind. There's something off kilter and I know it. I'm just not sure out of several choices, which issue is most pressing in Shelby's mind.

We walk on and it's a few moments before Shelby speaks. When he does, he starts with a weary sigh. 'Molly, I've tried not to let it affect me, but I can't. It grieves me that Homewood Manor stands empty for most of the time. It's a beautiful house and it should be lived in.'

Ah. This one. I don't really want to comment as I know what's coming next. We've had this conversation several times before.

'You could move in with me,' he ventures. I go to put my case, but he raises a hand to stop me before continuing, 'There's a housekeeper and a gardener. I know that housework isn't your thing. You wouldn't have to lift a finger.'

'I like my van,' I remind him. 'I *love* it.'

'I should never have bought it for you.'

'You should. Lucas and I are both very comfortable here. It has all we need.'

Look at this place. The vast expanse of unbroken sky, the glitter of stars above us. There's not a sound here at night except for those of nature. When there's not a full moon it's as black as pitch. Why would you ever want to be anywhere else?

'Is Lucas happy?' Shelby asks. 'I can never tell.'

'He's as happy as any highly sensitive teenager can be. But, yes, he loves it here too and I know he doesn't like to talk about it, but he's doing so well with his studies.'

'He doesn't want to talk about *anything* with me,' Shelby complains.

'I know. It's not easy to get Lucas to open up.' I've bought a firepit and we both like to sit out at night in our deckchairs, staring into the flames – or, more likely, Lucas at his phone. We don't talk much, but sometimes you don't need to. I wish Shelby could get that.

'Does he have friends?'

'Yes,' I say, cautiously. I'm not going to break Lucas's trust and tell Shelby about Aurora who seems to be the new girlfriend-not-girlfriend.

An owl hoots in a nearby tree and wild rabbits dart for their burrows when they see us approach. In the far field, there's the sound of a diminutive Muntjac deer barking and the dogs prick their ears. When they realise that he's no threat, they return to their sniffing.

'I have no idea what's going on in his life.'

'He tells me very little too,' I admit. 'He's a private person. You have to cherish the rare days when he is in a chatty mood.'

'And I'm never here to catch those.'

'You do the best you can. I know that. You have a lot of demands on your time.'

'I'm not sure that my son sees it like that,' Shelby says sadly. 'I feel as if I'm in the way when I come here.'

'You're not.' I'm horrified that he should think that way. 'Never think that.'

'You and Lucas have formed such a tight bond that I feel as if I'm encroaching into your special little bubble.'

'That's not how it is at all.'

'I confess that I'm a little jealous of how well you two get along.' He laughs but I realise there's a kernel of truth in his words. 'I feel surplus to requirements. I never expected that you'd become so involved in his life.'

'Aren't you glad that I care for him?'

'God, yes. I know that these things don't always go as smoothly. But he's close to you in a way that we lost when his mum died. You don't know how sad that makes me.'

'Lucas might not show it, but we'd both love to have you here more often.'

'I can't move in here, Molly,' he says. 'I like the animals well enough, but I don't love them like you do. I am trying but, as yet, I don't think it's cute when I wake up with a dog's bottom on my face.'

'The dogs never come into the bedroom.' My lover gives me side-eye. 'Hardly ever,' I correct. 'I'm also trying. I do understand that while I've been brought up on a farm, getting up close and personal with animals is a new thing for you.'

Even on *Flinton's Farm*, Shelby is kept well away from the animals with a body double standing in for him when contact is necessary.

'I want us all to be together,' Shelby says. 'Be a family.'

'Lucas loves living here and so do I.'

He sighs at me. 'I can't leave the manor standing empty for much longer. I have to do something. It's costing me too much money. I'm thinking of renting it out and getting a place nearer to the studios. I might even sell it.'

I know that will be a wrench for him as it was the family home he built with his late wife, Susie. I do appreciate that it means a lot and why. I'm only sad that I can't share it with him. But it's not for me. It could never be my home. It's too huge, too tidy, too pristine. It terrifies me.

'I have to be on-site for the animals,' I say. 'Look at tonight's goaty crisis. Dumb could have been seriously hurt if I hadn't been on hand. There's always someone who needs my attention.'

Shelby stops and turns to me. 'And what if that someone is me?' he asks.

'You know how it is here,' I counter. 'This was my life long before you came into it. I can't just turn my back on it.'

'Is there any chance that one day I'll come first or will it always be the animals?'

I can't answer that in the way that Shelby wishes and we both know that. I'd love to be able to say that it was different, but I can't give up everything I've worked for. It's too much to ask of me. 'Could we not just carry on the way we are? For now?'

'I love you.' Shelby pulls me close to him and kisses my hair. 'I want to be with you.' But he doesn't sound happy when he says it.

'I love you too.'

'That's all right then,' he teases. 'We'll work it out, somehow.'

Then he kisses me properly and my head swims and everything else melts away. My worries drift away into the night sky. When I'm in Shelby's arms I feel that, together, we can overcome any difficulties.

Chapter Thirteen

Shelby spends the night and we make love. It's fine – more than fine – and I feel it brings us closer together. There's a gentle intimacy that we haven't shared for a while and, when he says he loves me, I believe him. But when he turns over and goes to sleep, I spend the rest of the night wide awake with my head against his shoulder, holding him tight while he sleeps. I want to hold him here for ever, but I don't know if I can.

In the morning, long before dawn, he kisses me briefly before he dashes back to the studio. I saddle up and go out to feed the animals, who are slightly startled at me appearing so early. Even Little Dog struggles to keep his one eye open and he's usually full of beans at any time of day.

'I know it's early, guys,' I explain to the sheep. 'I couldn't sleep.'

Yet, whatever the hour, they're all still happy to eat.

Much later, when I'm back in the caravan and having my breakfast, Lucas appears. His mop of black hair is dishevelled and will stay like that for the rest of the day, but I'm hardly one to criticise his lack of grooming.

'Has he gone?'

'Yes. Your dad had an early call. He asked me to say goodbye.'

Lucas rolls his eyes. 'He can't even do that himself?'

'He didn't want to wake you. Should he have come into your room at four o'clock?'

Lucas decides not to answer that and instead grabs himself some cereal and slides into the seat opposite me. 'You've done the morning feed?'

'Yes, even the animals were surprised at how early I was up.'

He does smile at that. 'What's on today?'

'We've got Wendy the Winky Washer coming.'

Lucas's eyes widen. 'I don't even want to ask what that is.'

'We have a lady who comes to clean the horses'—

He holds up a hand. 'That's gross. I'm eating my breakfast!'

'You asked.'

'Is that even a job?' Lucas's face bears an expression of morbid fascination. 'Why would someone willingly do that?'

I laugh. 'You can watch, if you like.'

'No, I *wouldn't* like.' He tuts his disgust. 'The joys just keep on coming at this place.'

'Every day is a school day,' I agree. 'Just google . . .'

Lucas cuts me off. 'No. I will not. I'm not googling anything. There are some things in life you don't need to see.'

'When you first came here, you struggled with grooming the horses. Now, it's second nature. Look how far you've come.'

'There are some things I draw the line at.' Lucas gives a theatrical shudder. 'I'd be permanently scarred.'

Sometimes, he's more like his father than he thinks.

'How much does she charge for . . .' He can't even bring himself to say it.

'Twenty pounds a horse. More if they're . . . um . . . bigger.'

'Seriously?' He's horrified. 'I'd want SO much more.'

Then we both crack up and laugh together. I do love Lucas when I can make him forget he's supposed to treat everything with disdain.

'We've got quite a few students in today,' I continue when we've finished giggling. 'Anna, the Arts and Crafts teacher, is coming in too. You can help with that, if you like. She might want to make some natural decorations. If it's dry, the students could go out into the fields to collect some holly.'

'Holly? What does that look like?'

Now it's my turn to give him the evil eye.

He holds up his hands. 'I've only ever seen it on Christmas cards.'

'It's pretty much the same in the wild. I'll tell you where the best bushes are and you can take the secateurs and loppers out with you. I thought we'd do Christmassy bunting for the open day. It will make the barn look a bit jollier for our visitors.'

'I am *much* happier on bunting duty,' he says, looking horrified again at the thought of . . . well, you know. 'I can cope with that.'

'We'd like you to write and perform a poem for the nativity, if you would,' I venture. You have to catch Lucas at the right moment when you want him to share his gift for poetry with the world, and I'm hoping this is one of them.

'What do I know about the nativity? I know less about that than cleaning horses' knobs.'

'Lucas!' I hide my smile. 'Not appropriate.'

'I only know that Jesus wasn't eaten by three alpacas shortly after being born.'

Yes, we have still to discover the culprit of that particular misdemeanour.

'I can fill you in on the basics, but it doesn't have to be religious. It doesn't even have to be a conventional take on it. As long as the Virgin Mary doesn't tell the three wise men to "eff off", then I'm happy to give you free rein.' Though, in fairness, if I'd just given birth I wouldn't want three random men turning up with mainly smellies as gifts.

'On your own head be it,' Lucas says. 'I'll work on it with Aurora.'

'Is she coming to dinner tonight? Your *friend*?'

'No,' he replies crossly. 'She's busy.'

'That's a shame. I'd like to meet her.'

'Get a life, Molly.' He throws his cereal bowl in the sink and fusses with putting on his boots in a disgruntled manner.

'Don't be mad,' I say placatingly. 'I'm only teasing you because I love you.'

'Huh,' he grunts.

'If you wait for me, we can walk the fields together before the kids arrive. I'll show you where the best holly is.'

'OK. If you want to.' He puts on a front of doing this for me, but I know that it's one of his favourite things too. We just wander over our land, taking stock and enjoying the countryside. I'm trying to teach Lucas to appreciate the changing seasons and what they bring to our life on the farm. Though I've yet to convince him of the joys of winter.

Chapter Fourteen

After our invigorating walk – the mercury probably hasn't touched zero degrees yet – Lucas and I head straight to the tea room with our arms full of holly which we couldn't resist picking. We arrive at the same time as the rest of the students. We'll be busy for the rest of the day with plenty of kids booked in.

I pause before we go in. 'Band T-shirt bet?'

'Bugger,' Lucas says. 'I should have googled something.'

'I'm going with Blue Oyster Cult.' I've been giving this considerable thought while I've been walking. It's been a long time since I've seen Alan's Blue Oyster Cult-based wardrobe.

'Is that even a real band?' Lucas queries.

'Certainly is and it's a winner.'

'Pah,' he says with a sneering tone. 'Sounds more like a trendy seafood restaurant. I'll see your Blue Whatever and raise you a Van Halen.'

'Oh. Fighting talk.'

'They're the only ones I can think of that old people know. What's the prize?'

'Takeaway dinner paid for by the loser?'

'I'll have pizza, thanks.' Lucas is obviously feeling confident. Which is surprising as neither of us has ever been right.

When we open the door and step inside, Bev already has the kettle on and a row of cups set out. Jack is behind the counter with her, ready to serve, and from the broad smile on his face, I can tell that all is well in his world. Lucas and I pull a table to one side and we spread out the holly we've picked. Some of the leaves are still frosted and I don't want them to drip everywhere when they start to thaw out.

Bev indicates the band logo across her breasts. 'And what was your best guess today, lovelies?'

Today's T-shirt is Rage Against the Machine and both Lucas and I exchange bemused looks. Lucas shrugs at me and I'm none the wiser.

'No idea,' he whispers. 'But I like the sound of them.'

'No winner today,' I tell Bev who is well aware that we have taken up the band T-shirt mantle.

'Ah well. Tomorrow is another band T-shirt day,' Bev says. 'But seeing that neither of you have any taste in music, Alan and I can stay ahead of the curve.'

Which is true.

'I've got pains in my hands,' Lucas complains as he tucks them under his arms. 'I'm so numb, I can't tell whether they're hot or cold.' He stamps his feet, his boots covered in frost.

'Good job we've got indoor activities,' I say, rubbing my own hands together. 'It's a cold one out there. I think everyone would dig their heels in if we tried to make them go outside today. We can set up the crafting activities in here where it's nice and warm.'

'We had trouble starting the car this morning. Bloody thing. Alan's going to have a look at it later.'

I wish that I could pay Bev more as that would help them both out. Alan volunteers here too and I know from Bev that he has a good pension, but they could probably do with some extra money coming in. Everyone likes a few quid put by for a rainy day or a broken-down car.

'Asha's here. He can help Alan.' We have an eleven-year-old boy with ADHD who can strip down and fix any machinery you care to mention. Getting stuck into Alan's car engine would make his day. The pair of them often hang out in the barn, exchanging barely a word all day bar asking to pass a spanner or something. It's when they're both at their happiest.

'Would you like a hot drink, Molly? I'm using my favourite kettle today.' Making tea is Jack's comfort zone. He's a fantastic kid, always willing and he just needs a bit of a support. It's rare now that he has a bad day. 'We have Yorkshire Tea today and a selection of excellent coffees – Gold Blend, Nescafé or Kenco. I can offer you semi-skimmed or soya milk.'

Our tea break offers are generally reliant on donations from our supporters. We are gifted a lot of biscuits. We also get nearly-out-of-date bread and cakes from our nearest supermarket chain.

'Thanks, Jack. Tea would be great with a bit of semi-skimmed.'

'How much is a bit?' Jack queries. 'Is that more than a splash? Bev had a splash and that was quite difficult to judge.'

'Shall I put my own milk in, Jack?'

'Yes.' He looks relieved that the responsibility has been taken away from him. 'Would you like a biscuit with that? We have chocolate digestives.'

'Excellent up-selling.'

He holds the packet of biscuits to his chest, protectively. 'I don't know what that means.'

'In a coffee shop you'd ask your customers if they'd like something else with their drink so that it makes more money for the café.'

'But this is free.'

'I know. I was pretending to be in a coffee shop.'

'Oh. Why?'

'For a bit of fun, Jack. I was paying you a compliment.'

'So do you want a biscuit or not?'

'Yes, please.' You know when you wish you'd never started something? Jack carefully hands over my biscuit. Just the one. For a moment he looks as if he might not let go of it. 'Thanks, Jack.' I prise it from his fingers.

'They're my favourite biscuits.' He looks longingly at it.

'I know. You can have one too. Just don't spoil your lunch.' He's wolfed one down before I get the sentence out. 'Do you want to help Bev with preparation today?'

'What is it?'

I look to Bev who supplies, 'Jacket potato and baked beans.'

'I don't really like baked beans,' Jack says firmly. 'It's the colour. And they're slimy.'

'I'm sure you can manage. It would be good experience.'

Jack grimaces at me. 'I'll try.'

'Good lad. Bev will right there with you.'

'By the way, Mols,' Bev says over her shoulder. 'The new mayor is popping by today.'

'He's what?'

'He wants to see what we get up to here before he comes to the open day. I said it would be OK.'

'Are you going to deal with him?'

Bev stops what she's doing and puts her hands on her hips. 'No,' she says. 'You are.'

'I can't.' What would I say to the mayor?

'I'm sure you can manage.' Bev echoes me with a mischievous glint in her eye. 'It would be good experience.'

'Sometimes I dislike you intensely,' I tell her.

'But you love me more,' she bats back.

'You see the mayor,' I beg. 'Please. I'll make lunch.'

'No. You've got this, Molly. Charm him so that he wants to make us his Christmas charity.'

'Good luck with that,' Lucas says, sarcastically.

'Shut up or I'll rope you in too.'

'I'd rather wash horse dicks.'

All the students titter behind their hands. This is why they love Lucas. They see him as cool and untameable. To be honest, it's why I love him too.

Chapter Fifteen

I'm in the alpaca stall rooting through their droppings as I bag them up. We sell the manure as fertiliser for gardens and as well as still trying to identify the Baby Jesus-eating culprit, I don't want there to be a bag with bits of plastic doll in it. Tina, Johnny and Rod are watching me with great interest.

'You're all naughty,' I tell them. 'But that doesn't mean I love you less.'

I turn as I hear a noise and Alan stands behind me. 'Mayor's here.'

'Thanks, Alan.' I stand and wipe my hands on my jeans. 'Where is he? I'm dreading it.'

'Behind you,' Alan says and wanders off, giving a wave as he goes.

Slowly, I force myself to turn and there's a slightly perplexed and rather attractive gentleman standing by the pen flanked by our honking guard geese. My face is now a nice shade of beetroot with embarrassment.

I look at him, suitably mortified. 'I can only apologise.'

'No problem.'

'I'm so sorry that I didn't realise you'd arrived. Usually, I hear a car horn.'

'It looks as if you were preoccupied.' The mayor nods towards my pile of alpaca poo.

'I'm on a mission,' I tell him. 'It's a long story.'

He holds out a hand for me to shake, but I show him my palms, which are caked with all kinds of unspeakable things.

'Maybe not,' he says with a smile and it's really a very lovely smile. 'I'm Matt Eastman.'

'Molly Baker. I like to think I'm in charge here, but I'm never quite sure.'

He laughs and that makes me relax a bit. My only dealings with authority in recent times have been in connection with HS2 going through our land and I'm still feeling a bit bruised.

And you'll have to excuse me if I sound a bit thick here, but I thought that all mayors looked like Jeremy Corbyn or had dandruff and bad beards. Not that my experience with mayors is extensive, or even minimal.

This mayor is dark-haired, tall and well-built in the manner of a seasoned rugby player. He looks as if he hasn't shaved today and there's a fine stubble on his chin. I also imagined that he'd rock up in his official robes and neck-chain but, instead, he's all casual in a black polo-neck sweater under a khaki padded jacket. It suits him. His jean-clad legs are largely covered by a pair of green wellies that look like they've seen some action. His appearance is every inch the country squire rather than a townie council official. I'd guess he's about the same age as me, late thirties, and seems to have a shy charm.

I climb out of the alpaca pen and clean my grubby hands with gel. The geese, happy that the mayor isn't a threat to our safety, waddle away with more honking as they go. 'Sorry, I should have been ready to greet you properly.'

'I don't stand on ceremony,' he says. 'I've been dying to get up here and have a look ever since Beverly Adams got in touch with me.'

'Oh, Bev. She usually does anything that requires contact with the outside world. I prefer to hide away here with the animals.'

'I can understand why,' he says. 'I was brought up on a farm and miss it terribly.'

'Oh.' Hadn't expected that. 'Whereabouts?'

'A dairy farm in Lancashire.'

'Ah. Now I recognise the accent.'

'It's had the edges knocked off it over the years. I've been down south since I left university and moved to London to work. I've lived round here for a while now, though.' He looks around him. 'Yet I had no idea that this place existed.'

'Well, it's our pleasure to welcome you to Hope Farm. Can I give you a tour?'

'I'd like that.'

Just as I'm about to introduce the mayor to our atrociously behaved alpacas, Bev comes bustling over.

'Hiya! Hiya!' She's slightly breathless and flustered. 'Got caught up with making lunch. I only just found out you were here. I'm Bev. Pleased to meet you.'

I'll swear she does a little curtsy. It reminds me of the time when Shelby first arrived at Hope Farm and Bev went completely ga-ga and turned into a teenager again. Then it makes me feel a little bit sad that things aren't quite as they were.

The mayor smiles again. 'Thanks for inviting me, Bev. This looks like a great place. Molly's just about to give me a tour.'

'She is?' Bev looks at me, slightly stunned.

Yeah. Look at me being all friendly and not remotely trau-matised by having to deal with a figure of authority.

'You could join us for lunch too, if you like,' I offer. 'It will give you a chance to meet some of our regular students. They're not doing outdoor activities today due to the cold. They'd normally be out in the barns or the fields, helping with the animals. Instead, we've got them all tucked up in our nice warm tea room making bunting for the open day.'

He checks his watch. 'I'm not pushed for time so that would be great. Thanks.'

'I'll be serving up in about half an hour,' Bev says.

'Perfect. We'd better get a move on, then.'

'Right,' Bev says. 'I'll leave you to it.'

As the mayor turns away, Bev gives me the double thumbs-up behind his back. *HOT STUFF!* she mouths.

And I have to say that I think she's probably right.

Chapter Sixteen

The mayor and I lean on the gate of the pen. Tina Turner, Rod Stewart and Johnny Rotten all look quite frisky today. Always worrying. I point them out as appropriate.

The alpacas come over to the gate, hoping there will be food. Tina flutters her long eyelashes at Matt Eastman.

'Hey,' he says and softly strokes her muzzle. Pushover.

'Don't let their cute looks fool you, they're in disgrace at the moment.' I scratch Rod's neck which he just about tolerates. 'Aren't you?'

They hum in unison and give us their collective butter-wouldn't-melt looks.

Pah.

'Tina is definitely our diva. She gives great selfies and likes Abba music. Rod, the one with skinny white legs, will back-kick you whenever he gets the chance. Johnny Rotten is our bad boy of the alpaca world and likes nothing better than making mischief. But they're all a handful.'

'Aren't you all lovely,' Matt says.

'Because of their looks, people think that alpacas are cute. They, quite categorically, are not. They are feisty buggers, one

71

and all, with a nose for trouble. They don't like to be handled, touched too much and, if you are foolish enough to go near their fancy hair on their heads, they will bite you.'

And we take them into care homes! This was Bev's idea.

'Duly warned.' The mayor takes a step backwards.

'Let me show you some of our other residents.'

'Are they any better behaved?'

I laugh. 'Not necessarily. Bad behaviour seems to be our speciality – animals and humans. Most of the animals here, if not all, have been rescued from difficult circumstances. We tend to be quite lenient with them.'

Little Dog appears and grins at our visitor, who instantly falls in love with him. 'You're a fine fellow.' Matt ruffles his ears confirming mutual adoration. Always happens.

'Ready for our cuddle corner?'

'Animals or people?' he quips and ensures that I blush once more.

'Therapy bunnies.' We stroll along to the cuddle corner with Little Dog at our heels. 'If the kids are distressed they can come and sit on the straw in here to chill out. It's not usually very long before an obliging bunny hops onto their laps. Though the Flemish giant bunnies, Ant and Dec, are a tad big for that. They'd squash some of our youngsters.'

'They're whoppers,' he agrees.

'Gentle giants.' We move on and then stop at the sheep pen. 'I daren't count how many sheep we have. Despite Bev telling me not to, I take on more orphans every year. We have quite a flock now. This is Anthony our anti-social sheep. He has to be kept in his own pen as he likes to charge humans and other sheep alike. Never turn your back on him,' I caution. 'We love him dearly, but the feeling isn't mutual.'

Anthony stares down the mayor.

'I'll try not to get on the wrong side of him,' Matt says.

'Wise move.' I take him further into the barn. 'I don't know what happened to Anthony before we got him, but some of our animals prove too much of a handful for anyone else, some have been maltreated, some are here simply because they've outgrown their cuteness. All of these things could apply to our students too.'

'I'm looking to get involved in a local community project,' Matt tells me. 'Both while I'm mayor and then afterwards when my term ends too. This would be ideal.'

'We'd love to have you on board.' I gesture at our buildings, our animals. 'All this costs a lot to keep. We get some funding for the students and Bev manages to pick up a few grants here and there, but we're largely on our own for the rest of it.'

'You have a board of trustees?'

'Yes. My partner and a group of businessmen own the land. They've granted us the lease here for ten years at a modest rent, but we'll have to do a lot of fundraising. More than we currently do.' I smile at him. 'As you've probably gathered, that takes me well out of my comfort zone.'

'I'd like to be able to help.'

'We'd be grateful for any input.' I take him past our two spotted Kunekune pigs, Salt and Pepper, who always look so smiley even though Pepper is a hen-pecked husband. We head towards Teacup's stall. 'Does that mean you'll come and turn our lights on at the open day?'

'Of course. It would be my pleasure. Not just that. I want to get my hands dirty too,' he says. 'I realise how much I've missed this. My sister runs the family farm now. She has a fairly big dairy herd. I opted for a career that's nothing to do with agriculture and just being here makes me feel how much I miss farming and how much it's still in my blood.'

'That's music to my ears.' If I could change one thing about Shelby it would be that he enjoyed the animals here as much

73

as I do. I know that he tries, but he's not comfortable covered in mud or handling the working ends of livestock. Sometimes he's not even sure which end is which. Despite saying he hates celebrity parties, he's actually much happier chit-chatting with a glass of champagne in his hand than attempting to bottle-feed a lamb.

'I mean it,' Matt reiterates.

'And I'll take any help you can give.' We cross the yard and stop at the next pen. 'Here's Teacup, our giant "miniature" pig.' Teacup hauls himself to his feet and comes to greet us with some grunts. Fifty is right beside him.

'This is Fifty, our pet sheep. He couldn't stand up when he was born, but Bev and I nursed him night and day. And now here he is.' Another one of our little successes. 'We could walk Teacup up to our new piggy hollow, if you like. Before the weather turned too cold, the students spent a few weeks digging it out and putting some fencing round it.'

Let's see what this mayor is really made of, I think, as I let our lovely pig and Fifty out of the pen. I give the mayor a bucket of pig nuts which will ensure that Teacup follows us. Fifty runs ahead with his awkward gait while Teacup totters after us – or, more accurately, after the pig nuts – as we walk along the track up to the muddy wallowing hole. I need to get some more pigs, I think. A curly tail corner would make everyone's heart glad.

The mayor proves himself a natural with our porcine friend and Little Dog has already attached himself to Matt – and I think my dog is, generally, a very good judge of character. I think it will be a great addition to have the mayor around the farm. Look at the size of him for a start. He's a man who could manage our massive Shire horses or sort out a stroppy sheep. It amazes me how comfortable I already feel with him, as that almost never happens.

When Teacup is settled in the wallow – literally as happy as a pig in muck – I take the mayor on a walk across the fields. Fifty turns and heads back towards the yard, clearly worried that he might miss something. We climb the stile and head towards the big field.

'You've certainly got a beautiful piece of land here,' he says. 'No wonder you're so happy.'

'We were evicted from our previous farm to make way for HS2. Thankfully, my partner helped to save us.' And I mustn't ever forget how much Shelby has done for us. If he hadn't stepped in we could have so easily gone under.

'Does he live here too? I take it that's your caravan I saw as I came in.'

'Shelby has a home nearby,' I say. 'He works long hours so he's not here as often as he'd like.' Or, more accurately, as often as I'd like. 'I live in the caravan with his son, Lucas. He came initially as a student and now works here. That's how his father and I met.' I see him frown. 'It's complicated, but somehow it works.'

'Relationships seem to be these days,' he agrees. 'That's why, at my grand age, I'm still free and single.'

As I said, I'd put him at less than forty, but you know what my judgement is like. Bev will find out. 'You've never been married?'

'No. Came close once, but I think I dodged a bullet there.' There's a sadness in his eyes when he says, 'It didn't feel like it at the time.'

'I came to love late in life,' I admit.

'You're lucky to have found it.'

'I am. I was in very grave danger of turning into a mad old recluse who only had conversations with her dogs.' Now look at me, chatting away on a very personal level with a complete stranger. Go me!

Our fields slope gently and I find the highest viewing point so that we can look over the land. 'This is us,' I say.

'I love it.' Matt Eastman is a little out of puff after the exertion. Perhaps he spends too much time behind a desk. 'I'd give my right arm for a place like this.'

'You're welcome here any time you like,' I tell him, earnestly. 'Are you DBS checked?'

'Yes.'

'That's great.' He's had a screening so that means he can be around our vulnerable kids. 'We are always grateful for a willing pair of hands.'

He grins. 'You won't be able to get rid of me now that I've found you.'

'Good.' I like the sound of that.

'Thanks for taking the time to show me round.' The corners of his eyes crinkle when he smiles. He has a genuine, open face. I like him. And you know that I'm not all that keen on people as a rule.

'My pleasure. But we should get back. Bev will be dishing out lunch and she doesn't take kindly to latecomers.'

'I'll race you,' says the mayor and I'm so surprised at his challenge that he's already taken off by the time I respond. So I chase after him and, with Little Dog barking excitedly, we run all the way back to the farmyard.

Chapter Seventeen

We're still laughing when we burst through the door of the tea room and everyone turns around to look at us. I must also say at this point that I was the victor by the narrowest of margins.

'Well done,' the mayor says, panting.

'I think you might have let me win there.' I'm equally breathless.

'Not at all,' he insists. 'You won fair and square.' But I still think he's fibbing.

We pull ourselves up short when we realise that everyone is staring at us and try to regain some decorum. Even Bev looks startled by our entrance.

'Hi, everyone.' I address the students who are sitting at the big table waiting for lunch. 'This is Mr Eastman; he's the mayor of our local town and he's here today to have a look at what we do. He's also very kindly agreed to come and turn on the Christmas lights at our open day.'

Some of our students clap excitedly and are as thrilled as if we had a pop star in the house. The rest are, of course, seriously underwhelmed. It would take an actual pop star in the house to get them interested – and not just a minor one, probably 'like' the whole of One Direction or Little Mix.

The tea room is warm and welcoming and there's the appetising scent of Bev's jacket potatoes in the air. We spend a lot of time in here with the students and want it to feel like a safe space, so we try to make it as comfortable as possible. Today, it looks especially pretty as the bunting the students have been making has been hung around the walls. It features pictures mostly taken by Tamara of the animals, students and farm activities. Surprisingly, it brings a lump to my throat to look at it. We do well here, I think. The smiling faces reflected back at me say that we're making a difference. Some of these kids wouldn't even talk when they arrived.

'Do sit down,' I say to the mayor. 'This is Lucas, who I told you about.'

Lucas regards him with deep suspicion. If the mayor notices it, then he pretends not to and chats amiably to Lucas about what he's seen on the farm. I think if anyone has the ability to relate to Lucas and grind him down then Matt does.

I take the chance to go and help Bev and Jack with serving.

'How's Hot Stuff?' Bev whispers when I'm next to her.

'He's very nice,' I whisper back. 'Keen to help us and not just with the Christmas lights. He'd like to do something more permanent. Better than that, he's got a farming background.'

'Praise the Lord and all that's holy,' she says. 'We need someone else on our board with a bit of clout now that Shelby is more absent than present.' She raises her eyebrows at me.

'I'm not sure what else I can do on that front.'

'We'll work on it,' she promises. 'But, for now, you can get that big spoon and start dishing up beans or we'll be here all afternoon.'

Immediately, the mayor jumps up and comes to lend a hand, giving out plates to the students and cracking jokes.

He has a natural way with him and it's a wonder that he hasn't got kids. He'd make a great dad. When he sits down again next to Lucas, he even manages to engage him in conversation and, as you know, that's no mean feat. At one point he even makes Lucas laugh out loud and both Bev and I exchange a startled glance. I wonder what on earth he's said to elicit that response.

I take my lunch and go to join them. 'Isn't it nice that the mayor has agreed to join us for our open day and turn on the Christmas lights?'

'I thought you-know-who was doing that?' Lucas says.

'Your dad can't guarantee making it,' I tell him.

'Who's your dad?' the mayor asks.

Lucas shoots me a filthy look, but he brought it up.

'My partner, Shelby, is an actor in a soap opera,' I explain. 'We have, in the past, tended to rely on him for this kind of thing.'

'Shelby Dacre?'

'Yes, you know of him?'

'Who doesn't?' the mayor says. 'I don't watch it myself but my mum is a huge fan of *Flinton's Farm*.'

'That is hil-*ar*-ious,' Lucas says. 'My father likes to think his fan base is nubile nineteen-year-olds. Most of his girlfriends have been.'

That stings and, to deflect the direction of the conversation, I interject, 'Did Lucas tell you that he's writing some poetry for the nativity?'

'No,' the mayor says. 'You're a poet? What a great talent.'

I get another death-stare for my trouble.

'He is *very* talented,' I add, defiantly. I'm hoping that Lucas will make a start on his contribution soon as that will be one less thing for me to worry about.

'I'm a big fan of poetry,' Matt tells us. 'Who's your favourite?'

Lucas seems startled by his response. 'Er . . . you won't have heard of him . . . Harry Baker.'

'He's great,' Matt says. 'My favourite is "A Love Poem for Lonely Prime Numbers".'

'Seriously? You really know his stuff?' Lucas, rather grudgingly, looks impressed. 'I like "The Sunshine Kid" and "Paper People".'

'I follow him on YouTube and have listened to his TED Talk a dozen times. I haven't seen him live, have you?'

'No, but I'd like to,' Lucas admits.

'I think he's doing a tour next year. I should try to get tickets for us all.'

'Yeah, well . . .' Lucas glares at me as if I'm the orchestrator of this unexpected burst of enthusiasm.

It's sad, but I know that part of his reticence is that he's been let down too many times in the past. Things that Shelby has promised that he hasn't delivered, times he's cancelled due to filming schedules. I can see that Lucas can't let himself trust Matt's promises. I understand that.

'That would be great,' I say to Matt. 'You'll hear some of Lucas's poetry at Christmas.'

'*If* I do it,' Lucas says, trying to sound uninterested. But I'm not fooled and neither is our mayor. Behind Lucas's back, I give the thumbs-up to Matt. 'A' for effort.

When we've finished our lunch, Lucas and our crafts teacher, Anna, take the students out for a brief walk round the yard while we get the room ready for this afternoon's card-making session. As soon as they're wrapped up against the cold and out of the way, the mayor helps us to clear up and proves himself a dab hand with a tea towel. Bev's looking at him in a slightly dreamy way. If she weren't so smitten with Alan, I think she'd be in deep.

She sidles up next to me and whispers. 'Nothing turns me on more than the sight of a strong man with a tea towel in his hand.'

That makes me laugh and the mayor turns to smile at us both.

When Matt's completed his chores, he puts down the tea towel and says, 'I need to go. I've got to cut the ribbon at a new playgroup this afternoon and shake some hands.'

'Busy life,' I say.

'Have I passed the test here?' he asks. 'Will you have me back? You're doing great work and I'd like to be involved.'

'You're welcome any time.'

'Thanks for a great lunch, Bev,' he says and makes her face go a nice shade of pink and her eyelashes all fluttery.

I suspect that she's fanning herself with the tea towel as I walk Matt to his car by the gate.

'Thanks, Molly. I've really enjoyed myself.'

'It's been nice to have you here.' And then I do my usual thing and go all shy. We stand there by his car, not quite knowing how to part.

Then Wendy the Winky Washer rocks up in her rickety old truck and I open the gate for her.

'Hiya!' she says as she jumps out. Wendy is always the most cheerful of souls. I'm hoping it's not entirely due to job satisfaction.

'Hi, Wendy. Let me introduce you to Matt Eastman. He's the local mayor.'

'Nice to meet you.' Wendy shakes his hand then says, 'Are my boys ready for me?'

'Wendy's here to give the horses a . . . um . . . er . . . *spa* treatment.'

'Sounds great,' the mayor says. 'Can I book myself in?'

'I don't normally do humans,' Wendy replies with a wide grin, 'but I'd make an exception for you, sweetheart.'

I try to hide my own smile and think it's best if I don't reveal the true nature of Wendy's regular visits or the fact that she charges by the inch.

81

'It's a date,' the mayor says and then climbs into his car. I go to the gate and let him out, waving as he drives away. I hope it's not long before he comes back.

'You're very naughty,' I say to Wendy as we walk up to the horses' field together. 'He had no idea what he was agreeing to.'

'Shame.' Wendy winks at me. 'As I'd do that one for free.'

Chapter Eighteen

It's been a long day, and when I get back to the caravan after the evening feeding frenzy, I'm exhausted. Even the dogs look knackered as they slope in behind me – except for Betty Bad, of course: The Dog Who's Never Tired. Oh, to have her energy. Me, I'm looking forward to nothing more taxing than settling with the radio and my book. In the living room, Lucas is already showered and is sitting writing on his laptop. He looks up when I walk in.

'Hi. You got finished early,' I note.

'Speed and efficiency,' he deadpans.

I try to look over his shoulder at what he's writing, but he's having none of it and moves his body to block my view. I never manage to catch him out. 'How's it going?'

'OK.' He shrugs. 'What's for dinner?'

'I hadn't even given it a thought.' I open the fridge and peer into it, hopefully. 'There's some leftover rice. Shall I zhoosh it up with some veg and a bit of curry powder? Maybe put an egg on top?'

'We're vegan.'

'Right.' No eggs.

'Is there enough for Aurora?'

Oh, goodness. I'd entirely forgotten about the possibility of Aurora. 'I thought that had been cancelled.'

'It's uncancelled,' is all Lucas says.

'I can make it stretch, but wouldn't you like me to rustle up something a bit more fancy?' Not sure how I might follow up on that offer, though. There must be some pasta lurking in the depths of the cupboard.

'You don't have to impress her,' Lucas says. 'She's cool.'

But impress her I want to.

'What time is she coming? Do I need to go and collect her?'

'Stop panicking, Molly. She's just a friend. I said to come about seven and she's got a car so she'll drive herself.'

'Oh. Right.' Her own car. That must mean she's older than Lucas, if she's already driving.

I check the time. I feel that I'll be subject to scrutiny and hope that I've got time for a quick run round the shower. What's happening here? I've already met one stranger today and that seems like more than enough. Yet I don't want to ask Lucas to put off Aurora as he's never brought anyone home before and, despite his protestations, I feel she must be important to him.

'Can you chop some veg while I have a shower?' I plonk an onion, some mushrooms and a red pepper on the work surface. That should liven up the rice a bit.

'Sure.' He closes his laptop and jumps up.

Lucas is surprisingly perky tonight. That's a good thing, right?

'I won't be long.'

I get a nearly-smile. 'OK.'

Feeling more anxious than is probably necessary, I go through to the bedroom. I'm used to dealing with teenagers at work, but this new relationship with Lucas is a steep learning curve. There are times, precious ones, when we seem in tune and can relax together. Other times, I feel as if I'm constantly walking on eggshells, and being permanent referee between Lucas and Shelby is definitely challenging.

The dogs follow me through to the bedroom, jump onto the bed and curl up together. 'You're not allowed in here,' I remind them. 'Much as I love you all, your fur makes Shelby sneeze.'

They look at me dolefully and snuggle tighter.

'Banned territory,' I reiterate.

None of them budge. They do look quite comfortable.

'OK,' I say, 'You can stay in here while I'm in the shower, but that's all. Then you're back in the kitchen.' I try to sound stern. They don't look convinced.

Stripping off, I grab a towel and go to luxuriate in my indoor shower with hot water on tap. At times like this, I'm very grateful that Shelby has supplied me with such amenities. I hope he can find time to Skype me tonight, although I know his filming schedule is manic. I linger in the shower as long as I can possibly justify.

When I go back to the bedroom, the dogs are fast asleep in a huddle and don't even rouse as I potter round getting dressed. It seems such a shame to wake them when they look so cute together. I'll just leave them for a bit longer and make sure that I change the cover and give the room an extra hoover before Shelby's next visit. Though I should point out that this caravan is immaculate compared to my last one. Bev says I'm turning into Mrs Hinch. I've no idea what that means.

I leave my hair wet and go back to the kitchen where Lucas is still busy chopping. He's doing it with meticulous care and I sidle up next to him. 'Better?'

'Yes, you don't smell of farm.'

'Neither do you,' I tell him. 'I think there might even be a hint of aftershave.'

'Stop that now,' he warns.

I get the frying pan and glug in some oil. Lucas tips in the chopped veg while I find some pasta. The leftover rice can go into the animal feed. People say you shouldn't reheat rice, but it hasn't killed me yet. Though I would be mortified if I accidentally killed Lucas's first girlfriend, so I'll not risk it. Teacup will wolf it down gratefully.

While I get a pan for the pasta, I venture, 'Do you want to tell me anything more about Aurora?'

'Nothing much to say.' Lucas concentrates on stirring the veg. 'She'll be here in a bit, you can see for yourself.'

I feel honoured and terrified about that in equal measure.

Lucas's text alert sounds and he checks his phone. 'She's here,' he says. 'I'll get the gate.'

So I take over the stirring while Lucas slips on his boots. 'Don't embarrass me,' he says over his shoulder as he bolts outside.

'I'll try my best,' I shout, but he's already gone.

I tip a tin of tomatoes into the veg and sprinkle it with herbs. I hope Aurora likes this kind of food. Then I wait with trepidation until she arrives.

Lucas is beaming widely when he opens the door. His pale skin is flushed and I can't recall a moment when I've seen him look so happy. It brings a lump to my throat. There's a trace of lipstick on his mouth – not his own.

Behind him, there's a tall, willowy girl. She's a real beauty with dark, glossy hair in corkscrew curls and skin the colour of wild honey. Wow. If this is Lucas's 'girlfriend' he really has hit the jackpot. I'm no expert in these things, but she could be a model, I'm sure.

'Molly, this is Aurora.' There's no denying the shy pride in his voice.

'Hey,' she says to me, all self-assured and confident. We shake hands.

'Lovely to meet you. Welcome to our humble home.' She's definitely a few years older than Lucas. Nineteen, I'd say? Or maybe she's not that old, it's just the air that she has.

'Let me take your coat,' Lucas says, fussing round her.

She slips out of a fake sheepskin jacket and underneath she's wearing a chunky cream sweater, ripped jeans – fashionable ones, not ripped from climbing over fences as mine are – and sturdy laced boots. She looks like she's out of one of those clothing catalogues that Bev likes to browse.

'Sit, sit,' I say. 'Make yourself comfortable. Dinner's nearly ready. Can I get you a drink? Tea, coffee?'

Lucas shoots me a look to say that I'm babbling. I shut up.

'I'm good, thanks.' She slides into the bench seat at the table.

I'm bowled over by her poise. At her age, I was a total wimp and, as you know, I'm not all that much better now. I can't help but admire her but – and don't judge me for this – I can't help wondering what she's doing with Lucas.

There are times when Lucas is very mature – however, there are an equal number of times when he's just a lost and lonely boy. I can't put my finger on why, but I'm worried for him. From the outset this doesn't seem like an equal relationship, but then some would say that's the same for me and Shelby. I'm making snap judgements and I shouldn't. It's nice for Lucas to be in love, but I only hope that he doesn't get hurt as he's doing so well. Any small thing can upset the equilibrium and first love is always a big thing. As you can imagine, I'm not going to be the one to tell Lucas that.

I serve up my modest offering, wishing it was something infinitely more impressive. Aurora greets it as if I'm handing over something cooked by a celebrity chef.

'Oh, wow. This looks *totally* delicious, Molly. Thank you.'

'It's no trouble at all,' I say as I slip in beside them, feeling ever so slightly gooseberryish. 'Glad that you're here.'

Lucas shoots me a 'shut up' look again. I shut up.

Yet, even with my speaking ban, during the course of our thrown-together dinner, I find out that Aurora is at art college studying textiles, she's been writing and performing poetry for the last two years and that she still lives with her family on the other side of town. She's nicely spoken, polite and chatty. Lucas, I notice, hangs on her every word. He is clearly smitten and that makes me smile.

'Thank you, Molly,' she says as she delicately dabs at her mouth with piece of kitchen roll that serves as a napkin. I did fold it into a triangle, though. 'Can I help you to clear up?'

'It won't take me a minute. Are you going to show Aurora around the farm?'

'It's too cold,' Lucas says. 'We're going to go into my room to write together.'

'Right.' What do I say to that? I've never had to deal with Lucas taking a girl – *woman* – into his room before. Do I get them to leave the door open, hover outside, or are they at an age where I just leave them to get on with it? Has he tidied it up or is it still a health-hazard? Surrogate parenting is tricky. I wish Shelby were here to advise me, but he doesn't even know about Aurora yet.

They get up from the table and leave me to tidy up and wash the dishes. As I wipe round with a tea towel, I can hear laughter coming from Lucas's room – mainly Aurora's – which is nice but also weird. It's even more strange when I can't hear a single sound. What are they doing? Concentrating on their writing? I flipping hope so. I feel I'm dealing with a Lucas that I don't know, one that's emerging from being a child into a man.

Eeeek.

Tomorrow, I'll talk to Bev. She'll know what to do.

Chapter Nineteen

I try to settle into reading, then try listening to something soothing on the radio, but I feel as if I'm on high-alert to every sound – or lack thereof – from Lucas's bedroom. I want to check on the dogs and get them off my bed, but I daren't go near that part of the caravan or Lucas will think I'm snooping on them. This is traumatic.

About two hours later, when I'm just considering that I need to head to my room and how to approach that scenario, Lucas and Aurora emerge. Lucas is definitely flushed and Aurora is more dishevelled than when she went in.

'Aurora's going now,' Lucas says.

'Oh, right. Good. Lovely to meet you.'

'Thank you for having me, Molly. Supper was delightful.'

'My pleasure. It's nice for Lucas to bring a . . . friend . . . home.'

I get the usual death stare.

'Aurora's coat?' I remind him.

So he fusses with helping her on with it, while she giggles.

'I look forward to seeing you again. Maybe Lucas will invite you to our open day.'

89

'I'd love that,' she says. 'He's told me all about it. I can't wait to meet the animals.'

That has to be a good thing? He knows his father is likely to be there and yet he's still asked her to come.

Just as Lucas is opening the door to the caravan, I hear a car pull up at the gate. And not just *any* car. Lucas and I exchange a glance.

'Damn,' Lucas mutters.

The quiet purring sound of Shelby's Bentley is quite distinctive. It can only be him.

I feel guilty, as if I'm caught in a clandestine act. Which I am, in some ways. Lucas's face changes too.

'What?' Aurora says, as well she might.

'You have to go now,' Lucas says and tries to hurry her into her coat.

But it's too late, Shelby has let himself through and is already parking in the yard outside the caravan, right next to Aurora's more modest car. There's no way that Lucas can get his girlfriend out without her meeting his father.

While Aurora looks puzzled and Lucas and I behave as guiltily as we possibly can, the door opens and Shelby steps inside. 'Hello, there,' he says and then stops in his tracks when he sees Aurora. 'I didn't know you had company.'

'This is Aurora,' I say when Lucas fails to speak.

'She's just leaving.' Lucas pushes the poor, bewildered girl towards the door.

'Don't hurry away on my account.' Shelby turns on the full force of his charm. Which is exactly what Lucas will hate.

'Are you . . .' she stammers.

'I am.' Shelby beams at her. Not just a normal beam, his mega-watt, starry beam. Lucas's face grows dark. Oh, dear.

Aurora turns to Lucas. 'You didn't say.'

'It's no big deal.' Lucas has reverted to angry teenager, which is sad to see.

I step between Shelby and Lucas. 'Aurora has things to do,' I say. 'We shouldn't keep her.'

'I don't,' she says. 'I can stay longer.'

'Lucas, you see your friend to her car and I'll put the kettle on.'

Lucas takes Aurora's elbow and steers her out.

'Thank you again for dinner,' she shouts as she leaves rather unceremoniously.

I turn to Shelby. 'Tea?'

'I think I need a double brandy,' he says. 'Is that what I think it was?'

'She's a *friend*,' I tell him.

'My eye,' is Shelby's verdict. 'My son has a cracker of a girlfriend and I'm the last to know, as always.'

His tone is crisper than it needs to be.

'It was a last-minute arrangement,' I offer placatingly. 'I wasn't expecting Aurora and I wasn't expecting you.'

'Evidently.'

Lucas comes back in, rubbing his hands nipped by the cold. His face is like thunder.

'Well,' Shelby says. 'Are you going to let your old dad in on this?'

'There's nothing to tell. She's a friend.'

'A very pretty one.'

Lucas's eyes narrow and, if I'm honest with you, I wish Shelby hadn't turned up. Lucas is obviously feeling very sensitive and sometimes Shelby needs his mouth taping up. Why does he have to say all the wrong things when it comes to Lucas?

'Come on then, spill the beans. Why are you keeping her hidden?'

'Shelby,' I say. 'Let it drop. We'll have a nice cuppa and you can tell us all about how your filming went today.'

'Yeah, let's turn the subject back to you, Daddy,' Lucas snarls. 'We wouldn't want anyone else having any attention.'

Shelby's face tightens and I feel resignation wash over me. Here we go again.

'I know you and Molly like your little secrets, but I'm the one who pays all the bills round here. I think I'm entitled to know what's going on.'

Now it's my turn to look shocked. 'I don't think there's any need to play that card.' I turn to Lucas. 'I'm sorry, Lucas, but would you mind going to your room. I'd like to speak to your father privately.'

He goes to speak, but I hold up a hand and so he turns on his heels and marches towards his room. As he does, the dogs start to bark and Lucas opens the door to my bedroom, letting them out. Thanks for that, Lucas. Sensing that Shelby's here, they bound into the living room and try to jump all over him and lick him to death.

'Down,' I say. 'No jumping!' The dogs, too pleased to see Shelby, bounce with joy and ignore every word I utter. Much jumping is involved. They love him. What can I say?

'Can't you control these hounds?' he snaps. 'I've spent all day on set with bloody animals. I don't need any more of it.'

'I'm sorry, but I live on a *bloody* farm, I don't just play at it. What do you want me to do?'

'Did they come out of the bedroom? That's my one rule, Molly.'

'Rule?'

'The only thing I require of you is that you keep them out of the bedroom. Is that too much to ask?'

Then Betty Good Girl barks, worriedly, at the sound of raised voices and reverts to type. She squats and wees all over Shelby's shoes. His expensive ones.

Shelby looks down in horror. We both do. His face goes an alarming shade of puce.

'Betty Bad Dog,' I say and hurriedly push her out of the caravan, which now smells of dog wee. Little Dog and Big Dog looked perplexed as I push them out too in case there are any further mishaps.

'Right,' Shelby says. 'I've had enough.'

'You frightened her by shouting.'

'It's all *my* fault again? Why did you need another bloody dog? They're everywhere.'

'That is a slight exaggeration.'

And, suddenly, we're in a full-blown argument out of nowhere.

'I came to surprise you,' he shouts. 'Filming has been hell today and I thought it would be a nice thing to do. Instead, I walk in to find my son with a woman I know nothing about and dogs all over the bloody place.'

'I think you need to calm down,' I say quietly. 'This is helping no one. We were having a lovely evening until you turned up.'

'I can rectify that,' Shelby spits and he marches into the bedroom, snatches a case from the top shelf of the cupboard and starts to stuff it with his clothes.

'Where are you going?'

'Home,' he says. 'I can't stay here any longer. It's too cramped, too full of dog hair.'

'I'll hoover,' I offer. 'And I'll change the bedding. Please don't leave like this.'

'I have a perfectly good, pet-free manor house ten minutes down the road. I'm going there. I can't stand living in such close quarters.'

'Is this the end for us?'

'No.' He calms down a little and breathes deeply before he

says, 'Come with me. We could all move back there. Most women would jump at the chance of that lifestyle.'

'I'm not most women,' I remind him. 'I thought that's what you liked about me.'

'I can't stay,' Shelby says and there's a sadness in his voice as if it really is the end and he's only just realised it.

'And I can't come with you.'

'Then where does that leave us?'

'You'll have to decide.' I sound calmer than I feel. Inside my heart is pounding and my knees are weak. I don't want Shelby to go, yet I will not beg him to stay.

'Lucas,' he shouts. 'Get your stuff.'

Now I'm horrified. 'What?'

'Get your stuff,' he shouts again.

Lucas appears at the bedroom door. 'Why are you shouting your mouth off? We're not your minions on set.'

'Get your stuff. We're going back to Homewood Manor.'

'You might be,' Lucas says flatly. 'I'm going nowhere.'

'You're my son,' Shelby points out, needlessly. 'You do as I say.'

'No.' Lucas leans on the door jamb. 'I'm not going anywhere with you. I'm staying here with Molly.'

'Look,' I say. 'This is all very heated and it doesn't need to be. Shelby, I'm sorry the dogs were in here, it was a mistake. Also, Lucas is allowed to have friends here without your permission. It wasn't some master plan or conspiracy to exclude you. It's just the way it happened. We can arrange another dinner, if Lucas wants that, so you can meet Aurora properly.'

'I didn't want him to meet her at all,' Lucas shouts. 'You've seen what she looks like! *He'll* probably want to go out with her!'

Oh, God.

Shelby zips his case closed. 'I'm clearly not wanted here,' he says and flounces towards the door.

'This is ridiculous,' I say. 'Let's all sit down and talk it through.'

I follow Shelby to the door, but I won't trail after him. He's across the yard in a nano-second and yanks the gate open.

'Shelby,' I shout. 'Please listen to reason.'

Yet he jumps straight into his car, slamming the door decisively. Turning the Bentley with a screech of wheels on gravel, he shoots off down the lane. He doesn't close the gate behind him. Cardinal sin.

As Lucas comes to stand by my side, I sigh heavily.

'He's a complete and utter tit,' Lucas says.

At this moment, I can't really disagree with him. I thought that love had finally found me, but now I'm not so sure.

Chapter Twenty

The next morning, I have a monster headache. It's as if I have a hangover without having had the pleasure of getting that way. There's a bitter taste in my mouth.

It took me ages to get to sleep after Shelby had gone. I don't think I've ever had a row like that before, and it's shaken me. After many years in the romantic wilderness, I trusted Shelby implicitly with my love and feel I've had it thrown back in my face.

Dick the Cock is, for once, heralding the dawn and I peer out of my caravan window to see a landscape covered with a sugar coating of frost. The sunrise is a beautiful display of pastel pink sun and lilac-purple clouds. I let the dogs sleep on the bed last night as an act of defiance and they snuggle closer, reluctant for me to get up and disturb them. I also let them sleep with me as I needed a cuddle. In all forms of crisis, they are reliable with their comfort.

I didn't manage to talk properly with Lucas last night. He locked himself in his bedroom and refused to come out despite my entreaties through the closed door. What a mess.

Despite our domestic upsets, we'll have to get on with it as we have a busy day ahead of us. Bev has invited a local mental health charity to bring a group of their members and walk around the fields with the animals. This is another new fund-raising venture for us and it fills me with trepidation too. The last thing we need is one of the alpacas tipping someone who's already suffering from depression into the pond. I agreed to this! What was I thinking? I hope they all behave.

When I manage to stagger up and out of bed, Lucas is already at the table in the living room, angrily bashing his laptop. It seems that his rage has not subsided.

'Good material?' I say to him by way of greeting.

'Total knob,' he says and, from his pallor, I know that Lucas has also stayed awake half the night brooding. This is all too tragic. An argument should never have sparked so quickly, and it's spoiled what should have been a memorable evening for Lucas. I wonder if he'll ever risk bringing Aurora here again. I do hope so.

'Are you all right?'

'No,' Lucas says. 'But I'll live.'

'I'm sorry last night ended like that. She seems like a lovely girl.'

'Huh,' is all Lucas says. Now is not the time to try to draw him on the subject. We both know what went wrong.

I could swing for Shelby. Yet still my instinct is to phone him and check that he's OK. My heart says that I should apologise, but my head says it wasn't me who was in the wrong. I'll talk to Bev first; she's more worldly in these ways than I am. In the meantime, despite my heavy heart, I have animals to feed who don't care if I've had a lovers' tiff and am feeling utterly wretched.

I dress and go out to the barn and Lucas trails after me, face like thunder. I fear it's going to be a long day.

'We've got the people for the mental health outreach in today,' I remind him. 'Are you going to help us?'

'Sure,' he says. 'Just tell me what you want doing.' But his voice is flat and his body language is projecting extreme reluctance.

We set to with our morning tasks and, despite both Lucas and me being on auto-pilot, the animals don't care. They're still inordinately pleased to see us – albeit because we're bearing buckets of food. It's not long before they work their magic, and after I've fussed and fed the alpacas, pigs, sheep and bunnies, I'm feeling in a much better place. Lucas is whistling softly to himself, so I hope that means he is too.

It's not long before Bev and Alan arrive. And this is how upset Lucas and I are – we haven't even discussed what their matching band T-shirts might be today. They are both sporting a picture of The Cure, if you'd like to know.

Lucas says, 'I've no clue who the band are, but I really like that bloke's hair and make-up.'

'Robert Smith, style icon,' Bev informs us.

Lucas looks suitably impressed. I can see the guy-liner coming out later. That might cheer him up.

Bev gives me a hug. 'You two both look like you were on the razzle-dazzle-do last night.'

'Hardly,' I say. 'We didn't have our best evening ever, did we, Lucas?'

'No,' he agrees. 'Mainly due to that tit of a father of mine.'

'It's a long story,' I tell Bev. 'One best told over a cup of tea.'

'I'm going to finish off the feed,' Lucas says. 'I'll be up with the horses if you need me when the depressed people arrive.'

'Lucas,' I admonish.

He shrugs at me. Political correctness is obviously not high on his agenda today.

'Come back for a cup of tea as soon as you're done. It's cold out.' I feel as if I want to mollycoddle Lucas which, of course, he pretends to hate. 'You'll need some sustenance before we round up the animals for a walk.'

Getting any of them into a harness is always a challenge.

With a quick and cursory 'morning,' to no one in particular, Alan disappears into the depths of his workshop where he's always happiest – though it is hard to tell. I follow Bev into the tea room. The students haven't yet arrived, so we have time to take a few minutes to have a catch-up. Usually, it's to do with the day's activities and not a spectacular nose-dive in my love life.

I sit on a stool at the counter while Bev clatters about with the cups and the kettle, she says, 'OK, then. Tell Aunty Beverly why you look like you've found a pound and lost a fiver.'

I puff out a disgruntled breath before launching in. 'Lucas brought his girlfriend – who he insists isn't his girlfriend – home last night for the first time. It had all gone quite well and then Shelby turned up unexpectedly as she was leaving. Within minutes it had all kicked off. Lucas didn't want her to meet his dad. Shelby said all the wrong things. I was in trouble too for letting the dogs sleep on the bed and, before I knew it, he'd packed his stuff and had stomped off back to the manor house.'

'No wonder Lucas is fuming,' she says.

'I'm treading a fine line between them. Lucas doesn't want Shelby involved in his life and when Shelby does crash in he makes a complete hash of it. I'm so annoyed that he never learned how to handle his own son.'

'Or his partner?'

That makes me smile. 'That too.'

'Let him stew,' Bev says as she pushes a mug of builder-strength tea towards me. 'Don't you be phoning him.'

'I hate there being bad feeling between us.'

'It's up to him to come and sort this out. He'll be back with his tail between his legs. Trust me, he won't be gone for good.'

'I hope you're right.' We owe a lot to Shelby here and I don't want to lose sight of that.

Bev joins me on the next stool. 'So Lucas has a girlfriend?'

'Someone he met at his poetry club. Aurora. But he insists she's just a friend.'

'What's she like?'

'Very pretty, confident, polite. She's quite sophisticated. I'm just a little bit worried that she's a few years older than him, but Lucas is clearly very taken with her.'

'Oh, bless him.'

'Yes, they look very cute together.'

'Ah, young love,' she coos. 'There's nothing like it.'

'Except finding love when you're old and think you're past it.'

'Are you talking about you or me?' Bev wants to know.

I laugh. 'Both of us.'

My friend drains her tea and plonks the mug down. 'I'd better go and see my lover,' she says. 'He's making some bits for the nativity scene so that it looks more Bethlehem and less Buckinghamshire.'

'I'll drop in on him too later. Is it all coming along well? Please reassure me.'

'It's all fine and you seemed to be a big hit with our Hot Mayor yesterday. He was putty in your hands.'

'He seems like a really nice guy.' But we all know that I'm a terrible judge of people. 'I hope we see some more of him, as promised.'

Bev kisses my cheek. 'I'll leave you to worry about that as you wait for the walkers. As soon as they're here, they can have a cuppa while we harness the animals. In the meantime, I've got a load of tinsel to unload from the back of my car to pretty the place up.'

And worry I do, because until I've seen Shelby I won't know whether or not it's all over between us.

Chapter Twenty-One

Our morning is busier than usual. The timetable is all upside down for a start, which no one likes – many of our kids rely on the gentle routine we instil here. It takes me much longer than usual to settle our regular students to their lessons before a dozen people arrive for our first mental health walk. The idea is that we all take the animals on a stroll around the farm, giving our visitors a chance to just chat or air their troubles or lose themselves in hanging onto one of our four-legged charges – unless you count Big Dog who only has three legs.

For me, the influx of new people is a good thing. I'm so stretched that I don't even have time to dwell on Shelby and what he may or may not be thinking.

The visitors have a cup of tea and we get out the good biscuits for them – in date and with chocolate on. Then we harness a few of the animals, which is often a bit of a trial. Today, they are all reasonably compliant – even Johnny Rotten doesn't bolt when he sees his harness. When we introduce them to our group of eager walkers, none of the animals try to bite or back-heel our visitors. Small mercies.

Bev's plan is that each of our visitors takes an animal to

look after during their walk. When we have the three alpacas on halters, I hand them over to the sturdiest looking blokes, with strict instructions to hang on to them. Given their head, those tinkers will run and run. Then we take the little ponies which Lucas has brought down from the field. They're generally the most compliant and are always popular with youngsters, so they are given to the more youthful visitors to walk. Lucas also brings out a selection of our smaller, happier sheep which aren't too skittish – Teddy with the cuddly coat, Midnight with the black fleece and Baa-bara with the pretty face. Anthony the Anti-Social Sheep is deemed to be too much of a health risk to be allowed on what is intended to be a calming walk, even though he is eyeing up Baa-bara longingly. We harness the donkeys, Harriet and Hilda, too. This will be their first trial and, as they are usually extremely gentle, I have high hopes for them. Finally, we take two of the pygmy goats – Laurel and Hardy – who like any excuse to be out and about in the fields.

Eventually, when everyone has an animal to walk, we set off across the fields with Little Dog, Big Dog and Betty Bad Dog (fingers crossed that she's channelling Betty Good Girl today). Pet lamb, Fifty, joins us too. He won't go on a harness – he generally won't do anything we want him to do – but is quite happy to wander after us. As we go, we become a little band of merriment, and there's much chatter and laughter, which is nice to see. Bev looks over at me and grins. It is an I-told-you-so grin. I know that it won't magically solve the problems they're facing, but I like to think walking in the countryside with an alpaca, tiny goat or cheerful sheep on a regular basis might make those suffering feel just a little bit brighter for a short while.

It's a beautiful if cold day, but we take our time walking out across the fields and down along the river. We circle the pond and, as usual, the alpacas like to have a dip. Tina Turner paddles at the edges, but Johnny Rotten ploughs straight into the middle and lies down – nearly taking his handler with him. It's only a swift intervention from Lucas that prevents an unexpected dunking. But that's our only near-miss, everything else goes unnervingly smoothly. The donkeys are impeccably behaved. Betty Bad Dog only wees on fence posts and hedgerows rather than on expensive shoes. The visitors really enjoy their time and it does, to my utmost relief, go without a hitch.

Bev high-fives me as we get back to the yard. 'You can breathe again now.'

She's not wrong. I think I have been holding my breath most of the way round and am in desperate need of a restorative cup of tea. But the session could definitely be classed as an unmitigated success, and I hope that they'll book another one soon as it was a joy to have them here and will also bring in some most welcome funds. After last night's argument it makes me even more determined not to be reliant for Shelby on our funding.

'That went well,' Lucas says as he brings Johnny Rotten to a halt beside me.

'Yes. Thanks for your help.' He seems to be in a much better humour – I even noticed him talking to a young man of a similar age on the way round, which was nice.

'I'll take the ponies back up to the field.'

'Thanks, Lucas.' I squeeze his skinny shoulders and he doesn't shrug me off.

He grabs all of their leads and they trot after him.

After I've watched him go, I turn my attention to the visitors. I'm just helping them put their animals back into their pens when I see Shelby's Bentley pull into the farmyard. I swear to you that my heart skips a beat.

'Can you take over, Bev?' I ask.

'No problem.' She takes Laurel's lead from my hand and ushers him into his pen.

As always, Shelby looks very debonair as he steps out of the car – every inch the television star. He's dressed very smartly in a grey sweater and jeans. And – ahem – new shoes. I check, anxiously, to see if Betty Bad Dog is in the vicinity, but she's not. I'm also relieved to see that he grabs a huge bunch of red roses from the back seat of his car. This must be Shelby in conciliatory mood. I leave the visitors with Bev, cleanse my hands and head towards him.

'I'm an idiot,' he says as I approach.

I go to open my mouth.

'Don't disagree,' he says. 'I am.'

'Actually, I was going to *agree* with you.'

He gives me one of his heart-breaking smiles and holds out his roses. I take them from him with a sigh. He gives me puppy-dog eyes. 'Does that mean I'm forgiven?'

'You were out of order last night,' I remind him. 'I'm not sure that two dozen utterly beautiful roses are enough. There was no need for you to carry on as you did.'

'I know. I've come with my heart in my hand to apologise.'

'You can't pack your case and stomp off just because things don't go your way.'

'I behaved like a child,' he says. 'Let me take you to dinner. We need some time by ourselves, away from this place, the animals, Lucas.'

He knows how difficult this is for me, but I can't have it all my own way either. Relationships are about compromise. Having lived alone for so long, I need to keep reminding myself of this.

'Yes. That would be nice.'

'I'll book somewhere special.'

I'd really rather go to the local pub and hide in the corner, away from the prying eyes and head swivellers that invariably accompany Shelby wherever he goes. But I have to meet him halfway. 'Perfect.'

'Where's Lucas?'

'Up in the field with the ponies. We've just had a group of walkers from a mental health charity.'

'I thought you looked busy.'

'It was a great success and some welcome funds too.'

'I've got to head to the studio. I'll see you later.'

'You don't want to speak to Lucas?'

He looks down at his brand new, expensive shoes, his immaculate jeans. 'I'll catch him another time.'

'We could all go out together tonight,' I venture. 'A curry or something?'

'I don't think that would work,' Shelby says. 'Lucas makes it very clear that he doesn't want me around.'

'He does. You simply have to treat him with kid gloves.'

Shelby sighs. 'And when does that stop? When does he accept that I'm not perfect and I'm allowed to make mistakes?'

'In time,' I tell him. 'Just be patient.'

'I'll pick you up at seven o'clock.'

'Can we make it a bit later?' I ask, hesitantly. 'I've got the animals to feed.'

'Ah, yes,' Shelby says. 'The animals. Always the animals.'

'They can't order a takeaway.' It comes out more crisply than I'd intended. 'I'll be ready as soon as I can.'

'Seven-thirty,' he says and kisses my cheek briefly before he returns to his shiny car.

I watch him drive away and clutch the roses to my chest.

Chapter Twenty-Two

'Big gesture,' Lucas says when he sees the rather large bouquet of roses in my rather small vase.

'We're going out to dinner tonight too,' I say.

'He's still a knob.'

'Your dad's under a lot of pressure.'

'He's a fucking actor in a third-rate soap. How much pressure can that be? I talked to a kid today who's been thinking of topping himself. My dad has no idea about anything in the real world.'

I don't want to get into an argument with Lucas about it and, if I'm honest with you, a small part of me agrees with him. There are people with bigger problems to deal with.

'I saw you chatting to him. Did it go OK?'

'Yeah. I got him to talk to the supervisor and I'm going keep in touch with him.'

'Thank you, Lucas. You did well.'

He tuts at my praise.

'I don't like to go out and leave you here by yourself.'

'I'm not five.'

'You'll be all right, though?'

'Of course,' he says.

'I won't be late.'

'You can party until dawn for all I care,' is his parting shot before he disappears into his room.

I don't want to leave Lucas like this, but I do want to see Shelby too. I seem to spend a lot of my life similarly torn. I put on my one and only nice dress again. I do my hair. I even think about make-up, but tend to end up looking like Coco the Clown without Bev's assistance, so I think better of it. Natural. That's me.

I'm just about ready when the dogs start barking, heralding Shelby's car turning up at the gate.

I go to Lucas's bedroom and hover in the doorway. 'I'm off now.'

But he's still cross about everything and scowls at me.

'I won't be late,' I promise again.

'You said. Enjoy yourself,' he snaps. 'Fill your boots with our star while he deigns to be around.'

I'm not going to win with him in this mood, so I take my leave and totter across the farmyard on high heels that I'm not accustomed too. It isn't Shelby in the car, it's his driver, Ken. And I know that shouldn't disappoint me as he's a really nice guy, but it does. He's not Shelby and it feels like it's not a great start to Date Night.

'Hi, Ken.' I slide into the car next to him.

'Evening, Molly. I've already dropped Shelby off at the restaurant.'

'Right.'

'It's not far, so you'll be there in a few minutes.'

'Thanks, Ken.' We make small talk as we drive through the lanes, until he drops me off outside Crispin House restaurant. It's a posh place in the quaint high street of one of the more upmarket villages near to the farm. I haven't been here before, obvs, but I know of its reputation. Normally, you have to book months ahead, but I bet your bottom dollar that Shelby – or his assistant – got a table today with one well-aimed phone call. Such is the power of celebrity.

I thank Ken, climb out of the car and make my way into the restaurant. The only good thing about not arriving with Shelby is that no one turns to look at me. It's very fancy in here and already quite busy. There's a kind of hush in the place and conversation is muted. Classical music plays softly in the background and the furnishings are plush yet contemporary. I feel hideously out of place.

The place is all decked for Christmas with a huge tree covered in gold and red baubles. Swags of holly are draped from every beam. A basket of oranges sprayed with gold lustre adorns the reception desk. The air is scented with pine, citrus and cinnamon. I realise that I need to seriously up my Christmas game.

When I've whispered my name to the maître d', I'm shown to a table in the far corner of the restaurant where Shelby is already seated and is studying the menu.

He stands up when he sees me and, for a moment, his eyes sparkle and I get a glimpse of how he used to look at me.

'Hi.'

He kisses me and the waiter pulls out my chair. 'This looks very nice,' I say as I sit.

'One of my favourite places,' Shelby replies. 'The food is sublime.'

'I've heard all about it.' The chef is much-celebrated and is always on the telly, apparently. Guess who told me that? Thanks, Bev.

'You look lovely,' my date says.

The lighting in here is soft, flattering. There's a candle burning on the table. But Shelby needs no such devices, he always looks beautiful. He's in a dark suit tonight with a sharp white shirt and looks like he's off to some swanky awards ceremony. My heart tightens as I get an image of us entwined together, his body against mine.

'A glass of champagne, madam.' The waiter, who I thought had gone, is at my elbow.

'Oh, yes. Thanks.' He pours, taking time over the ritual, and then this time he does disappear.

Shelby picks up his glass and clinks it against mine. 'To us,' he says.

'I did wonder,' I admit.

'I've already said I'm sorry.' He looks duly penitent. 'I've got a lot on at the moment.'

'I know. I've forgiven you.'

He raises an eyebrow. 'And Lucas?'

'Not so much.'

Shelby sighs. 'I'll put a couple of hundred quid in his bank account, that will smooth things over.'

'That's not really the answer,' I tell him. 'You know that.'

'I never know what to do with Lucas,' he admits. 'He complains when I'm not there, hates me when I am. I can't win.'

'It's always a balancing act and I realise that you have a lot of commitments, but all he wants is for you to spend time with him. If you were with us more regularly, then the abrasive edges would wear down.'

Shelby's handsome face darkens.

I hold up my hands. 'I'm not judging. I'm just telling you as it is.'

'We have things we need to discuss,' Shelby says, cryptically. 'But let's order first. Would you like to see the festive menu?'

I shake my head. 'Too soon.'

So he hands me the à la carte menu and my eyes travel over it. I have no idea what to choose.

Shelby must see the terror in my eyes. 'I recommend the baked figs followed by, perhaps, the confit cauliflower steak?'

'OK. Great.' That's me sorted. With relief, I close the menu.

The waiter miraculously appears as I do and Shelby orders for us both. The baked figs with pomegranate and blackberries, then cauliflower with turnip tops and sweet potato for me. Shelby chooses salt and pepper squid followed by roast loin of cod with charred kale and parsnip puree. All sounds nice.

'Festive menu.' I give a shudder. 'I can't even believe they've already got their Christmas decorations up,' I whisper. 'It's still November. I'm barely getting started.'

'There's no holding it back,' Shelby says. 'It's beginning to look a lot like Christmas.'

'Tell me about it. We need to get a move on. There's so much to organise for the open day and nativity.' I don't want to spoil the convivial mood of the evening, but I decide to bite the bullet and address a looming issue. 'The new mayor came to visit us. Seemed like a nice chap. He's got some money to spend on a community charity and Bev's keen to have a slice of it.'

'Sounds good.'

'We've kind of told him that he can cut the ribbon or turn on the lights.' I give a slight wince to indicate that I know it's potentially a slight for him. 'One of the two. Bev thought a bit of flattery might do the trick.'

'I see,' Shelby says.

I'm dreading that he'll feel snubbed if he thinks the mayor is stealing his thunder. I hope he doesn't mind sharing. 'You'll still be around to do celebrity duties, won't you?'

'Ah,' he says and suddenly looks very guilty. 'That's what we need to talk about.'

Chapter Twenty-Three

At that moment, the waiter arrives with our food and I'm left hanging. Shelby is clearly uncomfortable too. We look at each other over the salt and pepper squid and whatever it is I've got. The last thing I can focus on is eating.

When Shelby isn't immediately forthcoming, I say, 'You'd better come clean, then.'

My stomach is in knots and, until I've heard what's got him looking so shifty, I won't manage a mouthful.

'You see, I have a bit of a problem,' he says. 'It could be a good problem.'

'For who?'

'Things are tough at work.' Shelby checks round to see that no one is within hearing distance, then lowers his voice as he confides in me. 'We've got a new producer who wants the storylines to be racier.'

'Bev will be pleased about that.'

He manages a smile. 'Not for me, unfortunately. We have a "hot" young actor joining the cast. He's going to be introduced in the Christmas special. He's an insufferable tosser, if you ask me, but he's the new generation.'

Bev will still be pleased about that, but I don't voice that particular opinion.

'He made his name on *Love Island* or something. I did three fucking years at RADA.'

There's a bitter note in his voice and it's not really surprising. In an industry that's all about ego, it must be hard to be forced to stand aside.

'He's getting all the best stories next year.' Shelby's face looks sad. 'I've been top dog on *Flinton's Farm* for years, but I fear that I'm being sidelined. Too old to be the romantic lead.'

'Never in my book,' I offer.

He smiles thinly. 'Thanks for the support, but I don't think I'm going to survive this cull. New broom sweeps clean, and all that.' His expression is bleak when he adds, 'I heard a rumour that I'm going to die in a tractor accident.'

'Oh.' That can't be good.

'Which is why I really want to take on this project that I've been offered.'

'Hence all the meetings in London?'

'I didn't want to say anything until it was cut and dried.'

My food is still untouched, but Shelby tucks into his. I pick up my knife and fork, but I've not much appetite for my baked figs. I knew something was happening in the background, but I've chosen to ignore it.

'I've landed a plum role in a panto,' he says.

'Oh no, you've haven't!'

'It's already been done, Molly.'

'Sorry, couldn't help it.' But we do both smile. And I'm relieved that it's simply the offer of a job and not something more. 'Panto, though? Why?'

'Panto is fantastic now. It's an all-star cast – some great names – and I'll be the villain. *Nebuchadnezzar*!' He says it in a pantomime villain voice, which makes the people on the next

112

table jump. 'The money is huge too. I really want to give it a go. The guy booked to do it had to drop out . . .' He checks round again and mouths a name at me. It means nothing. 'Rehab.'

'Ah.' Lucky for Shelby, not so lucky for him.

'This is a great opportunity, Molly. I can't stress it enough.'

'If it's what you want . . .'

'It is.' He takes my hands. 'Thanks for being so understanding.'

'So, I take it that you won't be at the open day?' I can't tell you how disappointed I am.

'You have the mayor,' he says, and I'm not sure if there's an edge creeping into his voice.

'But he's not you.'

'I'll try my best to be there, but this is a big commitment. Once a day and twice on Wednesday and Saturday. I'll only get Sunday off and then there may be press interviews and promotions to do.'

'That does sound like a lot.'

'Because I've had my storylines cut back, I can do my filming for *Flinton's Farm* in short snatches, but I'll have to be back in Birmingham every night.'

'*Birmingham?*'

'It's not the end of the world.'

'But it's pretty far.'

'I'll come back whenever I can and it's only for December.'

'All of it?' I can't keep the surprise out of my voice.

'Most of it,' he admits. 'The last show is on Christmas Eve. I'll definitely be with you both on Christmas Day.'

'Thank goodness for that.'

'The run will be over by then and I might be asleep on the sofa all afternoon, but I'll definitely be there. I wouldn't miss it for the world. Our first Christmas together. I know it's not going to be easy for either of us, but the money will be like a windfall – I can't turn it down. And I promise that I'll make it up to you.'

He looks like he means it. But then I have Lucas's voice ringing in my ears. 'He's an *actor*.' Looking sincere was probably day one of acting school.

I've always spent Christmas Day alone with the animals and I've never minded, but this year I wanted it to be different. And, as you've probably gathered, it's not only me that I'm worried about. It is, of course, Lucas. He's hardly going to see his father at all and we're having a tricky time anyway. The timing couldn't be worse. 'When do you start?'

'Opening night is the beginning of the month.'

'But that's not far away at all.' Shelby can't meet my gaze and I realise that he must have known about this for a long time. 'Have rehearsals already started?'

He nods. 'I wanted to tell you, but I didn't know how you'd feel.'

Of course he must have been involved by now. The show is starting in a few short weeks, the publicity needs to be done. It's probably being advertised and I hadn't even realised. I'm not sure how I feel about that. Seemingly, it's only a pretence that he's seeking my approval.

'It's your job,' I concede. 'What can I say? This is who you are. This is what you do. And, whatever you choose, I'm very proud of you.'

'Thanks, Molly. That means a lot to me.'

But does it? I can't tell him that I was depending on him to be there for us, that Lucas will be crushed by this. I don't know if Shelby is grasping at straws with this panto role or whether it is something that he really wants. He seems very enthusiastic, so how can I rain on his parade? He's been so supportive in the past, I kind of hoped we could rely on him

114

again. I have this awful feeling that Shelby is slipping away from me.

'I'll do all I can to help at the farm,' he says, obviously reading my face. 'I'm not abandoning you. Far from it.'

But, if I'm honest with you, it feels like he is.

Chapter Twenty-Four

We finish dinner and I'd like to say that it's in companionable silence, but it's not really. Things are a bit awkward between us and, though Shelby initially tries to be chatty, I'm unable to pretend. I'm still trying to process all that he's told me.

At the end of the evening he says, 'Come back to my place.'

'I can't,' I tell him. 'I've got Lucas to think about. I don't like to leave him alone at the farm for too long. It's too isolated.'

'I just wanted another hour of you all to myself.' Shelby sighs. 'I love Lucas, but I can't face his disapproval again. Not now.'

I do know what he means, but the longer he avoids Lucas, the worse it gets. 'Come back to the caravan. Stay over.'

'I took all my stuff home. Remember?'

'Ah, yes.'

'I'll get Ken to drop you off.'

'Thanks.'

Shelby texts his driver and pays the bill. The waiter appears with my coat and, with much fawning over Shelby, we head towards the door. It feels to have been more of an ordeal than a date night.

When we're out on the street, Shelby takes me in his arms and kisses me. I want to respond, but I'm aware that Ken is sitting in the car just a few metres away and I'm not prone to public displays of affection.

'Thank you,' I say. 'That was lovely.'

We both know that I'm lying.

'I'm sorry I dropped that on you,' he says. 'I had to get it off my chest.'

'It's fine. And I am pleased for you.'

Shelby stares earnestly at me. 'Friends?'

'Always,' I tell him.

We walk to the car hand-in-hand. 'Do you mind if Ken drops me off first? I've got an early start.'

'No problem.' I don't point out that I'm up every day at 5.30 a.m. to feed impatient animals.

So Ken takes Shelby home to Homewood Manor, the gravel of the sweeping drive crunching beneath the tyres. It's a beautiful house and, if I was a normal person, surely I'd move in like a shot.

Shelby kisses me again and, as he gets out of the car, says, 'You won't change your mind?'

Sadly, I shake my head. He looks lonely as he closes the door and heads towards the house, which is all in darkness. I can hardly bear to watch him go. I worry constantly about Lucas, but I know that Shelby is still grieving too and needs someone there for him. I know that I'm not giving him what he needs. When he's done with all this panto stuff, we do need to discuss our living arrangements, or is it too soon to do that? I want Lucas to have a stable home base, and Shelby should want that too. I hope that living in my caravan with me is providing that, but I think we all need to talk about the future. I want to reassure Shelby that he is at the top of my list – or, at least, very near it.

Ken drives me back to Hope Farm. As I'm still sitting in the back we don't chat, so I close my eyes and let the fuggy warmth of the car soothe me. We're soon at my gate.

'Goodnight, Molly,' Ken says. 'See you next time.'

'Thanks, Ken. I appreciate the lift.'

'He needs looking after,' Ken adds.

'I know.' I get out of the car, worrying that even Shelby's driver is pointing out my shortcomings. Perhaps everyone is used to pandering to Shelby's every whim.

I should feel light after our evening out but, instead, I'm heavy of heart. As I cross the yard, I see that Aurora's car is parked by the caravan. I didn't know she was coming over tonight, but why shouldn't Lucas have friends to visit? This, to all intents and purposes, is his home now.

The dogs bark when they hear me and just that simple thing makes me instantly feel much better. As I open the caravan door, the living room is in darkness, but I can hear scuffling sounds. Puzzled, I click on the light. On the sofa by the table, Aurora and Lucas are . . . oh . . . ah . . . er . . . getting 'friendly'. Really very friendly. I stand, frozen, blinking like a mad thing.

Lucas is lying down while she is sitting astride him, her hands on his bare chest. Aurora and her jumper also appear to have parted company. Her bra is on the floor. Oh my giddy aunt. I only met her for the first time last night and now I'm acquainted with her . . . well, you don't need me to spell it out.

Lucas looks suitably horrified, but maybe still not as horrified as me. 'What are you doing home?'

'I live here,' I remind him.

Aurora is covering her boobs with her hands – which aren't quite big enough to do a proper job. 'Hi, Molly.'

Then we all just stay like statues, unable to break the moment.

Finally, I manage to mobilise my brain. 'I just have to see to the animals,' I say, hurriedly. 'It will take me a while. Ten minutes, maybe longer. Bye.'

I bolt out of the door, taking the dogs with me. I stand with my back to the caravan and can hear myself breathing heavily. That was terrible, awful, traumatic. Did I really just see what I thought I saw? I did. Christ alive. I wanted to get to know Aurora better, but not that well.

I hear movement in the van behind me, frantic scrabbling. I hope that means they're getting dressed. True to my word, I plan to stay out here for as long as it takes. So I totter across the yard in my ridiculous shoes as I didn't hang around long enough to put my wellies on. The dogs, however, are happy that they're out of the confines of the caravan, whatever the circumstances. Yet, now I'm out here, I don't quite know what to do with myself, so I head into the barn to take a bit of solace with my beloved animals. I'm wearing a dress and silly shoes and it's the weather for a big parka and boots.

The animals are all snuggled up asleep. Only Tina Turner rouses when I go to their pens. She stands up and comes over to me, ever hopeful that a midnight snack might be on offer.

'Oh, Tina. What shall I do now?' I lean against her neck and she lets me. She must know that I'm troubled as she doesn't even try to eat my hair or my dress.

Never in a million years did I think that, while I was away, Lucas would be doing . . . *that*. He's only known Aurora for five minutes. My heart is pounding in my chest. I never expected this to happen, not yet, not on my watch. What would Shelby do? What would he say? Lucas might be of legal age to . . . well. But he's just a child. And not even my child. Oh, bollocky bollocks.

I stroke Tina's neck and she tolerates it. Bringing up animals, it seems, is less fraught than bringing up a kid.

A few minutes later, just as deep shivering is setting in, I hear the slam of Aurora's car door and her engine starts up. Then the gate closes after her and she heads up the lane. I need to catch my breath and marshal my thoughts before I speak to Lucas. I can't ignore this, but I'm not sure that I'm equipped to deal with it either.

Chapter Twenty-Five

As I'm still pondering my quandary, Lucas appears. He's got my big coat and my wellies.

'It's cold out here,' he says as he hands them to me.

'Yes.' I shrug on my coat, kick off my shoes and slip my cold feet into fur-lined boots.

'Aurora's gone.'

'I heard.'

'We could walk up the field,' he offers. 'If you want to.'

'OK.'

So we head out of the barn, Lucas shining a torch at the ground as we climb the stile. The dogs squeeze through the gap in the hedge and run ahead chasing each other, so pleased to be on an impromptu walk. I'm not sure whether I am or not. It's a still night, but it's freezing out. We walk in silence.

Eventually, Lucas turns to me in the darkness. 'Well? Aren't you going to say something?'

'Fuck, Lucas,' is all I manage.

'We did, thanks,' he says sarcastically.

'I know!'

'It's no big deal.' He sounds defensive. 'Everyone does it.'

'You've only known her a short while. You keep insisting that she's not even your girlfriend. It was the last thing I imagined. I didn't expect to see you like that.'

'It just happened.' Lucas shrugs. 'What can I say?'

'I thought I could trust you at home alone.'

'You can. It's only sex. I didn't burn the place down.'

We both let that hang in the air. The reason Lucas came here is that he was accused of arson at his last school, but he swears he wasn't responsible.

'Bad choice of words,' he says after a moment.

'I care for you. I want you to be safe. I'm responsible for you while you're here. I don't want you getting into trouble.'

'I know what I'm doing.'

I stop walking and face him. 'Do you?' Our breath puffs out into the air, mingling into a cloud of angry steam. Lucas's eyes are glittering with tears. 'Did you use contraception?'

'I'm not a kid.'

'You are. That's kind of my point.'

He holds up a hand. 'I don't want to be having this conversation with you.'

'If you think you're old enough to have sex, then you're old enough to talk about it. Did you?'

He grinds his toe into the frosty ground, unable to meet my eyes. Sometimes he's more like his father than he thinks. Eventually, he says, 'We didn't actually . . . I was just . . . It was only a bit . . .' Lucas dries up at this point. 'You arrived too soon, if you really want to know.'

Or in the nick of time. I hide my smile in the darkness. 'Has your dad ever sat you down and given you The Talk?'

'What? No! We can't even discuss what to have for dinner without getting into a row. Don't tell him, Molly. Please don't tell him.'

'One minute you're insisting that you're not a kid, then next you're begging me not to tell your dad. Make your mind up, Lucas. Which is it to be? A kid or an adult?'

'We were only dry humping,' he says. 'Then I don't know what happened. It went a bit further.'

'Dry humping?'

He scowls at me, his face as dark as the night. 'Work it out.'

I do. Then we both smile warily at each other. 'Oh, Lucas.'

'Fuck off,' he says.

'I'm worried that Aurora is older and more worldly than you.'

'You don't like her?'

'I do, but is she the right person for you?' I don't like to tell him that I still see him as vulnerable. But he is. Although Lucas has made great progress, he's not out of the woods yet.

'Girls my age are just kids,' he complains. 'I like that she's older.'

'Let's go back to the van and finish this conversation over tea. We do need to talk about the birds and the bees. I want you to understand what you're getting into.'

'You shag my father,' he says, but not unkindly. 'You're not exactly a role model.'

I let it pass, even though it wounds. Lucas is a master of the sharp cut. 'I want your first experience to be positive, with someone you love who loves you back.'

'I'm a teenage boy. I'm taking what I can get.'

We turn back towards the yard and I throw my arm round his scrawny shoulders. 'Do you love her?'

'Yeah. I think so. I don't know. I really *like* her.'

Is sixteen too young to experience true love? It was for me, but is it the same for everyone? Is it what Lucas is searching for? I know that he still has a terrible emptiness in his heart after losing his mum, but I'm scared that the first chance of love he has might not be right for him. How do I tell him all that?

We climb the stile and Lucas holds out a hand to help me over even though he knows that I don't really need it.

'What does love feel like?' he asks.

I stand and put my hands on his shoulders. He looks sadder than he should. 'It feels like the other person makes you a better version of yourself. They make you tremble inside and every minute without them is torture.'

He looks at me. 'Is that how you feel about Dad?'

That catches me off balance for a second. I think of the stilted evening I've had with Shelby, the fact that he's heading off to Birmingham for a couple of months without a backward glance or any thought of what I or Lucas might do. Is that love? Do I feel love? But, as I think Lucas has got more than enough on his plate to deal with, despite my misgivings, I say, 'Yes, it is.'

Chapter Twenty-Six

Relationships all round feel strained. Lucas is stomping about being cross about everything. With much cajoling, I manage to get him to agree to sit down and talk about sex. I try to tell Lucas about contraception, responsibility, respect, boundaries – everything I can think of. To his credit, he does sit and listen to me. I think. I hope.

'How old were you when you first had sex?' he asks.

'I don't want to have that conversation with you,' I reply, feeling a bit hot under the collar.

'That's what I hate about adults.' He scowls at me to indicate that I'm the particular adult he hates right now. 'You think you can preach to me and have "grown up" chats where you pick through my sex life, but you don't want to do the same for me.'

'I was a late-starter,' I concede. 'By today's standards.'

'What? Twenties? Thirties? So you think that should be the same for me?'

'Not necessarily.'

'I have surging hormones. I can't wait that long.'

'This is all about wanting to protect you. I don't want to see you hurt, Lucas.'

'Aurora isn't like that,' he insists.

And I don't want to stamp on a tender heart, so we leave our discussion at that – but that doesn't stop me from worrying.

This, of course, should be Shelby's job, but he's currently absent as he's busy shuttling between *Flinton's Farm* and panto rehearsals in Birmingham. It's nigh on impossible to even catch him on the phone and our recent conversations have been snatched and unsatisfactory. Lucas says it's a relief that Shelby's not here and takes every opportunity he can find to call him a 'dickhead'. He's obviously smarting that Shelby has gone away. Me? I'm missing him terribly.

I don't know if the students can sense that the atmosphere is not as laid-back as usual, but we seem to be having more than our fair share of problems. The run-up to Christmas is so often difficult for people with autism, whether adults or children – the forced air of excitement and disruption to routine can be very unsettling for them. So we're trying to manage it here and, while making it a fun thing, keep the preparations for our open day as calm and structured as possible. But there are always issues. Jack, who has been with us for years, may not have his funding for much longer. The council are threatening to withdraw it and his parents certainly can't pay for him. I wonder, not for the first time, if we could take him on as staff as I know the possible disruption to his future is troubling him greatly. Another of our long-term students, who's been doing so well, suffers a terrible setback. Tamara, who has a history of self-harming, cuts herself badly for the first time in over a year and is now in hospital. I'm worried that she might be sectioned. The news saddens and distresses everyone and for those who can't process emotions well, it results in a lot of challenging behaviour. Penny, in particular, is argumentative and difficult. I vow to make more of an effort to spend some quality time with her – I don't know how things are at home, but it doesn't look like it's improving.

Even the animals are playing up today. Anthony manages to escape his pen and spends half an hour careening round the farmyard until, finally, Asha puts on an impressive spurt and catches him. Johnny Rotten bites Jody on the elbow when she goes to fuss him and he has to be entered into the accident book – again. Harriet and Hilda haven't stopped braying at the top of their voices all morning. At first, their incessant hee-hawing is amusing and then it just becomes a terrible, ear-splitting din. Nothing I can do settles them. Betty Bad Dog knocks over all the feed bins and then makes herself sick by eating pig nuts. I've spent the last hour clearing it all up. I feel as if I'm being stretched to breaking point and have the headache to end all headaches.

The only upside is that today it's bright and relatively warm – given that we seem to have our own microclimate here, which always makes it chillier than anywhere else. A bit of physical activity is always a good thing on their difficult days, so the students are in the big barn helping to make wooden planters for our planned kitchen garden. I've been threatening to do a bit of grow-your-own since we were at our last home, and I'm determined we'll be ready to plant up some herbs and a few vegetables in time for next spring. We inherited some decking from a friend of a friend who was remodelling their garden, which has proved ideal. Alan has supervised the sawing of the planks and nailing them together. No one has lost a finger or an eye, so that's all good. Now the kids are all suitably overall-clad and are painting them up in rainbow colours. You'd think that it might be a nice activity, a change from things involving mud and manure, but they're all squabbling like mad. There's paint everywhere – more on the kids than the planters. Lucas is supposed to be in charge, but I see him flick his hood up on his sweatshirt and march off across the fields. Clearly he's had enough of them. My instinct is to follow him, but perhaps it would be good for him to have a bit of time on his own, so I let him be.

Aurora has been here a few times since 'that night' but she's more cautious around me now and they disappear straight into Lucas's bedroom the minute she arrives. I try not to stress over the amount of giggling that I hear through the closed door. I can't watch him every minute of the day and I know that he sees her at the poetry nights too. I have my fingers crossed that it all works out well for him.

The only light relief is that Alan and Bev are still so loved up. It's a joy to see. There's a sparkle in Bev's eyes that has been missing for a long time and who would have thought that our strong, silent Alan would have been the one to rekindle her flame. I tell you, the world is a strange place. The whole love thing is even more weird. They say that love makes the world go round, but I'm not so sure. It just seems to fuck it up, if you ask me.

Currently, Alan and Bev are canoodling by the Kunekune pigs. Well, Bev is twined round Alan coochy-cooing at him, while he grins benignly at her. It brings a smile to my own face too.

Bev turns round. 'That's known as voyeurism, Molly.'

'I can't avoid it.' I laugh. 'You two are like teenagers.' And I should know, having recently experienced teenagers in action.

Of course, I confided all about Lucas and Aurora to Bev and she assured me that I'd done the correct thing. I hope she's right as I rely on her greater experience in these matters.

'I'm telling him what a lucky man he is.'

'He is,' I agree. 'However, if you can put each other down for a moment, there's work to do.'

'You spoil all my fun,' Bev complains. Nevertheless, she gives Alan one last kiss.

'Better get back to kids before they kill each other,' Alan adds.

'I was coming to tell you that Lucas has abandoned them and gone walkabout,' I say.

'Want me to find him?' Alan asks.

I shake my head. 'He probably needs a bit of time to calm down. If he's not back in time for lunch, I'll go and look for him.' Like most teenage boys, Lucas runs on stomach time. As soon as he's hungry he'll return.

So Alan heads off to referee the arguments and bickering while Bev comes with me. We link arms as we walk across the farmyard, three dogs and two guard geese in tow. Betty Bad Dog is trying to bite the geese but they're having none of it. If she carries on, I know who'll come off worse.

I squeeze Bev. 'It's so nice to see you two happy.'

'He's moving in with me,' she confides.

'Wow. That's good news. And a big step for you.'

'Yeah. I've tried him out and found him sufficiently domesticated. He's going to put his cottage up for rent. With a bit of luck, we could even be together for Christmas.'

'That's lovely.'

'What are you and Shelby up to over the holiday?'

'I don't know,' I admit. 'He says that he'll be back from his stint in panto by then. In the nick of time. It only finishes on Christmas Eve, so a quiet one at home, I guess.'

'He'll want you to spend it at Homewood Manor.'

'I expect so.' The thought fills me with dread. How will I look after all the animals? I can't leave them alone.

'Your van isn't the most festive place,' Bev scolds.

'I could pretty it up.' I grimace. 'Lights and stuff.'

'Don't sound so flipping enthusiastic.'

'This is more your kind of thing. Help me. What shall I do?'

'We could go shopping this afternoon.' She looks back at the barn. 'Any excuse to leave this flipping lot to it and hit the charity shops.'

'I do need to find another Baby Jesus.'

'They'll have them coming out of their ears,' Bev assures me.

I hate shopping in all of its forms. Bev usually does it all for me or I make Lucas do it online.

'We can pop into one of the DIY sheds and get some Christmas lights.'

'We haven't got a tree yet.' I think it's a moot point to make.

'Didn't I tell you? The Hot Mayor is sending us one.'

'Is he? That's very kind.' I confess that I haven't given Matt Eastman much thought as I've been so busy, so it's nice to know that he's still thinking of us.

'It's coming in a couple of days. So we should get some decorations.' I must still look reluctant as she adds, 'I'll treat us to a coffee and some cake as you're being so brave.'

'After lunch?'

'Yeah. I've got a lentil shepherd's pie for the hungry hordes today.'

'Sounds good. It'll warm them up.'

'Should I put some drugs in it?'

'As tempting as it is, it might be ever so slightly illegal,' I say.

'Ah. There is always that.'

'You love them all really.'

'I do. It's just that some days they test us more than others.'

'They do, indeed.' And we go into my caravan so that Bev can fill me in on the preparations for the open day.

Chapter Twenty-Seven

When lunch is over we take Bev's car into town. While she drives I look out at the rolling fields, beautifully stark in their winter garb. In town we find another Baby Jesus in the Oxfam shop. It's probably a bit more boss-eyed and moth-eaten than a Messiah should be, but it's big and only costs four pounds. The plastic doll has also got blonde hair and a pink romper suit but, once it's well-swaddled and viewed from a distance, Bev assures me it will be fine. Frankly, I'm still in mourning for my expensive and realistic baby that the alpacas munched and it's hard to view any replacement as adequate.

Doll bought and bagged, we go into B&Q and load up a cart with Christmas lights. I prefer the tasteful and understated white but Bev – my trusted companion and self-appointed style advisor – is having none of it. We get the most colourful ones on display. Hundreds of them. All with variable flashing options. This is going to be a nativity crossed with Blackpool illuminations.

'I'll get in touch with the Hot Mayor,' Bev says. 'Find out when the tree is coming.'

'It'll need to be about twenty feet tall to take all these flipping lights.'

'I'll tell him that,' she jokes. 'Go big or go home.'

When we're spent up, we load up the car and then head to a little café for a recuperative cup of tea and a slice of lemon drizzle – things that will put everything in the world to rights. We sit in the window, too, which always seems like an extra treat.

We both make appreciative noises as we enjoy our refreshment.

'So?' Bev asks between sips. 'How's Widow Twanky?'

'He's the villain,' I remind her. '*Nebuchadnezzar!*' I try to mimic Shelby's villain voice, but don't quite do it justice.

'Ah. We should have an outing to go and see him do his *thang*.' Bev picks all the crumbs from her plate with her fingertip. 'The kids would love that.'

'Would they? I haven't been to a panto since I was about four and I hated it then. My mum took me and I cried all the way through it.'

'They've got better since then,' Bev assures me.

She's probably right. The early press reviews are great and Shelby, surprisingly, seems to be really enjoying it. I'm still not convinced it's for our kids, though. 'They're struggling enough with all the fuss of Christmas. Wouldn't it be too much of a trial to drag them en masse to Birmingham? Besides, I'm sure some of our teenagers would think it "totally" uncool to go to a panto.'

'Maybe,' Bev agrees. 'Perhaps something local, a bit more low-key just for the littlies? I'll see what there is. Surely you'll go to Brum to see Shelby's production, though?'

'Shelby hasn't mentioned it. But then he's been so engrossed that he probably hasn't thought of it.' Neither had I, if I'm truthful. Our worlds have always been kept firmly apart until now.

My friend frowns at me. 'Is everything OK between you?'

'Yes.' I nod, maybe too vigorously. 'I'm sure it is.'

'Hmm.' Bev doesn't look convinced. 'When did you last see him?'

'Over a week ago now,' I have to admit. 'He's hoping to come home on Sunday though.'

'So he should. Love by Skype isn't quite the same.'

'No.' Never a truer word spoken. 'It's the official opening night next week, so it's only going to get worse from here on in.'

Bev's frown deepens.

'It is just a temporary thing,' I assure her. 'After Christmas, everything will be back to normal.'

But Bev doesn't realise that I have my fingers crossed when I say that.

After we've finished in town, we take our booty back to the farm. It's dark early in the day now and all the lights are on – a welcoming sight. Bev drops me off and parks the car while I shut the gate. All the students will have gone home now, their tasks finished for the day.

Alan comes out of the barn and they hug each other as if they haven't seen each other for months. I get a little pang of loneliness.

'I've seen kids off,' Alan says. 'And fed animals.'

'Thanks, that's very kind. Saves me a job.'

Alan nods.

'Were the kids OK this afternoon?' I ask.

'Depends what you mean by OK? No one died.'

That's good enough for me. Some days you have to be grateful for small mercies and hope that tomorrow will be better.

'Come on, lover,' Bev says. 'Take me home and ravish me.'

'Can we have us tea first?' Alan asks. 'I'm starving.'

'I'd never expect you to *lurrrrve* on an empty stomach,' she purrs.

In reality she'll be on her sofa watching *Flinton's Farm* with a cup of tea. Perhaps I should start watching it. I can get it on my phone. That would be a surefire way of seeing Shelby every day. Though, as Lucas bans it in our humble abode, I'd have to watch it in secret.

I say goodnight to Alan and Bev, then do a quick tour of the animals. They're all happy to settle down early and most are already curled up, comfy in their straw. Oh, for the life of a pampered animal. Mind you, it wasn't always thus for our charges so they deserve a bit of love and TLC.

When I'm done, I head to the caravan. The lights are blazing out and the kitchen window is steamed up. The second I'm through the door, the dogs go into a barking frenzy and hurl themselves at me and I fuss them while saying 'Inside voices, doggies. Inside voices.'

Lucas is at the stove stirring a pot. The raising of one eyebrow is his more muted response to my homecoming.

'Hey,' I say.

'Successful trip into town?'

I hold up my plastic saviour of mankind. 'New Baby Jesus.'

'Cool,' he says. 'It looks a bit creepy though.'

'It's a doll. They're all creepy.'

'I've made some supper.' Lucas nods at the pan he's stirring. 'I've been a total shitbag for the last few days. This is an apology in the form of a curry.'

'Smells wonderful.' And it does. A waft of spices fills the air.

'Sweet potato and spinach dhal,' he says. 'Downloaded the recipe.'

'You modern thing, you.'

Lucas chuckles. 'I'm not modern, you're a dinosaur.'

'It's nice to see you laugh,' I tell him.

'Yeah, well. I'm a moody teenager. What can I say?'

I'd like to give him a hug, but that might be a step too far. 'Have I got time for a shower before dinner?'

'If you don't hang about. Ready in five.'

'OK.' So I do as I'm told and rush round in the shower and throw on some clean clothes. Then I set the table and, as soon as I'm done, Lucas dishes up, ladling the curry into bowls with dairy-free bread on the side.

'Where did you get this lot?'

'I walked down to the village shop. A new guy has taken it over and they stock some amazing stuff.'

'I'll have to check it out.'

'Yeah, but you've been off the farm once this week, so you'll have to wait until you've plucked up courage again.'

'True.'

Lucas laughs again as he spoons the dahl into his mouth. He seems much cheerier and I wonder why.

'If you think you can manage it, I've got a poetry slam coming up.'

'I've no idea what that is.'

'It's like a poetry competition, generally judged by people who know nothing about poetry, but I've kind of entered it.' Then he goes all shy. 'No big deal if it's not your thing.'

'Of course it is. I'd love to come along. You know that I always want to hear more of your poetry.'

'It would be nice to have your support,' he says. 'Plus I need a lift there and back.'

Ah, that's more like it. But then I would do that anyway and Lucas knows it.

'What about your dad? Do you think he'd be able to come?'

Instantly, Lucas's demeanour changes. 'You can't tell him.'

'Don't ask me to keep more secrets, Lucas. It's not fair. This should be something we could enjoy together – all three of us.'

My troubled teen puts on his mardy face. 'He'd just spoil it for me.'

'But he's so proud of you. Remember what the fundraiser was like in the summer when you and he were on the stage together? Wasn't that great?'

'He *always* wants to steal my thunder,' he complains – which is not my memory of it at all. In reality, Shelby was nothing but encouraging and kind. He was so proud of Lucas's performance. 'I *seriously* don't want him there. He can't help but hog the limelight. It's in his DNA. This is something that I want for myself. It *has* to be our secret.'

'OK. That's fine.' Lucas is quite impassioned, so I don't push it. I'm simply glad that he's asked me to be there. If I have to keep it from Shelby, then that's how it has to be. 'When is it?'

'Next week. I'll let you know the details.'

That's another consideration. I doubt Shelby would be able to attend anyway with it being his first proper week of shows, but I think it's best that I don't mention that. If I tell Lucas that his dad can't go, then he'll definitely want him there.

'I'd love to hear what you've got planned. Do you want to try out your poem on me after supper?'

'No,' Lucas says and returns to eating his curry.

And that's pretty much the end of that. So much for me being supportive.

Chapter Twenty-Eight

Bev has been scheming behind my back. Clearly, she was worried after our tea room conversation and has secretly been Skyping Shelby to organise for him to come home today. It's all been taken out of my hands and is planned to the nth degree. In true Bev style, she's volunteered herself to look after the animals and Lucas. I'm not sure which will be the more demanding.

She's been here since six o'clock this morning and everyone's fed and watered. Except Lucas, who is still in bed. In fairness, this is the one day he does get a lie-in as he's usually up every weekday to help me with the animals, so I'm happy to let him be.

It's ten o'clock and Bev and I are tucking into hard-earned hot buttered toast when her phone rings. *It's the Hot Mayor*, she mouths to me.

She chats away to him while I concentrate on my toast, and when she hangs up she says, 'One Christmas tree arriving on Monday.'

'Wow.'

'What size?'

'Extra large, I hope.' She widens her eyes lasciviously.

'You're terrible,' I tell her. Then, before I can ask any more, Shelby turns up and I can't tell you how excited I am to see him.

I take Bev's example and rush out to the yard, hugging him tightly when he gets out of his car.

'That's an unexpectedly enthusiastic greeting,' he says as we hold onto each other.

'I've missed you,' I say. 'I'm so glad that Bev organised this.'

'Me too.'

We hold hands as we walk to the caravan. Inside, Lucas has just surfaced. He's in his pants and a T-shirt, his legs pale and scrawny. His hair is a bird's nest.

'Lucas!' Shelby is all smiles and good cheer.

'Morning, Father,' Lucas mutters back. He's not at his best when he's just woken up.

'All good, son?'

Lucas shrugs. 'Other than the fact that we're killing our planet one piece of plastic at a time, everything's hunky dory.'

'Great.' Shelby gives me a perplexed glance.

To Bev's delight, Shelby kisses her and she puts the kettle on again. 'Toast, Superstar?'

'I'd love some. Thanks.' Shelby flops down on the sofa. 'My stomach's been rumbling through the entire drive. I was going to head back last night, but we finished really late. I left as soon as I could this morning.'

'I'm just glad you could be here.' And I am.

'I thought we could do something all together,' Shelby says, brightly. 'It's a glorious day out there. Freezing cold, but the sun is doing its best.'

'If we wrap up, a walk would be nice.' I look across at Lucas for his approval.

He looks horrified. 'What? Me too?'

'It would be fun,' I assure him.

'In whose world? I want to stay here and play *Fortnite*. By myself.' He gives me a pointed stare. 'I don't need a babysitter either. No offence, Bev.'

'None taken, you ungrateful little shit,' she says mildly.

Lucas does smile at that.

She pushes toast to him and Shelby and they sit opposite each other in reasonably companionable silence though, these days, I always feel an undercurrent of tension. Perhaps that's just me.

'I'm going to cook you a roasty dins,' she tells Lucas. 'Let these two have some "grown-up" time together.'

'Thanks for that image,' Lucas bats back. 'Now I'll have to bleach my brain.'

I hope that Shelby doesn't jump in because, if he says one word wrong, Lucas will go into a huff.

'Come out with us oldies during the day and then you can have the evening with Bev,' I suggest.

He sighs at me. 'Must I?'

'Yes,' I tell him. 'You absolutely must.'

'Come on, Lucas,' Shelby urges. 'I'm not going to be around for a while. Spend the day with your old man.'

Lucas's expression is one of extreme resignation, but it says he's coming.

So, much faffing later, we're all wrapped up and two out of the three of us are raring to go.

'See you later,' Bev says. 'Don't worry.' That comment directed to me. 'It will all still be here when you get back.'

'I have every faith in you,' I assure her.

'I might have eaten all your chocolate, though,' she quips.

I kiss her cheek. 'You'll be very welcome to it.'

'Have fun.' She waves to us all as we go.

Wellies donned and multiple dogs in tow, we set out over

the stile and across the fields. There's a public footpath that runs along the left-hand edge of our property and, if you follow that for a couple of miles, you come out onto Moreland Nature Reserve. It's an old flooded quarry that's been turned into a haven for wildlife and has spectacular views across the countryside. In the summer you can't move for people but, today, it's relatively quiet. Only the hardcore walkers are out. And us.

As family outings go, I'd say that it turns out to be a reasonable success. There are no full-on arguments. No bloodshed. Lucas only moans a bit – well, *quite* a bit. Shelby wears a flat cap and sunglasses, so is only recognised twice. I can hear Lucas grinding his teeth as Shelby poses for smiling selfies with his fans, but it doesn't last for long and Lucas seems to get over it quickly. To entertain us, Shelby tells some funny stories about the panto rehearsals as we stroll the entire way round the quarry and Lucas even laughs at some of them. It sounds as if Shelby is having a ball and this is the most relaxed I've seen them together for a long time.

After our walk, we stop for tea and cake in the café which is all dressed up for Christmas and the waitresses are wearing elf hats. They even have a vegan Victoria sponge, so Lucas can't complain about that either. Shelby and I go seasonal with mince pies – recklessly non-vegan. A few hours later, as the sun is sinking in the sky and there's a fresh nip in the air, we walk home, muddy but happy.

Shelby stops at his car and, with a kiss, says, 'I'll send Ken for you later. About seven-thirty?'

'Sounds ideal. Do I dress up?'

Shelby thinks for a moment. 'Yes. I think you should.'

So I assume we're going out somewhere fancy when, in truth, I'd rather the three of us were staying in together with a soya mince spag bol.

I put the dogs in the barn as they're not allowed in the caravan when they're up to the eyeballs in mud. I could hose them down, but I'm sure Bev will do it for me later if I ask nicely. Lucas and I kick off our boots at the door.

'How was that?' Bev asks when we're back inside.

'A trial,' Lucas says. 'I'm going to play *Fortnite*.' He disappears into his bedroom and closes the door firmly.

'Was it?' Bev asks as her eyes follow him.

'No. It was fine. They got on quite well. Though it would kill Lucas to admit it.'

She tuts. 'It's such a shame they rarely see eye-to-eye.'

I can't help but agree. 'I hope that one day they'll appreciate each other more.'

'I'm sure they will.'

Until then I'll just try to keep the peace between them as best I can.

'Want me to sort the dogs out later?' Bev says.

'You might regret offering. They're all filthy dirty and holed up in the barn.'

She laughs. 'I don't mind.'

'You're an angel,' I tell her.

'I am. A fallen one.' She winks at me. 'I'll make us a cuppa and then you'd better go and get ready for your date night.'

'I feel quite nervous about it,' I admit. 'Do you know where we're going?'

'Of course I do, but like I'm going to tell you. Duh!'

'Spoilsport.'

'It'll be nice. Relax. He's your bloody *boyfriend*. Why are you getting all angsty, woman?'

It's a good question and I don't know why.

Bev sees to my tea needs and then lowers her voice as we drink. 'Have you seen anything of Lucas's girlfriend-not-girlfriend? What was her name?'

'Aurora.' I shake my head. 'No. He hasn't mentioned her and she certainly hasn't been here.'

'Wonder if it's all off?'

'I don't know. He still spends hours on his phone and he doesn't seem to have been upset or anything,' I point out. 'No more than usual, anyway.'

'Fingers crossed that it's all going smoothly.'

'Yeah,' I agree. But then I start wondering if everything really is OK.

Chapter Twenty-Nine

The dogs are hosed down and tucked up in the caravan for the night. They're also slightly surprised that I'm going out again. They're not the only ones.

'I won't be late,' I promise Lucas as I get ready to leave. A well-worn phrase.

'You might be late,' Bev says. 'You never know your luck.'

She looks very smug.

'What have you been plotting?' I turn to Lucas. 'Are you in on this?'

'Don't look at me,' he says. 'I'm only ever told anything on a need-to-know basis. I guess I'll see you when I see you.'

He disappears back into his bedroom.

'Thank you,' I say to Bev. 'I'm very grateful to you.'

'My pleasure. Alan's coming over in a short while so I'm not going to have to rely on Lucas for sparkling company.' She throws a nod towards his closed bedroom door.

'He loves you really.'

'I know. He's a good kid.' The dogs start to bark and she grabs me by the shoulders and turns me round to face the door. 'That's Ken at the gate. Have a good time.'

'You'll call me if anything goes wrong?'

'I won't,' Bev says. 'All you have to think of tonight is you and Shelby. Off you go. He's waiting.'

So I climb into Shelby's car and Ken drives us smoothly through the lanes until a few minutes later we're arriving at Homewood Manor. The house looks as if it is all in darkness, so Shelby must be ready for us to collect him.

Ken pulls up outside and comes round to open my door.

'Are we going anywhere else?'

'I'll leave that for Shelby to explain,' he says, mysteriously.

So I get out and walk to the front door, which is bearing a huge holly wreath, over-loaded with shiny red berries. As I get to the door, it swings open. There's a butler standing there in full livery. I'm so shocked that I just gape at him. My heart sinks a little bit. I really hope that Shelby hasn't organised some kind of chi-chi party without telling me and there's a houseful of posh people who I don't know.

'Come in, madam,' he says when he realises that I'm frozen on the doorstep.

I step into a hallway that's lined with flickering candles and the impressive Imperial staircase is draped with swags of Christmassy foliage. The butler takes my coat and I follow him towards the living room, which is also filled with candles. There's an enormous Christmas tree in the corner, shimmering with red and gold baubles. Shelby is standing there in full evening dress and looks every inch like an old-fashioned movie star. His dark-blond hair is swept back, immaculately styled. He's so beautiful that I could just stand and stare at him all night.

'This is lovely,' I manage to say. 'When did you do all this?'

'I had someone in,' he confesses. 'You like it?'

'Love it.' The festive decorations make it look warmer, more intimate than usual.

The butler appears at my elbow with a tray and I take a glass of champagne. 'Are we having a party?' I ask Shelby.

'Yes,' he says. 'But just the two of us.'

'You've gone to a lot of trouble.'

'I haven't been fair to you,' he says. 'I shot off to Birmingham without consulting you and I shouldn't have. The decision ought to have been a joint one.'

'It's your work . . .'

'I know and, now I'm not going to be around for the rest of the month, I am regretting it.'

'You should make the most of it. Sounds like you're having a lot of fun.'

'I am.' His eyes sparkle in the candlelight. 'It's years since I've been on a stage. On television, if anything goes wrong we can retake a scene.'

'Like when a bunch of unruly alpacas decided to trash the set?'

He laughs. 'Thankfully, that doesn't happen very often.'

I don't think, even if I live to be a hundred, that I'll forget the humiliation of that day.

'When in front of an audience, it's pure adrenaline,' he continues. 'Anything can go wrong and frequently does. It makes me feel very alive.'

'Then it was the right decision,' I tell him.

'I wanted tonight to be special,' he says. 'It was partly Bev's doing. She volunteered to step in while we spent some time alone.'

'She's wonderful. I don't know what I'd do without her.'

'You should be relying on *me*,' he points out. 'I'm sorry to be abandoning you in the run up to Christmas.'

'It will be all hands to the pump,' I agree. In fact, I really need to get going tomorrow. If the Christmas tree is arriving that will spur us all into action. We have to do something with the five million dancing lights that Bev's bought.

'Want to see what's on the menu?' Shelby asks.

I nod and he steers me through to the kitchen where a chef is busy at the enormous range stove with its plethora of doors and hotplates. That's another thing that terrifies me. How do you cook on that monster?

'Evening,' the chef says to us over his shoulder.

'This is Stephen. He's been here most of the day preparing dinner especially for us.'

'Wow.' Whatever it is, it smells divine. So we sit on the stools at the kitchen island, watching the chef as he works and explains to us what he's cooking.

Dinner is served in the vast main dining room where candles abound again, there are arrangements of deep red roses entwined with holly on the table and it's all very fancy. I try not to think that I'd be equally happy with a takeaway on the sofa with Shelby and appreciate all that he's done for me. The food is wonderful. The house looks spectacular. The champagne is going to my head. He's made a huge effort and I love him for it. I look across the table at him as he's telling me a story about one of the actors in the panto and realise that, at this moment, I could not love him more.

After dinner, the chef and the butler leave and, finally, it's just Shelby and me. He puts some slow music on and, in the living room, we dance by the Christmas tree, holding each other close. I rest my head on his shoulder and enjoy feeling the warmth of his hands on my skin.

We go to bed and I discover that Cunning Bev has packed an overnight bag for me and has brought it here – every eventuality catered for. I must thank her profusely for doing this.

Shelby and I make love and it's just how it used to be. When he falls asleep, I lie awake curled against him, feeling happy, content. The moonlight streams through the window and bathes the room in a mellow glow. It could be like this, I think. Always.

I know how much Shelby wants it. And it's a beautiful home. Shelby is much more relaxed here than he is at the farm. Would it be too hard for me to leave Hope Farm and live here permanently? It's a thought that keeps me awake until dawn.

Chapter Thirty

Too soon it's morning and we're back to normal. I'd like to say that we luxuriate in each other's arms, but no – we're both rushing around, hurtling into the day. Shelby has to head straight back to Birmingham. I need to get back to see if the farm is still standing.

'This has been wonderful,' I say. 'Just what we needed.'

He takes me in his arms and holds me tightly. 'Come to opening night,' he says. 'Ken will bring you. There's a party afterwards. Put on your glad rags again.'

'I don't know . . .'

'It would mean a lot to me to have you there.'

'Could Ken bring me back afterwards? I don't like to leave the farm two nights in one week.' It's unheard of and I can't take Bev for granted. But how can I refuse? It's hardly a lot to ask that I be there to support him.

'OK,' he says. 'Let's compromise. Come for the show and party, then Ken can drive you home. It will be a late one, but you'll be back with your precious animals.'

I ignore the slight barb. 'Can Lucas come too?'

'Of course. Nothing would make me happier. If you can persuade him.'

That might take some doing. His father isn't on his 'favourites' list and I'm pretty sure panto won't be up there either.

As you know, I lay awake most of the night and my brain was very busy. I'd have to make a lot of sacrifices to move in with Shelby, but don't I owe it to him to try? If this relationship is to work, then I have to be more open to his lifestyle and he to mine. Could I get a manager in to run the farm full time, I wonder? That someone would have to live on-site in the caravan as we need someone here 24/7. But then that would be more expense and eat into our valuable resources. What would I do with the dogs? I couldn't bring them here. Betty Bad Dog would wreck the place within five minutes. That beautiful Christmas tree would be a goner. Valuable ornaments? All smashed. And what of Lucas? If we lived here would he want come back? My gut feeling is that he'd prefer to stay at the farm in the caravan and, in truth, that's where I'm most comfortable too. I'd hate to move here and leave him behind. I couldn't do it.

'I'm sorry, but I have to run.' Shelby's voice breaks into the workings of my frenzied brain. 'If you're ready, Ken can drop you off on the way.'

'I'm good to go.' I have my overnight bag that I was very grateful for. My nice dress is safely packed away and I'm in my more customary jeans and jumper.

We jump into the car and Ken whisks me back to the farm. Bev opens the gate. The dogs hurl themselves at me as if I've been away for six months. Little Dog runs round and round in circles chasing his own tail in excitement. I step in front of Betty Bad Dog before she wees on Shelby's shoes again. They'll all be attached to me like limpets today in case I have the audacity to want to go anywhere without them.

'Look,' my friend says as she greets us. 'All is just as you left it.'

'I owe you one, my co-conspirator.' Shelby hugs her.

149

Bev gives me side-eye. I can be in no doubt about what she'd like that 'one' to be. Naughty lady.

I kiss Shelby goodbye, embarrassed to have so many onlookers. 'See you Wednesday,' he says. 'Don't forget.' Then he's in the car and gone.

Bev and I watch him leave.

'Was it utterly romantic?' Bev asks.

'It really was.'

'And did you shag each other ragged?'

I laugh at her, outraged. 'You're so very *rude*.'

'I'm so very *jealous*,' she says.

'Thank you for being sneaky enough to organise it.' I link my arm through hers as we walk to the caravan. 'I think it did us good to spend some time together.'

'You're seeing him on Wednesday?'

'I doubt it.' My heart sinks. 'It's opening night and he wants me to be there. But I can't go out two nights in a week. I can't put upon you again.'

'You can,' Bev says. 'You know I don't mind.'

But it's not just that. I don't mind seeing the panto, though it's not really my thing. The after-show party is another matter. Since meeting Shelby, I've only been to a couple of social gatherings with his actor friends, but I'm so out of my comfort zone. I'd rather stick pins in my own eyes.

'I did begin to think whether we might need a full-time manager on site.'

'Blimey.' Bev stares at me, aghast. 'That's radical for you.'

'I know. But Shelby's not comfortable here and, he's right, there's a massive house down the road standing empty.'

'This is your life,' she says. 'You've worked so hard for it. Don't rush into anything.'

'I won't. I have Lucas to think about, above all else.'

'Lucas should be Shelby's responsibility. He seems to be quite happy to have abdicated that and handed parental duties over to you.'

'I don't mind,' I counter. 'I'm hoping that if I hold the fort for now, it will be easier between them when Lucas is a bit older and more tolerant.'

'He was fine last night, our lovely boy,' she says. 'A bit moody but that could be down to anything.'

'Aurora didn't show up?'

Bev shakes her head. 'No.'

'I can't tell you how much I missed him.' One night away from him is too much. I wonder whether he would consider spending a few nights at Homewood Manor for Christmas. It looks so beautiful in its festive garb and Shelby has gone to a lot of trouble. Though I think I already know what the answer would be.

'He's up in the fields, but I've asked him to be back in the yard as soon as he can. The Christmas tree is coming any minute. I thought we'd gather the students around to watch. Might get them in the Christmas mood.'

'Most of them are already completely hyper.'

'I'm feeling a little buzzy myself,' she admits. 'First Christmas together with Alan and I'm looking forward to it.'

'That will be lovely for you.'

'Will Shelby definitely be at home too?'

I nod. 'He said so. Panto finishes on Christmas Eve.'

And I get a little unexpected thrill of excitement myself. It will be our first Christmas together – me, Shelby and Lucas. After so many Christmases spent alone, I can't wait. I want to make it wonderful for us all.

Chapter Thirty-One

I just have time to drop off my bag, fuss the dogs and swig down a quick cup of tea before a huge truck pulls up at the gate. Bev is already there with all the students gathered in the yard, so I dash outside.

I know the mayor said he'd donate a tree to us, but I hadn't expected anything on this scale. It's a bloody good job that Bev did bulk-purchase fairy lights. The entire flat-bed of the lorry is taken up with an enormous pine tree. The students go into a frenzy of excitement. So do the dogs.

Behind the truck is the mayor's car. He parks up and jumps out, grinning as he comes towards me.

'I never expected anything like this.' I feel slightly over-whelmed.

His eyes are bright, excited. 'You like it?'

'I *love* it. Thank you so much. Bev must have known. You won't believe how many lights she's bought.'

'I hope you'll let me stay and decorate it with you.'

'We'd be delighted to have you. Can I offer you some tea?'

'Let's get this beast unloaded,' he says. 'Once it's in place, with all its branches intact, I can relax.'

And I admit that I hadn't even considered where it might go. At that moment Lucas arrives. He has his hood up and his hands jammed in his pockets. It's a cold morning and will have been even chillier up in the fields. His breath is making clouds in the air.

I nod towards the tree. 'Look at this! Where do you think we should put it?'

'Wow. That is one bad motherfucker of a tree,' he says, gazing at it slightly wide-eyed.

'Lucas!'

He shrugs. 'We should put it by the barn where the nativity will be. We can secure it to the building, so it doesn't blow over if we get a gale.'

'Good plan. Do you want to help?'

'Do I have a choice?'

'Not really. Make sure it's far enough away from Anthony and the alpacas so that they can't eat it.'

It's a beautiful specimen and will not be improved by any of our lot deciding that it's a buffet lunch. The mayor holds out a hand to Lucas and they do a fist-bump and a grab handshake. 'Good to see you again, mate.'

Lucas isn't weird with him, which is a good sign.

Then Alan appears and together with the truck driver, Lucas and the mayor, they all unload the monster fir tree. With much heaving, grunting and shouting, they position it in the yard near the barn. When it's up, it looks even more beautiful, full and lush. The scent of pine from it is fresh and invigorating. The kids are enthralled and take loads of photos for social media. When it's fully secured, Alan climbs to the very top of our longest ladder and winds the lights down from the top.

'I told you we needed all those,' Bev says to me. 'I had a premonition. It's the gypsy blood in me.'

It's the shopaholic in her, more like.

In all the commotion, I notice that Lucas and the mayor are chatting away on the far side of the yard. If only he had such an easy relationship with his father.

As soon as the tree is finished, we decide to have a trial run for the lights and Bev asks the mayor to do the honours. After a fashion.

'Matt,' she yells at him. 'Do your Thang!'

He gives her a thumbs up and gets into position at the base of the tree. The kids all huddle round him as he stands and booms out, 'I declare this Christmas tree open.'

Then Alan flicks the necessary switch and all the lights shine out.

All the kids cheer and, even though it's not yet dark, the myriad colourful lights sparkle for all they're worth. The mayor looks very pleased with himself as well he might.

'Top job,' Bev shouts. 'You're booked!'

He stops and chats to all of our students, taking time with them all.

'Bloody big tree,' Alan mutters and gives it one last approving glance before he disappears into the depths of the barn again.

'I think you deserve a well-earned cup of tea and a piece of Bev's cake,' I say to the mayor. Though I don't know what she's brought in today.

'That would be great.'

'We need to go through some stuff for the open day,' Bev says. 'If you've got time.'

'I'm yours for the morning,' the mayor answers. 'Happy to do all I can to help.'

Once again, I find myself warming to this gentle, easy-going man. He has a calming way about him and the children respond well to it. I find myself smiling.

Matt Eastman turns to me and, when he sees my expression, says, 'What?'

'Nothing. I just wanted to thank you again. You've made a lot of people very happy.'

He grins at me. 'Then my work here is complete.'

'I hope not,' I say. 'We all like having you around.'

As the rest of the students head for the tea room, I see Penny hanging back and say to Bev and Matt, 'I'll catch up with you in a minute.'

I go over to her where she's standing staring at our latest addition. 'You like the tree?'

'It's nice.' But her answer doesn't hold any great enthusiasm.

'But? Not a fan of Christmas?'

She shakes her head. 'My dad's out nearly every night at some work party or another. Me and Mum dread him coming home.'

'He's drunk?'

'Usually.' Her look of resignation has me undone. 'Sometimes he passes out and we have to put him to bed. Sometimes he uses Mum as a punchbag. It could go either way.'

'This is a terrible situation,' I say to her. 'Would your mum consider leaving?'

'I don't know how she can put up with much more,' Penny says. 'He's getting worse. Every little thing sets him off. But where will we go? How will we live? Mum doesn't have a well-paid job or any money of her own. He's seen to that.'

Like so many of the students who've passed through our gates, they're dealing with situations that are beyond their years. When they should be feeling safe and cossetted, concentrating on their own lives and exams, instead they're up to their ears in adult issues. It makes me angry that people can be so selfish as to rob their own kids of their childhood.

'There are refuges that you could both go to.'

'I don't think she'd do that.' Penny folds her arms. I don't ever think I've seen her look so miserable. 'I've been googling places, but she doesn't seem interested.'

'Would it help if I talked to your mum?'

'I don't know,' she admits. 'She doesn't really talk to anyone but me. All her friends are gone. Just as *he* wants it. She pretends everything's OK, but we both know it isn't.'

'Is she coming to our open day with you?'

'She says so. It'll depend on whether her bruises are on show or not. If she's got a black eye or a split lip, then she'll likely stay at home.'

How terrible to live your life like that. How does anyone cope in that situation? I open my arms to her and, with only a slight hesitation, she steps into them and I give her a big hug. She feels so insubstantial, a wisp of a girl, all skin and bones. There's no doubt it's having an impact on her physical and mental health to live in so toxic a situation. If only her parents could put her welfare first. We stay like that and rock together for a few moments.

'I'll try to help,' I say. 'If I can. But you know you can always talk to me.'

'Yeah,' she says. 'But talking doesn't stop him hitting her.'

'No,' I agree. 'There has to be something else we can do.'

Penny shrugs. '*She* has to want to do it. I don't know if she does.'

As we walk arm-in-arm to join the others, I think there must be a way that I can help her mum to break this violent cycle, for the sake of herself and the sake of her daughter.

Chapter Thirty-Two

I worry about Penny for the rest of the day and it's only the fact that I have my own issues to deal with that makes me put those thoughts to one side.

As I can delay it no longer, I raise the matter of attending Shelby's panto with Lucas. The night has drawn in and the temperature has dropped. Nevertheless, we're in the barn and he's taken it upon himself to cut the alpacas' toenails before we put them to bed. You'd think he was trying to murder them, given the fuss they're making.

Tina Turner's already been done and is sulking in the corner. Now I'm holding Johnny Rotten's bitey end while Lucas deals with his hind legs. This is no one's favourite job.

'Calm down now,' Lucas coos as he tries to keep a firm hold on a wriggly alpaca. 'It will all be over in a moment.'

Johnny howls with indignation. There are many, many things that alpacas don't like doing and standing on three legs is one of them.

'This is for your own good,' I add.

Our bad boy of the alpacas is having none of it. He kicks out and hisses.

'To think I could be a record producer,' Lucas says flatly.

'There's still time,' I tell him. 'You're young enough and bright enough to do whatever you want.'

'You sound like my father.'

'That's no bad thing.' Then I take a deep breath. 'Speaking of which . . .'

Lucas scowls at me as he manoeuvres the nail clippers.

'It's his opening night on Wednesday and he's invited us both to go and watch the panto and then attend the after-show party.'

'I'd rather be stuck in a lift for two days with nothing but the soundtrack from *Frozen* playing,' Lucas says.

I can't tell him that I feel pretty much the same. 'Don't dismiss it out of hand. Ken will pick us up, whisk us there and then bring us back afterwards. We don't have to stay, but I think it would be a nice thing to do. It's a big step for your dad.'

'He's playing the baddie in a frigging *panto*. Get a grip.'

'We should be supportive, if we can.'

'You be supportive. I'm not going.'

'OK.' I'll give him time to think about it overnight and raise it tomorrow.

'There's no point raising it again tomorrow. I'm not going.'

I didn't even say that out loud. Hmm. Am I that predictable? Obviously.

Johnny hops around a bit as Lucas moves to his hind legs. 'Easy, boy. Easy,' he says as he settles in to clip the rear nails. 'The party will consist of warm wine, canapés based on dead animals and a room full of tossers all high on their own self-importance.'

He may have a point.

'It's not exactly my favourite way to spend an evening,' I remind him. 'But sometimes we have to do things for the ones we love.'

'You might have to,' Lucas says. 'I don't.'

Johnny kicks out and skitters away from Lucas, so I tie his halter to the fence and jump into the pen. I lean my weight against Johnny's back end to stop him bouncing away and try to soothe him as I do.

For my trouble he stamps on my big toe. 'Ouch. Thanks for that, John!' That will be another toenail lost for me. Seems to be a regular occurrence. I'll have to enter him in the accident book – again.

Lucas moves in once more and this time Johnny deigns to lift his leg so that Lucas can reach his toes.

'You're a stubborn old cuss,' Lucas murmurs to him. 'You know this will feel better when it's done.'

And we do them every couple of months, so it's not as if it's something new. After a few minutes of wrangling and some swift clipping, Lucas pats his rump. 'All done. There, that wasn't so bad, was it?'

Johnny has one last defiant kick out, but misses us both.

So we change animals and begin subjecting Rod Stewart to the ignominy of an alpaca pedicure. Lucas takes a firm grip and I move to the front to scratch his neck to distract him. Time for a change of subject with Lucas too. There's only so far you can push alpacas *and* teenagers.

'You seem to get on well with the mayor.'

'He's not a dickhead and he likes poetry. Not poncy dead poets either. Modern stuff.'

'It's nice that you have something in common.' A pause while he swears under his breath at Rod. 'How's the poem for the nativity coming along? Have you finished it yet?'

'Yeah. No. Sort of.'

'Oh good. That's one thing I don't have to worry about then.'

Lucas snorts. 'If I told you it was the best thing I'd ever written you'd still worry about it.'

'True.'

Lucas risks a smile. 'You're hopeless.'

'I have my moments,' I bat back. Then while we experience a brief time where Lucas is feeling relatively chatty, I venture, 'How's it going with Aurora?'

He doesn't look at me when he answers, 'All right.'

'You haven't seen her?'

'We're both busy,' he replies, but he's concentrating a little too hard on Rod's toes.

'Oh.'

'She's fine,' he says. 'I like her. Don't read anything more into it than that.'

'OK.' Clearly, that's out of bounds too. I'll move onto safer ground. 'What do you want for tea? We've got mushrooms.'

'Mushrooms it is.'

I stop and look at him. He's struggling with Rod, so I go round to help him again and steady the alpaca's back end. Sometimes Lucas looks so small, so vulnerable that I come over all protective. 'I want you to be happy.'

'I'll have some tofu with the mushrooms then.'

'I don't mean with your tea. I mean with life.'

'I am happy.' He pauses in his nail trimming and bares his teeth at me in a rictus smile. 'Delirious.'

'I might not be your mum, but I love you like one.'

'Weirdo.'

Then that's the last of the alpacas tortured and Lucas lets go. He stretches his shoulders.

'You've done a great job there.' Praise where praise is due. He might grumble a lot, but he does work very hard on the farm and has a great way with the animals. 'You can have first shower.'

'OK.'

We put the alpacas to bed and, when we walk across the yard, Lucas lets me put my arm round his shoulders.

160

Chapter Thirty-Three

It's agreed that I'll go to Shelby's opening night tomorrow. Gah! Ken will pick me up and take me straight to the theatre, which means I'll just about have time to do the last feed with Bev. It'll be tight, but we'll manage. After that, she's going to stay here for the evening with Alan until I come home.

'You don't mind?' I ask her.

'That's the forty-second time you've asked me the same thing,' Bev says. 'Ask me again and I might have to kill you.'

'But you really don't mind?'

'Where's that spade?' she says looking around the yard.

'OK.' I hold up a hand. 'I can take a hint.'

'Go. Enjoy yourself. It'll be fun.'

'Oh no, it won't.'

Bev points a finger at me. 'See what you did there.'

I'm dreading it. Of course I am. Plus I haven't yet told Shelby that Lucas isn't coming. He'll be so disappointed.

A car pulls up at the gate and it's Ringo's celebrity hairdresser, Christian Lee. Perfect timing for the little pony's star-quality cut as his fringe is starting to make his face itch.

We wave Christian into the yard and he gets out of the car.

As always he looks totally incongruous in our setting. Today he's dressed in his usual flamboyant style, wearing fuchsia pink chinos and a black silk shirt with white trainers. Obviously ideal for cutting the hair of a frisky pony.

He gives me one of his all-encompassing bear hugs. 'Darling, lovely to see you. Is this a good time? I was passing and thought I'd give my client a snip.'

'It's perfect timing. The ponies are down in the barn, so Ringo won't be too muddy.'

'Excellent. I hate it when you make me go yomping about in fields.' Christian curls his lips in distaste. 'It offends the city boy in me.'

'Is it all right if some of the new students watch you to see the kind of A-list treatment he gets?'

'Yes. Not a problem, sweetie.' He casts a critical glance over my own locks, as always. 'You look like you need a short back and sides too. I can't remember when you were last done.'

I can. A few weeks ago with my kitchen scissors. I'll not tell Christian that, though. My haircuts are distinctly more sporadic than Ringo's, but usually done by Christian or, failing that, by my own fair hand which drives him mad.

Our high-maintenance stylist gets his kit from the back of his car and we go through to the barn where he cuts Ringo's hair while entertaining his enthralled audience.

When he's finished, he says, 'I'm not in a rush. I've got time to do yours now if you like?'

'How can I possibly refuse?' So I get Jack to look after the dogs while we go into the caravan as Christian is less keen on an audience of inattentive puppies and it's too cold to cut my hair outside in the yard as he often does.

While he makes himself some tea, I quickly wash my hair. As Christian will see what state it's in, I throw on some conditioner too.

'I'm going to Shelby's opening night tomorrow,' I tell him when I'm seated in the kitchen area and he's snipping away. 'I suppose I should make an effort.'

He laughs at my reticence. 'That's the spirit.'

'You know that I prefer animals over people any day of the week.'

'I'm very honoured that you tolerate me,' he says. 'I'll be there too.'

'You will?' That cheers me immensely. 'At least there'll be one friendly face I know.'

'I'll see if we can sit together. Is my delicious godson coming?'

'Sore point. Lucas won't even consider it.'

'That's a shame. We could have fun together.'

'He's out riding at the moment, but I'll put it to him when he comes back. He might change his mind if he knows you'll be there.'

'I hope so. I haven't seen him for ages. Is he well? Behaving?'

'Yes, he's doing fine. He's such a bright boy.'

'Still writing his poetry?'

'Yes. I hope you'll come along to our open day and nativity. He's doing a poem for that.'

'Wouldn't miss it for the world, darling – diary permitting. It's my busiest time of the year.'

'I'm not sure Shelby will be around. He's so tied up with this panto.'

'Is everything OK with Shelby, too? I've only seen him a couple of times, but he seems strange, distracted.'

'I don't really see a lot of him now that he's based in Birmingham,' I confess.

'It's nothing personal, Molly. I know his lifestyle takes some adjusting to. It's just the way his job works.'

'I know.' But, if I'm honest, I'm only now beginning to realise just how much.

'There's nothing else on his mind?'

'I don't think so.'

'Good,' he says. 'It must be nerve-wracking for him being back on stage again. I'm probably being over-sensitive.'

I hadn't really considered that and I feel bad that Shelby and I haven't talked much about it. I'm determined that I'll put aside my desire to hide away on the farm and be by his side.

When Christian's finished, he dries my hair and I look in the mirror in my bedroom. My hair looks great. Like proper hair without additional straw. As always, he manages to make a silk purse out of a sow's ear.

He kisses my cheek. 'Catch you tomorrow night, sweetie.'

'Thanks, Christian.'

I see him out of the gate and lean on it as I watch him drive away. Bev comes to lean on the top rung next to me.

'Nice guy,' she says.

'The best.'

'I've booked you in for a manicure, pedicure and a full-leg and Hollywood wax tomorrow morning.'

'What?' I have no idea what this is, but I suspect I won't like it.

'Don't worry,' she says. 'It'll be fine. I can't have you turning up to a premiere looking like you've been dragged through a hedge. Especially now your hair's all fancy. I've asked her to do your make-up, too.'

There's no way I'm getting out of this, so I grit my teeth and say, 'Thanks Bev, you're a pal.'

Chapter Thirty-Four

I have EVERYTHING waxed. This is what they do in Hollywood? Seriously? I'm not entirely sure that I need it in Buckinghamshire. It's agony. And a bit chilly. The beautician complains at the state of my fingernails and toenails – one of which is a blossoming shade of black thanks to Johnny Rotten stamping on it. She does, however, make a marvellous job of making me look like a person who cares about these things. Then she puts many, many layers of make-up on my face. So much that I hardly recognise myself in the mirror. Plus, my hair still looks nice from its attention yesterday and that's a first too. Shelby had better appreciate all the trouble that Bev has gone through to pimp me up. Wait till I see her.

As I rush back toward my car, head down, arms pumping, I bump into the mayor.

'Molly!' he says and stares openly at me. He seems quite startled by my transformation. Perhaps he didn't recognise me without mud in my hair and looking borderline glamorous.

'Oh, hi.'

'Good to see you. What are you doing in town?'

'Just a few errands.' I'm hardly going to tell him about my newly groomed nether regions.

'I have half an hour before my car park ticket runs out. I don't suppose you've got time for a quick coffee?'

'I'm so sorry, but I can't stay.' I feel more disappointed by this than I should do. 'I'm going to Birmingham tonight and need to check that everything's in order at the farm.'

'It was an outside chance,' he admits.

'Another time though,' I say. 'I'd love to.'

He smiles at me. 'It's a date.'

And we both laugh awkwardly.

'Thank you again for the wonderful tree. The kids love it.'

'My pleasure.' He looks at me intensely again and I feel myself blush under his scrutiny. 'I'd better let you go.'

'We'll catch up soon,' I swear.

'Enjoy Birmingham,' he says.

Then the major and I head off in different directions, but I can't help but turn round to see where he goes and, when I do, he's watching me too.

Twenty minutes later, I'm back at Hope Farm and the yard is empty. Everyone, it seems, is having lunch in the tea room. It's an utterly miserable day and now it's started pouring with rain, but the lights shine out on our massive Christmas tree, bringing a little sparkle of cheer to the gloom. I hope that the kids will do some more work on decorations for the Christmas open day this afternoon if they're trapped inside.

'How did it go?' Bev wants to know as I shake the rain from my hairdo.

'I hate you with a vengeance.'

She only laughs.

Lowering my voice, I hiss at her, 'No one in life should have a bare noo-noo.'

'Perhaps this will make up for it.' She reaches beneath the counter and pulls out a bag. 'Black jumpsuit from Oxfam. You'll look like the dog's bollocks in it.'

I assume that's a good thing.

'I tried it on and it was too tight, so it should fit you perfectly.'

'Thanks,' I say.

'Tell me at least that you're starting to look forward to it a little bit?'

'I am.' And somewhere deep inside of me, I'm not actually dreading it any more. I think it's because Christian will be there and I know that I'll have someone to hang on to. I did tell Lucas that his godfather would be in attendance too, but his position was entrenched and he still wouldn't budge.

Bev dishes me out some lunch – lentil pie with a vegan cheese topping which looks delicious – and I go over to sit beside Lucas.

'Hey,' I say. 'What have you been up to this morning?'

'We cleaned out the goat's pen and then, when it started peeing down, I showed the students how to upload the photos they took yesterday to social media.'

'Good job.'

We tuck into our pie and it's delicious and most welcome. It warms me down to my toes.

Then Lucas says, 'It's tonight.'

'The panto?'

'No, the poetry slam competition.'

I stop eating and stare at him. 'You're kidding me.'

He stares back. 'Why would I?'

'How long have you known?'

A couple of pink spots appear on his cheeks. 'Aurora had sent it through, but I forgot.'

I'm speechless.

'I guess you won't be coming now.' His voice is tight. 'Even though you promised.'

'I also promised your dad that I'd go to his panto.'

'But you promised me first.'

'Oh, Lucas.' And here I am, right back in the middle of them, loyalty torn and with the distinct impression that I'm being manipulated.

'I've got to go,' he continues. 'The prize is a top spot at a festival next summer. A really funky venue. How can I miss it? This could be my big chance. You said you would come.'

'I know, but I didn't know it would be the same night as your father's big debut.' Though I suspect Lucas has known this all along.

His face darkens. 'It doesn't matter. I know he comes first in everything.'

'That's not true, Lucas, and you know it.'

But he's already in full-on sulk mode. Part of me knows that I shouldn't give in to this kind of behaviour, but I also know how important it is to him. It feels like he's forcing me to choose between supporting him or Shelby.

It's a tough one.

Let's face it, I can see Shelby any night during his panto run, but this is a one-off for Lucas. If I abandon Lucas and go to Birmingham, it will seriously damage our relationship. He needs someone reliable and steadfast. What to do? I can't be in two places at once.

With a heavy heart, I say, 'OK. I'll phone your dad and explain to him.'

'You can't tell him that I'm in a poetry slam,' he says, ratcheting up his emotional blackmail. 'Absolutely not. I don't want him to know.'

'You're making this very difficult for me. We should be open with him. It's not fair if I'm letting him down.'

'Don't tell him. You can't. This is about me, not him.'

I want to tell Lucas that he needs to be adult enough to deal with this, but then I see the childish look of pleading on his face and cave in. 'Let me think about it.'

And I'm cross and a little bit saddened to see that there's a smile of quiet triumph on Lucas's face.

Chapter Thirty-Five

Shelby is not best pleased. I can understand that. He huffs at me down the phone.

'It can't be helped,' I say into the tense silence. 'Something has come up.'

'This better not be about a sick chicken, Molly.'

'It's not.'

'For once, I'd like to rank above a dog with a dodgy stomach or an alpaca with anxiety issues.'

'It's not the animals.'

'So what's keeping you from being with me?'

'I can't say.'

His tone tightens further. 'Can't or won't?'

'A bit of both,' I admit. I daren't tell him that it's because of Lucas, as Shelby will fly off the handle at that.

'This isn't just about you wanting to stay at home on the farm? I know this isn't your thing, but I really wanted you to be there for me. It's important.'

'Believe me, if I could be there, I would. I've even had all of my bits and pieces waxed in honour – at Bev's insistence. Would I have put myself through that if I'd not planned on coming?'

He does laugh at that. Thankfully.

'Is it Lucas? Is he all right?'

'He's fine,' I say, honestly.

'I'm missing you all.' Shelby sounds sad. 'Much more than I imagined. I even miss those bloody unruly hounds.'

'It must be bad.' At this moment, I feel like jumping in the truck and speeding down there to surprise him. But I've promised Lucas and I know how much it means to him too.

'I love you,' he says, but the words carry all the weight of the world behind them.

'I love you too and I can come any night next week,' I offer. 'Any night, really. I'd be delighted to. And I'll bring Lucas with me.' Even if I have to drag him there screaming. After this, he owes me one.

'Barring all animal emergencies.'

'The sheep and alpacas can be running amok throughout Buckinghamshire and I'll still come.'

'Can I have that in writing?'

'In blood,' I promise. 'And sealed with a kiss.'

'I'm ridiculously nervous about tonight,' he confesses. 'I've got a lot riding on it and I'm out of my comfort zone, too.'

'You'll be wonderful, I'm sure. Can you call me when you're back from the after-show party? It doesn't matter what time. I just want to hear how it went.'

'Yes,' Shelby says. 'I'll phone as soon as I can. I'd better go.'

I cradle the phone closer to my ear. 'I *do* wish I was there.'

'Well, you're not and we both have to deal with that.'

'I'll speak to you later,' I tell him. 'Break a leg or whatever it is you actor-types say.'

Then we both hang up. I sit there with my waxed legs, unnaturally smooth under-carriage, painted face and blow-dried hair with Bev's nice jumpsuit still in a bag by my side, feeling unhappy and unsettled.

Chapter Thirty-Six

Lucas is excited and irritable. It's a testing combination. I'll tell you how bad he is – I'm wishing that I was at Shelby's after-show party with people I don't know and a glass of warm wine.

It's been hell getting him out of the caravan in time for the drive to the pub in Stony Stratford. For a start, I thought it was his usual venue in downtown Aylesbury and he only dropped it on me an hour ago that we were heading elsewhere. The King's Arms, apparently. Half an hour away, in completely the opposite direction.

Then he spent for ever on his appearance. Needless to say, much longer than I have. Eventually, he appears wearing more make-up than both me and the entire Rimmel counter put together – pale foundation, red lips and tons of black eyeliner. His hair is meticulously back-combed into a bird's nest. He's wearing a black shirt and skinny jeans with Converse High-Tops.

'Nice,' I say. 'Robert Smithesque.'

'Do I need more eyeliner?' He peers in the mirror by the door, anxiously.

'I don't think so.'

'Just a bit more,' he says and disappears again.

Now – finally! – we're in the truck and trundling through the lanes in the darkness while he whinges that we're going to be late. I put my foot down.

'What if I'm on first?' he grumbles. 'I might miss my slot and then it would all be pointless.'

'We'll be fine,' I say, reassuringly. Then I have to slow for a crossroads, which also allows me to double check that we're heading in the right direction as this is unknown territory for me. It gives me time for a quick panic, too. What if we *are* late? Lucas will never forgive me – even though it's his fault! 'I'll drop you off and then find somewhere to park. That will save some time.'

Thankfully, the country lanes get wider, then houses and streetlamps start to appear – which is always a good sign. I've been over this way before, but not for a long time and I'm struggling to get my bearings.

'I feel sick,' Lucas says giving me a bleak look. 'We should turn round and go home.'

'It's only natural to have nerves. Try to harness the feeling. It will add an edge to your performance.'

'As if you'd know,' he sneers.

Oh, give me a field full of unruly sheep any day over a stroppy teenager. I concentrate on my driving. To add to our woes, I think they've changed the road layout since I was last here and Google just keeps telling me we've arrived at our destination when we haven't. We do two turns round a one-way system before I spot the pub.

I pull up outside the King's Arms on the High Street. 'Jump out. We passed a car park round the corner. I'll try to get in there.'

Lucas does as he's told. 'Don't be long,' he says and, suddenly, all the grumpiness and bravado has gone and a scared boy stands on the pavement.

'Five minutes,' I promise. 'That's all.'

I drive away, and as I look in the rearview mirror, he's still standing there looking forlorn. I hurry to find a parking space so that he's not by himself for a moment longer than necessary. I know that Shelby isn't pleased, but I feel as if I've done the right thing in coming to support Lucas.

A few minutes later, I'm hurrying into the pub. There's a sign that indicates the poetry slam is taking place upstairs and I head towards it. The room is small and crowded – most of the seats already occupied. Lucas is hovering at the door.

'OK?'

'Yeah,' he says. 'I've registered and I'm on towards the end.'

'Good. We can relax a bit.'

'You might be able to, but I'm bricking it.' He fidgets anxiously.

'Do you want a Coke or something to take your mind off it?'

'Is a double voddy out of the question?'

I raise my eyebrows.

'Coke it is then,' he sighs.

I queue at the small bar, get our drinks and then we find a seat. There are lots of people dressed flamboyantly – poets, I guess. Lucas is younger than any of them, by quite a long way. I start to get nervous for him. There's a man at the front fiddling about with microphones and the like. Five people sit on chairs at the side of the tiny stage – the judges, I expect.

'Can we keep a seat for Aurora?' Lucas asks.

'Is she coming?'

'She said she would.'

First I've heard of it. Lucas tries to pretend that he's not bothered whether she does or not, but spoils the effect by turning to look at the door every few minutes. I put my handbag on the seat next to me as there are many people eyeing it up.

About fifteen minutes after the allotted start time, the poetry slam kicks off. A comedian, of sorts, tells a few off-colour jokes and then introduces the first act. I know very little about poetry, but it sounds OK to me. It's an earnest piece about the power of the internet and I wonder what Lucas's poem is about. I wish he'd let me listen to it ahead of time. I wish I knew more about poetry.

I whisper to Lucas, 'Why is it called a slam?'

'I don't know,' he admits. 'Maybe it's a vain attempt to make poetry sound sexy.'

Aurora arrives and Lucas waves to her. She squeezes along the row to sit next to us and I switch seats so that she's next to Lucas.

'Hi, Molly,' she whispers to me.

'Hi.'

She and Lucas exchange a brief kiss and he takes her hand, holding it tightly.

When the act finishes, there's much applause. I look to Lucas and Aurora to solicit their opinion, but they're too engrossed in each other to care what I think. So I take time to text Shelby even though he'll already be on stage by now and try not to feel that, already, I'm surplus to requirements.

Chapter Thirty-Seven

Several more acts strut their poetry stuff, then it's Lucas's turn to perform. In fairness, I think the standard has been very high tonight. All the performers seem, to me, to be quite polished.

Lucas takes to the stage and appears tiny, young and vaguely vampiric. In the harsh blue-white spotlight, he looks truly terrified and ready to make a run for it. My heart breaks for him. Surreptitiously, I take out my phone to capture his performance on video.

Lucas pulls the microphone down towards him. '"Say Something".'

There's an uneasy pause and the crowd fidgets. Aurora pulls a hopeful face at me. Then, clearing his throat, Lucas starts:

Say something to me,
But mean what you say;
Think it through,
Don't just trot out
A well-thumbed cliché.
Make it count;
Make it worthy

Of your dying breath:
Say your piece
Or forever be silent in death.
Say something about me,
If you feel you must,
Without hyperbole
Or betraying a trust.
It's easy to snitch
And to add in a touch:
Tell the world what you can,
Though it won't be that much.

When he's finished, the room bursts into spontaneous and enthusiastic applause. He was so confident and strong that it takes me by surprise. I wonder what on earth he was worried about. He's standing there commanding the room, the little lost boy all gone, replaced by a grown man. My eyes well with tears and I brush them away.

The compère announces that there will be an interval and then just six performers will go through to the second round. Everyone makes a dash for the bar.

Lucas comes back to us and his eyes are bright.

'That was brilliant,' I say. 'Were you pleased with how it went?'

'Yeah.' He shrugs, feigning nonchalance, but I know that he's happy.

Aurora throws her arms round him. 'I'm so proud of you,' she says and Lucas grows in stature in her embrace.

'I'll get us some drinks,' I say and, after taking their order, slope off to the bar.

While I wait, I watch them together. Aurora is flirty, confident. Lucas looks to be in awe of her, grateful for her attention. My heart squeezes.

I love having this boy in my life and as soon as he's here, I'll have to deal with letting him go. It's wonderful seeing him testing his wings, ready to fly, but part of me wants to hold him at the farm for ever. I don't know if he'll resume his studies and in the future, go off to university. Or whether another job will take him away from me. But, for now, I should enjoy what I can of him.

I return with the drinks and Lucas is getting a little more anxious now. The judges take their places and the lights are dimmed once more.

The compère takes the mic. 'In no particular order, the poets through to the next round are . . .'

He reels off some names and there's clapping and cheering from the audience. Lucas grows quieter, paler. I dig my fingernails into my palms.

' . . . and the final place goes to Lucas Dacre.'

Aurora and I cheer loudly and Lucas grins shyly. The poets are called to the stage one at a time and they're all good. Each one of them seems to have upped their game and I'm nervous for Lucas. He looks nervous for himself too.

Eventually, it's his turn. He wipes his palms on his jeans and whispers, 'Wish me luck,' as he heads into the spotlight.

Lucas stands at the microphone again and takes a couple of steadying breaths before saying, 'This one's for Molly.' He glances up at me through the heavy curtain of his fringe and my heart tightens. '"The Laws of Chaos".'

Every action I take;
every movement I make,
has a universal consequence
riding in its wake.

Every tree that I shake;
every twig that I break,

puts the intricately interwoven
balance at stake.

Each innocuous flake;
every tremulous quake,
has a repercussion for
the environment's sake.

So every species we slake,
our existence we forsake;
not to appreciate this law
will be our final mistake.

Again, he seems to have the most enthusiastic applause from the audience, but I may just be biased. Now we have an anxious wait while the judges confer. There's some heated debate going on. Then, after a few minutes, the compère steps up to the mic and announces, 'The winner of the King's Arms Poetry Slam with a slot at the prestigious Green Scene Literary Festival is . . .' Agonisingly lengthy theatrical pause. 'Lucas Dacre!'

Lucas looks at me in shock.

'You've done it,' I say. 'You've done it!'

Stunned, he goes to the stage and they give him a trophy. He looks at it as if it's an unexploded bomb.

'Thanks,' he says and then stares at the audience as if it's the first time he's seen them. For once, he's completely lost for words, so comes off the stage.

'I knew you could do it,' Aurora tells him.

I don't think that I've ever seen Lucas grin so widely. Everyone starts to drift away and we follow. Out on the street, Lucas and Aurora are still hand-in-hand.

'I'll go and get the truck and come back to pick you up.'

That will give them a few minutes alone together without me playing gooseberry.

'Aurora's going to drive me home,' Lucas says.

'Oh.'

'Have you got a problem with that?'

'Er . . . no. Of course not.' In truth, I feel slightly put out that he's not coming in the truck with me, but remind myself that this is part of letting go. Why wouldn't he want to be with his girlfriend? He clearly dotes on her. Coming back to the caravan with me for celebratory tea and toast probably holds little appeal.

'We might stop off at her place,' he says. 'Don't wait up.'

He's sixteen. Do I give him a curfew? Would that embarrass him in front of Aurora? Would it embarrass me? Where's Shelby when I need his advice?

There's no doubt that Lucas is as pleased as punch and glowing. Tonight has given him such a boost of confidence. He deserves to have fun with someone his own age.

'I'm so proud of you,' I tell him.

'Thanks.' Bashful again. 'I'm pretty proud of myself.'

'So you should be.' As I prepare to leave them to their own devices, I say as nonchalantly as possible, 'Can I tell your dad?'

'No,' he answers.

And that's pretty much the end of that.

Chapter Thirty-Eight

So I head to the car park, find the truck and drive home alone. I'm buzzing and I wonder what it feels like to perform on stage and then come off feeling high and invincible. How do you come down from that? I think of Shelby and am sad that I couldn't be there for him. As soon as I'm home, I'll text him to find out how he got on.

Hope Farm is in darkness as I approach, but a security light flicks on as I get to the gate and the dogs start to bark. I park, and as soon as I open the caravan door, they all mug me, bouncing up and down as if they've been abandoned for years.

'Calm down,' I say. 'I'm home now.'

Before I make tea or text Shelby, I should take them out across the fields. If they've been cooped up for a few hours, they'll need to run off some steam or they'll be restless all night.

'OK,' I say. 'Let me put my warm coat on and then I'll be with you.'

So I pull on my coat, kick off my trainers and don my boots. Within minutes, I'm striding across the fields and, as always, my soul settles. The night is bright and clear and, in

181

the bottom of the vale, frost tips the skeletal branches of the trees. There's a cloud above the dogs from their warm breath. On our way back, I call into the barn to check on everyone else. They're all tucked up and asleep, only a few of my charges rousing as we go in. I stand and watch them all snuffle and wriggle for space in their sleep. This is how it should be and this is where I should be. I'm not one for crowded pubs or swanky parties. I'm happiest when I'm here, straw in my hair and mud on my boots.

When we go back to the caravan and the dogs are settled once more, I text Shelby. *Hope you had a fabulous opening night. Thinking of you. Call me. M xx.*

I make a cuppa, get ready for bed and stress that Lucas isn't home yet. It's nearly one o'clock and it's not long before I have to get up again. I hope that nothing's happened to them. More specifically, that they're not upside down in a ditch somewhere. I chew at my fingernails. Should I call him? I don't want him to feel that I'm checking up on him but, of course, I *do* want to check up on him. I stare at the phone willing it to ring – with either Shelby or Lucas at the other end – but it doesn't.

I read, but keep the light low with the hope that I might slip into sleep but, as soon as I start to snooze, every little noise jolts me awake. Finally, just before 3 a.m. the dogs go barmy and I assume that Lucas has finally come home. I lift up the curtain on my window, just in time to see him vaulting over the gate. He waves to Aurora as she flicks her headlights and then reverses away down the track.

He crosses the yard, a spring in his step despite the hour. I can't tell you how relieved I am to have him home. It took me all my strength not to ring him earlier.

The door bangs and I hear him murmuring to the dogs. Then he's outside my bedroom door.

'I know you're not asleep, Mols.'

'No.' He knows me too well. I put the light on and he opens the door. 'Are you OK?'

'Yeah.' Lucas comes to sit on the edge of my bed. His face is flushed and his eyes are bright. I hope this is only to do with his success at the poetry slam, but I can't be sure. He does look really very happy. His hair was artfully tousled before, but you should see it now.

'I just wanted to say thanks,' he says. 'You know, for everything.'

He sounds a little bit drunk. I think he had that double voddy – or two – after all.

'I wouldn't have missed it for the world. I forgot to thank you for dedicating the second poem to me. That meant a lot.'

'I'm sorry when I'm a tit to you. I don't mean it.'

'I know. All part of growing up.'

'I don't want to be like my dad. I want to be kind and caring,' he says.

I want to tell him that he has his father all wrong. That Shelby is a good man, but now isn't the time. When Lucas is older he'll understand that.

'Thanks for being like a mum to me when I'm not even your kid.'

'Come here,' I say and he snuggles in for a hug. 'I love you to bits. I'll always be here for you.'

'I know.' He peels himself away from me. 'Better go to bed. I'm knackered.'

'You'll struggle to get up in the morning.'

'I do every day,' he points out.

'Sleep tight.'

'I'm gonna let Little Dog sleep on my bed.'

'OK. He'll fidget.'

'I'm so tired, I don't think I'll notice.'

'Will you read out your poems for the students tomorrow? I want to be all boasty about your success.'

And he must be feeling mellow as he says, 'Yeah, sure.'

Then he goes and, as I put down my book, a text comes in from Shelby.

It was a triumph. Still at the party. Speak tomorrow. S xx

That must be some party, I think. We're all going to be tired tomorrow. And so, at last, I turn off the light and go to sleep.

Chapter Thirty-Nine

Everyone is in a bad mood. Lucas, after his erudite and spectacular performance, has returned to grunt mode. He's barely said a word this morning. His eyes are red with tiredness and he's grumping around the yard doing nothing in particular in an irritable manner like a tetchy teenager.

The students are all stroppy today too and I'm exhausted from dealing with them before the day even starts. They're all squabbling about nothing. Even the sheep are bad-tempered and Anthony the Anti-Social Sheep has escaped his pen and headed off to the corner of the field where he currently has his head down ready to ram anyone who approaches. I'm going to leave him to his own devices, but have put one of the students on watch to make sure he doesn't make a bolt for the road. The geese are trying to nip everyone who passes and the donkeys are braying at the top of their voices. It's mayhem. Welcome to another sunny day at Hope Farm. Except it's pouring with rain. The huge Christmas tree might be doing its level best to be festive, but there's not much Christmas spirit here this morning.

Even Bev and Alan aren't immune to the dark cloud hanging over us today. They arrive wearing different band T-shirts.

Lucas nods towards them and mutters, 'Some *serious* shit must have gone down there.'

He might be right. If they've not discussed what they're wearing today, I'd say it's a sure sign that all is not well in their world. To be honest, Lucas and I were too tired to even have our usual bet this morning.

Alan disappears into the barn without a word, not all that unusual, but Bev also disappears into the tea room with nothing more than a wave and a curt shout of, 'Leave me alone. I'll talk to you later.'

So I do just that.

I hope the rain stops soon and we can get the kids doing something that burns off their energy, shifts their mood. The barn feels a bit dark and gloomy due to the grey day, but if I string up some fairy lights in here and have a cleaning and cuddling session with the bunnies that might cheer everyone up. Thankfully, the rabbits don't seem to be having any issues today.

Then, just as I'm feeling pleased with myself for thinking how to turn this around, a fight kicks off. Two of the girls, Lottie and Erin, start a full-on brawl in the yard. There's slapping, kicking, name-calling and swearing. Neither of them are much over five feet tall, but they're like banshees.

I dash to intervene and, as I try to pull them away from each other, get my own hair pulled and Lottie gouges the back of my hand in the process. 'Stop,' I say. 'Stop that right now.'

It's days like this when I dream of a nice, quiet office job.

'She started it,' Erin says, petulantly.

'Did not.'

But I'm in no mood to listen. 'You both need to calm down,' I say in my most placating tone.

'You can fuck off,' Lottie says. 'And you can stick your Christmas thing up your arse.'

'I'm not doing it either,' her opponent adds, now that they're ganging up on me. 'No one believes that Father Christmas is real now.'

Calling on all my reserves of patience, I calm the girls down and give them a little talk about boundaries, respect, violence, use of bad language and not taking chunks out of each other while they both glower at me. If looks could kill I would be stone dead.

'You don't have to take part in the open day or the nativity,' I say. 'That's entirely your choice, but I think you'd be missing out.'

That worries them more than anything – FOMO. Fear of Missing Out. Something all modern teenagers dread. Though now I have given myself another problem in that I have to think of something that two make-up-obsessed teenage girls might miss out on. I wish Bev had never come up with this. Christmas is stressful enough without all this added pressure.

Then I notice that someone's left the door of the chicken coop open and, even though it only takes me seconds to respond, the chickens are running free and my pep-talk is sharply curtailed. Instead, I'm running round – rather like a headless chicken – as thirty-plus of our sparsely feathered friends scatter to the four corners of the yard.

'Who let the chickens out?' I howl.

Little Dog and Betty Bad Dog decide to help round them up and bark excitedly as the chickens flap about which, of course, only serves to make things worse.

'Down, dogs,' I shout. So they jump up a bit more. Oh, to have animals that take a blind bit of notice of me. If that's not enough, then the geese join in, throwing back their heads to honk loudly and flap their wings, spooking the chickens even more.

I stop and watch the chaos around me, helplessly. Why can't I go back to bed and lie with the duvet over my head until tomorrow?

'Help,' I say to the students who are looking on, mouths gaping. 'Grab a chicken! You know how!'

But knowing how and actually being able to do it are two different matters. When chickens don't want to be caught, you are definitely up against it. Even our one-legged hen, Peg – who can topple over when standing still – can hop at an impressive rate of knots when she puts her mind to it. 'Go in the coop and grab some lettuce! Wave it at them!'

The students manage to do that and chase the chickens with lettuce offerings, but on this day contrary to every other day of the year, lettuce doesn't do the trick.

I don't know where Lucas is, but he's not here when I need him. 'Lucas!' I shout. 'Lucas!'

Our blind chicken, Mrs Magoo, is running round aimlessly, flapping her wings in fright. I need to catch hold of her before she does herself some damage.

Mrs Magoo makes a dash towards the gate and I can't let her get that far, so I hurl myself towards her. At the same time, so does Little Dog and, in a terrible accident of timing, I go flying over him and land full-length in the muddiest of puddles. I lay there in the cold, muddy water that smells of manure, weary down to my bones. If I don't laugh about this, then I will cry. My late night has left me tired and emotional. This threatens to push me over the edge. Not knowing quite what else to do, I sit myself up in the puddle and let the water seep through my jeans. I might not be able to catch the chickens, but I need to catch my breath. Muddy water drips from my hair. Betty Bad Dog decides to sit in the puddle with me. Her broad smile and waggy tail indicates that one of us is enjoying it rather more than the other.

Right at this moment, a car pulls up at the gate and the mayor gets out. Of course he does.

When he sees me, he leaves his car where it is and climbs

over the gate. 'You look like you could do with some assistance,' he shouts.

So he comes across to me, picking his way through marauding animals, barely able to supress his smile, and offers his hand.

As I grip onto him, he hauls me from my puddle. 'Thanks, Matt.'

He regards me with concern. 'You're not hurt?'

'Only my pride.' I start to brush myself down and then give up. It is beyond brushing. Hosing is more in order.

'I've got this,' he says and, in a calm and collected manner, he starts to round up the chickens and usher them back towards the waiting coop. 'Come on, ladies,' he coos. 'Calm down.'

I stand and watch with admiration and he works some kind of Dr Dolittle ninja magic on them. He gets the kids to join in and soon my surly bunch of obstreperous humans are giggling away. Hmm.

In case you're wondering, I do actually help too. I head to the hedge and pick up Mrs Magoo who has ensconced herself there and carry her safely back to her home. Soon, with minimum fuss, the hen house is back in its usual order, all our chicks clucking contentedly. Matt comes out, making sure to close the door securely behind him.

'There,' he says. 'All quiet on the western front.'

'I don't know how you did that. I'm very impressed.'

He dusts off his hands. 'My dad used to call me the chicken whisperer.'

That makes me laugh out loud.

'I'm serious,' he says, feigning affront. 'It's a much under-rated skill.'

'Well, I for one am very pleased that you have it. I think you've earned a cuppa and a piece of cake.'

'Any other miracles you'd like me to perform before I take my reward?'

'No, but I'm sure I can find you some more to do afterwards. If you're planning to stay around.'

'I'm yours for the day,' he says.

'Thank you, Matt.' I look at this laid-back man, earnestly. 'That was like the cavalry arriving.' Or a knight in shining armour.

'All in a day's work, ma'am.' He tips a non-existent hat.

We walk towards the tea room. Before I open the door, I pause and put my hand on his arm. 'I have to warn you that Bev's in a bad mood,' I say. 'And she might not be as easy to handle as the chickens.'

Chapter Forty

Bev is crashing pots and pans. Thankfully, Jack isn't helping her today or he'd be terrified. As it is, she's crashing about purely for her own entertainment.

'We have company,' I say to Bev and, for a moment, she lays down her weapons and beams widely at the mayor.

'Well, hello,' she says. 'This is an unexpected pleasure.'

'I have a rare day off and just dropped by to see how the plans are going for the open day.'

'Brilliantly,' Bev says. 'All under control. Tea?'

'That would be great.'

She sploshes tea into two mugs for us while I strip off my muddy coat and wash my hands. I put some antiseptic on my scratches and vow to sit the two girls down and finish my talk with them. I'm not letting that drop.

When I'm relatively clean, I slice us some banana bread – still warm – and we take it over to the table. When I sit down I realise that my bottom is still very damp and muddy.

'It's not going well,' I whisper to Matt. 'Lucas hasn't written his poem yet and some of the students are refusing to take part.

We're a few short weeks away and I can see no progress. The tree, however, is looking wonderful.'

'It'll come good,' he says. 'These things have a way of doing that.'

I wish I had Matt's optimism. As if I haven't already got enough to do. Christmas does feel like a pain in the bum this year. I've bought no presents, nothing. I haven't had a discussion yet with Shelby about what he wants to do. I'm assuming Lucas will be with us, but what if he wants to spend Christmas with Aurora? When it was simply me and the animals, I never had these dilemmas.

'I'm quite busy in the run-up to Christmas with official commitments, but I'll do all that I can to help. I can stay for the rest of the day if that's any use to you?'

'I have lots of jobs that you could do, if you don't mind.'

'I'll enjoy it. I like getting my hands dirty and have little chance to do it now.'

'Oh, I can definitely make sure you're covered in mud by the time you leave.' I hold out my hands to indicate the state of me and we both laugh.

'You have a lot on here,' he says. 'I admire what you do.'

'Keep telling me that,' I urge. 'This is one of those days when I could easily jack it all in.'

'There aren't enough places like this. If we're not careful, children like this fall through the cracks. This is a very valuable service you perform.'

'I like to think so, but I'm not sure all of the kids would agree with you. We try our best, but I worry that some of the students are unreachable.'

'You can't save the world, but if you can save some of it that's a very good start.'

'Thank you for your enthusiasm,' I say. 'That will keep me going until lunchtime.'

'Come on.' Matt nods towards the door. 'Let's get out there. It sounds like the rain has stopped for now.'

I glance out of the window and I think that he's right.

'I'd like to do some more preparation in the yard for the open day, if that's all right with you? There are lights to be strung for a start, if you don't mind getting up a ladder.'

'No problem. I should go and move my car. It's blocking the gate and I need to make a few phone calls, then I'm all yours.' He pushes away from the table.

'Before I join you, I'll have a quick word with Bev.'

The mayor goes outside and I take our mugs and plates back to the kitchen. 'Are you going to tell me why you and Alan have fallen out?' I ask.

She bangs her ladle into the pan of whatever she's making for lunch. 'Silly old sod only mentioned the M word,' she huffs.

Looking at her wide-eyed, I gasp out, 'Marriage? That M word? How exciting!'

My friend glares at me in return. 'Not you too!'

I hold up my hands in surrender. 'Is it not a good thing? I thought you two were getting on famously.'

'We are!'

'So why is Alan wanting to marry you a problem? I thought you were planning on moving in together before Christmas?'

'We are!'

I look at her blankly.

Bev sighs and she genuinely looks troubled. 'There's a whole world of difference between living together and getting married. When you get married it all goes tits up. They take you for granted and then bugger off with someone younger.'

That does make me smile. 'I can't see Alan doing that.'

Then Bev starts to cry – something that she rarely does.

'Hey, hey,' I say and go to put my arms around her. 'Just because that happened with your first husband, doesn't mean

193

it'll happen again. You're at a different stage in your life, Alan is a *completely* different person. He adores you.'

'It's going so well that I don't want anything to make it go wrong,' she sobs.

'I'm sure that's not his intention. Far from it.'

'What do you think I should do?'

'Stick to your plan. Move in together. See how it goes from there. There's no rush to get married, take your time.'

'I'm being stupid, aren't I?'

'Yes.' I put my hands on her shoulders. 'Relax. Enjoy this.' She sags beneath my touch. 'Stop damaging all the pots and go up to the barn. Take Alan some cake. Kiss and make up.'

She sniffs. 'I like the sound of the kissing bit.'

I hug her tightly. 'You silly sausage.'

'You'd better go, too.' She pulls off a bit of kitchen roll and wipes her nose. 'Don't keep that Hot Mayor waiting.'

Then Jack puts his head round the door. 'The alpacas have escaped and have tipped over the food bins.'

'Right. I'm coming.'

Bev and I exchange a weary glance. I think there must be something in the air today as everyone's having a crisis.

Chapter Forty-One

Once the alpacas are secured and admonished, I go up to the workshop and find the mayor. He turns out to be a whizz with a hammer. Together we spend the rest of the day repairing broken bits of barn so it looks smart for the open day. It's late afternoon when we're finishing stringing up the lights together and it feels like a job well done.

The students have calmed down too and they've had their lessons this afternoon with no reports of mass hysteria, brawls or refusals. I can rest easy tonight. I say goodbye to them all and it seems as if Erin and Lottie are the best of friends again. For now. I show Lottie the deep scratches to my hand and she looks suitably chastened.

Their guardians come to collect them all and I wait with Asha until his taxi arrives. Tomorrow is another day. Thank goodness.

Alan shuffles across the yard and leaves without saying goodbye. A few minutes later Bev comes out of the tea room. 'See you in the morning, Mols,' she shouts.

'Is Alan OK?'

'He's having a sulk. Says he's not feeling well. Attention-seeker!'

She waves and jumps in her car.

'Small domestic,' I explain to Matt. 'Alan has started to mention marriage and Bev's less than keen to jump into a white frock and race down the aisle again.'

'Ah. They seem well-suited.'

'They're perfect together. Bev's just got the collywobbles.'

Matt hooks up the last set of lights and climbs down the ladder. When we try them out, suddenly the yard is transformed. Just that little thing gives the place more of a Christmassy air.

'That looks great. So much better.'

Lucas appears as Matt and I are standing admiring the lights. He slopes into the yard and comes to stand with us.

'Hi, Lucas.' The mayor high-fives him and Lucas doesn't look at him as if he's a loser.

'Hey,' Lucas says. 'The lights look good.'

I risk putting my arm round his shoulders. 'Where have you been all day?'

'I had a long walk round the fields,' he says with a shrug.

He does really well with the kids that come here, but perhaps we all need time to ourselves and he gets very little of that.

'You missed lunch.' I'd called his phone, but he wasn't answering.

'I'll get something now.'

'I could do an early supper. What do you fancy?'

'I'm going out with Aurora tonight,' he says. 'She's picking me up soon.'

'Oh.'

'We're going to work on some poetry together. Hang out.'

I guess that's a good thing, though I'd rather he was doing it at the caravan where I can see him. 'Tell Matt of your triumph.'

'Molly,' Lucas huffs. 'Do you always have to be embarrassing?'

'Yes. I'm very proud of you. I want to show off.'

196

Lucas sighs and, as if it's no big deal, mutters, 'I won a poetry slam competition last night. At the King's Arms in Stony Stratford.'

The mayor looks suitably impressed. 'Brilliant. Well done.'

I go all showy-offy. 'He got a hundred quid and a slot at the Green Scene Literary Festival.'

'Fantastic,' Matt says. 'I always try to get to that. We should all go and make a day of it.'

'Sounds like a plan,' Lucas says, trying to appear as if none of this matters to him when I know how much it does.

I realise that he's yet to tell his dad about his triumph and I wonder whether Shelby will manage to find time to call today. I'd love to hear how his opening night and party went.

'I'm going to get a shower,' he says. 'See you later, Matt.'

'See you. And well done again.'

Lucas lopes away.

'Don't use all the hot water,' I shout after him.

'He's a good kid,' Matt says.

'Yes. I think so.' Then I look away from Lucas and turn towards the mayor. 'You've been brilliant today. Thank you for your help.'

'I've enjoyed it.'

'I feel a little less anxious for our Christmas preparations now that I can see *something* happening. But I should let you go. I'm sure you have things to do.'

'Not really,' Matt says. 'In fact, I was just planning to go to the local pub for something to eat. If you're going to be home alone, do you fancy joining me? My treat.'

And, for once in my life, the appeal of being by myself in the caravan with just the dogs for company doesn't seem all that great.

'I'll need some time to scrub up.'

'Fine by me. I can come back in an hour?'

I don't really like to say that my ablutions generally take me roughly five minutes, but an hour will give me time to try and catch Shelby before tonight's performance.

'An hour it is.'

I watch the mayor drive away and then go to hurry Lucas out of the shower.

Chapter Forty-Two

Shelby picks up on first ring. 'Hi,' he says. 'I'm missing you.'

It's good to hear his voice. I don't know if it's true that absence makes the heart grow fonder, but it certainly makes mine grow more anxious.

'I've meant to call all day,' he says apologetically. 'But it's been mad here with meetings.'

'Oh. What about?'

'This and that,' Shelby says. 'Work stuff. I won't bore you with the details.'

'How did last night go?'

'Wonderful. I got a standing ovation. I really think that I make a good baddie!'

'That's great to hear. And the party?'

'Went on far too long. I didn't get to bed until the wee hours. Too many cocktails drunk. I had to have a nap this afternoon or I wouldn't get through tonight's performance.'

'It must be exhausting.'

'I found it all very invigorating,' he says. 'There's nothing like sparking off a live audience, but ask me again at the end of the run. I might not be so sanguine. This is definitely a young man's game. What kind of day have you had?'

'Everything that could have gone wrong has gone wrong,' I admit. 'But it all came good in the end. The mayor rode in to rescue me.'

'Oh.' Shelby sounds put out by that.

'I just mean that he's good at rounding up chickens.' And putting up lights and fixing broken stuff, but I don't labour the point. 'They were all running amok in the yard after someone left the door to the coop open.'

'Another day on the happy farm.' His tone is right, but the words feel off and I can't tell what's underlying it.

'Something like that.'

'At least you can put your feet up this evening.'

I decide not to tell him that the mayor's taking me to the pub for dinner.

'Is Lucas OK?'

'Yes. He's out going out with Aurora tonight. I'm just waiting for him to come out of the shower.'

'It must be love if he's having a shower.'

'Yes.' Part of me wants to tell him about Lucas's success at the poetry slam, but the other part of me is determined to stay loyal to Lucas. I hope that he will tell his father in his own good time.

'Do you think you can persuade him to come to the show next week?'

'Yes.' That boy owes me big time. I'll get him there come hell or high water.

'I'm not going to make it back this weekend. Sorry, love.' Shelby rushes on before I can express my disappointment. 'The turnaround is too tight. I can get you tickets for next Wednesday's performance. Does that work for you?'

'I'll check with Bev that she can babysit the animals, but I'm sure it will be fine. Will Ken bring us back?'

'I was hoping you'd both stay over and come out to dinner with me. Wouldn't that be nice?'

'OK.' I don't feel that I can say no. And, of course, it will be nice to spend longer with Shelby. If we just go to the show, we'll hardly see him except for on the stage. I was simply thinking of the amount of time I could reasonably anticipate Lucas remaining civil.

'Let me know as soon as Bev agrees and then I can book the tickets.'

'I will.' Then we run out of words. I'm never at my easiest on the phone and am finding this long-distance chatting quite difficult.

'I'd better go,' Shelby says. 'My make-up takes a long time.'

'OK. Speak tomorrow?'

'Sure,' he says. 'Think of me while you have your feet up in front of the telly.'

I say bye and hang up. I don't tell him that I won't have my feet up or remind him that I don't have a telly.

Chapter Forty-Three

Unlike Shelby, my make-up doesn't take long. In fact, I don't put any on at all. I do, however, spend a lovely long time in the shower, wash the mud out of my hair and use the conditioner that Bev bought me that makes me smell like a strawberry. Clean jeans and a jumper, then I'm ready to rock.

'You look done up,' Lucas says. 'For you.'

'I'm going to the pub with the mayor.'

'Get you,' he says. 'Socialising and all that.'

'I find the mayor easy to talk to,' I tell him. 'He seems like a nice bloke and he gets farming.'

'Yeah,' Lucas agrees. 'I like him too.'

And, as you know, Lucas doesn't like anyone.

'By the way, your dad's getting us tickets for his show next Wednesday.'

Lucas pulls a face and goes to open his mouth.

'You're going,' I say firmly. 'You owe me and I'm calling it in.'

'I could have been about to say that I was looking forward to it.'

'But you weren't.'

'No.' Lucas does a surly child pose. 'Do we have to? Can't you go by yourself?'

'Do this one thing for me, Lucas. For your dad.'

'I'd rather eat my own eyeballs with a spoon.'

'You're vegan and I'm sure your own eyeballs would be classed as meat.'

That makes him smile. 'You're a difficult woman.'

'And you're a difficult teenager.'

'OK, but I'm not going to any shitty, showbizzy after-party.'

'There's no party. It's just you, me and your dad.'

'Huh,' he grunts, unconvinced.

Then any further conversation is curtailed by the arrival of Aurora's car.

'I'm outta here,' Lucas says. 'Laters.'

'Not too much "laters",' I warn. 'One late night in a week is enough.'

'Do I turn into a pumpkin at midnight?'

'No, but I'll give you the worst jobs to do tomorrow if you're out half of the night.'

He laughs in the face of my threat, bounds out of the door and runs across the yard. That boy is in love.

Putting my coat on, I say goodbye to the dogs and do one last tour of the animals to check that they're all right. I lean on the gate in the barn and look along the row of my charges. It's lovely when they're like this, all snuggled down and cosy, the scent of fresh hay and the clouds of their breath in the air.

Then I hear Matt's car and say, 'I won't be long. Be good without me,' before heading to the gate. He flashes his head-lights at me and, with only a small pang of anxiety about leaving the farm behind and going to dinner with a relative stranger, I climb into the car.

'Hey.' Matt is also freshly washed and groomed.

'This is an unexpected treat.'

'Nothing fancy. I've booked us a table at the local. I thought you wouldn't want to stray too far from the farm.'

Of course, he's right about that.

So we head to the pub in the village and, when we walk in, no heads turn in our direction. We sit in the middle of the bar without having to hide in a corner. The pub is bustling as there are a few groups who are having Christmas parties. A bunch of boisterous women sit with their paper hats on and there's much chatter and laughter. To add to the atmosphere, there's a fire roaring in the grate and the beams are strung with swags of red and gold tinsel. A bushy, real tree stands proudly in the corner by the bar, but its pine scent is hidden by the smell of roast dinners. We're shown to a table and we both order a soft drink and a veggie curry.

I look round and no one is taking the slightest bit of notice of us. It's nice being out with someone 'ordinary' like Matt. There's no drama, no people trying to take a sneaky selfie, no one talking behind their hands as we pass. I can relax and be myself. It's hard to acknowledge that it will never be like this with Shelby. When we're out together, there's always part of me that's on edge. I glance at my watch. He'll be about to go on stage now in front of an adoring audience and here I am having a rare night out in a low-key country pub. Our worlds could not be more different.

'You look lost in thought,' Matt says.

'Sorry.' That pulls me back from my musing. 'Because Shelby's a celebrity – whatever that is – he always feels as if he's on duty. We can never be ourselves when we're out and consequently, tend to avoid it.'

'That's a shame.'

'Yes, I hadn't realised how much. I'm not a great socialiser, as you might have gathered. My life is my farm – the animals and the kids.'

'It's all-consuming. I get that. But very rewarding.'

'Yes. Most days,' I say. 'Today wasn't necessarily one of them. Thanks for turning up at the right moment.'

Matt smiles. 'You did look like you were drowning and not just because you were sitting slap-bang in the middle of a puddle.'

I put my face in my hands. 'I can't believe what a state I must have looked.'

'But you look lovely now,' he says and then we're both a bit embarrassed.

The curry comes to our rescue and it's homemade, creamy and soothing. We concentrate on eating.

'Is the open day the first fundraising you've done?'

'Shelby hosted an event at his home for us,' I say. 'But we've never done anything like this before at the farm. We'll have to, though. It's a constant struggle to make ends meet,' I tell him. 'We rely heavily on Shelby and that isn't right.' Or where I want to be. 'I need to work on finding a wider raft of support.'

'I can help with applying for grants. Sometimes they don't make the criteria easy to understand, but that's part of my job. I'm well-versed in officialdom-speak.'

'I would appreciate it.'

'Consider it done.'

'I don't want to get too personal, if you're not comfortable,' Matt says, 'But have you and Shelby been together long?'

'No. Only since the summer. We met when he brought Lucas to the farm as a student.'

'You seem very close to him.'

'I love Lucas to bits. I couldn't care for him more if he was my real son.'

'Shelby is a very lucky man. Taking on step-kids can't be easy.'

'Lucas has been through a lot. He can be tricky, but I'm very forgiving. Perhaps too much.' I think of how he can twist me round his little finger and how I don't mind it one bit.

'He's a great kid. I like someone with a bit of spark. He's bright, too.'

'It's nice that you're taking time to talk with him. He needs a male role model. He and his father have a rather strained relationship.'

'I'm sorry to hear it. I would have loved a lad like Lucas. One of the reasons my last relationship split was that I wanted to settle down and have children. She was happy climbing the corporate ladder.' Matt shrugs. 'That's why I thought I could get involved with Hope Farm. I'd like to help mentor some of the kids. My way of giving back.'

'I'm sure we could organise that. It sounds like a brilliant idea.'

'You've never wanted your own children?'

'I've not been lucky enough to have a long-term relationship. Before Shelby, I'd not been in love. I never let myself think about having children. I simply assumed that it's something that wasn't to be for me.'

'You'd make a great mum.'

I like to think that it's the glow of the fire that's making my face red, but it's more to do with the intimacy of our conversation.

'Sorry,' Matt says. 'I didn't mean to embarrass you.'

'That's OK,' I tell him. 'I've spent years having conversations mainly with dogs. Other than with Bev, I don't really do much mingling. I've always been a bit of a loner.'

'Then I'm even more honoured that you agreed to have dinner with me.'

Before I can answer my phone rings and it's Bev's number on the call display. I wonder why she's calling me now?

'Hey,' I say. 'Everything all right?'

'Come quickly.' She sounds in a terrible panic. 'I need you.'

Chapter Forty-Four

It's Alan. He's has suffered a transient ischaemic attack, a TIA, a 'mini' stroke and Bev, understandably, is out of her mind with worry. Matt and I abandon our dinner, jump into his car and head straight to the hospital. I phone Lucas on the way, explain what's happened and ask if he can return to the farm as I have no idea how long I'll be. I don't mind leaving the animals alone for an hour or two, but that's all. He agrees that he'll go home straightaway, so that's one less thing I have to worry about.

My friend is in a waiting room by the ward when we arrive, breathless and worried. Her face is pale and she looks as if she needs to be in a hospital bed herself. We hug each other.

'Thanks for coming,' she says.

'Is he OK?'

'Yeah. I think so. The doctor's with him now, so I had to come out.'

'What happened?'

'He said he was making his dinner when he went numb all down one side. It lasted for about ten minutes and he thought it was something and nothing. Then it happened again about nine o'clock and for longer. Then he phoned 111. They sent an ambulance right away and he called me. I jumped in my car and arrived at the hospital at same time as him. I was all of a dither.' Bev bursts into tears. 'I'm so frightened. I don't want anything to happen to him.'

'I'm sure he'll be fine,' I say when I'm not really sure at all. 'Alan's as strong as an ox.'

'Hopefully, he'll know more when the doctor's talked to him.' She sniffs away her tears and I rub her back.

'Shall I find us all some tea?' Matt offers, reverting to the British answer to everything, especially a crisis.

'Yeah,' Bev says. 'That would be great.' I nod too.

So he disappears and Bev and I sit down on the hardest chairs known to man.

She gives me a look. 'What are you doing with the Hot Mayor?'

'We were having a pub dinner.'

'And I called you in the middle of it?'

'That doesn't matter at all. I'm glad I can be here. Tell me about Alan?'

'I feel such a shit,' Bev sniffles. 'He should have been with me, not on his own. I didn't believe him when he said he wasn't feeling well. I thought he was in a mood. What a cow I am.'

'Hardly. You'd just had a little skirmish. The timing was awful, but you can't blame yourself.'

'I don't know what I'll do if I lose him.' That starts her crying again.

'You won't,' I assure her. 'I'm not an expert on this, but I'm sure it's like a warning. Now that he's getting medical attention, they can sort it all out.'

She grabs my hands and wrings it. 'I hope to God that you're right.'

And we sit there holding each other tightly.

A few minutes later Matt brings us tea and I say, 'You really don't have to wait. I really appreciated the lift. If you want to leave, we'll be fine.'

'I'm going nowhere. If Lucas is OK holding the fort at the farm, I wouldn't dream of leaving you here. I'll stay as long as it takes.'

I look at him, grateful for his kindness. 'Thank you.'

So we drink our machine tea and watch the door anxiously until a nurse appears. 'You can go through now. Alan's comfortable.'

'I'll wait here,' Matt says. 'Take as long as you want.'

Bev and I go through to the ward. Alan is in the end bed, propped up with pillows. His face is grey and he looks older than his years.

My friend flings herself onto him. 'You bloody drama queen,' she blurts out. 'You had me scared to death.'

Alan holds her closely and when, eventually, they let each other go, we sit by his bedside.

'I've got to stay in.' His voice sounds gruff, emotional.

Bev looks horrified. 'How long for?'

'Few days,' he says. 'Tests and stuff.'

'Tests?' My friend is close to tears again.

'To be on safe side.'

'I want you home with me as soon as possible, you big soft lump.'

All words of love.

'I'm fine.' He pats Bev's hands. 'Don't you worry.'

This is possibly the most I've ever heard Alan talk.

We stay for a while until it's clear that Alan is worn out and needs to sleep. His eyes close and Bev kisses his head tenderly. 'See you in the morning, big guy.'

We tiptoe out, both weary but relieved that Alan is OK. Matt is still waiting patiently.

'He's going to be all right?' he asks.

Bev nods. 'Thank God. I don't think I'll sleep a wink tonight worrying about him though.'

'Take off as much time as you need,' I say. 'Alan's more important than anything.'

'Thanks, Molly. You're a pal.'

In Matt's car we follow Bev to her cottage to make sure she's home safely before heading back to the farm. I'm tired down to my bones.

He stops at the gate and I say, 'I'm knackered, but in desperate need for some tea. Do you want a quick cuppa?'

'Yes. I want to make sure you're safely settled too.'

Aurora's car is parked in the yard and we pull up next to it. Yet all the lights in the caravan are off. We go inside, and of course, the dogs go mad and I shush their barking.

Lucas's bedroom door opens and he sticks his head out. 'Hey.' He rubs his hands through his tousled bed hair. 'How's Alan?'

'OK,' I say. 'He'll live to fight another day. He's had a mini stroke. They're keeping him in hospital for a few more days.'

'Shit.'

'It could be a lot worse,' I assure him. 'Matt and I are going to have some tea. Do you want anything?'

'No. By the way, Aurora's here.'

'I saw her car.' I don't know if this is appropriate, but I can't have a conversation about it now. What do parents do in this situation? Her parents, I assume, are all right with it, but then she's older than Lucas.

'I'll say goodnight, then.'

Matt holds up a hand. 'Night, mate.'

'Night, night, Lucas.'

He ducks back into his room and I sigh as he shuts the door.

'He's growing up too fast,' I say to Matt. 'Do all parents want to keep their offspring as children?'

'That's beyond my paygrade,' Matt admits. 'As I said, the joys of parenting have, so far, eluded me. I'd love kids though. Maybe one day.'

'I'm finding it tough.' I need Shelby's input and he's rarely here to give it.

'Do you think you and Shelby will have your own children?'

'No.' It sounds sadder than I expected. 'Shelby doesn't want any more. I guess it's a big gap to think about starting again when your son is almost a man.'

Even though Lucas can be a pain in the backside some days, I feel my life is so much richer for having him in it, and it's only now that I've begun to think that I would have liked children of my own too. Previously, it was something that had never been on the cards. As you know, my relationships with the opposite sex have been few and far between. None of them struck me as potential father material. Yet, now that I have finally found someone to love, Shelby has made it very clear that he's done his bit and that becoming a daddy again isn't on the cards for him in the future. And I get that. So it looks like Lucas will be my one and only chance to satisfy my maternal instincts.

While I'm waiting for the kettle to boil, I slide a few slices of bread in the toaster too. I need a bit of comfort food to set me right and it seems like a lifetime ago since I ate dinner. I pile on lots of butter and heap it on a plate on the table between us. Matt and I pick at it.

'I'll take the rest of the week off,' Matt says. 'I need to call the office in the morning, but they'll understand.'

'You said you had lots of commitments,' I remind him.

'I do, but nothing that can't wait. This is important.'

'I can manage.'

He smiles at me and it brings me close to tears. I've been strong for Bev, but now I want to cry. 'I'm sure you can, but I can also help. If you'll let me.'

'I don't like to abuse your kindness.'

'I offered,' he says. 'You've simply got to say yes.'

'If you can, that would really take the pressure off me.'

'No problem. I've still got a week of leave I was going to write off, so now I'll take it. I'll make a few calls in the morning, then I'll be here as soon as I can.'

'I can't thank you enough.'

'Hopefully, Alan will be back on his feet soon. Until then, I'm sure I can help you here.'

We finish our tea and toast, then Matt takes his leave. He stands at his car door while I open the gate for him. He kisses my cheek. 'Tomorrow is another day,' he says. 'It will all be OK.'

And he is such a calming influence that I fully believe him.

Chapter Forty-Five

Aurora is at the stove frying mushrooms when I get back from feeding the animals. She's wearing her pants, quite small ones, and a T-shirt, also quite small. I have no idea where to look.

'Morning,' she says, quite unfazed at being found nearly naked in my kitchen.

'Morning,' I say and widen my eyes in disapproval at Lucas who is also just in his pants and T-shirt – though they do cover a bit more.

He is oblivious to my secret eye signals – or pretends he is – and says, 'Morning.'

'Do you want some mushrooms, Molly?' Aurora asks, pleasantly. 'There's plenty.'

'No, thanks. I had breakfast before I went out. I've just come back for some gloves.' I also wanted a word with Lucas about Aurora staying over, but that will clearly have to wait.

'Have you heard from Bev?' Lucas asks.

'Yes. Alan's OK. Thank goodness. He's still in hospital for today and she's going in to see him later. The mayor is coming here to help us while Bev has a few days off.'

'Cool. I'll have brekky and I'll be with you.' Aurora in her underwear comes to sit next to him. She twines her slender leg round Lucas's.

I wonder if youngsters have no shame or decorum these days, and then realise I'm sounding very middle-aged so shut myself up.

'I've got to get to college,' Aurora says sweetly. 'Time and textiles waits for no one.' She forks her food delicately into her mouth while batting her eyelashes at me.

There's absolutely nothing to dislike about her and, yet, dislike her I do. I can't put my finger on it, but there's something off. I'm sure of it.

I grab my gloves. 'See you later,' I say. 'Wrap up, Lucas. It's freezing out there. I had to break the ice off the water troughs this morning.'

'Brrrr.' Aurora does a mock shiver.

Perhaps she'd be warmer if she put some clothes on.

I bang out of the door and collect the dogs who are waiting patiently. There's stuff to do before the students arrive, but I head out across the fields. Stomping my niggling thoughts away. She's not right for Lucas. She's too old, too worldly wise, too . . . I don't know.

The fields are hard with frost, the tree branches glisten with it in the weak sunshine, the sky is milky pale. The frozen grass crunches beneath my boots and the dogs make zig-zag tracks where they run. It soothes my soul. Sort of.

When I get back to the yard, Aurora's car has gone and has been replaced by the mayor's. I go up to the barn and find him and Lucas looking at Alan's work in progress. Some kind of backdrop for the nativity.

'Morning,' I say to Matt. 'I really do appreciate your being here.' He's wearing a well-loved overall and a beanie hat and looks younger than his years. I get an unexpected rush of affection for him which startles and comforts me all at once.

214

'Looking forward to getting stuck in,' he says before I have time to analyse my feelings. Probably just as well. 'Thought we'd finish this and then the students could paint it if you've nothing else planned for them.'

'Sounds like a good idea and we're only a few in number today.' I think we've got six kids here and they're some of our better behaved students, thankfully. We're probably in for a thoroughly nice day. However, I've probably jinxed it by saying that. I'm sure we could manage without Bev and Alan for a few days, perhaps even longer, but it's good to have the mayor's reassuring presence here. It feels as if I'm not shouldering this alone.

'I'll go back to the tea room and see them all in.' I'll also be on lunch duty today, so I need to check what we've got on the menu. Bev is usually organised at least a week ahead and it's all written down on our kitchen chalk board, so I've just got to follow instructions. Instead of staying with the mayor, Lucas starts to follow me.

'I need a word,' he says.

'OK.' I need a word too. I have to set some boundaries about him sleeping here with Aurora until I've fully discussed it with Shelby. I have no idea whether he'd be absolutely against it or whether, these days, it's something that's accepted. Whichever way, the decision has to be his father's, not mine.

We walk down through the barn and as we do, I spot one of the sheep looking a bit different to usual. If I'm not mistaken, Fluffy looks decidedly fluffier.

I stop and lean on the gate. 'Does Fluffy look fatter to you?' Climbing over, I go to feel the sheep's stomach. Yes, there's definitely a milk sack there. Underneath all that fluff, I hadn't spotted the changes. But changes there definitely are.

'Oh, Fluffy,' I say with a puff of breath. 'What have you been up to?' I turn to Lucas. 'She's definitely with child. No idea how.'

'Usual way?' Lucas says.

'Yeah, but we've had Anthony the Anti-Social Sheep's 'gentleman's things' removed to try to make him more pleasant and he's usually the main culprit.'

'Virgin birth? They're quite the thing at this time of year.'

'Ha, ha.' I am perplexed though. 'I didn't think our other rams had "introduced" themselves to any of our ladies. Just goes to show what happens when you're not looking.'

It's those long, dark nights in the barn with nothing to do.

Climbing back out of their pen, I say, 'We'll have to keep an eye on her. It looks like she's not got too long to go.' I rub my hands together happily. That's given me a lovely lift. There's nothing like a baby lamb to make the heart melt. 'Yay! We're going to have a baby!'

'That's kind of what I wanted to talk to you about,' Lucas says, kicking at the hay on floor.

'Had you noticed too?'

He looks at me appalled. 'What? The sheep? No.'

'Then . . . ?' And, a moment too late, the penny drops. So does my stomach. And my heart. And my spirits. 'Oh, *Lucas*.'

'You should be pleased,' he says fiercely. 'I am.'

I need to sit down, drink hot, sweet tea, put a cushion over my head. Instead, I continue to stare at Lucas, unspeaking.

'Say something,' he prompts. '*Anything*!'

'Oh, Lucas.' My head is shaking from side to side and I can't stop it. Anything but this.

We stand looking at each other. Me growing paler as I consider the implications, Lucas getting redder as he waits for my response.

But I have no words, nothing. Shelby will be furious. Of course he will. And I'm – supposedly – Lucas's guardian. How can I have let this happen on my watch?

I look again at Lucas. He looks thrilled and terrified in equal measures. A child yet a man. Oh, God. He needs my support now more than ever.

When I finally manage to find my voice, all I can offer is, 'I'll put the kettle on, shall I?'

'That's it?' Lucas snaps. 'I drop this F-bomb on you. I'm going to be a *father* and all you can offer is tea?'

'Right now, I can't think of anything else, Lucas,' I say honestly.

'Fuck,' he grumbles, dropping the more usual F-bomb.

So we walk back to the tea room in stony silence while, in my head, I try to stop my thoughts from tumbling erratically and work out what on earth to do.

Chapter Forty-Six

The kids are arriving by the time we reach the yard, so I turn to Lucas and say, 'We can't do this now. We'll have to discuss it later.'

'This is important,' he snaps.

'I am fully aware.'

He huffs at me and marches off across the yard while I look helplessly after him. What else am I to do? I have no idea how to deal with this news and need some time to process it.

On autopilot, I sort the students out for the day and take them up to Matt in the workshop to help him. Even though my difficult conversation with Lucas is delayed, it hasn't helped me to get my head round the situation. To the casual observer, I might look vaguely in control, yet thoughts are crashing round my brain, scattered and random.

When I go back into the tea room to prepare for lunch, Lucas is waiting. Mud on his wellies, scowl on his face. I can put off our talk no longer and I'm still no wiser as to how I'll tackle this.

'There's veg to chop if you want to help me.' I go into the kitchen and nod towards the menu. Lucas follows me.

'Bev has decreed that we'll have Mexican wraps today.' So I pull peppers of every colour out of the fridge and hand Lucas a knife. We stand side by side at the counter with our pile of veg. Neither of us do anything.

'We're keeping it,' is his opening gambit. 'No matter what you say.' Then he chops furiously at the red pepper on the board.

'Do you love her?' I ask.

'Of course,' he snaps, defensively.

'And she feels the same about you?'

'Yes.'

'You've known each other such a short amount of time,' I point out. 'You should be having fun together.' Though maybe one could argue, they're in this mess because they've had a little *too* much 'fun'. 'This is a huge commitment.'

'You think I don't know that?'

I put down my unused knife and turn to him. 'No. I don't think you do.' I take a deep breath before adding. 'It's very easy to say you're going to keep the baby, but have you thought of the practicalities? Where will you live? How will you pay for a child? You earn very little here, Lucas, and Aurora is at college. Babies are bloody expensive.'

'We'll manage!'

'How?' I shout back at him in the face of his obstinacy.

'I don't know!' He shouts louder.

I'm not handling this well. I need Shelby here and I need him now. 'Have you told your dad?'

'No.' Lucas looks panicked. 'You can't tell him.'

'I might be able to cover up your appearance at a poetry slam, but you're not going to be able to keep a baby secret.'

'I know what he's like. He'll only kick off.'

'And quite rightly,' I point out. 'This is a tough one, Lucas. Accidents happen, now we're dealing with the fallout.'

'This is my child we're talking about,' he says tightly. 'Not "fallout".'

'You're right. I didn't mean that.'

'We don't need anyone.' Now an onion gets chopped into oblivion and flung into the waiting pan. 'Aurora and I can do this by ourselves.'

'You can't.' I rub my eyes. 'You'll need us more than ever.' It's going to take a whole network to look after this child and, whether Lucas likes it or not, it will probably be Shelby who ends up funding it. I'm not sure how to approach this, so I blunder in, 'Have you considered other options?'

He looks at me aghast. 'You mean get rid of it?'

'There's abortion or adoption. Have you even thought about either?'

'No.' He's appalled I could even raise it. 'Why would I want to kill my own kid or give it to someone else? That's fucking *mad*!'

Glancing across at Lucas, I see that tears have welled up in his eyes and my heart unravels. He *is* going to need our support and love. There's no putting this genie back in the bottle. Shouting at each other really isn't going to help either.

'Come here,' I say and, without his usual hesitation, he steps into my arms. I hold him tightly. 'It'll be OK. It will all be OK.'

'I want this child,' he sobs. 'I feel as if it's something I can do really well. I want to be the kind of dad that I've never had. I want to be around for him – or her – all the time. I love Aurora. She'll be a great mum. You'll be like a nana. Can't you be excited for me?'

How can I tell him of my myriad misgivings? Lucas is so young, so vulnerable. Left to his own devices, I don't think he could feed himself or get out of bed every day. I'm sure that he has no concept of the new reality a child will bring. Who does? Even the most prepared and mature parent would probably agree that a new baby is like a grenade being thrown into your life. He's naïve to think that this will be one big adventure. Plus there's something about Aurora I don't trust. Can I see her as a mother who wants to stay at home with a child? What if they bring a baby into the world and then their relationship breaks down? I don't want that for Lucas, Aurora or for the baby. I'd love to be thrilled for them both but, in truth, I'm terrified at what this means for us all.

'How far gone is Aurora?'

'Not much,' he says. 'Six weeks. I dunno. Something like that. We've only just found out.'

But that's much longer than I imagined they'd been intimate. Lucas swore to me that they hadn't . . . er . . . 'fully engaged'. Has he been lying to me about that too? It seems so. Damn. How could I have been gullible enough to believe him?

'She's told her parents?'

'Yeah.'

'What did they say?'

He wipes his face on his sleeve. 'They think we're young and stupid too.'

There's no doubt that he looks very, very young at the moment standing here before me in tears.

'We will have to tell your dad,' I say.

'Not yet,' he pleads. 'Just not yet. Let me enjoy it for a bit before he goes ballistic.'

I sigh and hug Lucas again. I had thought we were making so much progress and now this. Shelby will indeed go ballistic. That's one thing Lucas has got right.

221

Chapter Forty-Seven

I serve the students their lunch, but my mind isn't on the job at all. Lucas sits at the far end of the table, talking to no one. I try my best, but it's Matt who has to jolly everyone along. If it weren't for him, lunch would be a very subdued affair.

'Everything all right?' Matt asks quietly as we're clearing away.

'I'll tell you later. When everyone's gone.' I don't want this getting out until Shelby knows, but I feel I can confide in Matt and, goodness knows, I need to tell someone. Bev would usually be my first port of call, but how can I burden her with even more than she's already dealing with at the moment?

It's late afternoon when Shelby calls. Obviously no matinee today.

'Hey,' he says. 'How are you?'

I can't tell you how pleased I am to hear his voice. 'All the better for your call.'

'Something wrong?'

I should have made a list. 'Alan's in hospital. A mini-stroke. I'm waiting to hear from Bev to see how he's doing today.' She'll phone me when afternoon visiting finishes with an update, I'm sure. 'I might try to get to see him later, if I can.'

'That's awful. I always thought Alan was fit and strong for his age.'

'Me too.' It's a salutary lesson.

'Give him my best. And Bev too. How are you managing without them?'

'Lucas has stepped up to the plate.' Now that we've cleared the air between us, he's working really hard this afternoon.

'Good lad.'

'And the mayor has taken a few days off work and is here to help us.'

'Oh.' He sounds less thrilled about that.

Best to move on to safer ground and, of course, there is Lucas's revelation left unspoken. Having fully intending to pave the way for a conversation with Lucas about it, I now can't bring myself to tell him. Instead, I stick to 'How's the show going?'

'Good,' he says. 'Very good. I'm really enjoying being back on the stage and the show is different every performance. There's a well-known comedian playing Wishee-Washee – Joe Peters . . .'

Well-known to everyone except me, obvs.

' . . . and he goes off-script every night. He's known for it. We don't know what to expect next. Keeps us all on our toes. You'll love it. I take it you're still able to come on Wednesday evening?'

To be honest, with all that's going on, I hadn't given it another thought. 'I . . . er . . . um . . .'

'Don't let me down, Molly. You promised.' His voice hardens. 'I've already booked the tickets for you and Lucas.'

'Right,' I say. 'Right. I'm sure it will be fine.' How am I going to square this circle? There'll be students in the next day. 'Perhaps another night would be better?'

'Perhaps not at all?'

'No, no. I don't mean that. We'd love to come. Lucas and I

are both looking forward to it.' Lucas is refusing point blank to be there, but now I have bargaining power. I add brightly, 'Wouldn't miss it for the world.'

If Shelby thinks I'm telling big fat fibs then he lets it go. 'You'll come up for the evening show? We could grab some dinner beforehand?'

'Yes,' I say, still thinking that I've no idea how we'll both manage to leave the farm without Bev to babysit. This is all too complicated. The only good thing is that it might give us a chance to sit down with Shelby and tell him Lucas's news face to face. How else will we be able to break it to him? That would surely be better. 'That'll be great.'

'You could sound a bit more enthusiastic, Molly.'

'No, I am. Really. I'm distracted with all that's going on.'

'What else is there?'

'Oh . . .' I wrack my brains. 'This and that. Nothing for you to worry about.' That's a blatant lie. 'We've got a pregnant sheep,' I blurt out.

'I'm very pleased for you,' he says, but doesn't sound all that thrilled. I'm dreading his reaction when he finds out he's to be a grandfather. I groan inwardly. 'Well,' he sounds very decisive. 'I'll leave you to your sheep as I have to get ready for this evening's performance.'

'I'm glad it's working out well for you,' I say earnestly. 'I miss you.'

'Not too much longer. The weeks seem to be flying by.'

For some not for others, I think.

'Bye,' Shelby says. 'Give my best to the big guy. I'll try to catch you tomorrow.'

He hangs up and I stare at the phone, so much left unsaid.

Chapter Forty-Eight

I walk up to the workshop with a heavy heart. The dogs, perhaps sensing my mood, stay close to my heels. Little Dog keeps smiling up at me in an encouraging way. Does he know that my heart is wounded?

Lucas and the students are all gathered round the nativity backdrop, paintbrushes in hand. Matt looks over and grins at me as I appear. There's an inn with THE THREE KINGS painted in wonky letters across the top and a big yellow star at the top of it.

'Busy bees,' I say. 'Looks as if you've done a great job.'

I think there's more paint on the students than on their wooden scenery, which makes me smile, but they are obviously all quite pleased with their handiwork.

'Clean up, guys. Home time soon.'

I usher the students to the sinks and watch them scrub paint from their hands and faces. After that, I supervise them cleaning their brushes. Matt tidies away too and when we're done, we all walk down to the yard.

'Aurora's picking me up,' Lucas says.

'OK.' I don't want to see her, to have that awkward conversation, so I'll try to make myself scarce. 'Take your key to the van. I'm hoping to go up to the hospital later and might be out when you come home.'

'I can take you,' Matt say. 'And Bev, if she'd like a lift. I know how tiring it can be going back and forth for hospital visits.'

'That would be very kind of you. Can I offer you some supper as a thank you?'

'As long as you wouldn't mind me jumping in your shower? I've got clean clothes and stuff in the back of my car.'

'That's fine.'

So we see the kids off for the day and I keep out of the way when Aurora drives up in her car and toots her horn. Lucas rushes out. I think he's as keen to keep her away from me as I am to avoid seeing her. I feel cross that, in this day and age where it's so easy to avoid an unwanted pregnancy, they have both been so irresponsible.

Matt gets his clothes from the car and I find him some clean towels before showing him how my shower works. Then I go to find something for supper. I decide to have a night off being vegan – it feels too much like hard work – and opt for knocking together some omelettes. So I quickly nip out to the tea room to pinch some cheese from Bev's stash in the kitchen.

While I'm cracking eggs, I wedge the phone to my ear and call Bev. 'Matt's still here and we're going to come and collect you to take you to the hospital once we've had a bite to eat.'

'That's great. It feels like I've only just got home from visiting this afternoon and it's time to go back. I'm so glad not to be going alone.'

'How's Alan doing?'

'He's fine,' she says. 'Another couple of days and they think he'll be OK to come out.'

'Good. We'll pick you up about seven. See you then.'

We both hang up as Matt comes out of the bathroom in fresh clothes, rubbing his damp hair in a towel. Some of his 'stuff' must have involved aftershave as he smells of lemon, jasmine and musky amber.

'I'll swap with you and then I'll make us cheese omelettes. Does that suit?'

'I can do them while you shower,' he says. 'I'm a man of many talents.'

I grin at him. 'I'm beginning to realise that.'

So I shower, standing under the hot water and letting it pour over me. I close my eyes and breathe deeply, but it fails to soothe me. When I come out, Matt continues making the omelettes – really excellent ones – and my stomach unknots slightly. While we eat, I tell him Lucas's news.

'Aurora is pregnant and he's thrilled.' I shake my head, still perplexed. 'Me, less so. They've only been together for five minutes and I'm worried sick for them both. His dad will be beyond furious.' And, I hope that I'm wrong, but I can't help feeling that I'll be the one picking up the pieces.

'That's tough,' Matt says. 'I'd find the thought of fatherhood daunting even at my age. They're both so young.'

'It's because they're young they have no idea what any of this means. I'm dreading telling Shelby. I'll have to pick my moment.'

'You'll go up to Birmingham?'

'Lucas and I are both due to go up there on Wednesday to see him in his pantomime.' Though I feel as if my entire life is like one, right now. 'It'll depend on Bev being able to babysit the farm, and I don't want to put that on her at the moment. I can leave the animals for an hour or two, but not for any longer.'

'I'm happy to stand in,' Matt says without hesitation.

'I couldn't ask. You've done so much already.'

'Really, it's not a problem. I love being here.'

'Thank you.' Then I cry and it's like a floodgate has opened.

227

I cry for me, for Lucas, for the baby they're bringing into the world, for Shelby, for Alan in the hospital and for a whole host of other things that I can't even articulate.

Matt holds me gently and passes me a piece of kitchen roll that was serving as a napkin. 'It will all come right,' he murmurs softly. 'Not all of this is on your shoulders. Let people in to help.'

'I'm trying to,' I sniff. 'I'm just so used to being by myself.' All of it has been my responsibility for so long.

'Well, you're not alone any more. Lean on me if you need to, Molly.'

I let myself sag into his embrace. He feels warm, strong, reliable. It's comforting to have him here. I think I'd go mad, otherwise. There's part of me that's also disappointed that Shelby isn't here. He's the one who should be sharing this with me.

'We should go,' Matt says. 'It'll soon be visiting time. You sit for five minutes while I clear up.'

I do as he says and watch him as he moves about my caravan, his large frame filling the space, the sheer solidity of him reassuring. I'm glad that he can stay here to look after the animals as it means I can see Shelby. But, if I'm honest, I'm not entirely sure how I feel about that.

Chapter Forty-Nine

Alan, thank the Lord and all that is holy, is coming home from the hospital today. He looked a bit frail and tired when we saw him a few nights ago, but Bev says he's definitely on the mend. He's come out with a lengthy list of dos and don'ts. No smoking, healthy eating, moderate alcohol, regular exercise – which will mean a complete change of regime.

I wish I could be here to help Bev but, with perfect timing, it coincides with our trip to the pantomime. As much as I'd like to, I daren't cancel our tickets. Shelby would never forgive me, so I haven't even mentioned it. Plus I have actually persuaded – well, forced – Lucas to come with me and I might only get this one shot at it. In truth, I don't think I could manage it without him by my side.

Ken has just pulled up in the yard, ready to whisk us both off to pantoland. I'm scrubbed up and in the black jumpsuit Bev bought me for the opening night that we didn't make. My fancy manicure has long gone and, I haven't even looked, but I bet my legs are hairy again. On the plus side, I have got lipstick on and I've combed my hair. There's no hay in it, which is always a bonus and never a given. My overnight bag is at my feet as we're staying at the fancy hotel where Shelby lives during the week.

Matt is standing with the dogs, seeing us off. He's looking at me too hard.

'What?'

'You look lovely,' he says softly. 'Very posh.'

'Thank you.' I feel myself flush.

'Go and have fun. Remember to boo and hiss in all the right places.'

'I will. I can't thank you enough for this.'

'I look forward to hearing all about it tomorrow,' he says. 'Until then, rest assured everything is in safe hands.' He puts those safe hands on my shoulders. 'No need to look so worried.'

That makes me smile – a bit. The students will be here for another few hours and Anna, our craft lady, is here, but I don't like to put on him too much.

'You'll be OK?'

He nods. 'We will.'

He's capable, responsible and I don't need to worry. But I will worry.

Lucas comes out of the caravan, man-bag over his shoulder. Looks as if he's travelling light. He too has scrubbed up – having been ordered to under pain of death. His hair is styled, spiky. His make-up is meticulously applied – if only I could say the same for mine. He's wearing a white shirt, skinny blue jeans and looks about twelve. For the hundredth time, I think that I cannot see Lucas as a father. He's not even legally allowed to buy alcohol or to vote. Though it's lawful – if ill-advised – to have sex and get married? How can that be right?

However, the moment of truth will soon be upon us. Tonight, we've agreed that we'll tell Shelby that he's going to be a grandad. Lucas is not happy about this. Well, that's tough. I'm not prepared to bear the brunt of this by myself.

Ken opens the door and I climb in. Lucas sits in the front with him and then we're whisked away from the sanctuary of the farm and into Shelby's world.

The traffic is terrible and the journey is slow. It feels like we're going to the moon rather than Birmingham and I can feel my anxiety rising.

Lucas turns to me and says, 'Chill out. We've got plenty of time.'

But it's easier said than done.

Eventually – and not a moment too soon – Ken drops us at the front door of the hotel in the centre of the city and right by the theatre where *Aladdin* is showing. There's a Christmas market in the adjacent street in full festive flow. Myriad lights shine out from cheery stalls selling all manner of festive fayre. The scents of cinnamon and spices on the air are wonderful, but the crowds look terrifying. Even so, I wish we had more time to look around.

Instead, we check in and then leave our bags to be taken up to Shelby's rooms. Lucas is tense as we walk the few hundred metres to the stage door of the theatre and I'm not much better. At the reception we ask for Shelby and are told to wait. We stand in a narrow corridor that's painted beige and wait, then we wait a bit more. There's nowhere to sit and we're in the way. Every time a performer comes in or out, we have to jiggle round them.

Lucas is getting agitated. 'He's such a fucker,' he mutters.

'This is his job,' I remind Lucas. 'He's not keeping us waiting on purpose.'

I get a murderous look.

Another twenty minutes later and Shelby finally comes out, all beaming smiles and open arms.

Lucas glowers darkly.

Oblivious, Shelby kisses me and slaps Lucas on the back.

'Good to see you both. The place is madness tonight. Utter madness! The local BBC television station have sent a crew down to interview us. It should have started half an hour ago, but I'm still waiting. Can you forgive me?'

'Sure,' I say. 'Do what you have to do.'

'I'd booked a table at a nice Tex-Mex place further down the street. Do you want to head off there and I'll join you when I can?'

'How long do you think you'll be?'

'Not much longer.' Shelby glances over his shoulder. 'Five, ten minutes?'

'We'll wait. It's not a problem.'

'I'll be back as soon as I can. Promise.' He dashes off before I can say anything else.

Lucas rolls his eyes at me.

'Say nothing,' I warn him. Another gaggle of performers squeezes past us. 'Shall we wait outside?'

'It's December and I'm wearing a shirt.'

'You didn't think to bring a coat?'

'I assumed I'd be sitting in a theatre all night.'

Probably quite rightly.

In the event, it's a good forty-five minutes before Shelby resurfaces. He does, however, look flushed and excited.

'It went well?'

'Brilliantly.' Then he grimaces at me. 'Problem is, now I'm tight for time. I need to be in make-up in a few minutes. Dinner is off the cards, I'm afraid. It's not long before the show starts. Do you two want to grab a sandwich or something in the foyer and then we can have dinner afterwards?'

I dread to think what time that will be. Matt is staying over at the van, but I'll still need to be up early and away after breakfast. I don't want him holding the fort alone. We've got students in tomorrow, so I want to be back as soon as I can.

I'm assuming that Shelby can lie in until lunchtime and hasn't really considered this.

'Yes, that'll be fine,' I say.

'I hadn't planned it like this.' He does look terribly apologetic. 'I'll make it up to you.'

He thrusts two tickets into my hand and dashes off again. I stare after him.

'How many times have I heard that?' Lucas grumbles. 'This is typical of my father. All that fuss about us coming and he doesn't care if we're here or not.'

But I'm trying to keep the peace between them, so I say nothing. If we'd known that Shelby was going to be so delayed we could have gone round the Christmas market or had dinner. A lesson learned.

'Come on then. There's not much time before the show starts. We'll go round to the front and see what we can find.'

'I must remind you,' Lucas says, drily. 'That I am absolutely doing this under sufferance.'

His dad being late isn't a great start – I'll give Lucas that – but he'd better brace himself as I fear that the worst is yet to come.

Chapter Fifty

There are no sandwiches to be had in the foyer, or any other substantial snacks. They have plenty of chocolate, but Lucas can't find anything that's vegan, so he sulks a bit more. If it weren't for Lucas's censure, one of those large bags of Maltesers – vegan or not – would be mine. All mine.

In fairness, when the show starts it's very funny. It's not really my thing, nor Lucas's, yet, despite his best efforts not to, I catch him smiling a few times. There's no doubt that Shelby is very good. He plays the villain, Nebuchadnezzar, so well. In fact, he's probably doing too convincing a job of being a baddie.

I think again how different his world is to mine. He's in his element up there in front of an audience, whereas I'm not even that comfortable being in the audience. I don't like crowds or being confined to a chair for two hours. I'd much rather be in my wellies striding across the fields.

But both Lucas and I get through it with something approaching aplomb. I'm proud of Shelby. He's a good actor, probably wasted in this role. When it's over we stand and cheer along with the rest of them. Well, I do. Lucas sits on his hands.

We leave the theatre and head round to the stage door.

'That's two hours of my life I'll never get back,' Lucas complains.

'Didn't you enjoy that just a little bit?'

'No,' he says. 'It's an utterly crass and pointless art form.'

'Don't tell your dad that. Smile sweetly and tell him he was wonderful.' I look at him with my most serious face on. 'You'll need him on side when we tell him your news.'

Lucas sighs heavily.

We wait outside the stage door, Lucas shivering in the cold, and he's almost turned to ice by the time Shelby sweeps out. It's a good half an hour before he joins us. I stifle a hearty yawn as it's approaching ten-thirty and I was up at the crack of dawn.

Magnanimously, Shelby signs autographs for the hardy fans who have waited in the bitter cold alongside us. When they're satisfied and the crowd thins out, eventually, he's ours. He takes my hands. 'Did you enjoy the show?'

'It was marvellous,' I gush. 'You were magnificent.' And he was. I dig Lucas in the ribs.

'Excellent,' he mutters. 'You aced it.'

Shelby is flying high on adrenaline. 'There's a bit of a get-together at a bar down the road. Caroline Curtis – Princess Jasmine – has a birthday party. I said we'd go along for just one drink. It would be rude of me not to.'

This is the time we need to go back to the hotel and sit quietly with Shelby, but it seems like a bad idea at the moment. I look at Lucas and he shrugs.

'OK.'

I'm not sure that we actually have much choice. Party, it is.

So we tramp along beside Shelby as we head to the bar, while he waxes lyrical about the performance and what happened on his side of the curtain. It's so alien to me and I should find it exciting, shouldn't I? But half of the time I've no idea what or who he's talking about.

We reach our destination, Club Escape, and open the door to a crush of people and bright lights. Definitely a place I'd be happy to escape from. Shelby and I appear to be the only ones inside who are over thirty. Lucas cheers up considerably and, thankfully, as he's with Shelby, he's nodded through rather than being asked for ID at the door.

The music is loud, pounding out. We push through the throng and are shown to a separate VIP area and are all handed a glass of champagne.

Lucas looks at it with disdain. 'WTF?' he mouths at me. 'Where's the beer?'

I shrug as speaking to him would be pointless. Shelby is immediately swamped by his actor friends and we hang about on the periphery.

'This is fun,' Lucas yells in my ear.

I'm getting a headache already and I think it's a bad idea to knock back the champagne, but we've had nothing to eat or drink for hours.

A tray of canapes passes us by. Pigs in blankets, tiny bites of barbequed ribs, mini Yorkshire puddings with beef in them. In fact, they all appear to be meat-based.

'Dead animals,' Lucas grumbles. 'I just knew it.'

Shelby is busy, surrounded by his co-stars. There's much joking and laughter. A couple of the younger girls flirt with him and giggle at his stories. It makes my heart tighten and reminds me of when we met and he was dating Scarlett Vincent, an actress half his age. It doesn't help that I hang back, avoiding the limelight. I should try to join in, be by his side, part of his circle, but I realise that my social skills and capacity for small talk are still woefully lacking.

'I saw a vegan place across the road,' I say to Lucas. 'I think it was still open. Want to duck out and get something to eat?'

'Yeah.' Lucas looks weak with relief.

I try to catch Shelby's eye to tell him that we're popping out for a few minutes to grab some food, but I can't and there's no hope of getting across the room to him. Instead, I send him a text. Hopefully, we'll be back before he notices we're gone.

After the fug of the bar, the fresh air on the street hits me and a gulp it down gratefully.

'That was hideous,' I say to Lucas as we dash over the road.

'The bar was the best bit,' he counters and makes me laugh.

The vegan café – Green World – is still open and we order wraps with falafel, red pepper hummus and spinach. But it's the cup of hot tea that I'm most grateful for.

I text Matt. *Everything OK?*

All still standing. Don't worry.

At last, some good news.

We sit and eat in silence, Lucas wolfing down his food as if he hasn't been fed for a week rather than a few hours. Eventually, Lucas stops chewing long enough to say, 'It's better when it's just me and you.'

'Soon it will be a lot more than that.'

'We're not going to be able to tell him tonight,' Lucas notes. 'He's in his own little Shelby World.'

'I know.' I look at Lucas and smile sadly. 'We can't put it off for ever, but now isn't the right time. Perhaps there'll be an opportunity.'

We both know our chances are slim.

'I know you think he's the best thing since sliced bread, but we're barely on his radar. His poncy actor friends are more important to him. You saw that. This is your future,' he warns with an insight that belies his years.

'It's his world, his work.'

'You keep telling yourself that,' Lucas says as he polishes off his wrap.

When he pushes away his plate, I venture, 'We'd better get back before he misses us.'

Lucas groans, but stands up and we walk back to Club Escape. It's late now, the street only peopled by drunks and those soon to be drunk. I have never wanted my own bed more in my life.

We go into the bar and, sure enough, Shelby is still holding court.

'We should just go back to the hotel,' Lucas says. 'He doesn't give a fuck.'

'We'll say we're leaving,' I tell him. 'Then we'll head back there.'

So we squeeze and ease through the crowd until I reach Shelby's elbow.

'Hey,' I say over the noise and he turns round.

Rather than being pleased to see me, his face darkens. 'Where the hell have you been? I've looked everywhere for you!'

'Where?' I ask. Seems to me he's in exactly the same place as when we left half an hour ago.

'I didn't know where you'd gone,' he insists.

'I couldn't attract your attention. You were busy.' It sounds barbed. 'I texted you.'

He pulls his phone out of his pocket and reads my text. 'I didn't hear it. It's so bloody noisy in here.'

Quite.

'Lucas and I are just heading back to the hotel. It's late and it's been a long day.'

'The party's still in full swing,' Shelby says.

'There's no need for you to leave. Stay. Enjoy yourself.'

Shelby steps away from his friends and pulls me to one side. 'Tonight didn't go as I'd planned,' he says. 'I'm truly sorry. I thought we'd have time for a nice dinner before the show.'

'It doesn't matter. Really.' I'm disappointed, but this is

Shelby's life and it's me who is the square peg in the round hole – as always. He could have made more effort, it's true, but – I sigh to myself – he didn't and that's life too.

'I should have introduced you around to the rest of the cast.' He takes my hand. 'Have another glass of champagne. Come and meet them now.'

I can't think of anything worse. 'I'm tired, Shelby,' I say. 'We'll leave you to it. I'll see you when you get back to the hotel.'

'Of course, I won't stay. Give me five minutes. Let me say goodnight to everyone and then I'm all yours.'

'If you're sure.'

Shelby moves back into his crowd. I turn to Lucas and puff out a heavy breath. He pulls out his phone. 'He'll be an hour,' he mutters.

In the end, Shelby is considerably longer than five minutes but less than an hour. Lucas and I wait, if not all that patiently.

Eventually, Shelby joins us all smiles and apologies and we walk together to the hotel. I'm glad it's not far as Lucas is all angles and tension. And I've got the mother of all headaches.

Chapter Fifty-One

'We should have a drink in the bar,' Shelby says when we're in reception. 'A last snifter.'

'I'm tired,' I say. 'I'd rather go to bed, if you don't mind.'

'I'm off.' Lucas turns towards the lifts, making his escape as soon as he can. 'I'll leave you two lovebirds to it.'

'Goodnight, son!' Shelby holds up a hand to wave. 'It's been great having you here.'

To Lucas's credit he doesn't say what I know will be going through his mind.

Then Shelby turns to me. 'He's a great kid. You've done a fantastic job with him.'

He's talking as if he's spent the entire evening chatting with his only child whereas he's pretty much ignored both of us. I'm sure if he really knew what was going on in Lucas's life – our life – he wouldn't be quite so jolly.

'One drink.' He takes my hand and pulls me towards the empty bar. 'A nightcap. Humour me.'

I feel that resistance is futile. Shelby is still wired and not ready to head to bed. So I follow him and we find a seat by the window that looks onto the street. Clearly, Shelby feels that no one will spot him at this hour. A weary-looking waiter comes to take our order.

'I'll have a Jack Daniel's,' he says. 'Molly?'

'I'm fine, thanks.' My headache isn't easing and I just want to lie down. The carpet is like a multi-coloured migraine and there's tinny muzak playing over a speaker right by our table.

'Have something!' He rolls his eyes at me. 'A Baileys.'

'A Baileys,' I echo to keep the peace and a few moments later the waiter reappears with a drink that I don't want.

This is my moment to tell Shelby, I guess. The two of us, alone. I could prepare him before he has to talk to Lucas about the forthcoming baby. Reluctantly, I sip my Baileys and think of how to frame the words to make the least impact.

'It's bloody hard work this, and I'm not getting any younger,' Shelby says. 'I have to hold my own with these kids. You've seen what it's like. The pace is relentless.'

'At least you don't get water thrown over you all the time like Wishee-Washee.'

'All that bloody dry ice, though. It's playing havoc with my throat.' He rubs it to demonstrate.

I'm sure it is, but my mind is saying *First world problems*.

'The hours are back-breaking. I've had to do this twice today. It's exhausting.'

I put down my glass and it clinks loudly on the table. 'But you don't have to do it,' I remind him. 'There's no need.'

He visibly bristles at that. 'I *have* to work.'

'Do you?' I think of the mansion standing empty, the posh car, the chauffeur, the housekeeper. There must be plenty of dosh in the coffers. If he sold the house and drove his own car, he'd never need to act again.

'Have you noticed, recently, who's funding Hope Farm? Those bloody animals are literally eating me out of house and home.'

241

Now it's my turn to bristle. 'You can stop at any time you like,' I say softly. 'We'll manage.'

'How?' Shelby snaps. 'Tell me how?'

It's not the time to say that I managed perfectly well before Shelby came on the scene. Perhaps that's stretching it, but we did muddle through. It was a hand-to-mouth existence and that has eased considerably since Shelby came along, but I don't want him holding that against me.

'I know that it's thanks to you that we found the current farm we occupy and you have, no doubt, been generous – extraordinarily so. It's been fantastic.' I keep my voice as calm as I can. 'You really helped to get us out of a hole, but I don't want you to feel beholden to us. I don't want you having to take jobs that you're not enjoying. We can do more fund-raising, like the nativity.'

'How's that coming along?'

I can't really tell him that it's shaping up to be a disaster. 'Fine,' I say. 'Slowly.'

'Christmas isn't far away.'

'I know. And this will soon be over and you'll be home again.' He doesn't look as thrilled by the thought as I'd hoped.

Then his expression changes and his face softens. Shelby drains his glass and then looks over at me.

'Shit. I'm an arse.' He grasps my hand. 'You've come all the way to see me and yet I've hardly spent any time with you. And now I'm doing nothing but complain. I'm sorry, Molly. It wasn't what I'd envisaged.'

I dredge up a smile. 'Me neither.'

'I'll make it up to you, I promise.' He stands and pulls me to my feet too. My toes hurt in my silly shoes. 'Let's go to bed.'

We take the lift up to Shelby's palatial room on the top floor of the hotel. I'd guess that it's one of the best as there's a view over the lights of Birmingham from the huge floor-to-ceiling windows. I stand looking out over the city feeling like a stranger, an intruder.

He closes the door and then comes to stand behind me, nuzzling my neck. He gathers me into his arms, kissing me deeply. I'd like to say that it feels like the connection between us comes flooding back, but it doesn't. I don't really want this intimacy. I wish I'd gone home, back to my comfy caravan and my dogs.

We make love. But, for the first time, I feel that both of us are acting.

Chapter Fifty-Two

I'm awake at dawn. Truth to tell, I didn't really sleep, only fitful bursts. I've not much experience of them, but I've decided I don't like hotel rooms. I was too hot, too cold, too troubled.

Shelby is fast asleep, out for the count. I tiptoe out of bed and look out of the panoramic window again. A pink blush is colouring the city and I wonder if it's the same at Hope Farm. We get the most beautiful sunrises there. I sigh to myself. Our adventure in pantoland is over. It's time for us to be heading home to the country.

I text Lucas. *Breakfast in five*.

Miraculously, he texts me a smiley face straight back.

Then I message Ken, who's also in the same hotel somewhere, and tell him that we'll be ready to head off in about half an hour.

Gathering my things, I put my bag by the door. On hotel notepaper, I write a note to Shelby. *Thanks for a lovely evening. Hope all goes well today. Speak soon.* I only hesitate briefly before I scribble, *Love Molly xx*

I put the note on the pillow next to him. He doesn't stir at all, so I creep out.

Downstairs, Lucas and I meet at the door to the breakfast room.

'Did you tell him?' are Lucas's first words.

I shake my head. 'I couldn't find the right moment,' I admit and feel as if I've failed Lucas. Though, it has to be said, Lucas looks relieved.

'I think we'll have to wait until he's home at Christmas. He might be in a more receptive mood then.'

Lucas looks hopeful. 'You think?'

'No, not really.'

'He's totally going to lose his shit when he finds out, isn't he?'

'Yes.'

I don't know why, but we both chuckle – it's not even funny. I link my arm through his as we walk into breakfast together.

'That was an utterly crap night,' is Lucas's verdict and, I have to say, I wholeheartedly agree.

The breakfast was good, so that's one thing. As we set off for home, I text Matt to say that we're on our way back and then nap in the car on the journey. Ken must drive smoothly, as I only wake as we pull up at the gate to Hope Farm.

'Rise and shine, sleepyhead,' Lucas says from the front seat. 'Wipe the dribble from your chin.'

I check, but there's no dribble. I do, however, feel an awful lot better for a doze.

'Home, sweet home,' Lucas adds and it certainly is. I could not be more relieved to get back here. I'm desperate to put my wellies on and get out in the fields. I might have only been away one night, but it feels like an eternity.

Matt comes to open the gate and he's beaming widely. All the dogs are going bonkers and I feel my spirits lift. I squat down and fuss them all. Little Dog pulls back his lips in the biggest smile. The geese come and honk hello. This is my home, where I am my happiest.

'Did you have a great time?' Matt asks.

'It was like the curate's egg,' I admit. 'Good in parts.'

'Panto is shit,' is Lucas's more succinct verdict. 'Never am I *ever* going to see it again even if my old man is in it.'

'I don't mind a bit of panto,' Matt says.

'The show was good, funny,' I tell him. 'The rest of it was a bit . . . complicated.'

'Ah.' He doesn't press the matter.

'How's everything here?'

'All present and correct,' he says. 'We only had one minor hiccup. Betty Bad Dog ate all my used tea bags from the draining board, but she's lived to tell the tale.'

'A favourite habit,' I say. 'I should have mentioned it.'

Betty wags her tail innocently.

'They all slept on the bed with me, too,' Matt says. 'That was interesting. I've never woken up with a dog on my head before. It was an experience.'

'I hope it was Little Dog rather than Big Dog.'

'We had fun didn't we, guys?' They all go into a frenzy of barking. He's obviously their new best friend and I wonder how many treats they had while I was away. There's some serious bonding gone on.

Ken flips the boot and gives us our overnight bags.

'Can't thank you enough, Ken.'

'I'll see you soon, Molly.' He ruffles Lucas's hair. Which Lucas hates, except when a few favoured people do it – Ken being one of them. 'Be good. Or, if you can't be good, be really awful.'

They high-five each other. Then we stand and wave as Ken drives away. I watch as the car trundles down the lane and turns into the road.

'Thank fuck that's over,' Lucas says and stomps off toward the caravan.

I have to agree with him. I'm relieved that our adventure is over too.

'I have a few surprises for you,' Matt says as he takes my bag from me.

'I'm not sure I can cope with surprises,' I warn him.

'These are nice surprises,' he assures me. 'You'll definitely like them.'

Chapter Fifty-Three

I follow Matt to the tea room and as he throws open the door I recoil. All the students shout 'Merry Christmas!'

Then I stare at him in awe. 'You've all been busy.'

'I hoped it would be completely finished, but you came back a bit earlier than I thought.'

The tea room has been draped with Christmassy bunting made in red, green and gold. It looks like the kids have each decorated their own as the style is definitely eclectic. In the corner of the tea room, there's another large tree, hung with handmade baubles.

Gaping, I try to take in all of their handiwork. 'How did you do this? *When* did you do this?'

'We got cracking as soon as you left and they put in some extra time too,' Matt says. 'Everyone came in early today and we worked our socks off this morning, didn't we kids?'

'This is fantastic. Well done, everyone.' The kids are giddy with excitement and I feel a thrill of joy too. Maybe now Christmas has finally kicked in. 'Give yourselves a round of applause.'

So we all clap and Matt shouts out, 'Guys! There are

biscuits and hot chocolate at the counter. Help yourselves.' As one, the kids dash over there to swamp Jack, who's on duty.

But the very best thing of all is that Alan and Bev are here decorating the tree too. I'm just so relieved to see them both, and I fly across the room to hug Alan. 'How are you?'

'Good.' He looks tired, a little more fragile, his band T-shirt hangs more loosely. But he's here and standing.

Lucas comes in and gapes at the decorations. 'Wow. You lot have been busy. We've only been gone one night. It's totally cool.'

The students glow from his approval.

Bev, at the top of the ladder, replies, 'The kids did most of this, under Matt's supervision.'

I turn to Matt again. 'I don't know how you managed it.'

'With some skill and much subterfuge,' he says. 'They've been brilliant. How they kept it a secret, I'll never know. I thought they were going to burst.'

What a guy. He's obviously skilled in mobilising our students. Seems I didn't need to worry at all about leaving Hope Farm in his care.

'They've been making decorations during their craft classes.' There are glittered pine cones, little paper baskets with sweets in them, wool pompoms and stars made from recycled straws. It looks fabulous.

'I've just been to The Range to buy a fairy to go on the top.' Bev fixes the fairy and climbs down. 'Likey?'

'Lovey!' I reply. 'But the best news of all is that you're back here.'

'Alan's got to walk every day, so we thought we'd suit up and head out across the fields. Coming?'

'I can think of nothing better.'

'No more scares,' I tell Alan. '*My* heart can't cope.'

'Matching band T-shirts again,' Lucas notes. 'All is well in the world.'

Alan glances shyly at Bev and she throws her arms round him. 'This one's not getting away from me again.'

We wait until the students have finished their drinks and then we decide to take them all out for a walk with some of the animals too. There's a great performance while we put halters on the alpacas, the donkeys, two of the pygmy goats and a couple of the sheep; and of course, our permanent doggy companions come along too.

As a noisy, unruly rabble – the kids and the animals – we head out across the fields. The kids are excitable, the alpacas are as skittish as always, the goats try to headbutt everyone. It's a bright, sunny day and we're all wrapped up against the cold. I feel that I can breathe again. I know that some people want to travel the world, but I don't even want to leave the farm. Why should I when I have all this?

Even Lucas has joined us which has made the girls very happy. They gather round him in a huddle, all sparkly ear muffs, fluffy gloves and lip gloss. They all hang on his every word and he doesn't seem to mind one bit. In fact, I think he's positively basking in the warmth of their adoration. And why not? Soon he'll be weighed down with responsibility. Penny is right by his side and she looks at him adoringly. She will be crushed when she finds out about Aurora and the impending baby. I wonder how different things would have been if he'd been seeing someone more his own age. Again my heart breaks for him, for his future.

We do a tour of the fields, visiting the ponies – Buzz Lightyear, Ringo, and our new little lady, Beyoncé – en route. Then we stop off to see how Sweeney and Carter, our Shire horses, are – and I've brought a bag of carrots as treats for them. As always, the students are all eager to feed them and these gentle giants are less likely to nip than the alpacas. We try to leave them outside as much as possible, but they have stalls up here and in the yard for when it's too cold.

'Do you ride?' I ask Matt.

'Yeah.' He's strokes Sweeney's neck. 'Haven't done so for ages, though.'

'We can take these boys out one weekend, if you like.'

'That would be great. I'll definitely be rusty.'

'Me too. I ride with Lucas sometimes, but not as often as I'd like.'

Bev comes over to me. 'I think we'll head back,' she says. 'Alan's done very well but he's tired now. I'll try to make him sit on the sofa and read while I make lunch.'

'Thanks, Bev.' I feel overwhelmed with love for them both. 'You don't know how pleased I am to have you back. Both of you.'

'It was such a scare,' she whispers. 'I want to wrap him up in cotton wool. I can't bear to let him out of my sight. I even follow him to the loo.'

'Too much information,' I say and we both laugh.

'It could have been so much worse.' I can tell from her face that this has been a terrible ordeal for them both. 'But we've had a warning. I'm going to mollycoddle him from now on.'

'He won't know what's hit him.'

'Half an hour until lunch. Don't be late.'

I watch as Bev and Alan amble slowly back towards the yard, arm-in-arm. Alan's steps are slow, hesitant, but I'm sure with Bev's tender loving care he'll soon be back on form. I've been on the receiving end of Bev's care before now and I know how good it is.

While I'm not watching, Johnny Rotten takes the opportunity

to slip his halter and sets off across the field at an impressive pace.

'Who let go of the flipping alpaca?' I shout.

Matt and I look at each other and, with a laugh, we both give chase.

Chapter Fifty-Four

When the day is done and all the animals are fed, watered and put to bed, I can finally wind down.

'Shall we have a takeaway?' I say to Lucas. I'm tired after my fitful night and can't face cooking.

'I'm supposed to be going to Aurora's place,' he says. 'I've been messaging her but she's not replying.'

'Could you try going old school and call her?'

I get a dark look for my suggestion. But he brings up her number, nevertheless. 'Still no reply.'

Matt is getting ready to leave and I say to him, 'Why don't you stay and join us for some food? If you're not rushing away. My treat after all you've done for us.'

'I have no plans for this evening,' he says.

'Chinese? The delivery man always complains that he can't find us, but he gets here eventually.'

'I'll nip out for it,' Matt says. 'Save him a job.'

I find the menu and we put our order together before calling it in. Then I find a bottle of wine gathering dust in the bottom of the cupboard and I open it and, something I rarely do, I pour myself a glass. As I'm putting some plates in the oven to warm, I send a text message to Shelby to thank him for our trip to the panto and wish him well for tonight. He replies to say that he enjoyed it too, but that he won't be back at the weekend as he has a meeting on Sunday. Funny he didn't mention it before, but then we didn't exactly have a lot of time to talk.

I know that it's wrong, but I'm rather glad that he's not going to be here as it puts off having to tell him about the baby. I shouldn't feel like that. But I do.

I potter about until Matt and Lucas arrive with the food and it smells delicious. We put the cartons out between us and help ourselves. The dogs all cram beneath the table hoping for titbits, but they're sadly disappointed. This mushroom chow mein is all mine. Matt and Lucas crack open some Tsingtao beer they bought at the Tesco Extra by the takeaway. There's lots of laughter and jokes. It's clear that Matt and Lucas get on well and I wish again that things could be so relaxed between Shelby and his son.

When we've eaten, the lads pile the dishes in the sink and I pull out the Scrabble.

'Oh, not board games,' Lucas complains.

'Yes. I am Scrabble champion of the world and I plan to whoop your sorry arses.'

'Oh, you think so,' Matt says. 'I am unbeaten in the Eastman family.'

'I see that as a challenge,' I tell him, spreading out the board.

Lucas holds up his hands. 'I'm always thrashed by everyone as my boredom threshold is very low.'

'Watch and learn,' I tell him.

So we refresh our glasses and settle down to play. Matt does, indeed, prove to be a worthy opponent. And, despite feeling that the men are ganging up on me, I easily trounce both of them. I get a 95 word-score for 'gherkin', slapping down my tiles and sealing their fate. They both mock-bow to me.

'Your prize for victory is that we wash up,' Matt says. 'Come on, Lucas. We must be magnanimous in our defeat.'

'That was a laugh,' Lucas says. 'I used to play with my mum and I'd forgotten what it was like. I want to have evenings like this with my kid.' Then he pulls himself up short and glances anxiously at me.

'I told Matt,' I confess. 'I didn't think you'd mind.'

'I don't,' Lucas agrees.

'Congratulations,' Matt says. 'That's going to be a tough gig. If you need any help from me, I'll support you all I can.'

'Thanks,' Lucas says.

Matt throws his arms round Lucas's shoulders and gives him a hug. Lucas leans into him, happily.

'That doesn't get you out of the washing up though, mate,' Matt says and he hands Lucas the tea towel.

It's been a great evening and, dishes done, I walk Matt to the gate. 'Thanks for everything.'

'I'll see you tomorrow.'

'I do appreciate it. And thanks for being supportive to Lucas. He's going to need all the help he can get.'

'No problem.' Then, before I know what's happening, he leans in and kisses me on the cheek. It's light, friendly, but it feels more than that. If I turned my head just slightly . . .

He squeezes my arm, his fingers lingering, and then gets into his car. I watch until he's gone from the lane. I like having him here. Perhaps too much.

Back in the caravan, Lucas is on his phone again.

'Still no Aurora?'

He shakes his head. 'I don't know why she's not replying.'

'Perhaps she's somewhere without a signal?'

He shrugs. 'She didn't say she was going out.'

255

'Perhaps she thought we were away tonight as well as last night. I'm sure she'll turn up tomorrow.'

'Yeah.' He still looks concerned. 'I'm off to bed.'

'It's nice to see you getting on with Matt,' I note.

'He's a good bloke.'

'One of the best.'

'He fancies you.'

I laugh. 'I don't think so.'

Lucas gives me a knowing look. 'He suits you better than my cockwomble of a father.'

'Cockwomble?'

We both giggle. 'It was the best I could think of,' he admits.

'Goodnight, Lucas. I'm just popping out to check on everyone, then I'll be right behind you.'

Lucas disappears into his room and I pull on my boots and coat. Outside, it's clear and bright. The dogs, snuggled up in the warmth, are reluctant to join me, but they still make the effort. I cross to the barn and go along the gates, looking into each pen to make sure that everyone is present and correct.

When I get to Fluffy, our mum-to-be sheep, I stand and look at her growing tummy. I should get the vet out to look at her and make up a lambing pen. We take in orphaned lambs nearly every year, but we don't often have them of our own. Seems as if everyone is getting pregnant round here.

And then a thought makes my stomach go cold.

When did I last have a period?

I try to calculate back. With all that's been going on, with Lucas, Alan, Shelby and Christmas, I admit that I've not paid much attention.

When I work it out, my heart is in my mouth. The truth of the matter is that I'm very, very late.

Chapter Fifty-Five

Bev is back and she's all bouncy. 'I've been busy over the weekend, Mols,' she announces. 'I've got the open day all planned out as well as what we're doing with the kids. Shall we go through it this morning?'

'I've got to pop into town,' I say and my voice sounds tight even to my ears.

She spins round and stares at me. 'What?'

'I've got an errand to run.'

My friend frowns at me, as well she might. 'You never "pop" into town. Any errands there are you get me to run.'

I shrug.

'Tell Aunty Bev,' she says, hands on hips. 'What's going on?'

I look round, checking there's no one in earshot, even though I know that all the students are packed off to their tasks for today. 'I have to buy a pregnancy test.'

Bev's eyes widen. 'For you?'

'Who else?'

Her eyes travel to my belly. 'You're not, are you?'

'That's exactly what I need to find out.'

'Fuck me, Molly,' is her verdict.

'I know.'

'I'll come with you,' she says. 'The bloody nativity can wait. This is more important. The Hot Mayor can hold the fort for a couple of hours.'

I'm dreading the day that the Hot Mayor has to go back to doing whatever it is that mayors do, as he's proving himself to be very handy round here.

'We'll go in my car,' Bev says. 'Get your coat on!'

So we leave Matt in charge with promises to be as quick as we can and drive into the town centre at breakneck pace. I stare out of the window as the hedges whizz by and Bev's brakes burn. My mind has been in turmoil since last night. I hardly slept a wink. How can this have happened? I know what you're thinking – the obvious way. But we've used contraception. Has it failed me? Don't you get other symptoms with pregnancy – morning sickness, sore boobs, that kind of thing? I feel nothing. I'm just the same as I ever was. Shouldn't I *know*? Shouldn't I be feeling something? Shouldn't I be aware if life is growing inside me? Instead, I am numb from head to toe.

'It will be fine,' Bev says, sensing my inner panic as only a best friend can. 'Whatever happens, it will all be fine.'

Bev screeches into the supermarket car park and throws her Fiesta into the first empty space we come to. Then we march into the store and straight to the pharmacy counter. There are a baffling array of pregnancy tests on the shelves and I gaze blankly at them.

'Get this one,' Bev says and grabs a box. She thrusts it into my hands and steers me to the counter where, on autopilot, I pay.

I could have gone to the little chemist's in the village, but I don't want anyone there knowing my business. It feels very public here but at least it's anonymous. No one in this place has a clue who I am.

Clutching my paper bag bearing my test, I say to Bev, 'I should go to the loo.'

'Not here!' Bev tuts. 'You can't find out if you're preggers in bloody ASDA! We'll go to that nice café down the road.'

So she grips my elbow and we rush out and head down the road to the café which is deemed a good place for a life-changing event. The window seat is empty again, which is a bright spot in a terrifying morning.

'Off you go,' Bev says.

'What do I need to do?' I whisper.

'Pee on it,' she whispers back. 'Then wait a couple of minutes. That's it.'

'Come with me,' I beg.

So we put our coats over the backs of the chairs to save the table and disappear into the loo together. The space is cramped and it's all pink and the smell of pot pourri makes me feel nauseous. My chest is tight and I feel barely able to breathe.

'Go on.' My friend nods to me in an encouraging way. 'Do it.'

I shut myself into the cubicle and, as ordered, pee on the stick. When I come out, it's already showing the result and my hands are shaking.

Bev is waiting anxiously. 'Well?'

'I'm going to have a baby,' I say.

'Right.' She wrings her hands. 'This calls for a cup of tea.'

I nod.

Then she pauses and adds, 'Are we celebrating?'

'I don't know,' I admit. Part of me is thrilled, the other part is utterly terrified. This wasn't planned, of course not. And it's not the thought of a baby that scares me, it's what Shelby's reaction will be. I know that he doesn't want children. It's not part of his life-plan at all. I've even been frightened to tell him that Lucas is about to become a dad. How can I tell him that both he *and* his son are about to be daddies? This is too difficult.

Bev hugs me tightly. 'Well, I think we are,' she says. 'Let's have cake too.'

We go back into the café and I sit at the table, stunned, while Bev fusses with ordering tea and cake.

She brings back two brimming mugs and huge slices of Victoria sponge. I stare at it blankly.

Bev pushes the cake at me. 'You're eating for two now.'

'I can't face it.'

'Has it sunk in yet?' she asks.

'No.' I shake my head, bewildered. 'I don't have time to be pregnant.'

Bev smiles at me. 'Life has a way of laughing in your face. We'll find time. That's the *least* of your worries. How far gone do you think you are?'

'I don't know.' Perhaps it was the romantic night we had at Homewood Manor. Were we as careful as usual then? I think so. But clearly not. Here I am lecturing Lucas about using contraception when I should, obviously, have been listening to my own advice. 'It can't be very long.'

Shelby and I have barely seen each other recently, let alone had time to do anything else. The 'occasions' are few and far between, so that should make it easy to work out. But I can't think straight, at the moment.

'Difficult question,' Bev says, 'But do you want to keep the baby?'

Then I get a rush of love, of emotion, like I've never experienced before and I know one hundred per cent what my answer is. 'Yes.' Tears well in my eyes. 'Yes.'

Bev squeezes my hand. 'Oh, I did hope you'd say that. You can allow yourself to be excited, then!'

I smile and cry a bit too. 'I don't think Shelby will be pleased, though,' I venture. 'How am I going to tell him?' And, just as importantly, how am I going to tell Lucas? I'm absolutely sure he won't be thrilled either.

'Wait until he comes back at Christmas,' Bev says. 'This is not an "over the phone" kind of thing. It will give you some breathing space to think and make some plans.'

'Yes, yes. You're right.'

She gives me her concerned face. 'Everything is OK between you guys?'

'I don't know,' I confess. 'We've hardly seen each other, especially since he's been in Birmingham.'

'How was the panto?'

'Fun,' I say. 'No, actually it was awful.' I don't tell Bev that Shelby was largely unavailable to us. 'Not really my kind of thing.'

'I didn't think so. But Shelby is enjoying it?'

'He seems to be in his element.' I get a vision of the young stars hanging on his every word and have a pang of jealousy.

'He'll come round to the idea of a baby.' Bev sounds more certain than I am. 'I'll be an aunty twice over! Yay! I'm looking forward to it already.'

Once I'm over the initial shock, I think I will be too. But it saddens me to say that part of me is aware that, somehow, someway, Shelby is slipping away from me.

Chapter Fifty-Six

Back at the farm, Bev runs through the plans for the open day while I try to pretend that my world hasn't turned upside down. My friend has printed out leaflets advertising the Christmas Open Day to put around the village. She volunteers me and the Hot Mayor for the job. Perhaps she appreciates that I need a bit of time out from the students to gather my scattered thoughts.

After lunch, she hands us both bundles of paper. There's a cartoon drawing of our alpacas at the top and all the details of the event. 'Stick them on lamp posts, ask the shops and pub if they'll put them up.'

Both Matt and I nod obediently.

'Lucas and I are going to start teaching the kids a song, maybe two. God help us.'

I think I'm glad to be putting up posters. Matt and I wrap up and set off down the lane together. The sky is milky, soft, but there's a fierce chill in the air and I wonder if we'll have snow this year, a white Christmas. The walk into the village is bracing, but helps to clear my head.

'Everything OK?' Matt says.

'Fine,' I assure him.

'You seem a bit quiet.'

'A lot on my mind. With the open day and that. Bev discussed her plans with me this morning. There's so much to take in.' I can't share with him what's really going on in my life. It's too new, too raw, too frightening. I can't tell anyone – except Bev – until I've shared it with Shelby and with Lucas. Though I have the feeling that Matt would understand.

We stop at a lamp post in the village and Matt gets first dibs on fixing his poster to it.

When we walk again, he says, 'The scenery is all finished and ready to put up. Is there anything else that you'd like me to do?'

'We should gather some holly with the kids,' I say. 'That would look nice around the farmyard, but there's nothing specific. There are a couple of holly trees in the fields that we can trim.'

'I've got tomorrow off too,' Matt says, 'But I need to go back to work after that. I can't put it off any longer.'

'Ah.' I turn to him. 'I've been dreading this,' I admit. 'It's been great having you around.'

'You're not getting rid of me that easily,' he laughs. 'This has been a godsend to me, Molly. I was feeling a bit lost and lonely. Don't get me wrong, it's great being mayor – an honour – but when all the shaking hands and cutting ribbons has finished, I go home to an empty flat. I've been looking for something but I didn't know what. I feel that coming here has given me purpose again.'

'That's lovely.'

'So I'll be here every weekend, evenings if you want me and I can spend some of my holiday time here too.'

'Whatever time you can spare will be greatly appreciated. You'll definitely be here for the open day?'

'I'm one of the turns,' he reminds me. 'Wouldn't miss it for the world.'

'I can't decide if it will be fabulous or a total car crash. This is a big thing for our students. I have everything crossed that it goes well.'

Our next stop is the village shop and the new owner agrees to put the poster in the window. He says that he can't come as the shop will be open, but is sure his wife and daughter would like a chance to come along to the farm. We have a standing invitation for the people of our village to visit us, but few take us up on the offer. I think Bev is right that an organised event will be more of a draw and it will be nice to meet some of the people who live here properly and on my own turf.

Before we move on Matt pauses and turns to me. 'I hope we've become good friends, Molly. I'd like to think so.'

'We have. Definitely.'

'You're very easy company.'

'I'm not. I'm socially awkward, a bit of a loner, a misfit. I struggle to make friends, yet we got on instantly. So this is very different for me. I really enjoy your company.'

'We should form a mutual admiration society,' he quips, but there's a serious look in his eyes. 'Shelby is a very lucky man.'

Perhaps. I'm not sure how lucky he'll feel when I tell him that he's going to be a father again. Would he really want a small child in tow? His relationship with Lucas isn't easy; I wonder whether he'll view it as a chance to do it all over and get it right this time or whether he'll want to run for the hills. Does it show how little I know the real Shelby, that I have no idea how he'll react to my news?

Chapter Fifty-Seven

When we get back to the farm, preparations for the open day are in full flow. Bev has taken the students out to gather holly and now they're knee-deep in it. There's also a basket full of pine cones from the woods that border our property. Anna is here showing them how to twist the holly into wreaths and garlands, threaded with the cones.

'Some of these are good enough to sell.' Bev holds up a particularly attractive specimen of glossy, dark green leaves heavy with the most scarlet of berries.

'That's beautiful.'

'Lottie's handiwork. We have some very talented crafters here,' Bev says while Lottie puffs up with pride. 'I'm going to turn her into a wreath-making machine. What do you think we'd get for them? A fiver?'

'I think that would be worth five pounds of anyone's money.'

'We are going to be swimming in cash after this,' Bev says, happily. 'Trust me.'

'Anything I can do?'

She lowers her voice so I'm the only one who can hear. 'I'd thought that Alan would dress up as Santa for a couple of hours, but I think it will be all too much for him. I don't want him traumatised by a ton of overexcited kids. Can you rope anyone else in?'

'I could ask Christian Lee,' I suggest. 'He said he was planning to drop in. I'm sure it would be right up his street.'

'Call him,' Bev says. 'Tell him we've already got a costume. That will be another thing crossed off my list.'

'Consider it done.' I can't see him putting up much resistance, though we may have the most camp Santa there ever was.

Bev throws a bunch of mistletoe to me. 'Look what Jack found in some of the apple trees. I didn't even know we had any here.'

I look at the mistletoe, its delicate leaves and berries like pearls. 'I haven't seen this in a long time. Or had the need for it,' I add.

'Do you want me to hang it in the yard for you?' Matt asks.

'Great idea,' Bev says. 'It will give me loads of excuses to snog Alan.'

'I'll help you.' So I follow Matt outside with an armful of mistletoe and he grabs the ladders, some nails and a hammer.

'Here?' He leans the ladders against the barn.

'Yeah. As good as anywhere, I think.'

I pass him a bunch of mistletoe and he hangs it from the beam. 'Not too high?'

'Just perfect.'

When he climbs down, we both look up to admire it.

'We should check it's the right height.'

So we both stand under it and it dangles, enticingly, above our heads. 'Told you it was perfect.'

Then we turn to each other and there's a moment where the temptation to kiss him is very strong. From the look on Matt's face, I think that he feels the same. We're close, our bodies

266

inches apart and it would be so very simple for our lips to meet. My heart is pounding and I wonder what magic this mistletoe is performing.

'Molly . . .'

That breaks the spell and I step away from him. This isn't right. I'm with someone else. I'm having his child. 'It's lovely, isn't it?'

'Yes, beautiful. But I wanted to ask you something.'

Now I'm all flustered. 'We have so much to do. We'd better get on.'

He puts his hands on my shoulders and holds me still. 'I'm having a charity ball in January. It usually raises thousands of pounds and I want Hope Farm to be the main beneficiary.'

'That's fantastic, Matt. I'm so grateful.'

'It's my pleasure. You know that I've fallen in love with this place.' We both look bashful at the choice of his words. 'I hold you in the greatest respect, Molly, and I'd also like to ask you to come along as my guest.'

'Me?'

'I'd be delighted if you'd be by my side.'

The telling thing is that I actually want to go with him, and you know from previous experience that this kind of event is usually my idea of hell. My mind is whirring. Should I go? I feel that we're becoming too close and, if I'm honest with you, I enjoy spending time with Matt far more than I should.

'Say something,' he urges.

'You should probably take someone else,' I say, sadly. 'I'm hopeless at socialising. I'd worry about it for weeks. Take someone who'll enjoy it.'

He goes to argue, but then thinks better of it. 'OK. But you'll be there in spirit with me.'

'I will.'

I don't want things to be awkward between us, as I've come to rely on Matt and I want him in my life – as a friend. A dear friend.

'I have been asked out on a date,' he confides.

'Oh.'

'A teacher at the local primary school. I went into one of their assemblies recently. We hit it off and she asked me to go for a drink with her.'

How readily I can imagine that happening. He's very easy to like.

'Sounds promising.' I sound as light as I can while acknowledging that it feels as if I've been stabbed in the heart.

'If you don't want to come, she might be a likely candidate for the ball?'

'Sounds ideal,' I agree, but the words almost stick in my throat.

He looks at me earnestly and it's almost too much to bear. 'Molly?' A beat. 'Is that *really* what you think I should do?'

This is a moment that could change our relationship for good and we both know it. We either step forward together or step back from the edge. Which is it to be? Do I go with Matt or do I watch from the sidelines while he goes with someone else?

'Yes,' I say. 'Go for it!' I force a bright smile.

He looks at me and I can't read his expression. Is it sadness I see or acceptance of our situation? Shelby will be coming home soon and I think that's a good thing. Absence should make the heart grow fonder but, at the moment, it just seems to be making our life more difficult. Surely it will be better when he's back.

'Thanks for your advice,' Matt says and there's a resigned note in his words. 'I'll call her.'

'Great. Let me know how you get on.'

'Friends,' Matt says.

'Friends,' I echo.

But I think that both of us have the feeling that we have lost a little bit of something unspoken.

Chapter Fifty-Eight

Finally, it's our Christmas Open Day. It seems to have been ages in the making and now, suddenly and in a last minute rush, it's here. And I can't tell you how nervous I am. I'm not comfortable with people at the best of times and yet we've got a crowd of them arriving today. I'm worried about how we're going to keep them all entertained, while being equally worried that they won't show up at all. The weather forecast is perfect, but what if they're wrong and it pours down? That won't feel very festive. I didn't sleep a wink all last night dwelling on everything that could go wrong, all the things I can't control, my animals being top of the list. I know. I can't help it. Call me a fatalist.

I'm up before dawn and, as I have done every day for the last week, I throw up in the loo, trying to be as quiet as I can so that Lucas doesn't hear. I've yet to tell him my news. Only Bev knows. But is this down to stress or morning sickness? I don't know. I look in the mirror and can see the start of a tiny bump, so small it's barely there. Is it a baby or could it simply be due to Bev force-feeding me mince pies on a daily basis?

I have no time to consider my predicament now. A few minutes later and I'm in my coat and wellies and out on the farm. Can't hang about today. Places to go, things to do, stuff to stress about. So far, the forecast is right. It's a bright, sunny day, but it's so cold that I can see my breath on the air.

Grabbing some buckets, I fill them from the food bins before heading into the barn. Everyone gets a little bit of extra grub to see them through the cold winter months.

'Morning, everyone,' I say. 'Breakfast is ready.' I hold out a bucket for the alpacas, who nearly pull me over in their enthusiasm. 'I need you lot in particular to be on your best behaviour. Remember what that is?'

Tina flicks her pom-pom hair at me.

'Just try, for once,' I say. 'Would it kill you?'

I move on to give our sheep their breakfast. Fluffy gets a little bit of extra 'extra'. I'm feeling great empathy with her at the moment.

'We're in this together,' I whisper to her as she turns her big eyes to me. 'I'll look after you.'

The students have groomed all the ponies and they look sparkly and clean – for the moment. I feed them next. The girls are coming in early today to make the ponies look Christmassy. They're going to get red ribbons threaded through their manes and, apparently, their hooves will be painted in glittery red varnish. This is the nearest we could get to reindeer.

The nativity scene is going to be set up in this part of the barn and the lads are going to move the scenery that everyone's been painting into place just as soon as they're all here. And, for a moment, I have a good feeling. My terror subsides. This is going to be all right. Bev has been working very hard behind the scenes and I should put my trust in her. We couldn't have done it without Matt, either. I've not seen so much of him since he's been back on mayor duties full-time. I think he's trying to

271

catch up with the backlog of commitments he put on hold to help us out. I can't lie to you, I miss him.

Shelby called last night. He's going to get here as soon as he can. Technically, Sunday should be his day off but he always seems to have meetings or press interviews or something that keeps him away from us. But he has promised and I'll hold him to that. I'm looking forward to seeing him – of course, I am – but part of me is dreading our conversation about our surprise arrival. I just have to hope that he takes it well. It seems odd, but I've been trying to curb my own excitement until I know how he's going to react.

Animals fed, I head back to the caravan. In the middle of the yard, I stop and look around me. Fairy lights hang from every beam and we've got festive bunting strung here, there and everywhere. The kids have been very busy with their crafting endeavours. There are holly garlands and wreaths, the dangerously tempting bunches of mistletoe that you already know about and, in the corner, our huge tree. It all looks quite magical and I feel my eyes fill with tears. Perhaps it's my hormones being all stirred up, but I think we do good here. I know we do.

Our kick-off isn't until two o'clock, so we have plenty of time to get ourselves ready, but many tasks to complete. My next one is to get Lucas out of bed.

He's been quiet the last few days and, as far as I know, he hasn't seen or had much contact with Aurora. I need to sit down with him and find out what their plans are for the baby but, then, I've had enough to think about of my own.

Back in the caravan, I take him a mug of tea in bed. Lucas burrows down into his duvet and it's hard to see him beneath the pile of covers.

'Wake up, sleepyhead,' I say and put his tea down on his side table. 'Lots on the agenda today.'

272

He opens one eye. 'I'm good to go.'

I laugh. 'Looks like it.'

He opens the other eye and peers at his phone. 'Christ on a bike,' he complains with a groan. 'Have you seen the time? You're not stressing already, are you?'

'Of course.'

'Chill out. It'll be good,' he assures me. 'We've got it all under control. You can relax and enjoy yourself.'

'I'll try,' I tell him. 'I know you've been working hard with Bev.'

'It's my job,' he shrugs. But I know that it is much more than that to him. He takes great pride in the work he does at the farm.

'Is your poem ready?'

'You worry too much.'

'No swear words in it?'

'Fucking LOADS of them,' he says with a grin.

That means there's not. Phew.

'Is Aurora coming today?'

'Yeah,' he says. 'Supposedly.'

'All OK there?' I ask tentatively.

'I dunno,' he admits. 'She's being a bit off with me. Moody and that.'

'Probably hormones.' Mine are definitely in a tizzy. I also wonder if she's beginning to realise the enormity of what's heading her way. I know that I am. Could I have handled this at nineteen? I don't think so. I'm not sure I can handle it at thirty-several.

'Make sure you spend some quality time with her today. We're having a bit of a get-together afterwards for the staff and students, a celebration. You can have a few beers, some food.' A soft drink for Aurora. 'See if she can stay around for that.'

'Yeah,' he says, then he asks, 'Is Daddy Dearest coming today?'

'I hope so. He said he was.'

'Knowing him, he'll rock up late when all the work is done and then take all the glory.'

'He's not as bad as you think,' I tell him, hoping that I'm right. Shelby knows how important this is to me, to all of us at Hope Farm. 'Christian's coming later. He's going to be Santa.'

Lucas grins at that. 'Cool.'

I stand up and resist the urge to ruffle Lucas's bed-hair. 'Want some porridge for breakfast? It's that kind of day.'

He nods. 'Give me five to get my shit together.'

'This will be a good day for us,' I say. 'I can feel it in my bones.'

Lucas snuggles down into his pillow and lets his eyes close again. 'Weirdo,' he murmurs.

Chapter Fifty-Nine

By the time Lucas has risen from his pit and downed two bowls of porridge for breakfast, Alan and Bev have arrived.

Thankfully, Alan is looking stronger every day, but that doesn't stop Bev from fussing over him. Preferably, she likes to be no more than an inch away from him now. And I don't blame her. It all must have been a terrible shock for them both.

'Hey,' I say and give her a hug.

'Look what I brought.' In the backseat of the car, in a mesh pen, are two handsome turkeys. 'Before you give me any grief, I know we're not taking on any more animals, but I had to rescue two turkeys at Christmas, no?'

I roll my eyes. 'How could we not?'

'Meet Holly and Ivy.'

'Hi, girls,' I say. 'Where are we going to put them?'

'I'll sort that out,' Bev assures me. 'I couldn't let them be someone's lunch.'

'Where did you get them?'

'Best you don't ask. I'll drive them up to the barn. I don't think the chickens will mind sharing for a couple of days.'

Like me, I'm not sure the chickens will have much choice.

'Before I go, I've got the cakes from the WI too. They're in the boot. Treble-wrapped, in boxes and under a table cloth. I think we're OK hygiene-wise.'

God forbid we give food poisoning to our visitors via the medium of WI cupcakes.

Alan goes to the back of the car.

'Don't lift them if they're too heavy!' she shouts. 'I'll do it.'

'It's fine,' Alan says. 'Don't fret.'

Bev gives me a sideways glance but Alan takes the cakes in, nevertheless.

'I'll put them out in the tea room and set up the cups and stuff,' I tell her.

My friend nods. 'When he's unloaded, I'll get the turkeys settled. Then we'll set up the nativity tableau with Lucas in the barn and I'll put the parking signs up.' Thankfully, the ground in the field is dry. No having to tow anyone out with a tractor.

She turns to me and grins. 'D-day!'

'I'm terrified.'

'It will be perfect,' she says. 'Look how hard we've worked. The students have been brilliant. You could eat your dinner off the ground in the yard. Our animals look like they're out of the pages of a kid's story book. We are fully locked and loaded on the festive front. It's up to everyone else now. We can do no more.'

She's right. Of course.

'Shelby's coming?'

I shrug. 'I hope so. He's promised.'

'The Hot Mayor messaged me to say that he'll be here in a few minutes. He can help with the nativity scene. A bit of extra muscle will take the load off Alan.'

I shouldn't feel funny because Matt's texting Bev rather than me, but I do. Is it because I made it clear we could be nothing more than friends? Did he want something more from me?

276

Alan comes out of the tea room. 'Cakes are in.'

'Right.' I rub my hands together in a purposeful manner. 'I'll go and get sorted in there. There's a tombola to fix up, too.'

'It's not a proper do without a tombola,' Bev says wisely.

'I'll get horses down,' Alan says and wanders off.

Sweeney and Carter are coming into the stables by the yard for the event as I'm sure everyone would like to admire our gentle giants. Their doors have been framed with holly decorations – out of range so they don't get munched.

'I'll come to the barn when I'm finished,' I tell Bev.

She moves towards me and whispers, 'No lifting! Are you going to tell Shelby your good news today?'

I pull a worried face as I answer, 'That's my plan.'

'It'll be great,' Bev says. 'You'll see. He'll be thrilled.'

It's fair to say that I'm less confident about his reaction than my friend.

'We'd better get on,' Bev adds. 'You go and titivate the cakes. I'll supervise scenery shifting.'

'I'll be with you as soon as I can.'

She nods and we go our separate ways. In the tea room, the boxes of cakes from the WI are all lined up on the counter and I set about displaying them nicely before covering the mouth-watering array of mince pies and Christmas cupcakes in cling film until opening time. I put out a table to hold our array of tombola prizes and stick the necessary numbers on them before adding their counterparts to the drum. Among the terror, I get a flutter of excitement. Everything will be all right. I know it will.

Before I leave the tea room to help the others, I stop and have a look around me. The students have done a brilliant job in here. The walls are filled with photographs of them and our animals in action, there's homemade bunting too and an abundance of tinsel in swags. The Christmas tree is laden with their own baubles from our craft sessions and I go over and switch on the lights. It looks lovely. My eyes fill with tears. I look at their faces adorning our walls – Jack, Asha, Lottie, Erin, Tamara, Seb, Jody, Penny; each and every one of our students and my dear Lucas. Sometimes the kids here drive us mad – they can be difficult, demanding, challenging and, on occasion, prone to violence. There are days when they test our patience to the limit, when we get kicked, bitten, scratched and sworn at. But we love them, we all do. And on the days when they are adorable, kind, co-operative, eager, loving and funny, it makes it all seem worthwhile.

Today is for them.

Chapter Sixty

I walk across the yard to the barn, my trio of faithful hounds in tow. Bev's right, the place is shining like a new pin. How long will that last? For the rest of the day, I hope. The kids have worked really hard on scrubbing, brushing and hosing down. I'd like to say 'without complaint', but that's pushing it a bit. However, it was – mostly – done without too much grumbling.

In the barn, the nativity scenery has already been erected. Matt is standing there in shirt sleeves, despite the cold, and is a little red in the face. I get a warm feeling in the pit of my stomach that shouldn't be there. Just seeing him brightens my day. He and Lucas are laughing with each other and I think it's wonderful that Lucas has a role model to look up to even though it's not his own father. They are comfortable, at ease together. I can only hope that, one day, he'll have that with Shelby.

'You've obviously been busy,' I say.

Matt turns to me and his eyes shine. 'You like?'

My mouth is a little dry when I say, 'It's great.'

And it is. At the back of the barn, there's a wooden shelter and next to it the frontage of an old Bethlehem inn – that looks rather like a high street pub – called the Three Kings. Above it, there's a huge star painted bright yellow and covered with glitter. That will be Lottie and Erin's handiwork. Neither of them are never knowingly under-glittered. It looks brilliant and I know how much work has gone into it.

At the front is a crib with my plastic-fantastic Baby Jesus already in there. As Lucas noted, it does look a tad scary. More devil-possessed than beatific with its alarming shock of blonde hair and bright blue eyes.

'What are the chances of that remaining uneaten?' I'm still aware that the previous culprit hasn't been identified.

'I've tied it in tightly,' Lucas says. 'Not taking any chances. Tina, Rod and Johnny will be right here.' He indicates a pen at the front of the barn. 'The donkeys are going at the back with Teacup. The goats will be close, but in a separate area in case they get the urge to run amok. Ponies in their Christmas livery will be front right. And we thought we'd let Fifty and a few more of the amenable sheep mill around as they're least likely to do any damage.'

'Apart from Anthony.'

'We are taking the precaution of moving Anthony out of the way to one of the furthest pens. For his own good and the good of our visitors.'

'Probably a good call.' Though it's such as shame as I love having our belligerent boy around and he would be much admired for his huge head and impressive shoulders.

'The guinea pigs and bunnies have been cleaned within an inch of their lives and we're charging two pounds to go in for a cuddle. I've put Seb in charge.'

I love how Lucas is in control of it all.

'What?' he says. 'Why are you looking at me all funny?'

'I'm proud of you,' I tell him.

He tuts. 'Are you listening or not?'

'Yes. Of course.'

'When we've done our songs and I've read out my poem, the ponies and alpacas will be available for walks around the field. The girls are sorting that out and Alan is supervising the walks. Again, two pounds a head.'

I nod attentively. It's a good job for Alan as it will keep him away from the throng.

'The rest of the students will have collection buckets and there's the stall selling wreaths and crafts. There'll be mulled wine and spiced cider too, but we can't technically sell that, so it will be by donation only – suggested at three pounds. Some of the parents have volunteered to look after those. We've got some games set up for the kids – Pin the Tail on the Donkey.'

I give him a pretend panicked look. 'Not the real one?'

'Not intentionally,' Lucas says. 'There's Smack the Rat.'

'I daren't ask.'

'And the obligatory face-painting woman will be here soon.'

'What about Christian?'

'We've set up Santa's grotto over there.' He points it out. 'Bev borrowed a throne from somewhere.'

'Local theatre group,' she supplies as she comes to join us.

'Christian texted me to say he'll be here shortly,' Lucas continues. 'There's no charge for seeing Santa. He's just going to sit there, take selfies and make false promises to kids about their hopes and dreams.'

'Lucas!'

'I'm kidding!' he says. 'There's paper and stuff set out so the more gullible can write letters to him begging for expensive presents.'

I'm astonished at all the things they've put in place for today. I had no idea that all this was going on. It's probably a good thing they've kept it from me or I'd have had a complete melt-down.

Lucas looks at Bev. 'Anything else?'

'I think you've covered all bases,' she says. 'Our new turkeys are enjoying some lunch. The students should be arriving soon. Most are bringing their own costumes and I've organised them for the ones who can't get help at home.'

'How did I ever doubt that this wasn't going to run like clockwork? Thank you so much for all your hard work.'

'Will you *finally* relax and enjoy it?' Bev asks.

'Yes.' I laugh. 'I promise I'll try!'

'Anything we've missed?'

'The dogs,' I say. 'I think it will all be a bit much for them. Especially Betty Bad Dog. I don't want her weeing up anyone's leg in excitement.' Particularly not Matt's as he's turning the lights on. No one needs that in their lives. 'I'll put them in the caravan with the radio on for company until it's all over.'

Bev checks her watch. 'Not long to go. I think we can bring the animals in now.' She turns to me. 'You can go and get changed now, Mols.'

I look down at my clothes. 'I thought I'd stay like this.'

'Get changed,' she instructs. 'Clean stuff. Comb your hair, put some slap on. Like it or not, you're on show.'

I sigh at her in the manner of Lucas.

'Do it,' she says in a voice that means she'll have no argument from me.

Looks like I'm getting changed. 'OK.'

Clearly they're trying to keep me out of the way, so I head to the caravan and notice that Matt slips away to follow me.

He catches my arm. 'Hey.'

Alarmingly, I like the feel of his strong hand on my arm.

'You're coping very well,' he says.

I smile. 'I'm doing my best. Everyone has worked so hard and I can't thank you enough for all your help. I owe you dinner.'

Then we're both awkward for a moment.

282

'I'm bringing someone today,' he says. 'I mentioned her to you.'

'Oh. The primary school teacher?'

'Yes. Victoria.'

'Good. Good.' And now I really don't know what to say. I hadn't envisaged that she'd come with him today. But why wouldn't she?

'You're OK with that?'

'Oh, heavens, yes. Why wouldn't I be? I hope she loves it here.' I can't read the expression on his face.

'Shelby's coming?'

'I hope so. You never know with these actor types. So unreliable.' I realise that I'm babbling and stop.

'I have to say this, Molly.' He looks at me, suddenly serious. 'With different timing, in a different life, I think we could have been good together.'

'Yes.' Unexpected tears prickle behind my eyes.

'I'm glad I'm not imagining it,' Matt says.

'No, you're not.' I can't tell him the reason why this *has* to work out with Shelby. There's not just me to consider. This is more than *us*. This is about the baby, Lucas, the farm.

He steps forward and, tentatively, takes me into his arms. We hold each other tightly.

'Sometimes the universe is an awkward bugger,' Matt whispers against my hair.

I couldn't agree more.

We break away and, without another word, he marches away across the yard. I stand and watch and wonder what on earth to think.

Chapter Sixty-One

At two o'clock the crowds flood in. I think the whole of the village has turned out to support us and I couldn't be more grateful. Soon the yard is filled with happy people buying wreaths and mulled wine or cider. The air is heavy with the scent of Christmas – cinnamon, cloves, citrus from the wine and fresh pine from our humungous tree.

Bev has put a speaker out and Christmas songs drift over us. The place is full of festive love. All the kids are in costume, including our own, and there's a prize for the best outfit. Most are dressed as elves or something similarly Christmassy – though Lottie and Erin look a little more sexy than perhaps elves and young teen girls should. Seb is in a reindeer onesie and Asha has come as a Christmas tree which is severely restricting his movement. Someone has come as a Stormtrooper, but I haven't yet had the chance to find out who. I expect they're one of ours. The students who can cope with it are, with supervision, going round with collection buckets or are helping out on the stalls

The only person missing is Shelby. I glance at my watch – as I have done a dozen times in the last five minutes. He will be here. I know he will.

Bev appears at my shoulder. 'Don't stress,' she instructs. 'Have a glass of something, mingle.'

I glance down at my stomach to remind her that anything strong is off the agenda.

'Non-alcoholic,' she adds. 'Just chill. Be the face of Hope Farm. Show the world – or at least the village – how wonderful we are.'

'Shelby's not here.'

'I know, but we can manage without him. I didn't put him on the posters when he buggered off to Brummieland, so it will be an extra surprise if he does rock up. Besides, the Hot Mayor is here. What more could we want? Two hotties might be overload.'

'Yeah,' I agree distractedly, while my eyes search him out.

Bev's eyes, however, narrow. 'Is everything all right between you two?'

'Why wouldn't it be?'

'You tell me, Mols.' Nothing slides past my friend.

'He's bringing a date today and I feel weird about it.'

'Hmm,' Bev says. 'Would you like to unpack that emotion?'

'Not now. I like him,' I say. 'That's all.'

'It's understandable. He's hot stuff and he's here for you, for all of us.'

I let out a weary huff of breath.

'It will be better when Shelby's back. His head is up his own panto arse at the mo. Wait until he hears your news.'

I wish I had Bev's confidence in my own relationship.

She takes my hand and pulls me to the spiced cider stall and grabs a paper cup filled with warm, delicious-smelling apple juice. 'Get this down your neck and enjoy.'

'Heard and understood,' I say as, obediently, I drink it down. It warms me to my toes. 'I could get to like this.'

She looks round. 'Have you seen how many people have turned up? This is a roaring success. Relax and enjoy it.'

Grinning at her, I say, 'I will, and thank you, Bev. This is all down to you.'

She grabs a more potent cider for herself and knocks her paper cup against mine. 'To us,' she toasts. 'We are flipping BRILLIANT!'

'We are,' I agree.

At that moment, I see Christian Lee heading across the yard to us. He's looking very festive and rather rotund in a glittery and seriously sequined red Santa outfit. A white beard flows down to rest on his pillowy tummy and is decorated with stars. He has matching red nails and lips. Quite possibly false eyelashes. Our borrowed Santa outfit would clearly have been found wanting.

He comes and kisses us both.

'You look fabulous.'

'And you look positively glowing,' he says to me at which I flush. 'It's obviously the good, clean living.'

If only he knew. 'Thanks so much for doing this, Christian.'

'I wouldn't have missed it for the world.'

'Can I get you something to drink and then we'll set you up? Bev's got you a very fancy throne.'

'I can't wait.'

'Stay as long as you can. We really appreciate it. We're having a get-together afterwards if you can hang around?'

'I'll be here for a couple of hours, after that I've got to shoot into London for a party. It is the festive season after all. Where's that delicious godson of mine?'

'I'm sure he'll be here as soon as he knows you've arrived.'

'Penny and her mum have just turned up,' Bev says. 'Mum looks in a bad way.'

'I'll go and find them once I've settled Santa. Shout if you need me for anything else.'

'It's all under control,' Bev says, confidently. 'I can see some more cars arriving, so I'll go and open the gate to the other field. Overflow parking!' She grins at me in a slightly manic way. 'After that, I'll give it another half an hour or so for people to have a look around, then I'll get the nativity set up and we can do our Thang!'

'I can't wait,' I say.

'You nearly made that sound genuine,' Bev laughs. 'It will be fine!'

So I leave her and head off with Christian. I get him settled in his throne beneath a sign which says SANTA SELFIES and issue him with a list of dos and don'ts. I'm sure he'll be an excellent Santa and won't scare any of the kids. Fingers crossed.

Then I set off to find Penny and her mum. When I track them down, they're over by the craft stall picking through the cards that our students have made.

'Hey,' I say. 'Good to see you both.'

Penny's mum lets her hair fall over her eyes, but it doesn't disguise the fact that one of them bears a livid bruise. Her daughter looks exhausted. I'm guessing they've both had yet another rough night.

'I'm Molly.'

'Jess,' she replies.

I hold out my hand. Penny's mum takes it, but I see her wince when I touch her fingers. I'd like to get my hands on the man who does this. Jess is a petite woman – she looks as if a stiff wind would blow her over. How could someone begin to think it's right to do this to her, let alone her own husband?

'A sprain,' she says, nursing it to her. 'A fall. I'm very clumsy.'

'Penny's told me,' I say quietly. 'There's no need to make excuses here, Jess. You're among friends.'

She flushes, but says nothing else.

'If I can help, will you let me? This is an awful situation for both of you.'

Then she does look at me and I see the pain in her face that's not just because of her bruises. The emotional toll is written large too. 'What can you do? I have no money, nowhere to go.'

'Will you leave it with me?' I hope that I do have a plan and have everything crossed that I'll be able to find a solution. 'You know that you can't stay.'

It's awful to see the resignation on Jess's face.

'You can lean on me,' I say. 'I'm used to hefting around hay bales and sheep. My shoulders are broader than they look.'

Jess manages a laugh at that. 'Thanks,' she says. 'Penny tells me that you're a good woman. This . . . situation . . . makes you distrust everyone.'

'I can understand.' I open my arms and, with only a slight hesitation, she steps into them for a hug. 'Come up for coffee one morning next week. We can have a proper chat then. But, for now, enjoy the afternoon. Penny has proved to be quite a dab hand with the crafts.' I give Penny an encouraging wink. 'I'll catch you again later.'

As I move away, my blood is boiling. If it's within my power, I *will* do something about this. It's been going on for too long and has to stop. And I know exactly who can help.

Chapter Sixty-Two

Up by the barn, I see Lucas mooching about and looking a bit lost. There's no sign of Aurora either, so I head straight for him.

'Have you seen Christian?'

'Yeah. Cool Santa. He looks like something out of *RuPaul's Drag Race*.'

'I don't know what that is.' I hope it's a good thing.

He huffs at me. 'It doesn't matter.'

'Everything OK?' I ask. He looks a bit down in the dumps.

'Yeah. Just waiting to bring the animals out. Bev didn't want to get them set up too early or they'd all get tetchy.'

'She's a wise woman.'

'The alpacas already seem a bit frisky.'

'That's worrying.'

'I'll keep my eye on them,' Lucas says.

Then, before I can stop myself, I ask, 'No Aurora?'

Lucas hangs his head and now I can tell just how miserable he is – which is a shame as he should be enjoying the fruits of all his hard work. 'She should be here by now, but I've messaged her and she's not replying.'

'I'm sure she wouldn't miss it intentionally. She knows that this is important to you. Perhaps she's not feeling well. She might be having a nap.'

He looks at me as if to say that's something only old people do. Lucas has much to learn.

'If she doesn't turn up, could you have a chat with Penny and her mum later? They're here by themselves and I think they'd appreciate it.'

'Sure,' he says. 'Where's my old man? Another absentee?'

'I haven't heard from him either,' I admit.

Lucas shakes his head, tutting. 'And he thinks I'm the flaky one.'

Then I see that Matt is standing by the Christmas tree. He's in a smart coat and he's wearing his heavy, gold mayoral chain of office. By his side is a very pretty young woman. She dresses like Aurora does, in faded jeans and boots with a chunky jacket. Her hair is dark and wavy. She is wearing make-up and has combed hair. They're laughing together and his manner is easy and relaxed with her, as it is with everyone.

Matt must sense me watching them as he turns around and our eyes meet. He smiles and ushers his date towards me. My stomach rolls as they approach.

'I love the bling,' I say when they're in front of me.

'Fancy, eh? Comes with the turf.' He strokes his gold chain. 'How are you coping with all this?'

'I'm doing surprisingly well,' I tell him.

'This is Victoria,' he says, turning to his date. 'She teaches at Ashlands primary school in Aylesbury.'

'Nice to meet you.' Victoria has a warm smile and a gentle face. I bet she's a hit with her pupils. We shake hands. 'Thanks for coming.'

'I wouldn't have missed it for the world. This is a great place you have,' Victoria says. 'Matt has been telling me all about it and how much he loves coming up here.'

'We very much appreciate that he does.' I avoid looking at him as I've no idea what the expression on my face is doing.

'I'd love to bring my school kids up here for a day out. Do you do that kind of thing?'

'We haven't. As yet,' I admit. 'But it's something my marketing manager, Bev, is considering.' Bev will be pleased that I've promoted her. No pay rise, obvs.

'We should talk, then,' Victoria says. 'At the start of the new term, I'll call her.'

'Great.'

They look good together. A perfect couple. And she seems like a really nice woman. Ideal girlfriend material. In fact, she'd probably make an even better wife. So why am I not pleased?

'I've come to give a hand with the animals, if you need help,' Matt says and stops my musings.

'I think we've got it covered.' I turn to Lucas, who nods that we have. 'You can relax until it's light-switching-on time. Have some wine, try your hand at the tombola!' I sound too jolly.

'Let me know if there's anything you need,' he says.

'I will. Lovely to meet you, Victoria.'

'Likewise.' She's endearingly earnest and enthusiastic. 'Matt talks about you a lot.'

Does he? Again, an exchanged glance between us that's loaded and unfathomable. I hope that she doesn't notice.

'See you shortly,' Matt says, taking his gaze from mine.

'Yeah.' I pin a smile on my face and stay like that until they move away.

'New girlfriend?' Lucas looks disappointed. 'I thought you two were going to get it together.'

'I'm with your father,' I remind him.

'You think he's being faithful while he's away?' Lucas snorts. 'You saw all those young girls fawning over him. Good luck with that one.'

'You have a very low opinion of him.'

'That's because I know him better than you. You're more suited to Matt, you know that. Bev says so, too.'

But Bev also knows why this needs to work with Shelby, whereas Lucas does not. I think he'll be furious when he finds out, and I'm dreading telling him. If I'm honest, more so than Shelby.

'We should get the animals set up,' I say. 'Time's getting on.'

'He's not coming, you know,' Lucas says.

'He'll be here,' I counter. 'I'm sure of it.'

'Don't hold your breath,' Lucas says. 'Daddy doesn't care that this is a big day for us and for the students. Daddy Dearest just thinks of himself.'

'You're wrong,' I tell him and hope to goodness that I'm right. I need Shelby here, otherwise I think I might go a little bit mad.

Chapter Sixty-Three

We take the animals out of their pens and lead them into the barn where they take up their places in the nativity scene. They have been beautifully dressed in festive livery and it makes me laugh out loud to see them. I'm guessing that Bev must have been busy on eBay.

The sheep and goats have little Santa hats on, held by elastic under their chins, and they look unbearably cute. The geese must be in an agreeable mood as they're wearing jaunty Christmassy neckerchiefs and aren't currently trying to nip anyone. Teacup has a festive scarf which he's currently trying to eat. Sweeny and Carter are in situ in the adjacent stables which are framed by arches of holly. Just their huge presence is calming. Everyone is looking very spruce and angelic.

And, something that gladdens my heart, our feral farmyard cat – Phantom – with his half-face and goosestep gait is up in the rafters of the barn looking down on the scene. We rarely get a glimpse of him and it's nice that even he has deigned to join in on this our special day.

The only problem – as usual – is the alpacas. As Lucas said, they're already strangely frisky and are skittering about. Perhaps it's because they've been haltered for a while and it's one of the very many things that they don't like. No one has even tried to get near them with Christmas adornments.

'We'll stay here,' I say to Lucas. 'Until they calm down.'

'OK.'

To prove my point Johnny bounces round in a circle and takes me with him.

'Chill out, man,' Lucas tells him and rubs his neck.

As there's activity in the barn, the crowd start to gather around, even though we're not quite ready for them.

The donkeys, Harriet and Hilda, are much more relaxed and settle in their corner of our Bethlehem/deepest Buckinghamshire stable. Lottie and Erin have been busy behind the scenes and they lead in Ringo, Buzz Lightyear and Beyoncé all dressed for the occasion – humans and ponies. The ponies have red sparkly ribbons threaded through their manes and tails plus, as promised, red glittery hooves. The ponies look quite pleased with their glamorous selves. Especially, Beyoncé. The sheep, as malleable as ever, mill about at the front of the scene, just content to look for something they can eat.

Jack and Tamara are dressed as Joseph and Mary. They take their places in the stable behind the crib. Three more students are dressed as the three wise men and even more as shepherds are ushered in. It's apparent that a lot of old tea towels and bed sheets have been pressed into service. I blame that on Bev. Joseph is totally ignoring Mary and, instead, is staring open-mouthed at the two rather skimpily dressed teen Christmas elves, which I don't remember being part of a traditional nativity set-up.

When they're all assembled, Lucas flicks a switch and lights come on all over the barn. It's late afternoon now and is getting dark, so they shine out brightly. The star twinkles and the stable is bathed in a mellow and suitably holy glow. Behind us is a painted backdrop of a city nightscape with little fairy lights peeping through the windows. Even the blond, blue-eyed Baby Jesus doesn't seem so freaky now he's in context. It all looks so much better than I'd hoped and I wonder how I ever doubted that we could pull this off.

Bev comes to the front of the barn and addresses the people who've braved the cold to be here.

'Thanks, everyone, for coming along today. I hope you've enjoyed some mulled wine, played some games, visited our sequined Santa, won something you want on the tombola and, last but not least, have learned something of the work we do here. If you haven't, then do speak to one of our staff or our students who are here today and are happy to tell you all about us.'

Everyone gives a big clap.

'The students are going to sing a couple of Christmas songs for you and then our resident poet, Lucas Dacre, will read his festive poem.'

Next to me, Lucas fidgets uncomfortably. I admit to being worried by this as I still haven't heard it.

The rest of the students come into the barn and gather round. Bev gives them the signal to start singing and, as one, they launch into a chorus of 'O, Holy Night.' It's beautiful and tuneful and I had no idea that our motley crew of badly behaved, troubled and autistic kids were capable of making such a wonderful sound. I don't know when they've been practising this – behind my back, obviously – but they've nailed it. By the time they finished, word and note-perfect – well almost – there's not a dry eye in the house.

Buoyed by success, they then launch straight into 'Jingle Bells' with equal aplomb. It's breathtaking – and I'm not just being biased because they're my miraculous misfits. The applause is enthusiastic and heartfelt. Encouraged by cheering, they do another round of 'Jingle Bells' and everyone sings along at the top of their voices. When the collection buckets go round the crowd, they jingle with spare change.

Across the barn, I see Matt standing with Victoria and he winks at me. Job well done. I smile back in acknowledgement and see Victoria take note of the exchange between us.

Then it's Lucas's turn and my heart is in my mouth. It's so disappointing that Shelby isn't here to see this and I grumble to myself under my breath.

Bev shouts out. 'Please put your hands together for our own award-winning poet, Lucas Dacre, with a specially written Christmas poem.'

'Take this,' Lucas says and hands me Tina's halter. Our diva also does a merry dance in a circle, nearly knocking me over. What on earth is wrong with them today?

'Woah,' I say, trying to calm her down.

Bev comes up next to me and takes Johnny and Rod.

'They're a nightmare,' I tell her. 'Even more twitchy than usual.'

'Performance pressure,' Bev says.

'I hope Lucas doesn't suffer from it. Now, I mean. Not . . . you know . . .'

She laughs at me. 'Do you ever stop worrying?'

'No.'

Lucas goes to the front of the barn and pulls a sheet of paper from his back pocket.

He looks squarely at the crowd. 'This is called "Nativity Schmativity"'.

Then he takes a deep breath and launches in, spitting it out in his usual style.

'You're forgetting the true meaning of Christmas!'
She said,

'I *am?*'
I *replied,*
'You mean that kid in the shed?'
'Our lord and our saviour was born in a stable.'
'*Are you sure?*'
I *baited,*
'I thought that was fable?'
It was pagan tradition to decorate trees,
At the solstice of winter,
their gods to appease.
The Roman god Bacchus said:
'Eat, drink, be merry,
Feast of the beast and the vine and the berry'.
The Americans stole European folklores,
creating the hybrid they called 'Santa Claus'.
Mix it all up with commercial allusions
And the meaning of Christmas is lost
. . . to confusion.

The crowd applaud and Lucas does a mock bow.

Bev turns to me. 'An interesting take on "write us a lovely, festive poem please, Lucas."'

'He always sounds so angry and unhappy,' I say, concerned.

Bev shrugs. 'That's poets for you. Miserable buggers.'

'Yeah.' I have limited experience of poets, but can only agree.

'We do have one extra surprise, though.' Bev claps her hands and shouts out, 'Is everyone ready for the big finale?'

My heart is in my mouth. A surprise? Oh, my goodness. What now?

Chapter Sixty-Four

Lucas takes centre stage again and this time he's wearing the most tasteless Christmas jumper I've ever seen. It has a tiny elf outfit on the front and mulit-coloured pom-poms all down the arms.

He gives me a wry smile and then turns to the kids. 'Ready to do your bit?'

They all shuffle about excitedly.

'This is called "Everybody, It's Christmas".'

Everybody, it's Christmas!

And the kids shout out their echo of, 'Christmas!'

Everybody, it's Christmas!
Christmas!
the happiest day of the year,
where everyone gathers together;
their hearts full of goodwill and cheer.

Everybody, it's Christmas!
Christmas!
that most wondrous day of the year,
the time for peace and celebration
and over-indulgence, draws near.

Everybody, it's Christmas!
Christmas!
that most magical day of the year,
children rapt in anticipation,
as they wait for St Nick to appear.

Everybody, it's Christmas!
Christmas!
the high point in everyone's year,
fifty-two weeks,
we've been waiting,
well, that day
it is finally here.

The atmosphere's intoxicating,
'cause that day
it is finally here.

Everyone's here celebrating,
'cause Christmas is finally here!

All the kids, now quite giddy with excitement, shout and cheer '*Christmas!*'. The audience go into a frenzy of applause once more. Lucas grins across at me and I blow him a kiss. His look says, *I can fake Christmas if required.* And he has. That poem was totally out of Lucas's comfort zone, but he delivered it at perfect pitch. I couldn't be more proud of him. He's even managed to put his anti-Christmas sentiments aside to do something for the students.

'I need to get the mayor to turn on the lights now,' Bev whispers to me. 'Still no sign of Shelby?'

'No.' No text either.

'I'll give him a piece of my mind when I see him,' Bev says. 'Do you want to leave the alpacas with the kids?'

'I'm not so sure. They're a bit of a handful today.'

'No change there, then.'

'Jack could probably cope with them. I think they'd pull the girls over. Where's Alan?'

'It's only for five minutes. I'd like you down at the front with me.'

'Do I have to?'

'Yes.' She pulls my arm.

I hope she's not going to give me a bouquet or anything like that. I've had enough of the limelight for one day.

Chapter Sixty-Five

'The moment we've all been waiting for!' Bev shouts out. 'Our mayor, Mr Matt Eastman, will be turning on the Christmas lights!'

Matt steps forward and says, 'I know it's already been said, but thank you to everyone for coming along and supporting Hope Farm. As I'm sure you've learned, they do great work here with challenging issues and limited funding. I hope you've all bought cakes, sampled the wine and cider on offer and will be taking home some of the crafts that the students have made. Dig deep and don't go home with any loose change in your pockets! There are plenty of buckets around waiting to be filled.'

Bev passes him the switch that Alan has rigged up for the lights and Matt continues, 'It gives me very great pleasure to turn on the Hope Farm Christmas lights!'

The lights shine out in a burst of multi-coloured twinkling and there's much applause. It's an idyllic scene with the beautiful Christmas tree and a backdrop of a nativity scene. Couldn't be more festive if we tried.

It's so perfect that I let out the breath I've been holding. Another thing gone without a hitch. Bev's right, I do worry too much. Our students have been brilliant. The animals have been a big hit. We have put our best foot forward and this day could not have been better. Well, Shelby could have been here, but you know how I feel about that.

Then, before the crowd can disperse, Bev says, 'Just one more thing before you go!' She waves over to Alan and, looking rather bemused, he reluctantly joins her.

Bev stands in front of him and immediately drops to one knee. 'I never thought I'd do this again at my time of life, but now that I've found you, you're not going anywhere. Alan Taylor, would you do me the very great honour of becoming my husband?'

It's fair to say that Alan could not look more surprised if he tried.

The crowd hold their breath while Alan tries to find his voice. When he does, he says, 'I will.'

Cheering ensues as Bev jumps to her feet and hugs her new fiancé. I find myself crying as I cheer too.

'Wow.' Lucas is at my side. 'Did you know about that?'

'No!' I laugh. 'I'm nearly as surprised as Alan.' I'm so pleased for them both. I think it was such a shock when he had his stroke that it's crystallised her feelings for him.

The local paper have sent a photographer and he comes up to take a photograph of the newly engaged couple. Then he asks Matt to pose in front of the Christmas tree.

As he does, there's a terrible racket from the nativity scene behind him. I know what it is instantly. 'Oh, shit! Not now! Not now!'

Rod Stewart has decided to mount Tina Turner. Jack is so shocked that he drops all of their halters. I knew it was wrong to leave one of the students in sole charge. When our boys go, they have a mind of their own and the strength of an ox.

And, believe me, when alpacas mate, they don't do it quietly.

302

As you would imagine, of course, our alpacas do it much louder than any others. Instantly, the racket starts up. Their mating call is known as 'orgling' and it sounds like someone blowing bubbles under water. Quite amusing, in its own way, but not exactly what you want at the end of your open day in the middle of the nativity scene.

Not content to be on the sidelines, Johnny Rotten joins in. They can do this any time of the year and they frequently do. Our students don't need sex education. They just watch this lot getting it on. But must they do it now? In front of a crowd? Do they sense that love is in the air and it's made them feel a bit romantic too? Heaven only knows. They could do it in the privacy of their own pen when everyone's gone home. But, no. Instead, we are treating our unsuspecting guests to an alpaca orgy. The noise of the three of them at it is ear-splitting. If this was going on in a hotel room next to yours, you'd be ringing the front desk to complain.

They bounce around in the straw. The stable is knocked over, as is Baby Jesus's crib. The press photographer steps forward and rattles off a dozen shots. Oh, Lord. I dash forward and shoot into the pen to try and grab them. In my haste, I commit the sin of all sins. I leave the gate open.

As I grab the alpacas and try to disentangle them, everyone else makes a break for it. The sheep spill out into the yard, followed by the donkeys. Buzz Lightyear, not being one to miss a chance of escape, also makes a bolt for it. The other ponies follow suit, red ribbons flowing in the breeze. Instantly, the farmyard is in chaos.

'Stop them!' I shout.

Our visitors dive this way and that, holding on to marauding sheep for all they're worth. Even Christian in his sparkly Santa outfit has a go. The donkeys, over-excited, bray at the top of their voices. Which, on the plus side, helps to drown out the sounds of over-enthusiastic courting alpacas. The press photographer is having a field day.

I see Bev, Lucas and Matt calmly taking control in the yard, while I try to regain some sort of order in here. I manage to grab their halters and stop the alpacas doing . . . er . . . what alpacas like to do.

'Oh, Rod,' I say. 'How could you?'

He looks at me in quite a lascivious manner. All comers are clearly looking attractive to him. Once they start, it's a hell of a job to stop them.

But stop them we finally do. With the help of our visitors, the sheep, goats, donkeys and ponies are rounded up. I'm mortified that our day has ended like this but, in the yard, there's much laughter and camaraderie. Everyone is saying how much they enjoyed getting involved and, apparently, found our shagging alpacas 'endearing'. I don't understand humans, really I don't.

So when we've got all the animals back to where they should be, our crowd of well-wishers drift away home. We've no cakes or crafts left for sale, the stalls have been stripped. Our buckets are full and jingling. We've had offers of support, people asking if they can volunteer and even enquires about taking on new students.

I'm stunned.

Chapter Sixty-Six

The yard seems weirdly still after everyone has gone and the animals are settled again. Peace has returned. I kiss Christian goodbye as he dashes off for his swanky party and thank him for his efforts. He's kept a constant queue of children very happy with Santa selfies.

Bev and I pull some deckchairs round the Christmas tree. I made the right call in putting aside some cakes and mince pies for us as a celebration, and I set them out on a picnic table that's been pressed into service. There's a crate of beer chilling and Bev is already dishing out the last of the mulled wine, cider and hot apple juice.

She hands a juice to me and we clink cups together. I flop down into one of the chairs with a contented sigh. Open days, I've decided, are exhausting – but worth it as we seem to have buckets of cash. A job for tomorrow is to total it all up.

Lucas has brought some blankets from the caravan and I wrap myself up against the cold. I'm pleased to see that Penny and Jess have stayed behind and that Lucas is being very solicitous towards them. They both have a chair and blankets and he's getting them a drink. He might have his moments but, on the whole, he's a good lad. Despite the fact that Aurora isn't here, he looks very chipper. Penny is bathing in his attention.

'Well done, Molly.' Bev sits beside me and pats my knee in a motherly way. 'You survived.'

'Next time you have the bright idea of throwing our doors open, remind me to emigrate.'

She laughs. 'It was brilliant and you know it.'

'Apart from the alpacas shagging.'

'That only served to enhance the atmosphere.'

That makes me laugh too. 'We might make the front page of the local paper. What with that and your impromptu proposal.'

'I've been so worried about Alan,' she confides. 'If anything happens like that again, I want to make sure that I'm his next of kin. Plus I fancy the pants off him. Thought I'd better grab him while he's still available.'

'Well done,' I say. 'I'm so pleased for you.'

She raises an eyebrow. 'You next?'

'My loved one isn't even here.'

Bev frowns. 'Shame he missed it. He'd better have a bloody good excuse.'

Then Matt appears and says, 'Is this a private party or can anyone crash it?'

'You are more than welcome.' I stand to get him a beer and I'm too aware that our fingers touch when I hand it over. 'I thought you'd gone without saying goodbye.'

'I just escorted Victoria back to her car. She couldn't stay. Prior commitment.'

'Ah. She seems very nice.'

Again, an expression I can't read. 'Yes,' he says. 'She is.'

But, if I'm honest with you, he doesn't really sound as if he thinks so.

'You'll see her again?'

He sighs. 'Molly, I have to tell you something . . .'

Then there's a horn tooting from our gate and Bev shouts. 'Shelby!'

'At last!' I left out a relieved breath. He might have missed all the festivities, but at least he's safe and sound. I turn back to Matt. 'What was it you wanted to say?'

He shakes his head. 'It doesn't matter.' He clinks his beer against my juice. 'Well done. I hope it's raised lots of money.'

'Thanks. I think it has. I'm so glad you were here. No one could have done a better job of turning on the lights. Anyone would think you were a pro.'

'I'm not as experienced as some,' he says as he looks over at Shelby striding across the yard.

'Sorry, sorry!' Shelby calls in a voice that would reach the back of the stalls. 'Traffic was hell!'

All day? I think. Matt and I exchange a glance. Seems as if he thinks the same.

Shelby comes over and seems a little put out that we're having a celebration without him. 'A party?' he says. 'I thought I'd missed it all.'

For the first time, I wonder if it was deliberate he's turned up so late. Did he not want to be involved in our open day?

'It went brilliantly,' I say and my voice sounds slightly brittle. 'Matt did a sterling job of switching on the Christmas tree lights.'

'Oh,' he says and Shelby's eyes appraise Matt.

'A handy reserve,' Matt says, mildly.

'You missed the poems that Lucas wrote for us too. They were very good.'

'Afternoon, Father,' Lucas says. 'You've managed to tear yourself away from Pantoland to come and bestow your Christmas wishes on us?'

'If you mean I've been sitting in gridlocked traffic for the last few hours to get here, then yes.'

'It went very well, thanks for asking, and we coped perfectly well without you,' Lucas snipes. I signal to him with my eyes that it's enough and, for once, he falls silent. I know how disappointed he is that his dad has, again, let him down.

'I'm sorry,' Shelby says and, this time, he does sound conciliatory. 'I really had intended to be here.'

'No matter,' I say, too brightly. 'It's all done and dusted now. No point worrying.' This from the Queen of Worrying. 'Come and join us. Have a beer, have a cake.'

The tension goes out of the atmosphere and Matt throws a tin of beer to Shelby who nods, gratefully.

'A toast!' Bev raises her glass of wine. 'To us for being flipping brilliant!'

'To us,' we echo.

'And to the newly engaged couple,' I propose.

Shelby looks at me blankly.

'Something else you missed. Bev asked Alan to marry her. Thankfully, he said yes.'

They both look bashful.

'Congratulations,' Shelby says and there are hugs all round. 'This is definitely a cause for a celebration.'

'Looks like we have a wedding to organise,' I add.

'It will be small,' Bev promises. 'A few friends and family only.'

'And definitely no alpacas,' I warn her.

'Strictly humans only,' she assures me. 'Could you cope with being a bridesmaid?'

'For you, anything.'

'I'll hold you to that,' Bev laughs. 'I have witnesses.'

So we relax and we laugh. Lucas keeps his distance from Shelby, but he does seem to be having fun with Penny and her mum. Matt chats mainly to Bev and Alan, but whenever I happen to look over at him, he's looking right back at me.

'You seem to have got on very well without me,' Shelby says and pulls my attention back to him.

We did. What can I say? At times we were so busy that I completely forgot about him.

'You're here now.' I smile up at him. He looks tired and I think this panto run is taking more out of him than he'll admit to. Thank goodness, it's nearly Christmas and it will soon be over. He'll be home with us permanently and we can get back onto a more secure footing. 'It's good to have you back.'

Even if it is only for a short while.

Chapter Sixty-Seven

When we've had a few drinks and are all feeling chilled, we tidy up and the yard looks more like a farm again. I let the dogs out of the caravan and they go into a frenzy of delight. They're long overdue a walk and I'll have to take them across the fields as soon as possible to run off their pent-up energy.

Matt comes across to me and takes my hands in his. There's a shock of electricity that we both ignore. 'Thanks for having me,' he says. 'That was a great day.'

'Again, thanks for your help.' I can't remember how many times I've had cause to thank this man over the last few weeks. 'Couldn't have done it without you.'

'I'll call you in a few days. To check on the total.'

'Don't be a stranger,' I tell him. 'You're welcome any time. You know that.'

He holds out his hand to Shelby and there's a moment's hesitation before Shelby takes it.

'Good to meet you,' Matt says. 'Enjoy the rest of your panto season.'

'Thanks,' Shelby replies.

Lucas comes over and stands by him. Matt grabs him in

great big bear hug and says, 'You, mate, blew me away. I don't know how you do it. You'd better take me to one of those poetry nights you do.'

'OK.'

Matt lets go of him. 'It's a date.'

Shelby looks taken aback by their casual interaction – as well he might. Sadly, he's never been able to be like this with his own son.

'See you all soon,' Matt says and, with a wave, he strides away.

Then Penny and her mum gather their belongings and get set to leave.

'Are you sure you're OK to go home?' I ask.

They nod, but both look uncertain. Penny looks particularly reluctant to leave.

'I'm going to do my very best for you. But if you need some-where to go, then just call me.'

'Thanks, Molly,' Jess says. 'You've been a pal.'

I hug her and then Penny. 'See you tomorrow.'

We walk to the gate complete with dog trio at my heels and then Lucas takes them across the road to the field where their car is. I look at Lucas and Penny together and feel they are much more suited as a couple. But it's all too late for that. Shelby and I need to have some tricky conversations and I can't really put them off any longer. He'll be wishing that he hadn't turned up today.

'Penny's nice,' I say to Lucas when he comes back.

'Yeah.' He shrugs. 'Hadn't really noticed before.'

'Nothing from Aurora.'

'Nah. I think she's ignoring me, but I don't know why. I'm going to get a shower and then message her again.'

'OK. I'll walk the dogs and your dad, if he'll come with me. Then I'll find us something for supper.'

'We should get a takeaway,' Lucas says. 'We deserve it.'

Then I throw caution to the wind and hug him.

I feel him tighten up in my arms. 'What's that for?'

'For being brilliant,' I tell him. 'Your poem was wonderful and you worked so hard today. Do you know how great you are?'

'Have you been at the mulled wine?' he asks and he unpeels himself from my grip.

I laugh. 'No. Definitely not. I just wanted to let you know that you're growing into a totally marvellous young man and I couldn't be more proud of you.'

'Huh,' he grunts, always unable to take praise. 'That's a yes to takeaway, then?'

'Of course.' I feel filled with Christmas spirit and goodwill to all men. 'I'll take the dogs to run off some steam and we'll get it as soon as I'm back.'

'OK.' Lucas heads towards the caravan. As he does, he turns and says over his shoulder. 'You're all right too, you know.'

And I smile, happily, as he disappears indoors.

Chapter Sixty-Eight

Shelby is waiting patiently – I think – by the Christmas tree. Already he's blowing his nose and rubbing his eyes. It doesn't take long for his allergies to kick in.

'Sorry to keep you hanging on,' I say. 'Fully histamined-up?'

'I couldn't take it until I'd driven up here,' he says.

'No Ken today?'

'Family get-together for Christmas. He brought the car up for me in the week.'

'Ah.'

'The tree looks amazing. A monster.' It does. It's shining out like a multi-coloured beacon in the darkness.

'Matt got it for us,' I tell him. 'One of his contacts donated it.'

'Useful.' Yet Shelby doesn't look impressed. Well, he bloody should be.

'He's been fantastic. He's helped us with the open day and we're going to be his charity for the Mayor's Ball in the New Year.'

'It seems as if my presence hasn't been missed,' he bristles.

Perhaps I did lay it on a bit thick. 'You were very much missed. You know that.'

313

'I need a drink and something to eat,' Shelby says. 'My blood sugar must be low.'

'I promised Lucas we'd have a takeaway.' Then I check my watch. 'First, I need to check on the animals, feed them and then take the dogs for a walk. Up for it?'

'Yes,' Shelby nods. But his face says he'd rather be sprawled out in front of a roaring fire with a good book and a glass of red.

'Are you sure your anti-histamine has kicked in?'

'I'll cope.' He's very crochety and I feel as if I'm walking on eggshells with him. Perhaps he is just tired after driving up here after a busy week on stage. Maybe he will relax when we've eaten.

So we head to the stables and I do my evening check on everyone. We look over the gate into the first pen. 'The alpacas disgraced themselves. Again. Matt was just posing for photos for the local paper and they decided to have an orgy behind him. I'm mortified. I hope they don't run it on the front page.'

'You're kidding me.'

'I don't need to make these things up.' Tina comes to have her neck scratched. 'You don't look the slightest bit ashamed of acting like a harlot in front of all those people. You saucy minx.'

'Seems as if I missed quite the afternoon.'

We walk up to check on the sheep and see that the chickens are all back in their coop. The goats are all safe and sound again too – already asleep in their hay.

'We've got two new rescue turkeys,' I tell him. 'Meet Holly and Ivy.'

'Hello, girls,' Shelby says but he seems distracted and not that interested in our latest arrivals.

'While I look in on the bunnies, can you check on Anthony, please?'

Shelby sighs. 'Do I have to? You know that thing hates me.'

'It will take you one minute,' I say. 'All you have to do is make sure he's in his pen and comfortable. And that his gate is securely locked.'

Reluctance emanates from him. He's as bad as any of the students. I can't bear to argue with him. 'You can do the bunnies, then, and I'll see to Anthony.'

'Can't Lucas help?' he asks. 'I thought this was his job?'

'He's not stopped all day and now he's having a well-earned shower.' I pause and turn to Shelby. 'Lucas is disappointed that you weren't here. His poems were very good. He taught the kids to join in with one as a surprise for me. He's a good lad. Be nice to him this evening.'

'What does that mean?'

'You seem out of sorts. We've had a nice day. It's been a great success. I don't want you two fighting and spoiling it all.'

'I'm beginning to wish I hadn't bothered to come. Seems as if Matt has quite easily slipped into my place. His feet are very much under the table here. With my son and with you.'

'That's unfair. He's a nice guy,' I counter. 'He's become a valuable fundraiser and a good friend to the farm.'

'And to you in particular?'

I ignore the barb. 'I'd like to think so.'

'More than a friend?' he snaps. 'Perhaps a boyfriend?'

'I thought I already had one of those,' I snap back. 'Is there something you want to tell me?'

Shelby's shoulders sag and he looks squarely at me. The drawn expression on his face is unbearable and my heart skips a beat when, in the saddest voice I've ever heard, he says, 'Actually, yes.'

Chapter Sixty-Nine

'Let's take the dogs across the fields and then we can talk.' I can tell this is serious and the sooner we get it over with, the better.

Shelby nods his agreement. 'I'll get my coat from the car.'

Watching him go, I wonder if his head has been turned by one of the young women in his company? Lucas warned me as much. Well, I guess I'm about to find out.

I call Lucas and ask him would he mind feeding the animals. I don't feel that I can put them ahead of this conversation – which I'm not expecting to be good. Lucas doesn't even ask why, he just agrees. I'm relieved about that.

When Shelby comes back, all wrapped up against the cold, I click the dogs to heel. We climb over the stile and head into the countryside. It's dark now, but the moon is bright and lights our way. There'll be a hard frost tonight, I'm sure, but it's a small price to pay. We're far enough from the nearest town to be able to see the stars in all their glory. This is such a beautiful place. Not for the first time, I think *Why would I ever want to be anywhere else?*

The dogs run ahead, happy to be free – unaccustomed as

they are to being cooped up in the caravan all day. They're playing with each other, tumbling and chasing and I can't help but smile.

Shelby and I walk side by side. There's a tension between us, so I link my arm through his.

'Want to tell me what it is?' I say when it doesn't look like he's going to start the conversation.

He doesn't answer right away, as if he's trying to form the right words, but then he says, 'I've been asked to go out to Hollywood again.' He looks over at me. 'Remember that zombie apocalypse series I told you about? *The Dead Don't Sleep*?'

Of course, I do. Not so long ago, Shelby was all set to turn our world upside down and hightail it to Hollywood without a backward glance to play a psycho zombie killer or something. 'Yes. The one you turned down.'

'Well.' There's a sigh and a long pause. 'They've offered it to me again.'

'And you're thinking about it?' We went through before how bad it would be for Lucas. Their relationship is strained at the best of times and Shelby was talking about going to live in Los Angeles for a year while it was filmed.

'I've accepted the role,' he says.

It hits me like a low blow, the breath taken away from me. He's *accepted* it?

All I manage to say is, 'Right.'

'I'll have to go to LA. Of course. I know it's going to be hard for me to be away, but I have to do this, Molly. You see that? I'm being elbowed out of *Flinton's Farm* – not so gently – and this role is huge, massive. I don't want to be consigned to the panto circuit.'

'I thought you were loving it?'

'I am, but I don't want to be defined by it. Once you get typecast, then you're doomed to panto season and celebrity reality shows. This role elevates me to a whole new level. It will invigorate my career.'

'I see.' And, believe me, I do.

'A year away and I could come back to fantastic parts. We're talking lead roles in primetime BBC dramas.'

This my moment to remind him that he has a son who needs him. I should tell him the reason why Lucas is going to need him more than ever. He also should know that he's not just going to be a grandfather but a father too. He is part of this child and has a right to know. But we've been here before and it's clear that the lure of Hollywood is strong.

What should I do?

As much as I want him here while I'm pregnant with his child, I don't want to be the reason why he stays. If I tied him here, would he, in time, come to resent the baby? Resent me too? I'm torn. Do I tell him so that he can make an informed choice or do I let him go and fulfil his dream? Should he be free to leave without knowing the complications in our lives? I'm barely two months' pregnant, if that. There's a long way to go yet. I can manage here with Bev's help. I wish I knew how things worked in Shelby's world. Can he come home regularly? Surely he must get time off from filming when he can do what he likes? Except, I have to face this, he's never really seen this as his home. I look around again and take in the expansive sky, the dark solitude. I don't know what Hollywood's like, but I know that I'd never want to leave here to try it.

'Say something,' he urges. 'What do you think?'

'Lucas would stay here?'

'Yes, yes. If he wants to.' He stuffs his hands deep into his pockets. 'I know he's doing well with his course and he loves it here. I don't want to cause him any disruption.' I don't point out that there's more than enough disruption coming Lucas's way. 'You're happy for him to live with you?'

'Of course.' I don't know how Lucas will handle his father going to Los Angeles. He'll be furious, of course, but when Shelby is here, Lucas doesn't want him interfering. How am I going to tiptoe my way through this minefield?

'I'll make a proper arrangement to pay you for his upkeep. You won't have to worry about money. The pay cheque is also very flattering.'

'You already do so much for us.' Financially, Shelby really looks after us and, now that we have some more fundraising ideas in place, I'm hoping we won't have to be so reliant on him.

He turns and puts his hands on my arms. 'I'm not turning my back on you,' he says. 'I promise.'

'I love you,' I tell him, frankly. I'm not a great one for expressions of emotion, but I do love him. I love him for who he is as a man, not as an actor or a Hollywood star. I'd be happier if none of that was in our lives, but that's who he is.

'I know that things haven't been easy recently,' he says. 'I should have discussed this with you. It's the meetings that have kept me from coming back, but I wanted to be sure. I didn't want it all to come to nothing and worry you unnecessarily.'

'I thought that you might have been seeing one of your younger, prettier, less animal-mad colleagues,' I confess.

'No, never.' He looks at me, dismayed. 'Did you really think that of me?'

'To be honest, I didn't know what to think.'

He takes me into his arms. 'This will be a temporary measure. If I can make it there, I can make it anywhere.'

'That's New York,' I remind him. 'Even I know that.'

'Ah, yes.' A wry smile. 'Do I have your blessing? It would mean everything to me.'

'If that's what you really want to do, then you should go.' How can I hold him back?

'I'll return to England as often as I can.'

'I'll make sure you do,' I say.' But if he hardly managed to visit from Birmingham, in reality how often will that be? 'When will you go?'

'Straight after Christmas. They start filming imminently. That's if we get the paperwork sorted. It's not a done deal quite yet. Until there's ink on a contract, these things can slip through your fingers.'

That's how I feel too. It seems as if Shelby is slipping through my fingers. I don't think I can keep him here on the farm. It's my love, not his.

Chapter Seventy

We walk back to the caravan. 'Shall I tell Lucas?' Shelby asks.

'It's probably better if I do,' I say. 'It's been a long day. Now really isn't the best time.'

I can't cope with any more emotion. All I need is to put my feet up.

I feed the dogs in the yard and decided to banish them for the night. They'll be fine snuggled up in the barn. Not quite as cosy as my bedroom, but it won't hurt them for once. Reluctantly, I turn off the Christmas tree lights. The tree looks so beautiful that I can't bear for it to fall into darkness. I click the switch. Until tomorrow.

However, I do leave the lights on that Lucas has strung around the caravan which is still a bright little spot. I like these so much I might leave them on all year round.

We phone for a takeaway and, eventually, it arrives. Lucas joins us, but it's a subdued affair. I don't ask in front of Shelby, but I'm pretty certain that he hasn't been able to speak to Aurora. He'd be a lot cheerier if he had. It was a shame she missed his performance today. I love to hear Lucas's poems and it's a rare occasion when he deigns to read them in public.

After dinner, Lucas beats a hasty retreat to his bedroom. Shelby and I cuddle up on the sofa. The windows are steamed up and I close the curtains, shutting out the night. I should get a little fake tree to put up in here as it's not very festive yet and Christmas is hurtling towards us.

I rest my head on Shelby's shoulder, savouring the short time I have him to myself. He's due back in Birmingham in the morning but, for tonight, he's mine.

'What will you do with the manor while you're away?' I ask. 'I know it's been on your mind.'

'I might rent it out,' he says. 'But I'm not that keen on doing so. I don't like it standing empty, though.'

'I have a possible solution to that,' I venture. 'One of our students is living in a terrible situation. Her father beats her mum. It's awful. They were still here when you arrived.'

'I noticed the woman with the black eye,' Shelby says. 'I meant to ask.'

'It's a regular occurrence and it seems to be getting worse. I've urged them to leave but the mother, Jess, says they've nowhere to go. I could try to get them into a refuge, but that's not ideal over Christmas. I was wondering if they could move into the manor cottage for the time being. Until they get sorted.'

'The manor is standing empty too. They could go there.'

'I don't think they'd like that. It's not very well . . . homely.'

'Is that why you don't like it?'

'It a beautiful house,' I say, honestly. 'But it's not a home. I think they'd be happier with somewhere smaller and cosier. I'm sure they'd feel safe in the cottage.' I like the idea that there are security gates, CCTV cameras. That would surely keep out any unwanted or unexpected visitors.

'I have no problem with that,' Shelby says. 'They're welcome to stay there as long as they need to.'

322

'Thank you.' I kiss his cheek. 'You're a good man.'

'I fall way short,' he says. 'But I do try.'

'I'll tell her tomorrow. It's a big step, but I bet they'll be relieved that there's a way out for them.'

'No one should have to live in fear.'

'No,' I agree.

'Lucas seemed to be getting on very well with the daughter. Is his girlfriend – what was her name? – still on the scene?'

'Very much so,' I say.

'She seemed a bit old for him.'

What can I say? I wholeheartedly agree, but it seems as if Aurora will be in our lives like it or not. 'Lucas is besotted.'

'Young love,' Shelby muses.

I steer him onto safer ground and we talk about the continuing dramas in Pantoland, until my eyes start to roll.

'To bed,' Shelby says and I'm so tired that I don't even do my usual night-time round of the animals before we hit the sack for the night.

We lie in bed and he takes me in his arms.

'Just hold me for tonight.' I don't want to make love. I'm tired, emotional and, with the baby, it would seem like a terrible intrusion. Once he's got his contract finalised, then I'll tell him. Hopefully, we can spend some quality time together over Christmas and he'll have time to get used to the idea.

Shelby falls asleep almost instantly, but I lie awake. I'm in the shelter of his embrace, but I feel there's a gulf between us. Our lives are becoming more like one of the storylines in his soap opera. Life might have been considerably lonelier before he arrived but, in truth, it was a lot more straightforward. I wonder how much I know the real man behind the façade. Something that Lucas frequently points out is that it's all an act. Shelby has been hiding his Hollywood negotiations from me and I'm hiding the fact that I'm pregnant. I think of Lucas's poem *Secrets 'n' Lies* – one of the first I knew he'd written. I guess that we all have secrets and lies. Putting my hands on my belly, I feel the secret of the life that I'm carrying there. And wonder just how long I can keep it that way.

Chapter Seventy-One

In the morning, Shelby leaves early. We are quiet and sad with each other. He gives me the keys to the cottage at Homewood Manor, so that I can offer it to Penny's mum. I kiss him as he gets into his car and wave at the gate as he drives away, trying to push away the overwhelming sorrow that I feel. This should be a happy time. It's Christmas and I'm having a baby. I should be basking in a glow that's currently eluding me. Perhaps because I need him more than ever, the separation seems all the harder. I don't know. New territory for me.

Routine, I think, is the way forward. So, as I do every day, I see to the animals, walk the dogs and try to bury my head in the sand. When I get back to the caravan, Lucas is up and dressed.

'Dad's gone?'

'Yes.'

'Did you tell him about me and Aurora? The baby?'

'Not yet. I think Christmas would be a good time.'

'Not the present he'll be expecting,' Lucas says.

'No.' I should tell him that his father may well be heading off to Los Angeles after Christmas, but there's time enough to do that too.

Hopefully, at Christmas, we'll be more relaxed, feeling good-will to all men and our various bombshells won't seem so bad at all. I have everything crossed.

'I'm going to see Aurora today.' Lucas looks relieved. 'Can I bunk off for a few hours?'

'Yes, sure. You worked really hard yesterday.' I look him squarely in the eye. 'And your poems were brilliant. Promise me you'll still try to find time to write when the baby comes.'

'Oh, yeah,' he says. 'Me and Aurora are going to keep it as real as we can. When you're young parents you have more energy.'

I don't point out to Lucas that, on the whole, he has very little energy now. His lie-ins until noon are soon to be a thing of the past. We've still yet to determine where and how they will live. Mind you, the same goes for me. I want Lucas here with me, but we can't all live in the caravan. Could we all move into Homewood Manor and be one big happy family? It would be a lovely idea. In reality, it might take some working out.

When Bev arrives, all bouncy and buoyant, she lifts my spirits.

'Yesterday was a flipping *triumph*!' she declares.

'Apart from the impromptu demonstration of alpaca love.'

'It only added to the atmosphere,' she says. 'Bless 'em.'

Bless 'em, indeed.

'I couldn't face doing it last night, so I'll total all the money today,' she continues. 'It's looking good though. Santa left us a nice present too. A cheque for a thousand quid.'

'He did?'

'Yeah. Top bloke.'

I must ring and thank Christian profusely. He's a good friend to us.

'So? While we're feeling flushed with success, do you fancy doing a spring open day?'

I groan. 'Let me get over this one first!'

Bev laughs. 'I've got a wedding to fit in before then.'

'Have you got a date yet?'

'No, but it will be soon. No point hanging about, eh? Strike while the iron's hot and all that.'

'Has Alan recovered from the shock?'

'Not quite,' she says. 'He did have a few large whiskies last night.'

We laugh together. 'I bet!'

'You really will be my bridesmaid, matron of honour, whatever?'

'Of course, I'll be delighted.'

Bev hugs me. 'How did it go with Shelby?'

'OK. I didn't tell him about the baby. The timing was wrong.'

She eyes my tummy. 'He didn't notice?'

If I'm honest, he was so caught up in his own dilemmas that I'm not sure he noticed me at all. 'No.'

'He'll need to know soon.'

'Christmas,' I say. 'I'll tell him then.'

Bev raises her eyebrows. 'That poor man's got a shock coming to him.'

'He's thinking of taking a job in Hollywood,' I admit. 'We might not be seeing much of him for the next year.'

'Surely, he won't go when he knows about the baby – both of them!'

'I wanted him to make his decision without complications. I can't be the one to hold him here, Bev.'

'You are a funny one,' my friend says. 'But you know that you'll have our support whatever you decide to do.'

'Thanks.'

'I'll get on and organise the students. We've a fair bit of tidying up to do today.'

'Lucas isn't going to be around. He's gone to see Aurora. I

327

hope they'll sort out some details of their situation. I was wondering – in an optimistic moment – whether we all might live together at Homewood Manor.'

'It would be a good idea,' Bev says. 'I think. It could work brilliantly, or you'd all kill each other within a fortnight.'

'One thing I did discuss with Shelby was the possibility of Penny and her mum living in the cottage there if she wants to and he agreed. I'm going to call her and see what she thinks.'

'Now that is an inspired idea.'

'Fingers crossed that she's willing to try. I can't bear to see how worn-down Penny looks. Potentially, this could transform their situation.'

'The cottage has been empty for a while,' Bev muses. 'It will need a good clean and freshen up.'

'I thought we could find a few hours to go over there this week.'

Bev nods. 'Shouldn't be a problem.'

'Penny's not here yet, but when Jess drops her off, I'll see if I can have a word with her.'

So, while Bev herds the students up to the barn, I clean up in the tea room while I wait for Penny and Jess to arrive. I set to and sweep the floor, swishing the broom vigorously to get rid of trodden-in cake. As I do, I get a sharp pain low down in my stomach which takes my breath away. I'm going to have to start taking things a little easier, I realise. I've been heaving feed bags around this morning and I probably shouldn't.

Then I hear a car at the gate and it's Jess dropping Penny off, so I dash outside.

'Morning!' They both look worn out and I wonder if they've had another difficult night. 'Everyone's in the barn,' I say to Penny as she climbs out of the car. 'Catch up with them. I want a word with your mum.'

'Nothing bad?' Penny says, anxiously.

'No. Nothing to worry about. I'll be up there in a minute.'

Jess has wound down her car window and I lean on the door. 'Fancy coming in for a quick cuppa? I have a proposal.'

'Sure.' She parks up and we walk to the tea room where I make a brew.

'I've got the keys to a small cottage,' I tell her when we're seated with our mugs of tea. 'It's tiny, but very lovely and not far from here. My partner is the owner and he says that you can stay there free of charge for as long as you need.'

Her eyes well with tears. 'Why would you do that for us?'

'Because no one should live in fear and, if I can help, I will.'

'Penny always says how lovely you are.'

'We can go and look at it if you'd like.'

Jess shakes her head. 'If you say it's nice then that's enough for me. Anywhere is better than where we are now. I'd rather live in a tent.'

'Give me a couple of days to sort it out. We could move you at the weekend?'

'He'll be around then.' She hangs her head. 'It would have to be during the week when he's at work.'

'Friday, then?'

'I'm afraid,' she admits. 'What if he finds out where we are?'

'The cottage is behind a high wall with security gates and cameras everywhere. I think you'll be safe there.' I take her hand. 'Safer than you are now. For Penny's sake, you have to try. This can't go on.'

Jess nods. 'Thank you, Molly.'

'We'll keep in touch this week. Bev and I will go and get it ready for you.'

We both stand up and hug each other.

Penny's mum looks at me with tears in her eyes. 'This will give us a new start, a second chance.'

I smile at her. 'That's what Hope Farm is all about.'

Chapter Seventy-Two

When Jess goes, I set off for the barn, but get another sharp pain that stops me in my tracks. This feels serious. I divert to the caravan and nip into the loo. There's blood, a lot of it, like a heavy period, and I know in my heart that the tiny speck of life that was my baby has gone.

I sit there for a long time, head in hands. It's gone. I'm not going to be a mum. Shelby isn't going to be a dad again. I can't begin to describe to you the emptiness I feel inside. Rationally, I know that the time wasn't right, that things would be difficult, that, possibly, Shelby wasn't even the right man for this, but I so wanted this child. I didn't realise just how much until now.

I don't know how much time passes but the next thing I know is that Bev has opened the caravan door and is shouting, 'Molly? Molly, are you there?'

'In here,' I call back.

'I wondered where you'd gone. Are you all right?'

It takes me a moment to answer.

'No,' I say. 'Not really. I'll be out in a mo.'

'Shall I come in?' Bev asks.

'No. But stay. Please.'

Then, when I've gathered my wits together, I mobilise myself and get up from the loo. I peel off my clothes and wrap a towel round me before emerging from the bathroom.

Bev only needs to take one look at my face to know what's wrong. 'Oh, my love.'

'It's gone,' I say.

She holds me tight and rocks me. I let out all the emotion that's been building up over the past month or so and cry my heart out. I should be able to turn to Shelby and am saddened to think that I can't.

'You will have another baby,' Bev insists as she lets me go. 'But next time it will be right. This little one obviously wasn't mean to be.'

It doesn't make me feel any better.

'Go and get a shower,' Bev says. 'I'll pop your things in the washing machine.'

'Thanks, Bev.'

She touches my arm. 'Will you tell Shelby?'

'No,' I say. 'You're the only one who knows.'

I head for the shower and let the hot water soothe me. I stay under the jets for as long as I can, eyes closed, trying to count my blessings. I'm young, relatively, healthy and I am loved. That's more than many people can say.

Bev is still waiting when I come out, clean and dressed again. The kettle has just boiled which makes me smile. Tea, the answer to everything.

'You'll be all right,' she says.

'I will.' It makes me think that I would like another chance to have a baby, but not like this, not now. If I want to try for a child, then I should discuss it properly with Shelby. The next year or more we should concentrate on Lucas and his needs. There's no doubt that he'll require a lot of support. I can get my baby fix that way. Plus, if we think about a child, then it should be when Shelby is back from Los Angeles. All very rational, but it doesn't stop my heart from breaking.

'Go and have a sleep,' Bev says. 'Alan and I will sort the kids out today.'

'Sure you can manage?'

'Yeah. They're all in good spirits today, so there are no problems.'

'Don't speak too soon,' I say.

'I did have my fingers crossed when I said it.' Bev turns me towards the bedroom and instructs, 'Bed.'

'OK.'

So I go to lie down and, within minutes, sleep takes me.

It's dark outside when I wake up and, for a moment, I'm completely disorientated. As I'm not usually in bed at this time of day, it takes time to work out where I am and why I'm here. Then it hits me again, but not quite so hard. Beneath the sadness, there's a kernel of acceptance.

'It wasn't our time,' I whisper out loud and hope that the baby can hear me.

Then there's a soft knock at the door and Bev pokes her head round it. 'Came to check on you, chick.'

'I'm fine,' I say and I know that, in time, I will be.

'I've got some visitors for you.' On cue, the three dogs barrel in and bounce onto the bed to lick me to death. They act as if they haven't seen me for at least three years and the cuddles of an excited doggy can soothe even the weariest of souls.

I push them off for a second so that I prop myself up and Bev comes to sit on the bed next to me.

'The kids have gone, the animals are fed and I've walked the dogs – not that you'd know from the state of them. It's impossible to tire this lot out, even the one with three legs.'

'You're an angel.'

'Try to have a quiet night. If you don't feel like work tomorrow, we can all cope. Stay in bed.'

But she knows me better than that.

'I mean it!'

'Physically, I'm all right.' Emotionally, it will take a little longer.

'You should still go and see the doctor.'

'Yes.' But we both know that I won't. 'Has Lucas come back yet?'

'Haven't seen him all day,' Bev says.

'I'm taking that as a good sign.' I hope that he and Aurora are enjoying some much-needed time together and are making plans for their future. That obviously doesn't stop me from fretting about him. I'll give him a call in a while to see what he's up to. I notice on my phone that Shelby has messaged me, but I can't reply to him now, not yet.

'I've checked your fridge and you've got stuff in for dinner. Do you want me to knock something together?'

'I can manage. Really. I'll just potter.'

'Well, if you're sure I can't do anything, then I'll be off.' She looks reluctant to leave. 'You know where I am. Call me and I'll be back in five minutes.'

'I know. Thanks.'

When Bev goes, I lie in bed, surrounded by dogs, letting my mind mull over all that's happened. I'm still worn out and drift in and out of sleep.

Then my phone rings. It's Lucas. 'Hi,' I say.

'I don't know what to do.' He's slurring his words and it sounds like he's crying.

'Lucas, are you OK? What's the matter? Where are you?'

There's snivelling down the line. 'I don't know.'

'Aren't you with Aurora? What's happened?'

'I'm in the park,' he says. 'Please Molly, come and get me.'

Then, helpfully, his phone goes dead.

Chapter Seventy-Three

Despite calling Lucas repeatedly, there's no answer. I don't know if his battery is dead or whether, for some reason, he's unable to answer. Why does technology never work when you need it most?

In a panic, I jump out of bed and hurriedly get dressed, my own problems instantly pushed aside. Still punching his number into my phone, I take Little Dog with me for company and comfort, then head for the car. He said he was in a park, but where?

Hands shaking, I sit in the driver's seat googling parks in this area and it's surprising how many there are. When you live on a farm, there's not really a great need to go to a park so I'm not familiar with them. I scroll through the list.

Shitshitshit! Where do I start? Which is the most likely one for him to be in? And where the hell is Aurora? I wonder if they've had an argument. Seems the most feasible explanation. Shamefully, I realise how little I know about Lucas's girlfriend. I don't have her surname, her telephone number or even know where she lives. I should know these things and I don't. Damn.

Taking a few calming breaths, I try to think about how I'm going to approach this. I come to the conclusion that I'm simply going to have to visit each local park, slowly, methodically until I find him. There's no other way. Checking there's a torch in the car, I set off.

Little Dog and I search the first two parks nearest to Hope Farm but that proves fruitless as, quite sensibly, no one is hanging around in a park on a cold winter's night. I decide, instead, to head straight to the main park in the town. It's not the best place to be after dark, but needs must. Little Dog, when riled, is an excellent barker and, though he's tiny, it feels nice not to be doing this alone. I'm sure, if provoked, he'd be a great ankle-biter.

When I reach the town park a few minutes later, I leave the car in a deserted side street and head through the gates – which, thankfully, aren't locked. It's pitch black, freezing and I'd rather be anywhere else than here.

'Come on, boy,' I say. 'Do your stuff. Find Lucas.' Little Dog trots ahead of me, sniffing everything. I follow behind, grateful for the comforting beam of my torch. 'Go on. Find him.'

When I reach the main grassy area, I call his name at the top of my voice. 'Lucas! Lucas!'

Then I follow the footpath, heading deeper into the worryingly empty park, shouting as I go. My torch beam lights on a scruffy man coming towards me out of the darkness and, for a moment, my heart stops. I hear Little Dog give a low growl and he backs up to be by my side.

'If you're looking for a kid,' the man says, 'there's a lad up on the playground by himself.'

'Thanks. Thank you so much.' In different times, I might ask why he didn't stop to find out what was wrong, but I can only hope that this is Lucas.

Little Dog, running ahead of me, starts to bark. I put a spurt on and, a minute later, come to the playground. There, sprawled in one of the nest swings, head hanging down, is Lucas. I feel sick with relief that I have found him and that he is safe.

I go over to him and he raises his head to peer at me. When I shine my torch at him, he winces.

'Hey,' he says and raises a hand in greeting.

'What the hell, Lucas? You scared the life out of me.'

'Soz.' He goes to get out of the swing and only succeeds in tipping himself onto the floor. Little Dog goes to lick his face and Lucas lies there, inert, while he does.

I help him up. 'Are you drunk?'

'Very,' he says, struggling to focus his glassy eyes.

Of course he is. And, now that I look, there's a plethora of Stella Artois cans around the area. 'Are all these yours?'

'Yes, Mummy,' he slurs.

I pick up the cans and put them in the nearest bin. It's a lot of cans.

'What the hell has happened? Have you fallen out with Aurora?'

He takes a few unsteady steps. 'You could say that.'

'Where is she now?'

'Fuck knows,' Lucas spits as he staggers.

'OK.' He's clearly in no fit state to have a reasonable conversation now. 'Let's get you home first and you can tell me all about it later.'

So I help him up and he puts his arm round me and sags heavily against me while we slowly make our way back to the car. Little Dog thinks it's a great game and dashes around us both.

'I love you,' Lucas slurs. 'Did I ever tell you that I really do bloody love you?'

336

'I love you too. Just keep walking,' I say to him. 'One foot in front of the other. You can do it.'

'You're my best friend,' he insists.

Then he stops and is violently sick in a flowerbed. I think this is going to be a long night.

Chapter Seventy-Four

Lucas sleeps in the car, snoring loudly, all the way back to Hope Farm. He only rouses as I get out to open the gate.

'Where are we?' he mutters.

'Home,' I tell him and very grateful I am for that. At least I found him without too much trouble and didn't spend half of the night tracking him down. I am thankful for small mercies. Bev and Alan will be furious that I didn't call them out, but how could I? They already do so much for me and I didn't want to worry them further. With Alan's health scare, they should be having a relaxing time too.

I help Lucas across the yard and into the caravan while Little Dog runs round our legs trying his best to trip us both. Inside, I make Lucas a strong cup of peppermint tea. He sits on the sofa, head an inch from the table, and sips at it.

I wasn't sure that he would keep it down, but it seems to be going OK, so I risk asking, 'Do you want anything to eat?'

'Bacon,' he slurs. 'Bacon sandwich.'

'We're vegan,' I remind him.

'Oh.'

'Toast?'

He shakes his head and seems to regret the sudden movement.

Sitting opposite him, I give him a long look. I think, after his sleep in the car, he appears a little more sober. 'Now then, what's to do?'

It takes a while for him to organise his lips to form the words before he says, 'Aurora and I have broken up.'

'Oh, dear.' Just as I suspected. 'These things happen. I'm sure it will blow over. You're both under a lot of pressure at the moment. There's a lot to think about with the baby and everything else.'

He looks up and tears fall from his eyes, tracking slowly down his cheeks.

'Oh, Lucas.' I go and sit next to him. This time, he doesn't resist my embrace, he wraps his arms around me and holds on tightly. I stroke his hair. 'Does it all seem too much? We can help. We need to tell your dad as soon as possible and then we can both be here to support you.'

He sobs louder.

'It's not ideal,' I offer. 'But it's not insurmountable either. I don't want you to worry. I know it's a daunting thing, a big step in both of your lives, but you should try to enjoy it.'

He prises himself away from me and takes in a great gulp of air. 'The baby's not mine.'

'What?'

Lucas turns huge, tearful eyes to mine and repeats, 'It's not mine.'

I'm struggling to take this in, so goodness only knows how Lucas feels.

'She's been seeing her tutor at college. For months. Probably longer. She wouldn't say. He's married and already has two kids.'

I don't voice what I'm thinking. So she needed a dad for her child and duped Lucas? This is terrible and Lucas's pain feeds into my own.

'She never thought he'd leave his wife, but he has. They're going to play happy families together and I'm binned.' He looks at me bleakly. 'He's as old as my fucking *dad*.'

'Oh, my darling boy.' We hug each other again.

'I don't know what to do,' he says. 'I feel like I did when Mum died.'

'It's only natural. You love her.'

'I really wanted that baby,' Lucas cries. 'I know everyone thinks I'm too young, but I'd have been a great dad. And, all along, she knew it was someone else's. How could she *do* that?'

'That's cruel of her,' I tell him. And it is. What a terrible thing to do to someone, especially someone as young and vulnerable as Lucas. I feel like I could kill her with my bare hands – perhaps that's my mothering instinct coming to the fore. But then I think that Aurora is young and foolish too and will soon find out that life is more difficult than she can have possibly imagined.

'I believed her,' Lucas wails. 'I believed all her lies.'

'I know you won't want to hear this now, but she wasn't the right girl for you. You'll look back on this and realise, but I know how it must feel now.'

'What if I never find anyone else to love?'

'You have years and years ahead of you. Plenty of time to meet someone else to love and to have a child with.'

'But what if I don't? What if I leave it too late, like you?'

Lucas has no idea how much that hurts. How could he? I have to bear my loss alone. 'That won't happen. I promise you.'

'I don't think I'm ever going to have sex again. Or at least not until I'm twenty-five.'

'The last bit sounds like a very good idea,' I joke in an attempt to add levity to this awful situation and he gives a weak, snotty laugh.

'How will I ever trust anyone?' He looks so crushed that it's heart-breaking.

'In time the pain will fade and you'll learn how to handle it – just as you have so brilliantly with losing your mum.'

'I went to the park and got royally pissed,' he points out.

'I don't blame you for that. Though please never do it again without telling me where you are.'

'It seems as if nothing ever works out well for me,' he sobs. 'All I want is to be loved and for someone to love me.'

'*I* adore you,' I tell him through my own tears. 'My life has been *infinitely* better with you in it.'

'Yeah,' he sniffs, 'but you had a shit life before.'

We both manage a laugh at that.

'I know you think your dad doesn't care, but he does.' Then I think about Shelby heading off to Los Angeles. That bombshell has yet to come. How will Lucas cope with that? 'Bev and Alan love you like family. And all of the students hero-worship you.'

'You can't tell my dad,' he insists. 'He can never know about this.'

'He would understand.'

'Promise me,' Lucas says. 'It has to be just us.'

'Bev and Matt know, too.'

'They won't tell, though, will they?'

'No. Because they love you as much as I do. You've made a very good friend in Matt. If you don't want to talk to me, you can always confide in him.'

He nods. 'I feel like such an idiot. I believed Aurora. I really believed her.'

Then he cries like the child he is for the child that he's lost. And, as I don't know what else to do, I join in and cry for Lucas and for my own loss too.

Chapter Seventy-Five

Lucas and I stay up well into the night talking and, for the first time ever, he really opens up to me. He tells me all about his mum and what she was like. I learn about his hopes and dreams for the future. He tells me how much he loves it here with the animals and it makes my chest swell with pride. For the first time, he's like an open book. I cherish it all and hold it in my heart as I feel it might not last. He drinks more tea, eats some toast and, by the time we fall into bed at three o'clock, I think we're both in a better place. Only time will tell.

I'm so sad for him that his hopes of love, of a family have ended in such a shattering way. It's sounds so trite to say 'it's for the best', but I'm sure that it is. From the start, I thought that Aurora wasn't right for him. Lucas is learning too fast that life isn't always easy and I hope that I can steer him through it.

I get up, as usual, at five-thirty, but I leave Lucas sleeping. I'm sure he'll have an almighty hangover when he does wake. I pull on my clothes, unleash the dogs, and go out into the fresh, frosty morning. My excitable hounds run round checking all their favourite spots. Whatever happens in the world, this place is an anchor. The dogs are still relentlessly cheerful, the sheep remain stupidly stoic and the alpacas will always be naughty.

After yesterday's drama and subsequent lack of sleep, I feel all wobbly today and it's more of an effort to heft the food around, but this lot won't wait for their breakfast. I take more time with each of them, handing out a little extra food, sneaking a little extra cuddle. It works with the students and it works with me too – animals are calming and their love is unconditional. I sit in with the bunnies and guinea pigs and they all come to have a snuggle on my lap – after which, my equilibrium is greatly restored.

Bev and Alan turn up. I wait while they kiss and cuddle as if they are to be parted for ten years. Eventually, Alan disappears into his workshop.

Bev scrutinises me with a laser gaze. 'How are you doing?'

'I'm OK. I did, however, not have the restful evening I'd planned.' I fill her in on the events of last night.

'You should have phoned me,' she admonishes, as I knew she would. 'We could have come to look with you. Fancy going out on your own – *after what you've been through*.' The last bit in a stage whisper.

'All's well that ends well,' I say. 'Lucas is still in bed for now.'

'That poor boy,' Bev tuts. 'He's had a bucketful.'

'Better that he's found out now.'

'You've not told Shelby?'

'He remains blissfully unaware of *all* of our issues.'

'Probably for the best,' she says.

'Least said, soonest mended.'

'Promise me that you'll take it easy today, Molly. Otherwise, I might just have to march you down to the doctor's.'

'I fed the animals, but promise that I'll do nothing more remotely strenuous.'

'It's a glorious day. We could take the animals out for a walk. I'm sure kids and creatures would appreciate that.'

'As long as they're all wrapped up.'

'I'm going over to clean the cottage tonight,' she says. 'And you're *not* coming. Alan and I will do it.'

'But . . .'

She holds up a hand. 'Talk to that.'

'Can I come if I promise to sit on a chair and watch?'

'Yes,' Bev says. 'But don't make me tie you to it.'

'OK.'

'I do have some good news,' my friend offers. 'We counted up the money from the open day last night and we took a shade over two thousand pounds. How about that?'

'We did? That's fantastic.'

'People were very generous and I have plans for *lots* more,' Bev says with a wicked twinkle in her eye.

'It'll be like Alton Towers,' I tease.

'Never,' she says, 'But it *will* help our finances considerably. More importantly, the kids love it too. It's good for them to be involved in something like this. They were all so proud of themselves, they were buzzing.'

'I know and I'm very grateful to you for pushing me out of my comfort zone too. Just be gentle with me. This is all very new.'

Then the students start to turn up. 'I'll sort this lot out,' Bev says. 'I bet they'll all still be hyper today. You tend to Lucas.'

'Thanks. You're an angel. I'll go and see how he is.' But before I can do that, Matt's car turns up too.

'Aye, aye.' Bev nudges me. 'Hot Mayor alert.'

With a grin at her, I go over to the gate and Matt jumps out of his car. 'Can't stop,' he says. 'On the way to an event. Christmas craft fair to open.'

'It's good to see you.' And seeing him has, indeed, lifted my spirits. 'I was going to contact you to thank you for all your help at the open day. Bev's just told me we raised over two grand plus we had a very generous donation from our celebrity Santa.'

'Wow. That's great.'

'Thank you for being part of it.'

'You know if there's anything else you want me to do, you only have to ask.'

'Well . . .' I say hesitantly. 'There is one thing. Penny and her mum are moving into the cottage at Shelby's manor. I was wondering if you were free at all on Friday. They need to get out while her husband is at work. If you have any time at all . . .'

'I'll make time,' Matt says. 'Tell me when and where you want me and I'll switch my diary around.'

'You're so very kind.'

'There is, however, a price,' he says with a grin. 'You *have* to come to my charity ball.'

'I thought you'd be taking Victoria. She seemed very nice.'

'She is.' He holds out his hands. 'It didn't quite work out for us. A few dates and the conversation ran dry. We're different people. She wants fancy bars and designer what-nots. Like you, I'd rather be a foot-deep in cow poo.'

I laugh. 'And I thought I came across as an elegant sophisticate.'

'Say you'll come,' he begs. 'It's for your cause and I hope it will raise a lot of money. It would be so much better if you were there.'

'How can I say no?'

'Excellent. I like a bit of gentle bribery and coercion.'

Weirdly, I no longer feel quite the terror that I would have done at the thought of attending a posh event like that. I've come a long way, I'll tell you. I have to thank Bev for that, and

Shelby. They've both forced me to do things that I could never have imagined before.

'Why are you grinning?' Matt asks.

'Not so long ago something like a charity ball would have filled me with dread, but I might actually be looking forward to it. Just a little bit.'

'I'll make sure you have a great night.'

And, the thing is, I know that he will. Matt won't ditch me while he talks to pretty young things or holds court. Above everything, he'll make sure that I'm all right, that I enjoy myself too. 'Stay for tea?'

'Can't,' he says. 'I have to dash. I just wanted to say hello while I was passing. Let me know what time on Friday and I'll be there.'

I lean on the gate and watch him go. It's totally and utterly wrong of me to be relieved that it didn't work out with Victoria, right? But I am.

Chapter Seventy-Six

Lucas is quiet and withdrawn but I'm sure that, given time, he'll learn to live with this new pain. But it's so sad that he has to. My heart still bleeds for him.

In the evening, I go with Bev and Alan to clean the cottage for Penny and her mum. Lucas comes along too and we add a few extra touches to make the place seem more welcoming.

On Friday morning, Matt turns up as promised and we drive to Penny and Jess's current home. I probably could have done this myself, but it's nice to have Matt as back up in case there's any trouble. When we arrive, they are both ready and waiting, anxiously, suitcases packed. As quickly as we can, we load them into Matt's car. Thankfully, there's no sign of her husband or any nosy neighbours, but I can tell that they're both nervous and keen to be gone.

'It'll be OK,' I assure them. 'We'll support you all we can.'

'There's so much to think about,' Jess says. 'My brain's in a spin.'

'I think you'll feel better when you see where you're going to live. It will give you some breathing space, if nothing else.'

So we set off, two fearful women in the back of the car, and head towards Homewood Manor. They're quiet en route and I understand that. They don't know what the future holds and have put a lot of trust in me to bring them this far. Yet as we turn up at Homewood Manor, punch in the security code and wait for the tall gates to swing open, I hear Jess gasp.

'Is this where we'll be living?'

'Yes,' I say. 'You'll be safe here.'

'Look at this place,' she whispers. 'Won't we be grand, Penny?'

'You're in the cottage next door to the main house,' I tell her. 'But there's a housekeeper who lives here and a gardener who comes in every day. So you won't be completely by yourselves. You need a code for the gate and the whole place is covered by CCTV. It's as private and secure as it can be.'

'Who lives here?'

'It belongs to my partner, Shelby. But he's away at the moment.' And for the foreseeable future. 'You can stay as long as you need to.'

We pull up next to the cottage and, with Jess and Penny still looking slightly dazed, go indoors.

Waiting inside are Bev and Lucas. Dear Bev has laid out a nice lunch ready for us all. She's also done a big shop for Penny and Jess and I know that the cupboards are filled with enough food to keep them going for the next few weeks, at least.

Lucas is standing by the Christmas tree that we put up as an extra surprise and, as soon as he sees us all, he turns on the lights. 'Ta-dah!'

They fill the room with a welcoming glow.

Jess looks at me astounded. 'You've done so much.'

'We wanted to make it as cosy as possible,' I say. 'I hope you'll be comfortable here, but do let me know if there's anything else you need. We've tried to think of everything.'

'We'll be happier here,' she says. 'I know. Won't we, Pen?' She hugs her daughter to her.

'Yeah.' Penny looks relieved to be here too and that's good to see.

'You have friends who'll support you through it,' I remind her. 'Don't struggle with this alone. If you need to chat or to see a friendly face, you're welcome at the farm anytime.'

She looks at the rest of the cottage and then we all sit to share lunch. There's a nice, festive atmosphere and it's good to see that Lucas and Penny are getting on famously. I even hear him laugh.

Matt looks across at me and winks. *Well done,* he mouths. *Thanks,* I mouth back.

After lunch, we leave them to settle in. They wave at the door as we head down the long drive and back towards the farm. We pull up at the gate and I sit in the car next to Matt, enjoying his company. I have much to do, but am reluctant to get out of the fuggy warmth with the heater on full blast, toasting my toes. My eyes are heavy and I'm drowsy, feeling the effects of my missing night of sleep earlier in the week that is now catching up with me.

'That was a job well done,' he says.

'I feel happier now they're out of that situation. I hope they like it there. Shelby says they can stay as long as they like.'

'That's very generous of him.'

'He's a good man,' I say honestly. This is a very kind thing for him to do.

'Lucas seemed a bit quiet,' Matt notes.

'Long story.' If there's one person I can confide in, it's Matt. 'He's no longer going to be a dad. The baby isn't his. She has a much older lover. Married. It seems that Aurora was possibly already pregnant when they met. She's been stringing him along all the time.'

'That's harsh, but there must be a part of you that's relieved.'

'There is,' I admit. 'But I'm hurting for Lucas. He's devastated.'

'Poor lad.'

'A tough lesson,' I agree. 'But he's young and I hope he'll bounce back. I'm trying to spoil him a bit at the moment. Help him through it.'

'Is Shelby supportive?'

'He doesn't even know,' I confess. 'Lucas won't hear of it.'

Matt nods. 'My lips are sealed.'

'I know that I can trust you.' And I do. I don't think I've ever met a more straightforward, genuine man.

'I'll look out for him,' Matt says. 'If you need me to.'

'I'm sure he'd appreciate that.' I smile. 'I know that he likes and respects you. With Lucas, that's a rare thing.'

Matt laughs. 'I take that as a very great honour.' Then he glances at his watch. 'I'll have to go. One last job to do for today.'

That means I have to get out of the lovely warmth of his car and the comfort of his steadfast company.

'I'll see you soon, Molly,' he says. 'Not long until Christmas now.'

'Do you know what you're doing yet?'

'Going home to my family,' Matt says. 'Just for a few days, but it will nice to see everyone. I haven't been up there for a few months.'

'I hope you have a wonderful time.'

'My sister will make sure that I'm fed on the hour, every hour. I'll come back as fat as a house.'

'That's what Christmas is all about.'

Matt laughs. 'What about you?'

'A quiet one. I expect it will just be me, Lucas and Shelby.' We have both been studiously avoiding making plans. I don't

350

even know if he wants to spend it here or at Homewood Manor and I've yet to hear if the contract is signed – though I feel it's a given.

We've still been Skyping each other while the panto continues unabated, but with less regularity. There are secrets hanging between us now and I feel that withholding so much from him makes conversation more stilted. We never really get beyond exchanging pleasantries. Perhaps this is the difficulty of long-distance relationships.

'I'll try to pop up again before I leave,' Matt says. 'I'd like to wish Lucas a merry Christmas.'

I look to see where Lucas is, but he came back with Bev and must have already disappeared into one of the barns. Having taken the morning off, we have a lot to catch up on this afternoon.

Reluctantly, it's time for me to go out into the cold and get on with my day. 'I should go.'

Matt leans over and gently kisses my cheek. 'Merry Christmas, Molly.'

'Merry Christmas, Matt.'

Then I open the door, get out and go through the gate. Matt reverses down the lane and I watch as he goes. My head is whirling with all kinds of thoughts and emotions, but I can't catch onto any of them. However, I do know that I'll be glad to see the back of this week.

Chapter Seventy-Seven

We don't have students here at the weekend, as a rule. So, today, it's just me and Lucas. Yesterday, he spent most of the day secreted in his room, only coming out for meals, so I hope he's feeling a little more amenable today. All I want is a nice, quiet Sunday with no drama.

All the animals seem fine this morning. The alpacas are well-behaved and even Anthony the Anti-Social Sheep is quite sociable. The temperature is dropping rapidly and we seem to have our own much chillier micro-climate here on our exposed site so I give everyone a little extra food as we'll do all through the winter.

When Lucas eventually wakes up, he's in a reasonably good mood, which is a relief. 'You seem a bit better today,' I venture as I pour some cereal into a bowl for him.

He puffs out a world-weary breath as he slides into a seat at the table. 'Life goes on, right?'

'It does.' I put his breakfast in front of him and, with a little more than lethargy, he tucks in. I join him and we eat in companionable silence.

Eventually, he looks up from his bowl of cereal. 'I wrote a poem about it.'

I glance at him hopefully.

Preceded by a lot of tutting and sighing, he says, 'I suppose you'd like to hear it.'

'Very much so.'

'OK.' Lucas flicks open his phone and, on a deep breath, says, '"The Unfired Bullet".'

My slate is clean
my page unwritten,
my slice of life
as yet unbitten.
My conscience clear
I'm indecision,
no prejudice to queer my vision.

No allegiance
no concern,
no moral compass to discern
no hopes,
no dreams,
no blind ambitions,
no regrets,
no learned repressions.

Everyone is equal
until the day they're born
a king is not a king
until his crown is worn.
Anything is possible
when nothing has been done,
I'm the unfired bullet
in the barrel of your gun.

'That's so sad,' I say. 'Beautiful, but very sad.'

Lucas flicks his phone closed. 'None of it is a barrel of laughs, is it?' He lifts his pale face to me. 'On the bright side, I'm finding misery quite motivational.'

'Oh, Lucas.'

'Yeah, well, let's face it, I'm never going to write bloody love sonnets, am I?'

'You did very well with your cheery Christmas poem.'

'That was definitely a one-off.'

That makes me laugh, but Lucas doesn't join in. 'Oh, my darling boy, what can I do to cheer you up?'

'Fuck knows.' His eyes are bright with tears. 'Just don't be too nice or I'll cry.'

'We could decorate the inside of the caravan for Christmas. If you like. We are the only bit lacking festivity. Even if you don't feel like it, I think it would be a good thing to do.'

Lucas shrugs his acceptance.

'There are some spare Christmas lights from Bev's splurge. That should do it.'

'I'll get the step ladders,' he says.

So Lucas brings them from the barn and I find the Christmas lights. I hand them up to Lucas, directing him how to drape them into garlands round the ceiling of the caravan, hooking them onto whatever we can as we go.

'I am an expert in this,' he tells me.

'I know. But let that bit dangle a bit more, just don't cover the door.'

He's in the middle of a heavy sigh when there's the sound of a car in the lane and all the dogs go into a frenzy of barking.

I look out of the window and it's Shelby. 'Your dad's here.'

'Now?'

I don't know who's more surprised, me or Lucas.

354

'Did you know he was coming?' Lucas asks as he climbs down the ladder, lights put aside.

'No. I haven't spoken to him for a few days, but he didn't say anything.' If I'd know he was coming I might have done something with myself. 'I'd better go and let him in.'

So I hurry across the yard to open the gate and Shelby pulls in, giving me a wave as he drives by.

'Hey,' he says as he climbs out of his unfeasibly shiny car. 'Good to see you.'

My heart, as always, tightens when I see him. But now there's a feeling behind it that I can't identify. He looks vibrant, glowing and altogether too polished to be in our humble yard. His pristine jeans, black jumper and jacket make him look like he should be modelling designer clothes or flogging after-shave.

'You should have told me you were coming,' I say as I go to hug him. 'I would have made something special for lunch.'

'Flying visit. As always.'

Arm-in-arm, we walk across to the caravan and, inside, I announce, unnecessarily, 'Look who's here!'

'Good of you to grace us with your precious time, Father,' Lucas replies and, already, we're off.

To his credit, Shelby ignores the barb. 'You look a bit down in the dumps, Son,' he says, cheerily. 'Everything OK?'

'Fine,' Lucas mutters.

I look at Shelby and indicate with my eyes that he should keep quiet. But no, he's not receiving my warning look.

'How's that hot girlfriend of yours?' he asks and, unwittingly, digs himself deeper.

Lucas winces and two spots of red appear on his cheeks. 'Fine,' he says tightly. 'Everything's fine and fucking dandy.'

I think I should separate these two quickly before it ends in pistols at dawn.

'We were trying to spruce up the caravan for Christmas,' I explain.

'Great idea. 'Looks like you're doing a good job there, Son.'

Lucas glowers at him. And Lucas does very good glower. 'Stop calling me "Son".'

'You are my son,' Shelby snaps back.

Oh my giddy aunt. I stand between them. 'Speaking of Christmas, we need to decide where we're going to spend it. I have to organise food and all that. I assume you'd prefer to be at Homewood.'

'Ah,' Shelby says. 'That's really why I'm here. We need to have a talk about that.'

Lucas rolls his eyes. 'Count me out of that one. Some people embrace Christmas, some people have Christmas foisted upon them.' He stomps back up the stepladder and snatches at the lights.

I turn to Shelby and grimace. As always, stuck in the middle. He's looking stony-faced.

'Shall we have a cup of tea or a walk across the fields?' A cup of tea equals not so bad. A walk, something terrible coming.

'A walk, I think,' Shelby says.

'I'll get my coat.' I smile and brace myself for the worst.

Chapter Seventy-Eight

We go over the stile and, instead of taking our usual route over the fields, I turn right and head into the woods that border our property on one side. The mulch of damp, fallen leaves is turning to mud. I'm glad that Shelby put on his wellington boots, even though they don't look like they've seen much in the way of mud action. Possibly another pair purloined from the *Flinton's Farm* prop store.

The dogs run ahead, picking their way along the path and through the trees. Betty Bad Dog bolts after every squirrel that she sees, ever hopeful that one day she might catch one. As she's so over-excited and uncoordinated, I think the squirrel population of Buckinghamshire is quite safe. Every now and then, Little Dog comes back to check that we're still here as Shelby and I follow on behind. The trees are bare skeletons, black silhouettes against the clear blue sky. I like the stripped back minimalism of nature at this time of year but, nevertheless, look forward to spring and wonder what next year will bring for us all at Hope Farm.

When Shelby fails to start a conversation, I revert to my stock question and ask, 'How's the panto going?'

'Good. Good. I'll be glad when it's done. This far into the run, the jokes are starting to wear thin. At least I don't get a custard pie in my face twice a day.'

'Not long until you finish now.'

'No.' He lapses into silence again.

'Penny and Jess have settled into the cottage,' I tell him. 'I can't thank you enough for that. They'll be so much safer there.'

'Not a problem. Glad to be able to help. I haven't been home yet. I'm pushed for time, so I'll head back after a bite of lunch.'

'So soon?'

'Stuff to do tonight,' he offers.

'Oh.'

We walk on, quiet again. I feel the weight of many unspoken words hang in the heavy air between us. Sometimes, when Shelby doesn't have a pre-prepared script, he seems at a loss. When we are deeper into the woods, he takes my hand in his. 'This is tough,' he says.

'You've taken the LA job.'

'Yes.'

'There's no surprise there. I know how much it means to you.'

'I'm planning to stay for a year. Initially. I want to make my mark while I'm there.'

I nod. 'Initially' is a big word.

'I'll get a nice place out there. The studio are being very generous. You can come out as often as you like. With Lucas too,' he says. 'And, of course, I'll come back regularly.'

But he won't and we both know that. It's been hard enough for him to find time to come back from Birmingham to see us.

He rubs at his chin, frowning. 'How do you think Lucas will take it?'

'As always with Lucas, that's anyone's guess.'

'Will you tell him?'

'No,' I say. 'You're his dad. You need to sit and discuss this with him.'

'Huh. You're so much better at talking to him than I am. I just make him cross.'

'You're going to leave him here with me, though?'

'If he wants to stay.'

I experience a moment of dread. I'm sure that Lucas will want to remain here at Hope Farm. He has me, Alan and Bev, the animals, his studies. Surely, he won't want to go? But Lucas is in a fragile place right now and he might think that a change of scene might do him good. Perhaps, like Shelby, his head will be turned by the lure of Hollywood. I simply don't know.

'They want me there as soon as this run has finished.' Shelby wrings his hands. 'Ideally, I'd take the flight on Christmas morning.'

'But you don't finish in panto until Christmas Eve.'

'That's the difficulty.'

'I see.' I jam my hands into my pockets. 'So you have no plans to see Lucas and me at all over Christmas?'

'I'm trying to juggle everything,' he pleads. 'It's just another day. I'd like to get out to America with a bit of time to spare. Filming starts straightaway and I need to get over the jet lag. I don't want to be going into the studio feeling fuddled. I have to be straight out of the starting gate. It's ruthless out there.'

And yet he's choosing it over his own son, over me.

In the middle of the path, I stop and look at him. I have loved this man so much. He has taught me a lot about myself over the last six months. 'I want this to work for you with all of my heart,' I tell him. 'Really I do.'

He places his hands on my arms, his face the picture of relief. 'I knew you'd understand, Molly. You always do.'

'I do understand and hope you do too.' A feeling of calm

359

descends on me. 'Shelby, we both know that this is the end of the road for us.'

He looks appalled. 'Why would you say that?'

'You want to be free to fly high and I don't blame you.'

'But what about you and Lucas?'

'We're happy here. If Lucas chooses to stay with me, I'll look after him to the very best of my ability. I couldn't love him more than I do. He's the closest to a son I'll ever have.' I get stab of pain in my heart for the child I've lost, but that's something that Shelby will never know about. 'Yet, we both have to face it, this isn't your ideal life. I think you like the idea of a quiet, natural existence without the trappings of fame and fortune, but it's an act.' Something that Lucas has always pointed out that Shelby does so well. 'It's something that you want on occasional weekends, whereas I'm grounded here and this is where I want to stay. I don't want to come to Los Angeles. I want to be here with my animals, up to my elbows in mud and manure. That's what I do best. It's who I am.' He goes to open his mouth to speak, but I press on before I lose my nerve. 'You love the person you are and the life you lead. And that's fine by me. That's a good thing. But my part in it ends here.'

'I love you.' His expression is bleak.

'And I will *always* love you,' I promise. 'But sometimes love isn't enough.' Shelby has been my first love. I think as it came later to me in life, I have cherished it all the more, but I can also recognise when it's over. For him and for me. 'You've been one of the very best things to happen in my life. I hope we'll stay the closest of friends.'

Shelby looks flabbergasted, but surely he must have seen this coming?

When he manages to speak, all he has to offer is, 'I don't know what to say.'

'Be happy. We have one life, Shelby. Go and enjoy yours.'

'This isn't over for us, Molly. I have to do this. You know that. If I don't, I fear I'll regret it for the rest of my life. But I promise you, I will come back to you.'

But what I can't tell him is that I don't think I'll be waiting.

Chapter Seventy-Nine

When we get back to the caravan, Lucas has strung up the Christmas lights and it looks amazing. They criss-cross the ceiling, giving a multi-coloured disco effect. There's a mini fake tree set up in the corner that's hung with baubles that are too big for it. A gold star shines out from the top.

'Behold,' he says, 'Yonder Christmas caravan!' He sounds chirpier now; sometimes, his mercurial moods catch me off balance.

'All this looks wonderful, Lucas.' I squeeze his arm. 'Very cosy.'

'I got a bit carried away,' he explains with a shrug.

'Well, I'm glad that you did.' I try to respond to his brightness. 'Fantastic job!'

Yet, when he sees our faces – or our body language – he frowns and says, 'What?'

'Your dad is going to take you out to lunch,' I tell him. 'Just the two of you.'

'Without you? Why?' He looks to each of us for an explanation.

'We've got things to talk about,' Shelby says.

'Then let's talk about them here.'

'Lucas, please go with your dad,' I beg. They need time together, and I know that sometimes Shelby says all the wrong things, but I can't do this one for him. He has to step up to the mark and be a proper parent to his son.

'We'll just go to the local pub,' Shelby offers. 'Come on. Let's have a bit of time to ourselves.'

Lucas looks horrified. 'Are you two splitting up? You are, aren't you?'

Shelby and I exchange a glance, both of us worried.

'I knew it.' Lucas huffs at us both. 'Well, I'm staying here with Molly. Whatever's going on, I'm not budging. This is my home now.'

My relief is palpable.

'Come to the pub with me,' Shelby cajoles. 'We can discuss it properly.'

'No,' Lucas says. 'Everyone will be looking at us. It'll be a fucking circus like it always is.'

'I can't help that,' Shelby says crossly. 'It's my life.'

'That doesn't mean it has to be mine,' Lucas snaps.

As usual, I end up refereeing. 'Let's scrap the whole pub idea,' I suggest, placatingly. 'I can make us some sandwiches and we can discuss it together.'

Lucas gives me a thankful look. Shelby also seems grateful that he won't have to do this with Lucas alone.

'Sit down, both of you, while I make lunch. Talk.'

Lucas goes straight on his phone and ignores his father while Shelby sits and looks as if he's no idea what he's doing here.

So, muttering silently to myself, I bang out some sandwiches and a big pot of tea. Then we sit awkwardly at the table beneath lights which are flashing on and off in random patterns, while Shelby explains that he won't be home for Christmas and that he'll be leaving us both behind to head to Hollywood for a fantastic role that will make his fame and fortune.

I thought he might come back to pack up his stuff, but apart from one suitcase, Ken will see to it all and ship it on to him. Ken, it transpires, will be joining him out there for the foreseeable future.

Lucas sits and calmly takes it all in. He doesn't rail or rant and I'm so proud of the mature way in which he handles this news – another blow, no doubt, on top of everything else. Shelby, on the other hand, looks devastated. Now that he's said it all out loud, perhaps it seems more real to him. He comes to the end of his speech and we all fall silent.

I jump in and say, 'It's a great opportunity for your dad.'

Lucas rolls his eyes at me and picks up his phone again.

Shelby looks at me, eyes pleading – for what, I don't know. He's leaving. There's very little else to be said.

Conversation is, at best, strained as we finish lunch and, as soon as we're done, we both walk Shelby to his car. He hugs Lucas and, for once, his son doesn't resist. Perhaps there's a small sign of capitulation here.

Then it's my turn and I step into the warmth of Shelby's arms. I remember how all this started and how I had so much hope for us all. For a moment, I'm almost undone. From the way that Shelby is holding me, I feel that he might be regretting accepting this move which has been on the cards for so long.

'I'll message you on Christmas Day.' He looks like he might cry or change his mind and not leave at all.

For a moment, I think about begging him to stay. Parting isn't 'sweet sorrow', Mr Shakespeare, it's bloody agony. The pain threatens to take my breath, but I don't want Lucas to know that I feel like this, so I hold it all together for his sake.

Shelby kisses my hair before reluctantly letting go of me, and climbs into his car. As he passes us to go out of the yard, Shelby leans out of the window and says, 'I'll be back as soon as I can.'

'Have a safe journey.'

We close the gate and Lucas climbs on it as we watch him go. As the car turns out of the lane, he looks at me and sighs. 'We've both been dumped.'

'I let him go, Lucas. It was the right thing to do.'

'He's a knob,' Lucas says as he jumps down next to me. 'He thinks it will make him happy out there, but it won't.'

'You might well be right,' I agree.

'It will be better with just you and me,' Lucas says. 'You wait and see.'

I think he's right about that too, but for now, my heart feels shattered into a thousand pieces.

Chapter Eighty

I have very little time to nurse my broken heart as Christmas Eve is, somehow, suddenly upon us. It's the last day for us to have students on the farm and I'm very pleased to say that we've got a full house. To celebrate, Bev is cooking us a veggie Christmas dinner with her special nut roast and, thanks to a generous donation from a local supermarket, Christmas pudding to follow.

Everyone is in an excitable mood. The tea room is full to bursting. The tables are laid out in a long line and are set with all the festive fripperies. Crackers that the kids have made in their craft sessions are given pride of place and are adorned with holly, berries, angels and stars. They are, without exception, totally wonky and all the more adorable for it. There are pretty centrepieces fashioned from holly that Anna has made in a much more professional style and Bev has splashed out on some red paper napkins. Everyone is wearing the traditionally awful paper hats – also handmade. The weather has been terrible for the last few days, so there has been a lot of indoor activities which are now in evidence.

It's all hands to the pump today and it takes time to get

everyone settled. It's like herding cats. Lucas is on serving duty and Penny's mum, Jess, is here to help too. The only person we're missing is Matt. And, if I'm honest with you, I am missing him.

'Jack, you sit here,' I instruct. 'Asha, will you go next to him, please?'

'Can I go to see the hens, Molly?' Jack asks. 'There might be more eggs.'

'This is a joining-in time, Jack,' I tell him. 'Remember we've talked about those?'

'Ah, yes,' he says. 'I'll join in, then.'

'That would be nice. You can collect the eggs when we've had our lunch and tidied up.'

'Right.' He looks worried. 'You won't forget?'

'I promise you. We'll do it together.'

'Good. Good.' He sets about straightening his knife and fork until their symmetry suits him.

'If you want a job to do, Jack, you could pour a glass of the sparkling clementine juice for everyone.'

He jumps up, always eager to please. 'Yes, I'd like to do that.'

'Do it slowly,' I remind him. 'And not too full. I don't want any spilled on the nice table. Think you can manage?'

'Slowly,' he parrots. 'Not too full. Yes, yes.'

'Good, lad. The bottles are on the table over there.' I point it out to him. 'Shout if you need help.'

'Erin, can you and Lottie go there, on the end?' I try to place them all with their particular friends, but by the time I've done that it *will* be Christmas. I suppose I could have written name cards, but they all would have just ignored them. I usher the rest of the students into empty chairs and hope that they'll stay there for at least a few minutes until we serve lunch. They start moving instantly, so I give up and just shout, 'Leave a space for me near the kitchen, please.'

That will have to do.

Lucas has found some Christmas songs on Spotify and they're blaring out, competing with the high level of chatter and general merriment. I head to the kitchen where Bev, Alan and Jess are already busy. I join Jess in laying out the plates ready for Bev to dish up.

'How are you liking the manor cottage?' I ask Jess as we work.

'It's great,' she says. 'I can't thank you enough, Molly. We've only been there for a short while, yet for the first time in years I feel that I can breathe properly.'

'Have you heard from your husband?' I venture.

'He started to bombard me – and Penny – with calls and texts. I didn't answer them and now I've changed my phone number. I'll have to contact him in the New Year to start divorce proceedings, but I hope I can do all of that through a solicitor.'

'Good for you. I'll help wherever I can. Meanwhile, try to relax and enjoy Christmas together. You've got plenty of food in?'

'Yes. It will be nice for me and Penny to spend a relaxing time together without worrying about . . .' She tails off. 'Christmas has always been a bit of a tinder box for us.'

I can imagine. 'Well, if you can bear some chaos, you're more than welcome to come to the caravan for Boxing Day. Alan and Bev will be there too, so it will be a tight squeeze and lunch will be completely random food, but it would be lovely to have you.'

'That's very kind of you. We'd really like to come.'

'Good.' We give each other a hug.

My Christmas gift shopping has all been very last minute and, with Lucas's help, entirely done online, but I did get a couple of little presents for them both. I've bought presents for Alan and Bev too and a little thank you for Matt, though we won't see him now. It will have to wait until January when, hopefully, he'll be back at Hope Farm again. I've bought nothing for Shelby, though. What do you buy for the man who has everything? I don't expect anything from him either. He supports the farm and that's all that matters to me.

It might not surprise you to know that he and I have hardly spoken since our last encounter. Shelby has been frantically busy with his last week of panto and getting prepared for his move to Los Angeles. I've been rushed off my feet here. But it's all excuses. You can find time for the one you love if you want to. In truth, the bonds have been broken and, though I am terribly sad that this didn't work out, I feel it's the right thing for both of us.

'Come on, Molly Dolly Daydream,' Bev says. 'Snap out of it. There are three trays of roast spuds ready and waiting to be dished up.'

'Right.' I pull myself out of my reverie and set to with my big spoon, doling out a few of Bev's golden, crispy potatoes onto each plate. Jess follows behind me with the veg and Alan adds a slice of nut roast and finishes with a flourish of gravy before Lucas serves the plates to the table. There are dishes of cranberry and bread sauce on the table.

It's hot work in the kitchen and Bev wipes her brow with her forearm before puffing out a breath. She and Alan were in here early this morning getting all the veg peeled and prepped for the hungry hordes. She looks over her shoulder at me. 'Where's that flipping Hot Mayor when we need him?'

'On his way up to see his family by now, I think.'

'It's a shame he's not here.'

'Yes.' I can only agree with that. He's been a good friend and great help over the last few weeks and I miss him more than I thought I would.

With a concerted effort, we get the dinners out to everyone

while they're still hot. 'Last few. Here you go, Jess. One for you too, Alan.' Then Bev pushes a plate at me. 'You're done here, Mols. You take yours now.'

'You've got one too?'

'Last one. Perfect portioning, if I do say so myself.'

'You're a wonder,' I agree.

So I take my plate and go out from the kitchen into the tea room. And, as I go to take my place at the head of the table, I stop in my tracks. The sight before me takes my breath away. Lucas has switched on LED candles and fairy lights, which are threaded all along the table. The Christmas tree, lights shining out, stands proudly in the corner. All our students are laughing and chatting together, pulling crackers, tucking into their lunch. It's a beautiful, festive moment. They look so happy here that it brings a lump to my throat. Sometimes they can be challenging, positively difficult and, on occasion, outright awkward little buggers, but I love all of our kids so dearly and I can't tell you how glad I am that, here at Hope Farm, we can make such a difference to their lives. Some are going to spend time at loving homes over Christmas, some less so, and I know that I will worry about them until we open again in January and they're safely back in our fold.

Bev comes out of the kitchen with her own dinner in hand. As she passes me, she touches my shoulder and gives me a wink. I know that she's thinking the same thing as I am.

'Right,' she shouts. 'Tuck in, everyone! Don't let your lunch get cold!'

She takes her seat next to Alan and I also notice that Lucas has pulled up his chair next to Penny which makes me smile. That's nice. He's not mentioned Aurora since our 'big talk' and I hope that it means his broken heart is beginning to heal.

Glancing out of the window, I see that it's started to snow. Great flakes fall in lazy circles to brush against the windows.

'Look! Snow!' Asha says. 'It's snowing.'

Everyone cranes their necks to look outside, then they start to clap and cheer.

A white Christmas. What could be better? I take a deep breath and feel a rush of festive warmth right down to my toes. This is how Christmas should be. Then I raise my glass of perfectly poured sparkling clementine juice and hold it high.

'Merry Christmas, everybody!' I say.

And when their shining faces turn back to me and say, 'Happy Christmas, Molly!' it's all I can do not to cry.

Chapter Eighty-One

The hedges are already tipped with white when Lucas and I – plus all the dogs – are waving all the students off after our lovely Christmas lunch. It's still snowing steadily and I catch a few flakes on my hands.

'We'll see you on Boxing Day,' I say to Penny and her mum. 'Hopefully, the lanes will still be passable. If not we'll get the tractor out and come to get you.'

'Thanks for everything, Molly,' Jess says. 'It's been a brilliant day.'

'Take care.' We hug each other and I note that Lucas and Penny exchange a shy glance which warms my heart.

'Have you enjoyed it too, Penny?'

'Yeah,' she says, but her eyes never leave Lucas.

I give them a dozen fresh eggs to take with them as Jack didn't let me forget he needed to collect them.

Alan and Bev are the last to leave. I hug them both. 'You two lovebirds have a wonderful first Christmas together.'

'We'll be round in time for lunch on Boxing Day and I'll bring a few bits.' Bev looks worried to be leaving us for a day to our own devices. 'You and Lucas will be OK by yourselves?'

'Yeah, yeah.' I turn to Lucas. 'We'll be fine, won't we?'

'Just the two of us snowed in together in a caravan.' Lucas rolls his eyes. 'Can't think of anywhere I'd rather be.'

That makes me laugh.

'We'll survive,' I assure Bev. 'I promise you.'

Bev still looks concerned. 'No word from Shelby.'

'Not as yet,' I say. 'But that's fine too.'

'Shitbag,' is Bev's verdict. 'I can't believe he's going away at Christmas.'

I shrug. 'Hollywood calls, you drop everything and run. So I'm told.'

'Huh.' Bev is still not impressed by this.

'Seriously, don't worry about us. We're happy.' I look to Lucas for his endorsement.

'Delirious,' he agrees.

'You know where we are if you need us,' Bev says.

'I do.' I kiss her again. She and Alan climb into their car and, despite my many assurances, I feel like crying as I watch them drive away. My eyes fill with tears and I brush them away with hands already damp with snowflakes.

In a world first, Lucas puts his arm round my shoulders and says, 'We will be all right, you know.'

'We will. I just feel ridiculously teary. Today was a lovely day and it's made me all emotional.'

Lucas gives an exaggerated sigh. 'I suppose that you'll want to go and see how all the animals are and then take a stupidly long walk across the fields with the dogs even though it's frigging snowing.'

I laugh through my tears. 'That sounds like a very good idea.'

'I suppose you'll want me to come with you.'

'I'd like that.'

He tuts and puffs, 'Some things never change.'

But I can tell he doesn't mean it.

Lucas and I go to the barn and do a tour of the animals. Instantly, my melancholy is lifted, my soul soothed. The alpacas are all present and correct, straw sticking out of their mad pom-pom hair, contentedly humming in unison. How can you stay cross or upset with these guys around? The animals are constant and have no care for whatever drama might be occurring in our lives. They just want food and attention. I stroke Johnny Rotten's neck and he tries to have a sly nip at my elbow. All is as it should be.

We walk on to the sheep, both Lucas and I falling into our well-trodden path. We have a look at our mum-to-be, Fluffy. 'She's getting huge,' I note. 'The vet said she might give us a Christmas baby.'

Lucas looks at me and there is sadness in his eyes. I assume he's thinking of his own baby that never was.

'You OK?'

'Yeah.' He tries to pull a philosophical expression, but doesn't quite cut it. 'I wish things had turned out differently, but it is what it is.'

'Your time will come and you'll appreciate it all the more.' I don't know if that will comfort him, but I hope so.

'I don't wish her ill,' he says. 'Aurora. I hope it works out with this bloke. Kind of. For the kid's sake.'

It's not the ideal situation to be bringing a child into, but I keep my counsel. 'I hope so, too.'

Anthony is obviously feeling less anti-social than usual as he comes over to say hello. It could, however, be the bucket of food that Lucas is carrying that lures him in. As a reward, our anti-social sheep gets a handful of our special mix. In contrast, Lucas's reward is Anthony pushing his head through the gate and trying to headbutt him in the nether regions.

'Bad sheep,' I admonish.

'True to form,' Lucas notes and we leave Anthony thwarted but still with an evil glint in his eye.

We check on the bunny run and they're all OK. Ant and Dec are nestled happily together in their huge hutch. The hens have gone into their shelter for the night. Fifty and Teacup are already snuggled up in their pen, content in each other's company. I can relax knowing that my beloved animals are safe and well – and, in some cases, as feisty as ever.

Calling the dogs to heel from the four corners of the yard, Lucas and I climb over the stile into the field. Lucas holds out his hand to help me down, when he normally wouldn't do that at all. He's being very solicitous today and I don't know if it's because he knows that Shelby going away is a blow, but it's nice whatever the reason.

The fields are already blanketed with snow and it looks so beautiful sparkling in the moonlight. A winter wonderland, indeed. It's bitterly cold, but the night air is still without a hint of breeze and our walk is bracing. Thank goodness that Sweeney and Carter are already in their stables in the yard and the ponies are beside them in a covered pen. Betty Bad Dog snuffles along, snout buried in the snow, occasionally making herself sneeze violently.

'Dozy mutt,' Lucas murmurs with a laugh.

'She'll never learn,' I agree.

We walk on in silence, until I risk venturing, 'Penny's very nice.'

'Yeah.'

'You seem to be getting on well with her.'

'Stop that now,' Lucas instructs. 'Don't even go there.'

Damn. I hoped that he would be feeling mellow enough to confide in me. So, not wanting to spoil our current closeness, I drop the topic. All I'll say is watch this space.

Chapter Eighty-Two

It's Christmas Day and I wake at four in the morning. I can tell from the crisp feel of the air, the muffled weight of the sound, that a lot more snow has fallen overnight. I budge the dogs over and push myself up in bed to look out of the caravan window. Sure enough, the yard is deep with snow and I feel a thrill of excitement.

Then my phone rings and I answer it.

'Hi.'

It's Shelby on the other end of the line. Who else would it be at this hour?

'I'm at the airport.' His voice sounds strained, anxious.

'Was it OK getting there?'

'Yes, yes.' His tone is dismissive.

'I thought the snow might have hampered you.'

'The motorway was clear enough.' It's obvious that he's not in the mood for small talk. 'Molly, I'm about to go through passport control.'

'I hope you have a great flight,' I tell him. 'Fingers crossed that it's not delayed. I'll be thinking of you.'

He takes a deep breath. I hear it wavering down the line. 'I don't have to go,' he says, tightly. 'Tell me not to go and I'll turn round and come home.'

My heart is pounding and I wonder if this is what I've waited to hear. At the eleventh hour, he's obviously having second thoughts and who wouldn't? It's a huge step. He's giving up life here to start anew. He's leaving me and his son behind. He might have convinced himself that it's a temporary situation, but we both know that it could well be much more than that.

'Say something,' Shelby urges.

What do I do? This is Shelby's big moment, his dream. Yet, should I think of Lucas and ask him to come home? If I did that, would Shelby hold it against me for ever? Even if he comes back now would this ending be happy ever after?

'Molly, I don't *have* to get on this plane.'

This is it. The moment that changes everything. I take time to gather my thoughts before I answer as I know there will be no going back.

'You do,' I say and my voice sounds stronger than it feels. 'This is what you want.'

'I don't know if it is,' he admits.

'You have a contract, commitments. You start filming in a couple of days.'

'I can ask my agent to sort it. I'm pretty sure he could get me out of it. You and Lucas are more important to me. My head has been so messed up, I've not been thinking straight. Say the word and I'll come home right now.'

It would be so tempting, so easy to ask him to stay. But what then? Are we already too far apart to bridge the gap?

'Molly?'

I try to steady my breath, but my heart is thumping and I take another interminable moment to make sure that this absolutely what I want.

'Go,' I say as calmly as I can. 'You're halfway there.' He

might have miles to travel, but emotionally he is already stepping out of our lives.

There's a long silence before he replies. 'I'll call you as soon as I arrive.'

'Safe journey, Shelby,' I offer. 'I hope that it's all you wish for.'

'I love you,' he says.

But I can't answer that. All I can manage is. 'Take care.'

Then I hang up the phone and stare at the wall wondering whether or not I've done the right thing. Is this for the best or have I just completely messed up my life?

Chapter Eighty-Three

Wrapping up warm before I head out into the snow, I go through the usual routine of feeding the animals and try not to think about my conversation with Shelby. He'll have gone through to the departure lounge by now and will be getting ready to board his flight. I feel numb. I feel sad. I feel relief.

I take care to wish all of my charges a very merry Christmas and sneak them an extra treat as it's a special day. I've got a Christmas carrot for one and all, so am very popular. As I watch them crunch and munch, I savour the peace, the unchanging nature of the farm and feel my soul settle once more.

When I get back to the caravan, Phantom is sitting at the bottom of the steps, staring at me. Our feral cat has never come anywhere near the van before and, as you know, is rarely even seen in the yard, preferring to be out in the fields or in the barn.

'Hello, boy.' I bend down towards him and he leans away from me, but holds his ground, regarding me with his one good eye. So I sit on the step next to him. 'This is a nice surprise that you've come to say hello to me.'

He meows and rubs against my leg, which is definitely a Christmas miracle.

'Would you like something to eat? I can probably rustle up some cheese as long as you don't tell Lucas.' I think there's some in the back of the fridge for my non-vegan emergencies. I'm frightened if I move, he'll bolt, but I want to give him a treat if I can. Moving slowly, I risk going to the fridge and do, indeed, find a morsel of cheese for him. Thankfully, he's still waiting when I go back outside.

I hold out my hand and Phantom takes the cheese, scoffing it down greedily. Perhaps it's a real luxury for a cat who's used to foraging for himself.

'Do you think you might like to live nearer to us, eventually?' I ask him. 'I'd love to look after you properly. I could put a bed under the van for you as a start?'

But he's too busy licking his whiskers to reply. Then he turns and walks off across the yard, flicking his paw in his strange goosestep as he goes. I hope he'll come back soon. Perhaps now he's made the first approach, we might have just turned a corner with him. It was a lovely Christmas present, nevertheless.

With a smile on my face, I go back indoors to find that Lucas is just emerging from his room in his T-shirt and torn joggers. He yawns and scratches his head.

'Merry Christmas,' I say.

'Oh yeah. Merry Christmas.'

Still in tactile mood, he hugs me. Then he looks out of the window. 'Christ, look at the snow.'

'It's lovely out there,' I tell him. 'The sun's out, the sky's blue. It's a gorgeous day.'

'A white Christmas. Who'd have thought?'

'I've got some vegan bacon. We can have sarnies for breakfast.'

'Top job,' Lucas says and curls himself into the sofa where Little Dog takes up residence on his lap.

So I fry the bacon and we eat our breakfast together while listening to Christmas songs on the radio.

'Your dad phoned early this morning.'

Lucas raises one eyebrow.

'He was at the airport and was thinking about not going to LA.'

'But he still did,' Lucas says.

'I told him he should.'

'Good call. We're better off without him.'

Only time will tell, I guess.

'It's OK to miss him,' I point out.

'For you,' he replies, crisply. 'I got over my dad years ago.'

I don't think that's entirely true. I'm sure this is tough for Lucas and he's putting on a brave face, but I let it go. It's Christmas Day and I want us to have a lovely time together.

'I don't suppose Superstar Daddy remembered to buy us any Christmas presents?'

'No,' I admit. 'But he has been very busy.'

Lucas tuts. 'Tell me something I don't know. He could have got a minion to do it, as he usually does. He'll put some money in my account when he remembers. Throw some cash at it. That always eases his conscience.'

I don't want to argue with Lucas and, in fairness, he's probably right. 'Well, I got you a present.'

In the cupboard, I find what I've wrapped for Lucas. There's a book of poems, *The Sunshine Kid*, by one of his favourite poets, Harry Baker, and a T-shirt that says POET – BUT ONLY BECAUSE SUPERHERO IS NOT A JOB TITLE. I think he'll like them.

He unwraps them enthusiastically. 'These are totally awesome. I've wanted this book for ages.' He holds the T-shirt against his skinny chest. 'I'll put this on tomorrow when we've got visitors. Thanks, Molly.'

'My pleasure. We've got gifts from Bev and Alan too.' I find those tucked in a box under the sofa.

There's a bottle of Aldi rum for me and a hand-knitted *Doctor Who*-style scarf for Lucas.

'Cool,' he says. 'Top presents.'

'That's very thoughtful of them.'

'I can wear the scarf on our obligatory walk.' He stands up and winds it round his neck. 'I've got a present for you, too. I didn't buy it, but I hope you like it.'

Lucas stands up and takes up position in the middle of the kitchen floor and says, 'Are you sitting comfortably?'

I turn to face him. 'I am.'

'This is for you. It's called "Without You Too".'

He lets out a wavering breath and, from memory, starts to recite.

To have lived my life without you
would've been to have lost all hope,
of ever standing on my own;
of learning how to cope,
with the pains I faced so early:
the loss you helped me through;
the second chance you offered me,
and from which our friendship grew.

I could have lived my life without you,
but how cold would I have felt,
without the warmth you gave so freely,
that caused this heart of ice to melt?
There'd been a fork in the road ahead;
a darker path that beckoned me,
but you were there:
your light
to guide my way;
encourage:
set me free.

And now I wouldn't be without you;
you mean that much to me,
you've been a friend;
a coach;
a mother;
made me the best that I could be.
And so from me to you this Christmas;
offered unreservedly:
my thanks;
my humble gratitude
for a life without you in it . . .
Is one I wouldn't want to see.

He stops and looks up at me, as if uncertain of my reaction.

'Oh, Lucas.' I don't even bother to hide the fact that I'm crying. 'That is the nicest present I've ever had.'

'Then you must have had some really shit presents in the past,' he says, but I can tell that he's secretly pleased that I like it. No, I don't just like it. I *love* it. I adore it.

I remember so well the moving poem that he wrote for his mother to express how he felt without her and this, I feel, is Lucas coming full circle. It's a statement of where he is now and I couldn't be more proud. I'm proud of myself too for being part of his life.

'Should have put on my poet T-shirt before I did that,' he says, shyly.

'You should because you are an *amazing* poet.'

'Heartbreak and misery, it turns out, are very good for creativity. Perhaps I wouldn't be a poet if I was deliriously happy.'

'Are you not happy?'

He thinks for a moment and then gives a rare smile. 'Yeah,' he says. 'I think I might be.'

'Hug?'

With only a moment's hesitation, he steps into my arms and I give him a good squeeze while I have the chance. I have so much hope for Lucas's future. He's made mistakes, had setbacks, experienced love and loss, endured moments of darkness and doubt, but he's turning into a fine young man and I can't wait to see what's to come.

'You can stop crying now,' Lucas says.

'Can you read it again?'

He sighs. 'Do I have to?'

'Yes. It's Christmas. Indulge me.'

So he recites it again and makes me cry a bit more.

Chapter Eighty-Four

Lucas and I have a lovely, chilled day together. I cook a traditional Christmas lunch for us except with vegan onion tarts instead of turkey. Holly and Ivy will be happy about that. We pull crackers that the students have made and wear our completely naff paper hats.

'I feel like a right wanker,' Lucas says as he checks out his reflection in the window. But he keeps it on, nevertheless.

In the afternoon, I potter about while Lucas, amidst a pile of cushions and dogs, reads his new poetry book. I cajole him into a game of cards, which he quite enjoys as he pays little attention and yet he still wins. The dogs flop about on the floor beneath us, untroubled even though they've been cooped up for hours.

The snow continues to fall throughout the day and, as they say, it's deep and crisp and even.

As it darkens into evening, I look out of the window. 'I should go and feed everyone. Want to come?'

'Yeah,' Lucas says, pushing himself out of the cosy nook he's created in the sofa. 'I'll get my coat.'

I look at him tenderly. 'It's been a nice day. I've enjoyed spending time together.'

'Yeah,' he agrees. 'And I whooped your arse at cards.'

I laugh. 'You did.'

'Return match tomorrow?'

'Don't forget we have a houseful – or caravanful.'

'Ah. I might challenge Penny to a game or two. See what she's made of.'

That makes me smile. 'I see.'

'You don't,' he says. 'We're friends. Don't start phoning the vicar.'

'I won't. I just want you to find a special friend.'

'A special friend?' He wrinkles his nose at me. 'Give me a break. You forget, I'm sworn off lurrrrve for the foreseeable future. Little Dog is the only companion I need.' He ruffles the dog's ears which sends him into a frenzy of delight.

Maybe. If not Penny, then I hope someone comes along for Lucas to care for, someone of his own age to share his life, his hopes and dreams.

We wrap up, pull on our boots and venture out into the snow. The fresh fall has obliterated our previous footsteps, so the yard is pristine until we crunch across it to reach the barn.

The animals are quite excited to have some human company and even more excited that dinner is on its way. Lucas and I set about feeding them all. When we get to the sheep, Fluffy has separated herself from everyone else and is pawing at the ground. Her belly looks lower than it was and she's stretching her back.

'I think that Fluffy's time is near,' I note.

Lucas looks anxious. 'Shall we phone the vet?'

'If it's a straightforward birth, she'll be able to manage,' I assure him. 'I don't want to drag out anyone on Christmas night unnecessarily. We'll keep a close eye on her.'

Then there's the sound of a car trundling its way up the lane and for one stupid moment I wonder whether it's Shelby. Maybe he didn't get on the plane after all and has come back to us for Christmas.

Leaving Lucas on sheep duty, I hurry out of the barn and to the gate. It's Matt's car that's waiting there and he's the last person I expected to see. I let him into the yard and when he gets out of the car, he says, 'I hope you don't mind me dropping by. This isn't a bad time?'

'It's the perfect time,' I tell him. 'But I thought you were on your way to stay with your family.'

'Couldn't get up there. The snow is much worse in the north. I decided not to risk it.'

'They must be disappointed.'

'Yes. I am too, but I'll see them as soon as I can. I didn't want to get stuck halfway up the M6.'

'Very wise.'

'You're sure I won't be in the way?'

'Not at all. It's just me and Lucas today.'

He looks puzzled. 'No Shelby?'

'I'm afraid not,' I tell him. 'He's gone to LA. He flew out this morning. He's taken a contract to be a baddie in a big drama out there.'

'How long for?'

'That's a moot point.' I might as well tell Matt what the situation is. 'If I'm honest with you, I don't think that he'll come back at all.'

He frowns at me. 'So where does that leave you?'

'Here. With Lucas. Just the two of us. I couldn't be happier.' I smile at him to show that I genuinely am OK. 'Shelby and I will always be friends, I hope. I love his son as my own and will be looking after Lucas here for as long as he needs me. Shelby is my landlord here too, so I have to keep on the right side of him.'

'He's a fool to go off chasing stardom when he has so much

here.' Matt looks round at the yard, the farm. From what I've already seen, I know that he's very comfortable in this setting.

'I'm not sure that he sees it in quite the same way. This isn't the life that Shelby wants.' Even though, sometimes, he thinks it is. 'Sheep poo and bitey alpacas are not really his scene. We all have to follow our dreams. It's just a shame that our dreams didn't coincide.'

He looks as if he wants to say something else, but changes his mind.

'I'm very pleased to see you, and Lucas will be delighted,' I say instead.

'I brought you both presents, if that's all right.'

'That's very thoughtful of you.'

'Just small gifts,' he says. 'Don't get too excited.' He delves into the back of the car and produces a beautiful red poinsettia, all wrapped in cellophane with a big bow. He offers it to me. 'My sister said this was a good present.'

'She's right.' I take it from him, gratefully. 'It's lovely. Thank you. It will certainly help to brighten our little caravan.'

'I've got something for Lucas, too.'

'He's in the barn. Our pregnant sheep has picked this moment to go into labour. Lucas is watching over her. Shall we take a look at how she's getting on?'

We head back to the barn and as we cross the yard, we walk beneath the mistletoe that we hung there together. Suddenly, mid-stride, Matt pauses and says 'Molly.'

I turn towards him, expectant.

'We missed out before,' he says and glances at the mistletoe.

'We did.'

Despite my arms being full of poinsettia, he moves towards me. His lips find mine and he tastes of Christmas spices, cinnamon and nutmeg. His kiss is warm, tender and makes my head spin and my knees weak.

'I've wanted to do that for a long time. It was worth waiting for,' he says. 'You don't mind?'

'No.' I smile shyly at him. 'I rather enjoyed it.'

We both laugh and he says softly, 'Merry Christmas, Molly.'

'Merry Christmas.'

But, such is my life, our romantic interlude doesn't last for long. I look anxiously at where I've left Lucas. 'I don't want to break the moment, but I should check that Fluffy's OK. It's her first lamb.'

'Come on, then,' Matt says and we head over to the barn where Lucas is standing on the gate, attentively watching over our mum-to-be.

'Look who's come calling,' I say, as I put down my poinsettia.

'Hey, Matt.' Lucas jumps down and Matt grabs him into a bear hug and slaps his back.

'Merry Christmas, mate,' Matt says. 'Having a good one?'

'Yeah. Watching a sheep in labour. What could be better?'

Matt laughs. 'Hope this will cheer you up.' He hands over an envelope and looks at me as he says, 'I thought we could all go.'

Lucas rips it open and looks at Matt, astonished. 'You're kidding me.'

'Tickets for the Harry Baker tour in the spring.' Matt looks pleased with his choice of present. 'You said you wanted to go, so I got three of them.'

'That's fantastic.' Lucas is obviously thrilled and I love how Matt has remembered their conversation about the poet and has done something so kind.

'Cheers, Matt. That'll be great.' Lucas's face is shining and it makes me think how easy it is to please him. It also makes me sad how little effort Shelby goes to when it comes to understanding his son.

'How's Fluffy doing?'

'I don't know,' Lucas admits. 'It's all new to me.' He wrinkles his nose. 'There's some kind of goo coming out of her bum. Is that right?'

I look over the gate and am quite worried by what I see.

Chapter Eighty-Five

Climbing into the pen, I examine Fluffy. Lucas's 'goo' is, in fact, the amniotic sac. Looks like Fluffy's ready to give birth to her first baby. However, she's straining to deliver the lamb and I think she's going to need some assistance. 'It looks like the legs are tucked up and trapped under the lamb. They need to be facing the other way for a smooth delivery. She'll never get this little one out by herself.'

I turn to look at Lucas, who has gone a pale shade of green. 'Don't look at me.' He holds up a hand. 'I draw the line at getting acquainted with a sheep's noo-noo.'

I've done this before in the past, with supervision, and it's a lot harder than it looks. However, it's a long time since I've had any practice in sheep midwifery and I feel nervous as I don't want to hurt Fluffy.

'I can do it,' Matt says.

Lucas and I both look at him with surprise. 'You can?'

'Sure. I've helped enough cows to calve in the past. It's got to be easier with a sheep. I can scrub up, if you've got some disinfectant.'

He certainly sounds confident and I could definitely do with some help. 'You're sure?'

Yet Matt is already taking off his jacket.

'There's disinfectant in the shed. Lucas, can you run and get it?'

He shoots off without being asked twice.

Our mayor rolls up his sleeves before climbing into the pen alongside me.

'You're all right, girl,' he coos to Fluffy. 'The cavalry's here.' Expertly, Matt turns the sheep onto her side. 'You have a little lie down while we sort you out.'

Lucas comes back with a bucket of water, soap, a clean towel and some disinfectant. Matt scrubs his hands and arms.

Then he tends to the sheep, taking a deep breath before he murmurs. 'Nothing to it.' He reaches into Fluffy as gently as he can and she bleats with the indignity of it all. 'I just need to hook the legs forward. Keep still for a second, Mum. Ah, here's one.'

Lucas and I are watching anxiously, hearts in our mouths.

'Got the other one too,' Matt says with a grunt. 'Here we go.' He pulls firmly and, next thing, a new lamb slithers into the world in the most ungainly way, landing in a mess of mucous in the straw. Matt clears its airways and rubs the body vigorously.

'Oh, well done.' Lucas and I look at each other, both relieved.

'A perfect delivery,' he says. 'Even though I say it myself.' Matt puts the lamb at Fluffy's head and the sheep gently starts to lick its new baby. 'We've got us a little girl. That's a bonny lamb.'

'She never would have popped it out by herself. You turned up in the nick of time.' I'm sure I could have done it if, literally, push had come to shove, but how grateful I am for his calm and assured intervention.

'Glad to be able to help.' Matt scrubs his arms again and dries them on the towel.

'What a delightful Christmas gift.' I look at Fluffy nuzzling her newborn and feel full of pride for her. 'This will be a nice surprise for Bev and Alan when they turn up to celebrate with us tomorrow.'

'I can't wait to show her to Penny, too,' Lucas says excitedly. 'What shall we call her?'

'Joy?' I suggest. 'That's suitably festive.'

'Yeah,' Lucas agrees. 'Joy. It's a good name.'

'I think we can leave mum and baby to bond now while we have a celebratory cup of tea.'

'Tea?' Lucas says. 'I'm all for cracking open that bottle of rum that Bev bought for you.'

I laugh. 'That sounds like a much better idea. Will you join us?' I say to Matt. 'If you've nothing to rush away for, you can stay over if you'd like. I'm happy to make up a bed on the sofa for you so that you don't have to drive home.'

I feel shy making the offer, but the roads must be hazardous by now and, after what's he's done, I'd really like him to stay around.

'I might take you up on that. A tot or three of rum sounds like a very good plan.'

'I'll take the sofa,' Lucas offers. 'Matt can have my bedroom.'

I'm not sure that he'll want to sleep in a teenage-created bio-hazard, but we can sort that out in good time.

Then I look round. 'Where's Anthony?'

Chapter Eighty-Six

In all the drama, it seems our dear anti-social sheep has taken advantage of our distraction and has slipped through the gate to make a break for it.

'Buggeration,' I huff. 'He's heading across the field at full tilt. How did he even squeeze through the hedge?'

Anthony is a fair old size and the gap in the hedge is quite small. So I thought.

'Don't worry,' Matt says. 'I'll get him.' He grabs his jacket before chasing off after our badly behaved sheep.

Lucas and I head to the stile where we perch and stare at the pair of them, Anthony gambolling in the snow and Matt in hot pursuit.

We both giggle.

'He has no idea what Anthony's like, does he?' Lucas says.

'I'm afraid not.'

We laugh again.

Lucas gives me a sideways glance. 'You should definitely get with Matt,' he says. 'He's cool.'

'You're giving me dating advice?'

'Well, it's clear that you need help with your choice in men,' he replies.

'Oh, Lucas.'

'Trust me. I know these things. He's a good bloke.'

'If it's any help, I think so too.'

'There you go, then. My dad's fucked off. There's nothing to stop you.'

My mind goes to Shelby across the miles, starting out on his glamorous Hollywood lifestyle, and think that it will suit him much more. He's a man who needs to be adored, feted, whereas I need a man who's here for me – one who will muck in *and* muck out. One who will roll up his sleeves and help a baby lamb in distress with aplomb.

In my heart I say goodbye to Shelby, the man that I've known and loved. It's over for us and we both know it. I'm entirely rubbish at this romantic stuff, but I think there is chemistry between me and Matt, a tentative attraction. Perhaps Lucas is right, he would be a good man for me. There's no doubt we have so much in common.

We watch as Matt gets closer to grabbing Anthony who then performs a perfect swerve to avoid him and runs the other way.

Lucas and I laugh so much that tears run down our faces.

My dear boy turns to me and, wipes away his tears. 'Molly,' he looks serious for a moment. 'This has been a good Christmas. One of the best.'

'For me too,' I tell him.

'We'll be OK,' he says. 'Just you and me.'

I nod, emotion tightening my throat. 'We will.'

I look above me. The stars are out, the landscape is white with snow as far as the eye can see, the air is crisp. The animals are snug and warm in their stalls. The dogs are at my feet. My dearest boy is content with the world and so am I. It feels exactly like a Christmas night should do.

'Don't just stand there,' Matt shouts over at us. 'This sheep is a damn sight speedier than he looks.'

We turn again to the antics carrying on in the field ahead of us and frown. 'I suppose we should go to help Matt out or he'll be there all night.'

'We could help,' Lucas notes. 'Or we could just go and pound Matt with snowballs.'

I look at Lucas and smile. 'That sounds like a very fine idea.'

Lucas's eyes twinkle mischievously. 'Let's do it!'

'You're on.'

So, side-by-side, we jump down from the stile and run into the field, scooping up snow to pat into snowballs as we go. Matt sees us coming and stops chasing Anthony who immediately stands still in disgust at being abandoned.

'Oh, no, you don't,' Matt shouts at us and bends to hastily make his own snowballs to repel our attack.

We all come together in a flurry of snow and playful shrieks. There's snow in my hair, ears, my mouth and down the back of my coat. Matt and Lucas roll on the ground, grappling together, and rubbing snow into each other's face. Their joyous guffaws fill the night air.

I don't know what the coming year might bring for me, for Lucas and for all of us at Hope Farm, but I'm sure that along the way there'll be a lot of love and even more laughter. I just need to open my heart, throw wide my arms and embrace whatever comes next.

Talented poet, Paul Eccentric, one half of the comedy performance act, The Antipoet, created these poems for Lucas in my
previous novel about Hope Farm, *Happiness for Beginners*, and
I thought it would be nice if you could enjoy them again.

For further information on his work, pop along and have a
look at www.pauleccentric.co.uk.

Without You

It still goes on without you;
life still goes on for me,
it'll never be the same, though;
not how it's meant to be.
They tell me it gets easier
with every passing day,
but how could I accept that cancer stole my mum away?
It still goes on without you;
life still goes on for us,
but it's a lacklustre alternative,
and ever will be thus,
without you here to guide me;
I won't know what to do,
without you here beside me:
on hand to help me through.
Life still goes on without you;
it still goes on for those,
who kill and maim and terrorise,
because that's just how it goes!
Life goes on without you,
and I'll do the best I can;
I just wish you could have stayed around 'til I was an
old man.

Secrets 'n' Lies

Who are you?
C'mon an' show me who ya are!
Is anything f'real,
Mr TV star?
Action!
Reaction!
Time t'pour out
y'heart,
but how'm I t'know
what's y'life and what's ya art?
Cards on the table:
time t'bare your soul,
but when you lie for a living,
ain't life just another role?
How will I know
if what y'telling me is true?
An' if nothing is f'real,
then, does it matter what I do?
Who are you?
I shouldn't really have t'arx,
but I really need to know
if there's a man behind the mask.
Action!
No action;
words are all you got,
scripted 'n' lifted from a cheap soap plot.
Well-versed, rehearsed;
in the character immersed,
two faces; two families,
but which a'them comes first?
They all think they know ya;

398

they see you as their friends,
but none a'them will be there when the story ends,
so —
Who are you?
That's what I need t'know;
when they turn off the camras
and they wrap up the show.
Action!
Interaction:
that's what I'm looking for,
I shouldn't have to queue at the stage door.
We all got a secret that we're burnin' t'yell,
we're defined by the lies that we're willin' t'tell.
Secrets 'n' lies;
I's no big deal;
all I'm arxin's that y'keep it
a little bit real.
All I'm arxin's that y'keep it
a little bit real.
All I'm arxin's that y'arx y'self:
how I might feel . . .

Save the Farm

It's nothing short of criminal:
It's a travesty; a scam.
We're another victim of that HS2 to Birmingham.
Because, despite the work we've done here,
For those with special needs,
The rich man's railway still comes first,
Yes, progress supersedes!
And that leaves us with a problem,
As our work here's far from done,

Our appeal needs to go viral
Reach the hearts of everyone.
All we need is twenty acres,
At a rent that's not too steep;
A place to keep our goats and pigs
And Tony, the angry sheep.

Save The Farm! Save The Farm!
With the alpacas we'll stand tall!
Save The Farm! Save The Farm!
Hear us all at Hope Farm call!
Save The Farm! Save The Farm!
Stand up for what you know is right,
So the work we do can con-tin-ue
Come join us in this fight.

'Cos the work we do here's vital,
It's a lifeline we provide;
For those for whom conventional education
Hasn't been an easy ride.
You see alpacas aren't judgemental,
And goats don't take the mick,
And pigs and sheep don't badger you
For being dyslexic.
They help to normalise anxieties,
Build the confidence to achieve;
They encourage us kids to integrate
And in ourselves believe.
They've been called iconoclastic;
Revolutionary; unique,
We've got all we need to make this work,
It's just the ground space that we seek.
Save The Farm! Save The Farm!

With the alpacas we'll stand tall
Save The Farm! Save The Farm!
Hear us all at Hope Farm call!
Save The Farm! Save The Farm!
Stand up for what you know is right,
So the work we do can con-tin-ue
Come join us in this fight.

There are people who depend on us;
We won't go down without a fight,
But we're an independent entity
And our finances are tight.
There's animal feed and vet bills,
Day-to-days, and at some stage,
Molly would like to draw herself at least a living wage.
So if you're rich and fancy helping us,
Or you've got some land to spare,
Or if you know anyone else who has,
Who could be convinced to care,
Then get in touch; we'd love to hear, or share my video,
On all your social media and with everyone you know!

Save The Farm! Save The Farm!
With the alpacas we'll stand tall
Save The Farm! Save The Farm!
Hear us all at Hope Farm call!
Save The Farm! Save The Farm!
Stand up for what you know is right,
So the work we do can con-tin-ue
Come join us in this fight.

Acknowledgements

To Donna and Paul Eccentric for all the help with this book and for perfect poems, friendship, tortoise traumas and really excellent afternoon tea.

🐦 @PaulEccentric
www.PaulEccentric.co.uk

To all the team – human and otherwise – at Animal Antiks for continued help with my research.

🐦 @animal_antiks
www.animalantiks.co.uk

And to Caenhill Countryside Centre for extra inspiration. We watch their morning 'rush hour' on Twitter to start every day with a smile. Do check them out.

🐦 @caenhillcc
📘 www.facebook.com/CaenhillCC

The poet who Lucas is so keen on is Harry Baker – very clever and entertaining – and I admire him just as much. His website is simply HarryBaker.co (that's not a mistake!) and is worth a look. You can also see some of his fabulous performances on YouTube.

🐦 @harrybakerpoet
📘 www.facebook.com/harrybakerpoetry

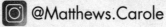

Help us make the next generation of readers

We – both author and publisher – hope you enjoyed this book.
We believe that you can become a reader at any time in your life,
but we'd love your help to give the next generation a head start.

Did you know that 9% of children don't have a book of their
own in their home, rising to 12% in disadvantaged families*?
We'd like to try to change that by asking you to consider the role
you could play in helping to build readers of the future.

We'd love you to think of sharing, borrowing, reading, buying or talking
about a book with a child in your life and spreading the love of reading.
We want to make sure the next generation continue to have access
to books, wherever they come from.

And if you would like to consider donating to charities that help
fund literacy projects, find out more at www.literacytrust.org.uk
and www.booktrust.org.uk.

Thank you.

hachette
CHILDREN'S GROUP

little, brown
BOOK GROUP

*As reported by the National Literacy Trust

Join us at